PLAYING AROUND

Gilda O'Neill was born and brought up in the East End, where her grandmother ran a pie and mash shop, her grandfather was a tug skipper and her great-uncle worked as a minder for a Chinese gambling den owner. She left school at fifteen but returned to education as a mature student, studying with the Open University and the Polytechnic of East London, and taking an MA at the University of Kent while lecturing part time. She is now a full-time writer, and has had seven novels and three non-fiction books published. She lives in Essex with her husband and family.

Praise for Gilda O'Neill

'Tarts with hearts, dastardly villains and a happy ending. A thumping good read'
Lesley Pearse

'This novel has everything . . . a cracking read'
Martina Cole

'A sharp eye, a warm heart and a gift for storytelling'
Elizabeth Buchan

'Peopled with an irresistible vivid cast of characters and told with warm-hearted sympathy . . . a great read'
Oxford Mail

'The characters are brightly and freshly drawn . . . the dialogue is sp‌͏   ͏eling for

D1080677

GILDA O'NEILL

Playing Around

ARROW

Published by Arrow Books in 2000

3 5 7 9 10 8 6 4

First published in the United Kingdom in 2000 by Heinemann

Arrow Books Limited
The Random House Group Limited
20 Vauxhall Bridge Road, London, SW1V 2SA

Random House Australia (Pty) Limited
20 Alfred Street, Milsons Point, Sydney,
New South Wales 2061, Australia

Random House New Zealand Limited
18 Poland Road, Glenfield
Auckland 10, New Zealand

Random House (Pty) Limited
Endulini, 5a Jubilee Road, Parktown 2193, South Africa

The Random House Group Limited Reg. No. 954009

www.randomhouse.co.uk

A CIP catalogue record for this book is available
from the British Library

Papers used by Random House are natural, recyclable products made
from wood grown in sustainable forests. The manufacturing processes
conform to the environmental regulations of the country of origin

ISBN 0 09 927997 5

Typeset by SX Composing DTP, Rayleigh, Essex
Printed and bound in Great Britain by
Bookmarque Ltd, Croydon, Surrey

For Lynne Drew

Chapter 1

As the twanging opening strains of 'Ticket to Ride' struck up on her transistor, Angie Knight closed her magazine with a sigh, and shoved it under the bed.

It was all right for Jackie – she looked like a fair-haired version of that Cathy McGowan off the telly – and for all the other girls who looked as though they belonged to the world that Angie could only glimpse in the glossy pages of *Honey*. They all knew how to dress, how to look good, and how to do their make-up.

On the secret occasion when Angie had experimented with cosmetics, she had wound up looking like a cross between Coco the Clown and a cheap tart: just like her mother, only without the fag hanging from the corner of her mouth. Mind you, men seemed to like the way Angie's mum looked. Lots of men.

It was a good job Angie didn't care what blokes thought about her, and that she didn't mind spending yet another Saturday night with no one for company except a bunch of pirate disc jockeys who sounded as though they were speaking with their heads stuck in a bucket. Although, Angie suspected, that had more to do with the radio her nan had bought her off Doris Barker than the quality of the actual broadcast, despite the fact that it was coming from somewhere out at sea instead of a nice, cosy, BBC studio.

The unexpected sound of a key turning in the street door had Angie hurriedly flicking off her crinoline lady bedside lamp and turning off the transistor with a metallic click, darkening the room and silencing Radio Caroline and the Beatles right in the middle of their final chorus.

She groaned inwardly and pulled the blankets up over her head. It was only a quarter past ten. She hadn't expected them home nearly so soon. Had the pubs run out of booze? She had hoped, really hoped, that she would be asleep by the time they got back.

Angie listened, in the muffled darkness, as Vi, her mother, and Chas, her mother's latest, useless, boyfriend, stumbled drunkenly up the stairs, their voices raised in anger over something or other.

She hadn't expected them to be rowing quite so soon either. It usually took at least a month for her mother to grow bored with her men – or rather her 'meal tickets', as she called them behind their backs, and sometimes to their faces as well if she'd had a few too many Snowballs – and then another week or two for the inevitable, and occasionally spectacular, battles to begin.

'All I said,' she heard her mother shriek, 'was I didn't like the way your nasty little brother was looking at her yesterday.'

'Vi, your daughter is meant to be how old?'

'She'll be seventeen next week, as you'd know if you'd listen to a single bloody word I say.'

Angie threw back the covers and propped herself up on her elbows. Had she heard right? Were they actually arguing about *her*?

'Seventeen. Exactly.' Chas was triumphant.

This was a first. Her mother was the centre of the universe, the only possible topic of interesting conversation, everyone knew that. Well, you did if you spent any time in this house, regardless of whether you were her daughter, or a visiting boyfriend, even if you were a

2

well-off, dodgy car dealer – sorry, businessman – from Chigwell, like Chas, rather than a casual pull off a local building site as the last one had been.

'Surely she can look after herself at that age.'

There was a pause, then the sound of her mother's bedroom door being swung back viciously on its hinges, and her mother snapping, 'You've seen how slow she is around fellers. She could get really conned. Specially by a nice-looking boy like your Matthew. You've got to do something, Chas. I mean it.'

Slow? Conned? Angie sank back on her pillows, her cheeks burning red with shame.

'Don't be daft.'

'I'm telling you, I didn't like the way that randy little so-and-so was looking at her.' Vi's voice was now whiny and low, as, in a customary display of acrobatic mood-swinging, she had leaped from banshee to pouty child in a single, accomplished swoop. 'He could take advantage.'

Angie heard Chas snort derisively, and then the twang of bedsprings. 'Be honest, sweetheart, who'd want to take advantage of that mousy little thing? She's as timid as a bloody rabbit. And twice as gormless.'

'Don't talk about her like that.'

Chas snorted again. 'I'm not saying she's got a furry coat, long, pointy ears and big teeth, I'm just saying—'

Angie could hear Vi laughing. 'Stop it, Chas. She can't help the way she is.'

She can't help the way she is? Angie felt her eyes begin to prickle with humiliation.

'Well, don't be so silly.' There was another pause, then she heard Chas say, 'Here, you're not jealous are you?'

'Jealous? Of her?' The sound of her mother's obvious outrage made Angie feel sick.

'I'm not a fool, Vi. I know as well as you what you're up to. As long as you keep her looking like some gawky schoolkid in those terrible clothes you make her wear, people'll look at her as if she's a child. And that makes you seem younger.'

'You bastard. You know I'm only thirty-four. And I don't tell her what to wear, I just sort of advise her, that's—'

'Come off it. If anyone did show interest in her, you'd be right up the Swannee. Who'd you have to skivvy for you then?'

'You know I've got my condition.'

'What? Lazyitis?'

'Don't be so rotten. The doctor said it was a very traumatic birth. He said I was to get plenty of rest. I had a lot of trouble. It affected me. Psychologically.'

'Vi. That was seventeen years ago.'

'You'd understand if you were a woman.'

'Well, I'm not, am I? As you can see.' There was another, brief pause, followed by Vi squealing in half-hearted annoyance. Then Chas went on, 'Come on, darling, don't let's fall out over a bloody kid. Show me how good even an old girl like you can be.'

As Angie felt the tears brim, and then trickle down her cheeks and flow into her ears, she pulled the blankets back over her head and tried to block out her treacherous mother's lascivious giggles, and the vision of what was happening in the next room, as the bedsprings began squeaking like a rhythmic, asthmatic donkey.

Chas was right, she was a mousy little thing, a timid little rabbit. She was too scared, or too stupid, to make it

4

clear how unhappy she was, how unhappy people could make her. Her nan was always telling her to stand up for herself, but somehow she never had. She knew she had to do something about it, or she would be trodden on for ever.

But knowing something didn't mean you could do it.

Angie sobbed as quietly as she could, hoping that they had no idea next door that she had heard every humiliating word.

The petite, expensively dressed blonde glanced down at her gold cocktail watch as she strode purposefully across the concrete floor of the private underground car park, her high heels tip-tipping like a metronome.

Nearly half past ten.

Without pausing, she looked over at the security booth. The guard wasn't there. He often wasn't at this time of night. She smiled indulgently. Lazy sod. Off having a crafty drink and a cigarette as usual. If only the other tenants of the exclusive Mayfair block knew that their precious E types and Bentleys, supposedly being defended to the death, were regularly abandoned to the mercy of any even half-way competent thief or resentful vandal, the guard would have been sacked on the spot. If you lived in these flats, you could afford the luxury of bypassing any sentimentality regarding the jobs and lives of lesser mortals such as car-park attendants.

She stopped beside a scarlet Mini Cooper, dropped her chin, opened her handbag and began to rifle through the lipsticks and screwed-up tissues, searching for her keys.

As a large, masculine hand clapped over her right shoulder, the woman froze.

'Don't turn round, and don't even think of screaming.' The voice was deep, husky. 'Understand?'

She swallowed hard, then nodded.

'Good.' The man laughed, a sound that rose from somewhere deep in his broad chest. 'Look at you. Birds like you, you're asking for it. Dress up your arse, flashing all you've got. Now. Now you can turn round. Slowly.'

Wide-eyed and with her open bag still in her hand, the woman did as she was told. But, before she had a chance to call for help, run, or even faint, the man, in what seemed a blur of movement, had slammed her back against the car, had pulled up her skirt with one hand, and had ripped open his flies with the other.

'Stockings and suspenders. Good.' His breath came in short, excited grunts as he made a wild grab for the triangle of sheer black lace that barely covered the mouse-coloured curls of her pubic hair – the woman was not a natural blonde.

She snapped upright, clapping her knees together. 'Careful!' She spoke in a refined, Home Counties accent, and she sounded annoyed: a middle-class woman complaining about the behaviour of the lower orders. 'David only bought these for me today. They cost a fortune.'

The man grinned. 'Glad I'm the first to appreciate them, Sonia.'

Sonia grinned back, and stepped delicately out of the panties. She tucked them neatly into her handbag, clicked the clasp shut, set it on the ground next to her, and then rolled her skirt tidily up her thighs.

'Get on with it then, Mikey, or the guard will be back.' She ran a perfectly manicured fingernail across his cheek, and peered up at him through suggestively lowered lashes. 'Or maybe you'd give a better performance with someone watching . . .'

As the man thrust into her, and the woman threw back her head with a gasp, neither of them realized that they did, in fact, actually have an audience.

Too busy with their game, they had failed to notice the hot, red glow of a cigarette, coming from the back seat of the nearby racing-green Jaguar, as her husband, David Fuller, took a draw on his rare, imported Turkish Imperial, before crushing it, without a flinch, in the palm of his hand.

'Coming.' Tilly Murray, a pleasant-looking woman in her early forties, walked along the passage to answer the door, wiping her floury hands on her apron. Sundays, especially the mornings, were all go for Tilly – even harder work than the other six days of the week were for her and her husband, Stan. And that was saying something.

'Hello, love. How are you, then?' She stepped aside to let Angie Knight into the hallway. Like a lot of other homes on the estate, the Murrays' house had a front room, kitchen and bathroom leading off the passage downstairs, and two main bedrooms and a box room leading off the tiny landing above. Being on the other end of the five-house terrace to the Knights', the layout was a perfect mirror image of Angie's own, but there the similarities ended: the Murrays grafted long and hard to make sure their house was warm, comfortable and full of the tantalizing smells of cooking, with Stan working all hours to pay the bills, and Tilly doing all the domestic chores, so they could make a decent home for their kids, while the Knight house offered none of those things, not

7

unless Angie herself did something about them when she got in from work. Violet Knight was not a bad woman, in fact she could be a loving, lovable, warm and funny person to be around, it was just that men, rather than her daughter's comfort and future opportunities, were her priority, and when one of them was in her life, which was most of the time, she was definitely above such banal matters as home-making.

'Hello, Mrs Murray. Is Jackie around?'

Tilly jerked her head towards the stairs. 'She's not out of bed yet, but go on up. I know she's awake.' She smiled warmly at Angie. 'I don't know how you youngsters manage to spend so much time laying about doing nothing. You're like little dormice in hibernation.' Immediately wishing she hadn't said something so stupid to a kid who spent just about every waking hour either at work or slaving to keep her idle, no-good mother's house in some sort of order, Tilly put her hand on Angie's shoulder. 'Stay for dinner if you like, love. I'm doing a nice shoulder of lamb with all the trimmings, and I'm making a jam roly-poly for afters, with loads of custard. It'll be no trouble, I'll just peel a few more spuds.' She nodded encouragingly. 'You know how Mr Murray likes his Sunday roast. And he deserves it, how hard he works.'

'Thanks all the same, but I'm going round to see Nan.'

Good for you, thought Tilly, you leave that lazy mare to sort herself out. 'Well, you're more than welcome if you change your mind, you know that.'

'Thanks, Mrs Murray, I know.' Angie grabbed hold of the banister and swung herself up the stairs.

'So much energy.' Tilly shook her head in affectionate wonder as she took herself back to the kitchen and the monumental task of cooking the Sunday dinner.

'It's only me, Jack. Can I come in?'

'Course.'

Going into Jackie's room always made Angie feel happy; no matter how often it was decorated, or changed round, it was just the way Angie would have chosen – if she had had the chance. The latest look involved the walls being emulsioned in white with a big red, white and blue target painted on the wall facing the door: the handiwork of Jackie's older brother, Martin. The carpet was plain navy – terrible to keep clean, according to Mrs Murray, but as beautiful as the finest velvet according to Angie – and had a thick, sheepskin rug by the bedside to warm Jackie's toes. The bed itself stood along the length of one wall, and was covered in a Union Jack bedspread, with matching pillowcases; opposite was the 'dressing unit', as Jackie called the combination white melamine dressing-table and wardrobe. Reflected in the mirrored wardrobe door was a much-kissed poster of the Beatles, which showed the Fab Four walking along a beach dressed in jokey, old-fashioned stripy swimsuits and straw hats; strange outfits, but, as Jackie said, they looked gear in whatever they wore, and Paul especially could get away with anything.

The only concession to the pink, girlie bedroom that it had been up until just a month before was the crinoline lady bedside lamp, with its deep rose, nylon skirts, through which the bulb glowed warmly: an altogether feminine accessory, and a match with Angie's own. Angie's nan had bought them for the girls from Doris Barker, a woman who lived in her buildings in Poplar, and who, considering she didn't go to work, seemed to spend all day, every day, at home being visited by people and always seemed to have a whole flat full of stuff to sell. Where it all came from was a mystery to Angie, but, as her nan told her, it wasn't polite to ask people about their private business; it was like a code in the East End, she had said.

Angie settled herself at the foot of Jackie's bed with her back leaning against the wall.

'You look so miserable, Ange.' Jackie made herself comfortable in her nest of pillows and blankets. 'Everything all right?'

'Not really. Mum's new boyfriend said something horrible.'

'How do you mean?' Jackie first frowned, then her mouth and eyes widened. 'Here, he didn't try it on or nothing, did he? Didn't try and get a feel up your kilt?'

'No, nothing like that.' Angie closed her eyes and rubbed her hands roughly over her cheeks, refusing to let the tears come. 'I heard him say to Mum', she said, her voice catching, 'that I was ugly, and stupid, and useless, that no one would ever fancy me, and that . . .' Too late. Her bottom lip began to tremble, and her eyes watered.

Jackie threw back the covers and scrambled to the other end of the bed to be close to her friend. Tugging down the hem of her blue-and-white striped, granddad-collared nightshirt that had recently usurped her pink baby dolls, she screwed up her face in anger. 'The buggery, rotten old sod. What did your mum say?'

All Angie could do was shake her head as the tears flowed.

'Was this last night?'

She nodded.

'Drunk, I suppose.'

Another nod.

'I told you, you should have come with me to the Palais.'

'I couldn't. You know I don't . . .'

'Angie, it's only the Ilford Palais we're talking about, not the Scotch of flipping St James or the Canvas Club.'

'I wouldn't fit in with your friends,' wailed Angie. 'You know I can't . . .'

'Angie, *you* are my friend. And you know I'd love you to come out with me. It's only because you won't that I still knock around with that lot from school.' Jackie put her arm round Angie's shoulder and gave her a little shake, in the mistaken belief that it would cheer her up. 'We had a right laugh.'

The door opened and a male voice asked, 'Who did? What have you pair been up to?'

Angie and Jackie looked round to see Martin Murray, Jackie's big brother, standing in the doorway.

'Hello, Squirt,' he said, smiling at Angie, 'you look pissed off. My little sister's not been upsetting you, has she? If she has I'll take her teddy off her. She still cuddles that ratty old bear every night, you know.'

Angie managed to wring out a feeble smile in reply. Last October, Martin had become an economics student at London University, but he didn't have a duffel coat or a scruffy beard. Martin was a mod, with a parka, a tonic mohair suit and a chrome-covered Lambretta, and, during the past couple of years, had grown into just about the most beautiful thing that Angie had set eyes on.

'Ignore him, Ange,' Jackie said haughtily. 'Being the first one in the family to go to college has gone to that fat head of his. But what he doesn't realize is, being clever doesn't mean he's got any sense.' She pointed to the box of tissues on her bedside table. 'Why don't you make

11

yourself useful and give Angie a paper hankie, then go down and brew up so me and Angie can have a cup of tea?'

Martin handed the tissues to Angie. 'Actually, I was going to offer to put the kettle on, sis, but, now you've asked, I think I've changed my mind.'

He ducked just in time to avoid the tissue box, expertly aimed by Jackie, from hitting him on the head.

'That was one sugar, wasn't it, Squirt?' he called as he ran down the stairs to the kitchen.

'Listen, you two.' Martin held out a tin tray bearing two cups of tea and a plate of Jammy Dodgers. 'Mum's bending my ear about persuading Angie to stay for lunch.'

'*Lunch*? Ooh, lah-dee-flaming-dah!' Jackie jeered at her brother in a high, mock-posh voice. 'Don't they have Sunday dinner at your toffee-nosed college, then? Too common for the likes of them?'

Martin did not rise to the bait. He had sworn he would never wind up in a job like his dad's: ruining his lungs as he cleaned out the crud from the boilers in the local car factory, with only a nightly pint of mild and bitter in the Fanshawe Tavern and a fortnight in a chalet in Leysdown to look forward to. He wanted more from life, a better life, but that hadn't stopped him being as scared as hell about going to university. Jackie knew all about his anxieties, and, despite being at times boastfully proud of her big brother, it didn't stop her exploiting them whenever she wanted to jerk his chain around.

'How about it, Squirt?' he went on, ignoring Jackie. 'How about helping us all out by giving Mum the chance to cook an extra mountain of food?'

Angie took one of the cups and handed it to Jackie, then took the other one for herself. 'It's really kind, but I already promised Nan I'd go over to see her.'

Jackie blew across the top of her steaming cup, while helping herself to the plate of biscuits. 'Go later.'

'I can't. Once I've got the underground to Mile End, I have to get the bus down Burdett Road, and you know what they're like on a Sunday.'

Angie sipped at her tea, agonizing over the choice of missing the chance of sitting down to eat with Martin or of letting down her beloved Nan. And even if she did stay, she would probably be too embarrassed to say anything much to him. It was so different trying to talk to him lately, not like it had been when they were kids. But she really liked him. Not like that, of course, but it was just . . .

'Come on, Squirt.'

'I suppose if I missed the bus, I could walk from Mile End.'

'Tell you what,' Martin slapped the empty tray with his hand as though it were a tambourine, 'I'm meant to be seeing someone from college about borrowing some books. I could go up there this afternoon and give you a lift on the Lambretta at the same time.'

Angie's mouth went dry. Was this like being asked out on a date or something?

'I couldn't let you do that, Martin.' *Oh yes she could.*

'Why not? They live in Mile End. Bancroft Road. Right along by the college. I could drop you at your nan's, then go on. And I do need the books today. I've got to finish some work I'm meant to be handing in by the end of the week.'

Jackie pulled a Jammy Dodger apart, separating the

13

biscuit into two, and thoughtfully licked at the filling. What was this all about then?

Angie could hardly breathe. Her world had just turned upside down: misery to pure joy in a matter of moments.

'You'd have to make your own way home, though. I don't know how long I'm going to be.' He paused. 'So? What d'you reckon?'

Angie stared up at him from the bed.

'It means you'll be doing us all a favour: keeping Mum happy by staying and having –' he paused and looked pointedly at his sister '– *lunch* with us first, means she'll be able to cook even more grub than usual.'

'If it makes Mrs Murray happy,' Angie finally managed to gasp.

'Great.' He smiled and winked at the poor little thing. What a life that kid had. He felt really sorry for her. She was so grateful for everything. If only she realized what a real favour she was doing him, giving him the excuse to get out for the afternoon. Living at home was driving Martin Murray stark, raving bonkers.

'Busy last night, David?' Sonia Fuller put down her cigarette and sipped her orange juice, as she flicked lazily through the *Sunday Times* colour supplement. Her attention was suddenly focused. She really had to have her hair done like that. An asymmetric cut would look wonderful with her jaw line, and would take at least five off her thirty-two – off her twenty-nine – years.

'Actually, I came home around half ten.' David, a look and soundalike for Michael Caine – the first thing, apart from all his money, that had attracted Sonia to him – calmly continued with his breakfast, despite knowing he had just dropped a bombshell right in the middle of the bizarre kitchen table that Sonia had 'found' in some 'wonderful little shop in Chelsea'. Until he'd met Sonia, David had had no idea that 'finding' things could be so expensive.

He shook another dollop of ketchup on to his plate. Regardless of his wife's attempts to get him to eat muesli – trendy, overpriced hamster food, in his opinion – and to drink orange juice, David was still a resolutely fry-up and dark brown tea man, especially on a Sunday, and even more especially when he'd had his appetite whetted by anger.

Sonia was no longer concerned with the shiny pages and their drooling displays of the latest, overpriced fashions.

'Half past ten?'

'Yeah, where were you?' He dipped his toast into the yolk of his fried egg, knowing how much she hated such 'common habits'.

'I popped out for cigarettes.' Sonia waved her hand breezily, as though the gold-tipped menthol she was currently smoking was proof of her story, a king-sized, Virginia alibi.

'Why didn't you send the doorman out for some? Or a cab?'

David was beginning to enjoy this, maybe even more than the crisply fried bacon that he had speared on his fork with half a grilled tomato. Sonia might have been a crappy liar – in fact, as a wife, she had proved to be a major let-down in most areas – but she could make a very tasty breakfast, and it had been a while since anything else about the little tart had interested him. But being made a mug of by people, that interested David Fuller, that interested David Fuller very much indeed. That guaranteed his full attention. And it made him think of all sorts of nasty things he wanted to do to people. Very nasty things. Things that would make Sonia's dainty little lips curl right up.

His appetite – for food – satisfied, David shoved the plate away from him.

'Enjoy your breakfast?' Sonia could have hit her husband right over the head with his nasty, greasy, egg-stained plate. God, she hated him. Why wouldn't the pig just say if he had seen her and Mikey together in the car park?

'Handsome, darling.' David belched into his fist, and then scratched his bare chest under the lapels of his navy silk robe.

'Do you mind?'

'Sorry.' He sucked noisily on his teeth trying to dislodge a piece of bacon.

He was driving her to bloody distraction. She stomped over to the sink and dumped the plate on the side, ready for the daily to deal with. Daily! That was a laugh. Despite how well Sonia treated her, the cow couldn't even be bothered to drag her fat, lazy arse over to the flat just because it was a Sunday, so the dirty dishes and clearing up just accumulated over the weekend until Monday morning. It was disgusting. Just like him.

'David, I have to know.' She stared down at the filthy plate, took a deep breath. 'You've been very quiet. Have I upset you in some way?'

David made a show of thinking about it. 'Nothing that occurs,' he lied, leaning back in his chair. He reached out and pinched her – hard – on her neat little backside. 'Just appreciating your cooking, darling.'

Sonia closed her eyes. Thank God for that. She wasn't

16

ready – not yet, anyway – to give up everything that the aggravating, uncivilized swine could give her. She intended to accumulate rather more in her private account before she did that.

So, Sonia Fuller, time to be nice.

She turned round to face him. 'I might change my hairstyle,' she said, flirting down at him through her lashes. 'What do you think?'

'I think you'd look the business whatever you do with that barnet of your'n.'

'You are sweet,' she pouted, and ran a perfectly manicured fingernail across his cheek.

Just like she'd done to him. To bloody Mikey Tilson. David could have killed her stone dead on the spot. But he wasn't going to. Not yet, anyway. He was a man who knew the value of hiding his hand.

By biding his time he could make a situation really work for him, when other men didn't realize that a situation even existed. He'd show the pair of them, and any other disloyal fucker, exactly who was in charge, that he couldn't be monkeyed around with. Any idiot who thought they could cross him would see exactly who called the tunes in David Fuller's organization. He'd make them suffer. All of them. In all sorts of ways.

He shoved his chair away from the table and stood up. He hadn't gone from errand boy to top man by being impatient; he'd got there by using his brain. He tightened the robe round his taut, muscled belly and smiled to himself. And by using his brawn, of course. What was more, he enjoyed playing games. It amused him. Even his teachers had said he was always playing around, always acting the goat. And they'd been right. Mind you, they'd been wrong about one thing. They'd all said he would never amount to anything. That he would never get anywhere, that he'd stay stuck in the same, poxy, Bethnal Green backstreet he'd been born in for the rest of his natural. He'd like to see their faces now. He'd rub their sneering, bastard noses right in it.

'Don't you drive that thing too fast, will you, love?' Tilly Murray and her daughter Jackie stood on the Cardinal-red doorstep, watching Martin and Angie standing on the other side of the privet hedge, preparing to set off on the Lambretta.

Jackie was grinning at them in bemusement. Did her big brother actually fancy Angie? She was her best friend, had been ever since she could remember, but *Angie*? Nobody could ever rate her as fanciable, and, as much as she teased her brother, Jackie had to admit Martin was considered something of a catch. It was all very strange.

While Jackie grinned, Tilly frowned: the concerned mother hen. Rotten scooters, why ever had she let Stan talk her into letting their boy get one in the first place? Bloody deathtraps. You heard such stories.

'Don't worry, Mum, I'll take care of her.' Martin handed Angie a crash helmet, a rarity amongst image-conscious mods, with a dramatic flourish. 'See, look how responsible I am.'

Tilly flapped her tea towel at her son in surrender and went back indoors to work her way through the mounds of clearing and washing-up that cooking a decent Sunday dinner for her family inevitably seemed to result in.

Jackie stayed where she was, watching her brother's every move with a confused fascination, but had she been close enough to notice how Angie was quivering as

18

Martin bent forward to fasten the helmet under her chin, she would have been genuinely amazed.

Misreading Angie's excitement for resistance, Martin whispered to her, 'Don't worry, Squirt, I know it's a bit big, but I'll stop round the corner and you can take it off again.' He winked conspiratorially. 'Don't want to mess up your hair, now, do we?'

Angie suddenly visualized what a shocking state her greasy brown hair, only partly dragged back in an elastic band, was in and what it must look like poking out from under the helmet. She snatched a crafty look at herself in one of Martin's long-stemmed side mirrors.

She looked ridiculous.

Why hadn't she washed it this morning?

Why? Because her mum never had any change for the gas meter, that's why, and any change Angie might have had in her purse would have disappeared, as usual, and boiling up kettles and saucepans to fill the plastic washing-up bowl in the sink took time, and all Angie could think of that morning was getting out of the house as soon as she could, and then—

'You all right?'

'Sorry?'

Martin zipped up his parka. 'You looked like you were about to pass out. Not that frightening, am I?'

As she shook her head, vigorously denying such a preposterous idea, the loose helmet slipped round.

Stopped only by her nose from covering her entire face, it still managed to completely cover one eye. Forget frightened, he must think she was a moron.

Why couldn't the ground just swallow her up and let her disappear?

'Here, you daft doughnut, come here.' Gently, he put

19

the helmet back in place, then threw his leg across the scooter, and twisted round to help her on behind him. 'Good job you don't wear miniskirts, eh, Squirt?'

This was getting worse. Not only did her hair look a complete mess, she was now all too aware that she was wearing her old, brown, corduroy slacks, the ones her mum said made her look like a refugee from the Land Army – whatever that was – and here she was about to get a lift from Martin. Martin! With his scooter, with all the chrome, the big, waving aerial with its foxtail flying out behind, the latest, long-stemmed, shiny mirrors, and, most of all, him, with his brains, his mod haircut, and looking just completely, totally, gorgeous in his parka. What was she – what was he – thinking of?

'Are you sure you're all right?'

'Too much roly-poly, Ange?' shouted Jackie with an encouraging wave. 'Why don't you hurry up and get on the back of that thing and clear off? The film's coming on in a minute and I don't want Dad settling down in front of the telly, thinking I'm going to let him watch some old rubbish on that BBC2.'

'I thought I might go out for a walk.' Sonia was peering round the door of what she referred to as the study, and what David called the spare room.

'Hang on.' David raised a finger to silence Sonia as he spoke into the telephone. 'I'll call you back.' He replaced the receiver. 'What did you say?'

'Such a lovely afternoon. I thought I might take a stroll over to the park and have a look at the daffodils.'

'Daffodils? You've got a flat full of sodding daffodils. And roses, and whatever else all them other flowers are.' He leaned back in his chair and folded his arms across his chest. 'But what do I know? I just pay the florist's bills.'

'I'm bored.'

'So why don't you go and clear up the kitchen?'

Sonia ignored such an insulting suggestion. Instead, she stepped into the room and lifted her chin dramatically. 'God, I hate Sundays. You're always working. The shops are closed.' She sighed loudly. 'I am *so* bored.'

Abruptly, David stood up, knocking over his chair. 'All right, you win. I'll go out with you.'

This wasn't the plan. 'But—'

'I'll drop you over at Speaker's Corner. You'll have plenty of company there. And I can drop into the office. Like you say, some of us have plenty of work to get on with.'

This was more like it. She could almost have kissed him.

Almost.

'Go and get your stuff, I'll see you down in the car park in five minutes.'

As soon as Sonia was safely in the bedroom, buried in the delights of her walk-in, room-sized wardrobe, David made a telephone call.

'Bobby. I've got a job for you.'

David watched Sonia hover around the edge of the throngs of tourists, as the regulars heckled and laughed at the placard-wearing preachers vying for the crowd's attention at Speaker's Corner. Exactly as he had expected, Sonia hung around, pretending she was interested in what was going on, but actually just waiting for him to leave.

David stayed where he was for a few more minutes, his blood pressure rising along with his temper, then, as soon as he caught sight of Bobby's shiny black Humber approaching in his rear-view mirror, he did a screeching U-turn in the middle of the Bayswater Road, drove off at speed along Oxford Street, and then suddenly stopped his car with a squeal of brakes and a surprising mouthful of expletives from a passing middle-aged female dog-walker.

David slapped a 'DOCTOR ON CALL' sign on his dashboard, and ran across the road, flipping a two-fingered salute at a taxi driver who had almost run into him, and yanked open the door of the telephone box that stood on the corner of Duke Street.

'Mikey?'

'Yeah.' He sounded put out. 'That you, Guv?'

David's jaw was rigid. 'I need you over at the office.'

'But, Guv—'

'I've got a job for you. Be over in Greek Street in fifteen minutes or I'll be all upset and think you don't want to work for me no more.'

David knew that was enough of a threat. Even for a hard little bastard like Mikey Tilson.

Mikey Tilson, the bloke who David was now sure was shafting him in more ways than one.

As they whizzed their way along Goresbrook Road, heading for the A13, Angie breathed in great gulps of air and was sure she could smell the sweet scent of the bright flowering bulbs that swayed gently in the spring breeze in the neat little front gardens behind the privet hedges.

She had nearly swooned when Martin told her she could either lean back and grip on to the chrome luggage holder behind her, or lean forward against him and put her arms, tightly, round his waist. She had, of course, opted for leaning back, although she had regretted it immediately. So, when Martin stopped the scooter on the corner of Flamstead Road for her to take off the helmet – just as he had promised! – she resolved, just as soon as they were mobile again, to hold on to him rather than on to the cold metal.

But Martin didn't seem in any immediate hurry to be on their way.

'Mind if I have a quick fag first?' he asked her a bit sheepishly, stowing away the helmet. 'I know I'm nearly twenty and shouldn't give a damn about what Mum says, but you know what she's like, she could nag the Krays into going straight.'

He offered Angie the packet of Player's No 6, but she shook her head.

'I think she means well. She's just being kind.' She stared down at her feet while Martin lit his cigarette and then took a deep lungful of smoke. 'I wish my mum would show a bit more interest in what I do.'

Martin took another drag. 'You don't know how lucky you are, Squirt, not having someone wanting to know everything you're up to every minute of the night and day. It's bad enough having to live at home still, without having a jailer thrown in for good measure.'

Angie's head snapped up. 'Do you want to leave home?'

'Are you kidding? The other students are all having a great time living up in London, and I'm stuck down here in Dagenham. Why wouldn't I leave?'

'So why haven't you?' Angie had to struggle to keep her voice steady.

'That's easy.' He looked at her, eyes narrowed against the smoke. 'Mum says they won't help me any more if I do, and that would mean using the money I earn working at the petrol pumps for living on.' He tapped the toe of his desert boot on the footrest of the scooter, then smiled wryly. 'And then I'd have to sell the scooter and I wouldn't be able to buy any more new clothes. Shallow, eh?'

'I don't think so.'

'You're a good kid, Squirt.'

Angie glowed under the light of his praise.

'But I am shallow. I really care about that sort of thing. Sometimes I feel right out of place at college. Sort of separate. The other students are so different from me. And not just in the way they dress. But the way they talk and . . .' He blew a plume of smoke down his nostrils and laughed, not entirely convincingly. 'They should see me when I've got my full mod gear on, eh? They wouldn't know what had hit them.'

He dropped the cigarette butt into the gutter and ground it out under his heel. 'I've wondered, you know, if I should try to be more like them. The other students. The way they do things. I'm just as clever as they are, but I don't really—' He stopped mid-sentence. 'Hark at me, going on to my little sister's mate, like she was Sigmund Freud or someone.'

Angie frowned, wondering what this Sigmund Freud looked like. Knowing her luck, she probably had squeaky clean hair and a really fashionable pair of trousers.

He nodded at the Lambretta. 'Come on, Squirt, let's get the wind in our faces.'

Angie climbed aboard. 'He must be nice, though.'

'Who?' Martin shouted above the noise of the revving engine.

'The boy who's lending you the books.'

Martin turned his head to check the traffic before

pulling out into the street. '*He*, Squirt, is a very nice young *she*.'

Jill Walker was wondering how all this had happened to her. Here she was, on a Sunday afternoon, ironing in the semi-darkness because she couldn't afford to waste the electricity – *Of course I can manage, Mummy* – in a dingy basement room in a house that she shared with two miserable biology students, who were more interested in things in jars than in going out anywhere. There was a world outside that everybody said was 'swinging'; but she had yet to see any evidence of it. To think she had actually chosen to live here: to leave her family, her friends and the beautiful Sussex countryside, and to come to London to study economics because everybody said what a fantastic place it was. Well, she had yet to see what was so fantastic about it. In the six months or so that she had been here, what had she seen? The Mile End Road, damp washing, and nasty things in formaldehyde left on the bathroom shelf. Oh, and don't forget the library, she'd seen that as well. Totally thrilling.

She blew out a long puff of air and smacked the iron down on the board in frustration.

What a swinger she was. They should do a feature on her in the papers.

She picked up the iron again and posed like a fashion model. 'Miss Jill Walker of Twycehurst', she said, simpering into an imaginary film camera, 'is taking London by storm. You will have noticed the faint sheen of grease on her hair that she has tried to disguise with a sprinkle of talc. This is not due to the lousy hot water supply in her flat, but is a statement of the very latest style. Soon, every dolly bird will be wearing theirs just

25

like it. Probably even greasier and positively caked with powder! Asked about her constant appearances at all the trendiest nightclubs, on the arms of Mr David Bailey, Miss Walker replied—'

The sound of the doorbell – even that had a dull, monotone buzz – jolted her back to reality. 'Coming,' she said, hurriedly getting rid of the pose and the iron.

She opened the door, forgetting, as usual, her mother's anxious warnings about the supposed terrors of city life and her instructions that she should never, ever, do so without first peering through the letterbox to find out who was there.

'Hello. Er . . .'

'Martin.'

'Yes, Martin. Of course. Er . . . Hello.'

'I came about the books?'

'Books?'

After a few moments' awkward silence, it dawned on Martin, that George, the bloke in his group who had assured him that Jill had every book anyone could possibly want – she was loaded apparently, a rich farmer's daughter – and that he, George, had asked her personally if Martin could borrow some of them and she had said 'Why not?', was maybe exaggerating a little bit. Or, more likely, he was a bloody, rotten liar who had just put him, Martin, in a really embarrassing situation. He'd kill the lying toe-rag when he saw him on Monday.

And then there was all that petrol he'd used. He could have put that towards the blue checked Ben Sherman shirt he'd set his heart on.

'Sorry, Martin, you'll have to explain.'

Martin ran his fingers through his short fair hair. 'It was George.'

26

'You've lost me already.'

'Red-haired bloke, bit of a know-all.'

Jill was none the wiser. 'Look, why don't you come in and have a quick cup of coffee? I could do with a break.'

Martin was sitting in a battered utility armchair, with threadbare upholstery and a broken spring, by a spitting, feeble gas fire, sipping chalky instant coffee, facing Jill Walker, who was perched on a similarly dodgy chair. And he was in heaven.

He had known her for less than ten minutes, but Martin had decided that Jill Walker was the nicest, sweetest, funniest girl he had met in his entire life. Not exactly the prettiest maybe, although she certainly had something really special about her: a lovely face, rather than a beautiful one, and flicked-up, dark hair that was sort of cute, like Emma Peel's in *The Avengers*. Gorgeous. But whoever she looked like, she was definitely the nicest, and poshest, girl he had ever met. And she also owned more books than anyone he had ever met before either, although she seemed to think she had hardly any compared with what she was used to at home. George appeared to be right about one thing at least: Jill Walker was obviously loaded.

'Honestly, Martin, take them.'

He looked at the pile of books at his feet. 'But you might need them.'

'I don't think so.' Jill curled her legs under her, and took another mouthful of coffee. 'I'm thinking about changing courses. Probably colleges as well. So I've not bothered even starting the latest essay.' She flashed her eyebrows. 'Or the one before that.'

Martin felt as if he'd been pole-axed. This wasn't

right, he'd only just met her and she was clearing off.

'That's a shame,' he said feebly. 'Why?'

Her smile lit up her face. 'Sounds pathetic, but I'm lonely. I just haven't settled in here.'

He wanted to say: You're lovely. How can you be lonely? Instead, he said: 'You've met me now.' He hid his fluster at his own boldness in a careful study of his coffee mug.

'That is so kind, Martin. Thank you.'

Say something else. Quick. 'Er, must be nice living in a flat,' he busked. 'Independence and all that.'

She grimaced around the room. 'If this is independence, I don't think it's all it's made out to be.'

Martin grinned back like a ninny. She was smashing.

'Maybe if I had a chic little bachelor-girl flat in Chelsea? What d'you think?'

'No! That's miles away!' He had blurted out the words before he had registered what he was actually saying. 'From college, I mean.' He stood up clumsily, gathering the books into an untidy heap. 'Thanks for the coffee, Jill. And, really, thanks a lot for these.'

'My pleasure.'

She followed him over to the door. 'Maybe it might be worth starting those essays after all.'

He spun round to face her, shedding a heavy volume on the basics of macroeconomics at her feet.

She bent down and retrieved it for him. As she returned it to the toppling tower in his arms, she looked up into his eyes.

Martin gulped. 'I could help you if you like. With the essays. You know, to say thanks for the—'

'Coffee?' That smile again.

'Yeah. And the books.'

'I'd be really grateful. Thanks.'

As she reached round him to open the door and her hand brushed his arm, Martin felt giddy from her touch and the smell of her standing so close to him.

'Perhaps we could meet up?' she suggested. 'Tomorrow? At college?'

Martin nodded enthusiastically. 'Sure. Yeah. Sure.'

'Good. I'll see you then.'

Martin backed up the basement steps, smiling down at the wonderful girl smiling back at him. Was this really happening to him? A girl with her own flat?

It was a dream come true.

Chapter 2

Sarah Pearson fussed around, arranging a box of jam tarts and a packet of chocolate Swiss rolls on a doily-covered plate. She had already emptied a tin of salmon on to a serving dish and, along with a bowl full of salad, Sarah was satisfied that she had created a perfect Sunday tea, with all her granddaughter's favourites.

She looked out of the kitchen window at the bright, clear sky and, knowing it wouldn't be dark for a good few hours, smiled happily. It was a treat now that spring was here at last; seeing blue skies made her feel as if a lid had been lifted and she could breathe again. And it was good to see the railings along the balcony looking smart after their fresh coat of paint.

The council hadn't done too bad a job in doing up the old flats: nice big windows, an Ascot heater in the tiny new bathroom they had put in, and a back boiler in the fireplace. But the best thing about the refurbishment of Lancaster Buildings was that it had saved the residents from having to move into one of the tower blocks that were all they seemed to build nowadays.

Sarah carried the food through to the front room, and placed it, just so, on the lace tablecloth. She might have lived on the fourth floor of a tenement block in Poplar, but Sarah still liked everything to be nice: spotlessly clean, and with all her things around her. And things were what Sarah had plenty of. Every flat surface, and every inch of cabbage-rose-patterned wallpaper, was covered with some little knick-knack, souvenir, or framed photograph, most of which were shots of a self-conscious-looking Angie that Sarah had snapped with her Box Brownie.

At the sound of the doorbell chiming its jingly greeting, Sarah snatched a hurried look in the mirror, patted her immaculately set hair, and hurried through to open the front door.

'My little Puddeny Pie!' She threw open her arms in welcome. 'Come and give me a great big kiss.'

'Hello, Nan.'

'Come in. Come in. Take your cardie off, sit down and I'll make us a nice cup of tea. And there's a bit of salad and a few cakes if you're feeling hungry.'

Sarah poured a generous measure of thick, sterilized milk into her cup and added two heaped spoons of sugar from the stemmed cut-glass bowl – a permanent feature on the dining-room table ever since Angie could remember – and then topped it up with dark orange, scalding tea. Then settled down into her armchair, as Angie perched on the edge of the sofa.

'You sure that's all you want to eat, love?'

'I've had loads, thanks, Nan.'

Sarah sipped her tea and frowned. Angie was never exactly a chatterbox, but she was being so quiet it was ridiculous, and she'd hardly touched her food. Sarah tried to sound casual: 'How's your mum?'

'You know.'

'Still seeing that . . . What's this one called?'

'Chas.'

'That's him. What do you think of him? Another five-minute wonder?'

'Suppose so.'

'You seem a bit down, pet.'

Angie shrugged. 'There was a sort of misunderstanding, Nan, that's all.'

'Had more words indoors? Your mum swinging the lead again?'

Angie chewed on her lip.

'I'm not making excuses for her, darling, but she's sort of got into a habit. She's made not doing anything for herself a way of life.' Sarah shook her head. 'I blame myself. When she had you I made such a fuss of her. Looked after her like she was an invalid.'

'Did having me really make her so ill?'

'No, love. Not ill. Look, don't let's talk about that now. Tell me how you're getting on at work. What have you and that Jackie been up to?'

'I should be going soon.'

'Why don't you phone her? Jackie. She can run along and tell Mum you're staying with me tonight. We could have a game of cards. Rummy. You always enjoy that.'

'I'd like to, Nan, but I've got work in the morning, and I've not got any of my things with me.' Angie stood up and listlessly pulled on her cardigan.

'OK, pet.' Sarah went over to the window that took up almost the whole wall behind the ornament-covered Formica-topped bar that she had recently had installed in the already crowded room.

She looked out at the darkening sky. The deep blue was studded with pinpricks of light, the terrestrial stars created by the lamps which glittered amongst the forests of derricks and cranes lining the nearby docks. There would be no foghorns on a lovely clear night like tonight.

She pulled a cord and the pink, nylon velvet curtains closed with the satisfying swish that always made Sarah

32

smile. Who ever would have thought she would have had curtains that drew themselves? That Doris Barker came up with some things.

Sarah smoothed her hand lovingly over the fabric, sending out a crackle of static. 'You promise me you'll be careful going home, babe. There's some funny blokes about, you know. Blokes what try and take liberties with young girls.'

Angie's breath came out in a little snort. 'Who'd want to take liberties with me?'

The wonders of her curtain track forgotten, Sarah spun round to face her granddaughter. 'What did you say?'

Angie stuck out her bottom lip. How could she ever have dreamed Martin was interested in her? Whatever would he say if he found out what had gone through her stupid, thick mind?

'Angie?'

'Well, not exactly pretty, am I? Not exactly a fashion model or someone a boy would—'

'You listen to me, young lady. You've got a lovely face and a beautiful little figure.' Sarah put up her hand to silence her granddaughter's protestations, then marched across the room and fished out a tartan zippered shopping bag from behind her chair. From its depths she pulled out a fat, leather purse. 'Angela, it's your birthday next week.' She flipped open the purse and took out two five-pound notes. 'I want you to take this.'

'But, Nan—'

'No buts, you just do as you're told.' She thrust the money into her granddaughter's hand. 'And don't tell your mum you've got it.' Sarah knew her daughter too well. 'Now, you wait there.'

Sarah disappeared into the front bedroom, the room

Angie had never known her grandmother share with anyone, her grandfather having died years before Angie had even been born.

'I got some things for you. Off Doris,' Angie heard her call from the depths of the wardrobe. 'I was saving them for next week.' Sarah's voice grew louder as she straightened up and came back into the living-room. 'But I'll give them to you now. To cheer you up.'

In one hand, Sarah held one of the crocheted flying helmets that, suddenly, no self-respecting dolly bird could be seen photographed without, and, in the other, she held a black leather box.

'Here.' She put the box on the mantelpiece. 'Let me put this on for you first, and you can open that in a minute.'

Angie stood in front of the chimney breast, staring into the brass sunburst-framed mirror, while her grandmother pulled the hat, with some difficulty, firmly on to her head, and buttoned it tightly under her chin.

They both looked mortified at Angie's reflection. Loose strands of greasy hair were plastered unflatteringly to her cheeks; her eyebrows had been shoved down into a single, scowling line; and she was left looking as if she was wearing the kind of rubber bathing cap sported by people who liked to lard themselves up in preparation for a swim across the Channel.

It looked even worse on her than Martin's crash helmet.

'Maybe if I loosen the button a bit.'

'Nan, it looks barmy.' Angie turned to face her grandmother, her features distorted into a troll-like grimace. '*I* look barmy.'

Sarah whisked off the hat and shoved it in her apron

34

pocket. 'She's given me the wrong bloody size. That's what she's done. I'll skin that Doris when I see her in the morning.'

Angie stared down at her feet. She couldn't stand much more of this.

'Here. Open this.' Sarah handed her the black leather case. 'And if that doesn't fit . . .'

Angie let out a resigned sigh. What was this, a false nose, glasses and moustache set? Something to make her look even more ridiculous? But she still did as she was told. Angie was like that.

Inside was a dainty marcasite watch with a narrow, black velvet strap.

Her voice quivered with self-pitying shame. 'Nan. It's lovely.'

'Just like you, sweetheart.'

'But I can't take the money. Or this. It's too much. Too nice.'

'Don't be silly. You are going to take yourself, and that money, up West, and you are going to buy yourself the prettiest dress you can find.'

Sarah bent down to put her purse back in her bag, automatically straightening the already perfectly tidy, lace chair-back as she stood up. She hesitated, then said, 'You mustn't let your mum get you down, you know, babe. She doesn't mean anything.'

'It's not Mum. Well, not only Mum. It's . . .' Angie's words trailed away.

'I know.' Sarah took her by the shoulders and turned her back to face the mirror. 'Here. Just look at yourself.'

Sarah unwound the elastic band and loosened her granddaughter's hair around her shoulders. 'Look at the thickness of it.' She weighed Angie's heavy, if oily, dark, chestnut hair in her hand. 'Plenty of girls would go mad for hair like yours. And look at those lovely green eyes. You're at a difficult age, that's all. You've just got to believe you're worth something.' She swallowed back her tears as she turned Angie back round to face her.

Kissing her tenderly on the forehead, she folded her granddaughter in her arms. 'You've just got to believe in yourself, darling, that's all.'

The glass-domed clock on the desk chimed nine. Another of Sonia's 'finds'. David Fuller hated the bloody thing. With its weird twists of this, and shiny bits of that, it looked like it was worth about two bob. It looked like it was worth that, but David had seen the bill.

It wasn't just the cost that made him so wild, he could afford it after all, but it actually looked like a piece of crap, that's what upset him. Sonia was a mug for any posh-speaking salesman who told her something was classy. At least she used to get it right most of the time, buying decent antiques and things David could under- stand, but since she'd started going for all this modern gear, it was like living on the set of some dodgy spy film.

Still, he never had to put up with any of her old nonsense littering up his office over in Greek Street – Sonia wouldn't soil her calfskin pumps walking the streets of Soho to get there.

Christ, that woman had changed.

He bit the end off a King Edward cigar and stuck it in his mouth, waiting for the bulky shape of Bobby Sykes to reach out and light it for him.

David savoured the first taste of tobacco in silence, then levered himself forward in his leather chair. 'Right. What have you got to tell me, then, Bob?'

Bobby clasped his hands in front of him, as though protecting himself from a kick in the groin, and gazed down at the rug in which his size elevens were almost half-submerged. He was puzzled by the bold, geometric design, wondering how someone would want such a monstrosity. His Maureen would never let a mat like that through the street door, let alone have it down on the floor of the prefab. Maureen liked nice things, in nice tasteful colours. Sometimes Bobby wondered how Dave let his old woman get away with buying such a load of old shit.

'Bob?'

'Yes, Dave?' Bobby looked up mournfully. He hated all this getting mixed up with other people's domestic bollocks. Especially Dave's. It was awkward. Tricky. You never knew if you were saying the right thing. He would much rather be out on the streets, straightening out some villain or other. He could handle that: keeping people in order. That was his job. But all this lark, this was a different matter. This got him down.

'Wake up, Sykesy. I was expecting some sort of a report, remember? On what happened this afternoon.'

A report. Bobby rubbed one of his massive hands over his shaven head. 'I, ummm . . .'

'Just spit it out.'

He took a deep breath. 'I watched her, like you said. Parked up and followed her on foot.' Bobby stared down at the patterns again, big pink triangles against deep orange squares and a sort of purply, swirly background. Weird.

David squinted up at him through a haze of cigar smoke. 'Do you know, Bob, you're getting on my nerves. Do me a favour: pull that chair over here, sit down, and tell me what happened.'

Bobby cheerlessly followed orders. 'As soon as you left, she ran across the street. In a right hurry, she was. Nearly got run—'

David slapped his palm on to the desk. 'Bob!'

'She went in a phone box.'

'She made a call?'

Bobby, accepting the glass of Scotch that David pushed across to him, shrugged. 'Yeah. I reckon so.'

'Yes or no?'

'Yeah.'

'Then what?'

'She come out looking all chuffed. Then started walking up and down this one bit of the park. Up and down, up and down. Like bloody Felix the Cat she was. Just kept on walking. I'm telling you, Dave, me legs are killing me.'

'Get on with it.'

'She kept looking at her watch, like she was expecting someone to turn up or something.' Bobby stared into his glass.

'Come on, Bob, I'm getting old here.'

'I've got to say it, Dave, she got herself worked up into one hell of a mood. All happy at first, then right agitated. Then she went back to the call box, looked like she never got through – as far as I could make out, like – then went off and got herself a cab. Then I followed her back here, waited for five minutes, then I called you from the phone box on the corner and you let me in.' He paused, then added, for want of something else to say, 'And, as you can see, here I am.'

'I'd have to be blind to miss a big old lump like you, Bob.' David stood up, took the barely touched glass of whisky from Bobby's hand and slipped him a tight roll of notes in its place. 'Go on home. Buy something nice for Maureen for spoiling her Sunday. I'll see you in the morning.'

As David padded along the broad, thickly carpeted corridor that led through to the bedrooms, loosening the collar of his sports shirt – Sonia liked him to 'look respectable', even at sodding weekends – he heard Bobby Sykes slam the front door from what sounded like about half a mile away. The size of this flat was a joke. Another of Sonia's bright ideas. It was bloody huge, easily big enough to house a family with three or four kids, rather than a miserable, sodding couple without a single one.

As David neared the master bedroom, he could hear Sonia talking on her private line.

He stood there, in the passageway, listening.

'It's all right, I just heard him going out. The pig slammed the door as usual.'

There was a pause.

'But are you really sure it was a coincidence? Why should he call you on a Sunday?'

Another pause.

'I suppose so. I missed seeing you, that's all. I had the room booked and everything.'

She giggled happily. 'Mikey Tilson, you are *such* a rude boy.'

David's lips twisted into an enraged snarl. 'I'll give him fucking rude.' He kicked the door open wide, just in time to see Sonia fumbling around as she tried to fit the receiver back into the cradle.

'Wrong number?' he said.

'Yes. That's right.'

David was pleased to see she was shaking.

The next morning, David was sitting in his Greek Street office, at a big, scratched dining-table that served as his desk, talking to someone called Peter about a business deal in West London.

Bobby Sykes stood in the corner of the room, waiting in respectful repose, as glad as his boss to be far away from the Mayfair mansion block where they had had their embarrassing conversation about Sonia Fuller's latest tricks the afternoon before.

Bobby could cope with this. This was a man's world. Sort of grubby, shabby, just the way he liked it. He wouldn't like to live in a grimy place like this, of course, your home was different, but women sorted all that out. This was his work, and even though the street betting business was finished now, they were still doing men's work. Proper graft. Bobby wasn't exactly sure what it was they did, apart from it being about getting people out of properties that Dave had acquired, and something to do with getting into import and export, but the actual mechanics of earning the dough, that was for the Guvnor to know, and for other people not to wonder about. Asking questions wasn't sensible in Bobby's world.

Another of the bank of telephones on the desk rang. David looked over at Bobby and gestured for him to answer it.

Bobby did so with a gruff, 'Yeah?' then hurriedly had to conceal his exasperation.

'Mrs Fuller's on the blower for you, Dave. What shall I say?' He had tried to mouth the words in a subtle sort of way, so as to minimize the interruption of his boss's other call, and to prevent Sonia from hearing him. He had failed on both counts.

40

David looked at his watch. It wasn't even nine thirty. 'Blimey, up this early on a Monday morning? She must've fell out of bed.' He sniffed loudly and cleared his throat. 'Tell her I'm busy.'

The big, burly man raised his eyebrows, and gave David a *don't do this to me* look. He held out the receiver. 'Dave.'

David could hear Sonia going on. And on. He shook his head.

Bobby swallowed hard. 'Er, Mrs Fuller? Dave says—'

David heard her screeching blue murder. 'Just give it here, Bob.'

Bobby handed him the telephone, relieved not to be part of whatever was going on.

'What is it, Sonia? I'm busy.'

Bobby thought it appropriate to make himself scarce, and disappeared into the outer office, where Bill and George sat in the comforting fug of old cigarette smoke and ripe language.

'I wondered if I could have the Jag.' Sonia paused for the briefest of moments, but long enough for David to notice. 'With a driver,' she continued. 'I want to go shopping.'

'What, fed up with the Mini already? Well, I suppose you must be; it's all of two weeks old.'

'David, don't be so unkind. You know what it's like trying to park in Kensington. And Monday-morning traffic is always dreadful.'

'You've got a terrible life, you have, girl.'

'Why are you being so grumpy?'

'All right, don't go on. I'll send the motor round with Bobby.'

'Bobby! But he's such a thug.'

41

'Sonia, I am a thug.'

'No, darling, you are a businessman.'

'Yeah. Yeah. So's everyone in the property and import games these days.'

'What?'

'Nothing. Who d'you want me to send round? George? Bill?' He waited. No reply. 'Or how about Mikey?'

'Mikey will be fine.'

David could hear the triumphant smile in her phoney, poshed-up voice. 'I bet he will,' he sneered.

'Sorry?'

'You will be, sweetheart,' he said, after he had put down the receiver.

'What are you doing here, Squirt?' Martin sank his teeth into the doorstep of hot, buttered toast that he held in one hand, and snatched his parka from the banister with the other. 'Can't stand the thought of going to work on this beautiful Monday morning?' He grinned and winked at her.

Angie blushed and concentrated on her feet. 'Jackie had to come back for something,' she mumbled.

They both looked up the stairs as they heard Jackie wail in alarm. 'Aw no, Mum, I can't wear them! What'll everyone think of me?'

Then they heard Tilly Murray making soft, cajoling noises, and then Jackie responding with a despairing moan.

Martin rolled his eyes. 'Hark at the fashion plate.' He checked through the folders in his canvas satchel and then slung it over his shoulder. 'You know, Squirt, I don't know why you two have stayed friends. You're nothing like one another.'

Angie managed a miserable little smile. She didn't need Martin to tell her that.

'You should have stayed on at school. Done your A levels and gone on to college like me. All Jackie's ever interested in is what she looks like. She could never be bothered with school, but you're different. You should use that brain of yours. Make something of yourself.'

Angie was momentarily stunned; of course she should have stayed on at school. She knew that. Maybe she wouldn't have made it as far as A levels, but she could have done her Os and got herself a better job than the dead-end, rubbishy one she had now. Unlike her friend, Angie had desperately wanted to do her GCEs, but her mum had insisted that she had to leave. Had to. Angie would never forget her words: 'You've got to go out into the world. Learn how to make your own living. Learn how to look after yourself. No other bugger will.' Ironic advice, considering her mum had hardly ever done a hand's turn herself, but had preferred to live off her never-ending succession of boyfriends.

But how did Martin know she had a brain? Know she was unhappy being a rotten filing clerk and rotten dogsbody in the head office of a rotten shipping and heating oil company? He wasn't interested in her.

Was he?

Before Angie had a chance to think of something bright, or funny, or even simply sensible to say in reply, Martin gently ruffled her hair and was off out of the street door.

Thank goodness she had got up an hour early to wash it this morning, and that her mum had left her hairdryer on the kitchen table. Her nan was right, her hair was nice when it was clean. Thick and shiny. And maybe

Martin did care about her. No, not maybe, he had to care about her. He had said such nice things. Had really noticed her.

She would buy a new dress with her nan's birthday money. A whole new outfit. And she'd . . . She'd . . . She'd do lots of things.

She felt hope and happiness rising in her heart, and even Jackie's groans and complaints as she stomped downstairs couldn't spoil her mood.

But as Angie stood on the platform of the local underground station twenty minutes later, looking along the tracks, willing a train to appear she was, again, well and truly fed up.

Not only was she late for work, all her attempts to tell her supposed best friend about her exciting plans for a new look had been ignored; all Jackie was interested in was the tragedy of how she came to be wearing such hideous hosiery.

It had all started when she and Angie had been hurrying down the steps at Becontree station for the first time that morning. They were dashing to catch the tube to Barking, from where they would take the mainline train to Fenchurch Street. But Jackie had caught her leg on the central banister and – disaster! – had laddered her sheer, cream tights. Being unable to contemplate going to work with a run in her tights, she had insisted on going home to change. She had also insisted, of course, that Angie accompany her. Then Jackie had almost passed out with shock when she discovered the only things to wear in the whole house were a pair of American Tan stockings belonging to her mother. Stockings were bad enough, but *American Tan*.

Now she and Angie were back on the platform, and Jackie was failing to come to terms with the indignity of it all.

'I hate these rotten things, Ange. I hate them. I only hope that shop in Leadenhall Street'll be open, so I can get some decent tights. Do you think it will be?' Still peering over her shoulder at her calves, she added, 'I don't know why I'm bothering asking you.'

'I'll ignore that.'

'Well, be honest, what do you know about fashion? It's important to me, how I look—'

'Charming.'

'Don't get touchy. It's because I'm a receptionist. You're stuck in that horrible little back office, so it doesn't matter. And you don't care anyway.'

'Thanks again. And, if you must know, I do care.'

Jackie bent down and ran her fingertips up her shin, trying to smooth the thick, orange nylon into something more acceptable. 'Yeah,' she said absently, 'course you do.'

'I mean it. I was looking at that magazine you gave me over the weekend.'

'What?'

'*Honey*. I read it and worked out what I want for my birthday.'

'What's that, then?' Jackie was still preoccupied, but Angie was her friend, so she had to at least sound interested.

'You're going to have to help me.'

'Course.'

'Did you hear me, Jack? I want you to help me.'

'*Yes*.'

'I want you to change me.'

45

'Change you?' Jackie giggled. 'Into what? A white rabbit? I'm not a bloody magician.'

'Don't laugh. I want you to help me look pretty.'

That had Jackie's full attention. 'Pretty?'

'I want to be a dolly bird. Like in *Honey*. Nan's given me some money for my birthday, and I'm going to use my savings to get a really fab hairdo.'

'A really fab hairdo,' she mimicked. 'Bloody hell, Ange, hark at you.'

'And hark at you. Your mum'd go mad if she heard you swearing like that, Jacqueline Murray.' Angie tossed back her hair. 'Anyway, why shouldn't I be a dolly bird?'

'Because, Angela Knight, whenever I suggest you put on even a little tiny bit of make-up, or try and lend you a skirt or something, you say you don't want to wind up looking like your mum.'

'Who said I want to look like her? I just want to look, like I say, like a dolly bird.'

Jackie pulled a face. 'Blimey.' Her mind began working overtime. It was obvious when she thought about it: Martin. Angie fancied Martin. But did he fancy Angie? She couldn't imagine he would. She would have to investigate this one. 'A dolly bird, eh?'

Angie said nothing, she just fiddled with the buttons of her navy mac, the same mac she had worn almost every day since she had started work in the City a week after her fifteenth birthday.

'Won the pools, has she?'

'Who?'

'Your nan. Giving you money.'

'Don't think so.'

'And what's your mum gonna say?'

'She probably won't even notice. So long as I don't bother her.'

Jackie narrowed her eyes. 'What's brought all this on?'

Before Angie could think of a more convincing reason than: I thought your gorgeous brother actually fancied me; then I didn't, but now I'm not so sure, but I think he just might, so I'd better tidy myself up a bit. Just in case. Or even a less pathetic reason than: I can't bear being the object of my mum's pity, and my mum's boyfriend's sneering, the District line train came into sight.

Jackie elbowed her way forward to get a good spot at the front of the platform. 'With a bit of luck we'll get into Barking in time for the twenty past.'

'Meet me later?' Angie gasped, as she struggled through the other tardy, Monday-morning commuters. 'To talk about it?'

'OK. I'll see you at the sandwich bar in Leadenhall Market just after one.' Jackie spat the words through her teeth, as she glared a warning at a middle-aged man who thought he could get on the train before her.

'Can't we go to the Wimpy in Wentworth Street?'

'Please yourself.'

'Good, I've got to get a few bits for indoors.'

'Your mum left the cupboard empty again?'

She had, but Angie would never have said so. She didn't like admitting how carelessly her mother treated her, not to other people. Not even to Jackie. It made Angie feel ashamed. But despite having to spend half her lunch hour doing food shopping, despite the crush on the train, and despite being late for work, Angie Knight was beaming with pleasure. She was going to be a dolly bird. And then Martin would really notice her.

Well, maybe she shouldn't quite jump the gun about Martin, maybe she had better wait and see, but he had definitely seemed interested in her.

Definitely.

'Martin.'

At the sound of his name being called in that unmistakable accent, Martin knew it could be nobody but Jill Walker. He took a deep breath and turned round to look for her in the sea of students moving listlessly along the corridors to their morning lectures.

She waved cheerily at him. 'I'm glad I found you,' she said, edging her way towards him. 'I've looked every-where.'

She was puffing. She must have been rushing around the place. *Looking for me.*

He grinned foolishly. 'Well, here I am.'

'I wanted to tell you that I'm going to see my personal tutor. This morning. To explain I'm behind, but I'm going to catch up. And I wanted to say thank you.'

'For what?'

'For being so nice to me.' She cocked her head to one side and smiled. 'I wondered if you'd let me say thank you properly. Wondered if you'd fancy coming round to the flat. On Saturday night. For something to eat.'

Martin's stomach did a back flip, just as if he was in an express lift that had screeched to a halt mid-way down a tower block. 'That'd be great.'

Great? It would be fantastic.

Recalling what happened next – at least two hundred times that wonderful Monday morning – Martin couldn't imagine that he would ever feel so elated again. Jill had smiled another one of those smiles, had raised herself up on her tip-toes, and had kissed him on the cheek. Just like that. In front of every one.

'About seven?'

He nodded dumbly.

'See you later?'

Martin nodded his head up and down again like a prize nit.

'It'll only be spaghetti bolognese and a bottle of Chianti,' she called over her shoulder, as she hurried off along the corridor. 'Will that do?'

Again the moronic nodding. But Martin genuinely could think of nothing to say. Jill Walker had asked him round to her flat on Saturday night. For spaghetti and wine.

Martin had never actually eaten spaghetti bolognese before, and he had certainly never had Chianti – it wasn't the sort of thing they went in for round their house – but, more important, as far as Martin was concerned, was the fact that he had never had sex before either.

As Sonia lowered herself on to Mikey, straddling him, with her skirt hitched up round her waist, she let out the gasp of pleasure that he had learned to expect from her when they 'made love', as Sonia insisted on calling it.

They were in the back of David's Jaguar, Mikey having suggested, with a wicked grin, that 'doing it in the motor' would be more fun than going to the hotel room that Sonia had booked for them. And Sonia had readily agreed.

She'd do it anywhere. Mikey liked that about her.

As she moved rhythmically up and down, her breath coming in short, increasingly loud gasps, Mikey closed his eyes, his chest rising and falling with the exertion, as he matched her movements, thrust for thrust.

With a low moan and a shudder, Sonia threw back her head and burst into satisfied, happy laughter.

Slowly, she opened her eyes, kissed him hard on the mouth, and wound her fingers roughly through his tight, black curly hair.

'All right for you, girl?'

'What do you think?'

'I think we should see what you can do for me now.'

Mikey tore open the buttons of her thin, lawn blouse and grabbed at her breast. Too far gone to protest, she laughed again as Mikey drove into her, and she bucked and reared like a liberated pony across his broad, muscled thighs.

Unusually, she began to speak. 'If only that pig . . .'

Mikey pushed harder and faster, and her words were reduced to short, gasping bursts.

'Could see . . . what we're doing . . . to his precious . . . upholstery . . . It would be . . .' She sank her nails into his back.

'What?'

'Perfect.'

Knowing that the man on the other side of the door – Jeff, the head of security at the Canvas Club – was staring at him through the peephole, David Fuller smiled pleasantly. 'Only me, Jeff. Let us in.'

Puzzled as to what his boss was doing there so early, he immediately slid back the bolts to let him in. But before Jeff had a chance to realize what was going on, Bobby had slammed the door back on its hinges, trapping him against the black painted wall.

'Sorry, mate,' said Bobby flatly. 'Never saw you there.' He ruffled the thick neck hair of the excited

Alsatians, cooing gently at them, 'Say hello to your Uncle Jeff,' and shoved the door shut behind them with his foot.

Jeff, six feet three of toned muscle, staggered away from the wall, trying to staunch the blood pouring from his nose with the back of his hand.

'You're not doing a very good job of that,' David said, offering him the blue silk handkerchief from his top pocket. 'Try this.'

Jeff took it with a nod.

'Now, let's go through to the office. I've got a few questions about the books.'

'So you reckon it's Mikey Tilson taking the dough from the nightly cash collection?'

'On my life, Dave. I wouldn't cross you, you know that.'

Bobby was standing with his back to the office door, with the dogs still straining on the leads.

'I'm not happy. You should have said something.'

'I didn't know nothing about it. I swear.' Jeff examined the blue silk square for any signs of fresh blood. 'I thought because he was working for you, he'd be kosher.'

David considered for a moment. 'Not a word to anyone. All right? I don't want him getting wind of what we know, and going off on the trot.'

'You can trust me, Dave. You know that, don't you?'

David didn't answer him. He had other things on his mind. 'I've decided to change things. Make them', he paused, 'more business-like.' He recalled the words Peter Burman had used. 'Diversify and that. I've been taking a bit of advice about expanding more in the property game.' He paused again. 'And a bit more on the import-export side. Distribution.'

'But the Canvas is still a good earner. You always say so. Like the snooker clubs.' Jeff didn't like the sound of this. He didn't fancy being put out of a job, especially not now his Jean had another baby on the way. It wasn't so easy to get a job when most of the adverts said 'no coloureds', even the completely trashy jobs, never mind well-paid, responsible ones like this.

'The snooker clubs I'm not so thrilled with any more, but you're right about the Canvas, Jeff. Clubs like this are getting a lot of very nice publicity at the minute.' David thought about the photographs in the Sunday papers of celebrities having a good time in West End night spots, including a few in his very own Canvas Club. That sort of publicity never did a business any harm. Who knows, maybe they'd have some of the nobs favouring the place. They seemed to spend as much time in night-clubs as rock-and-roll stars nowadays, and to use plenty of the merchandise he was about to get into in an even bigger way. 'And that's why I ain't going to let some two-bob little tool like Mikey Tilson go spoiling things.'

He wiped the back of his hand roughly across his mouth as he pictured punching Mikey Tilson's grinning, stupid, face to a pulp. 'Hold back five per cent of the takings, Jeff. That's what I reckon that arsehole's been pocketing every night. Let's see him get a bit worried. See what he does.'

'Sure.' Jeff dabbed gingerly at his nose. 'I'll let you know.'

'Be all right to handle this by yourself? Or shall I send Mad Albert round for back-up? He's due out soon, and I can easily get cover for him on his usual debt-collecting if you reckon you need him.'

'No, Dave. I'll be fine.'

'Good man, Jeff.'

'No offence about the bloody hooter, eh, mate?' Bobby held out his hand. Jeff shook it. He and Bobby both knew he was only following David Fuller's orders. And that he would have been very silly not to.

'This week's really going to drag, Jack. I don't know if I can wait till Saturday.'

Jackie, her arm linked through Angie's, jerked her friend to a rough halt, saving her from the 145 bus *en route* to the Heathway.

'I know you're excited, Ange, but pull yourself together. You nearly got us killed.'

'I'm sorry, Jack, I'm just really excited.'

'Angie, if you don't shut up, I'm going to wish I'd never bothered getting you that bloody appointment. It's all I've had out of you all the way home. You're only going to the sodding hairdresser's.'

'I know, but Michaelton's.'

'Let's just hope they do a better job on you than his barber did on him.' Jackie raised her chin to indicate the man standing outside Spicer's the greengrocer's, on the other side of Gale Street. He was in his thirties and was dressed in the drapes and brothel creepers that had once been favoured by the Teddy Boys. Stuck like a butterfly on a pin for the past ten years in the style of his youth, his hair was slicked and greased, moulded into an extravagant, gravity-defying quiff.

Jackie and Angie looked at each other and collapsed into giggles.

'How embarrassing,' snorted Jackie. 'What a prize twerp.'

'Yeah, what a twit,' agreed Angie, but as soon as she'd said it she felt guilty. Angie knew what it was like to look stupid, to be an object of derision.

It hurt.

Angie pushed open the front door with her shoulder – her mum never bothered to lock it – and hauled the two bags of groceries through to the kitchen. It had been a real rush at lunchtime. But she knew that if she didn't get some shopping in, they'd have nothing.

It was in a complete mess: an ashtray full of fag-ends on the table, a sink full of dishes, and a puddle of partly dissolved instant-coffee grains spreading out over the stainless steel draining board.

'Angie? Is that you?' a voice called from upstairs.

Angie stared up at the ceiling. She was getting ready early tonight, must be going to the West End. 'Yes, Mum.'

'Bring me up a cup of tea, there's a good girl.'

Angie made the tea and took it upstairs, all the while planning what she was going to say.

'You're still in bed,' she began as she put the mug on the bedside cabinet.

'I know.' Vi exhaled a long, lazy plume of smoke. 'I looked in that mirror this morning and knew that I'd been letting things get to me. I looked worn out. So I decided to catch up on a bit of beauty sleep. To have a little rest.'

She stubbed out her cigarette and sipped at her tea. 'I won't be wanting too much to eat just now, I'm going out with Chas later. A couple of poached eggs on toast'll do.'

Angie stood there, staring at her mother with her hair rollers bristling from under the pink chiffon scarf and the remnants of yesterday's make-up streaked round her eyes. She looked a real state.

'And have a little tidy up downstairs, Ange. I don't want Chas coming round and seeing all that mess.'

Angie swallowed hard. 'Shall I do the eggs before I do yesterday's washing-up? Or shall I clear up the front room first?'

'Don't you take that tone with me, Angela.'

'Mum, I've been working all day. And I even had to find time to do the rotten shopping, because you said you were busy.'

'You kids, nowadays,' sighed Violet, dramatically. 'You have it all too easy.'

Angie's mouth dropped open. She never usually confronted her mother about her demands, but then she at least usually got herself out of bed and dressed, even put the washing-up in to soak, and managed to drop a bit of washing round the launderette for a service wash. But this was ridiculous. And after what she'd heard her saying to Chas . . .

Angie steeled herself. 'Mum, I can't do everything any more. No. I don't mean I can't. I mean I won't. I'm fed up with it all.'

Violet's green eyes blazed with anger. 'Are you answering me back?'

'No, it's just—'

'Don't you get saucy with me. You're always the same when you've been round your bloody nan's. She puts ideas in your head. Interfering old cow.' Vi lit another cigarette. 'Treat you, did she?' she asked casually, picking a strand of tobacco off her tongue.

'No,' lied Angie, pulling down her sleeve to cover her new watch. 'I wouldn't let her.'

From her mother's scornful expression, Angie could see that Vi thought her daughter was little more than a fool. 'Just get down those stairs before I lose my temper,' she said wearily. 'Go on. Get the hoover out. I'll be down in a bit.'

Course you will, thought Angie as she ran down the stairs, the tears welling up in her eyes, as soon as I've done everything, that's when you'll be down.

Angie really had had enough. Wait till Saturday. Then she'd show her. She'd show everyone. She was going to change herself. Change her life. She'd show her what it was like to have to do things for herself. She'd show Jackie that she could be just as interested in what she looked like. And she'd prove to Martin that she was a whole lot more than just a little squirt.

Chapter 3

'Angie, if you don't get yourself in there. This minute. I'm going to start screaming.'

Angie, wide-eyed with fear, stared at her friend, knowing she was easily capable of doing something as embarrassing as screeching out loud in public, but still unable to force herself to go through the door and into the seriously posh-looking interior. 'I can't.'

'I told you, it's only a bloody hairdresser's.'

'But look at them.' Angie jabbed her thumb at the stylish young women sitting on the other side of the huge plate-glass window. 'And look at me.'

Jackie shrugged. 'You look all right.'

'I'd have looked a sight better, if you'd have got up in time and helped me get ready, like you said you would.'

'It's too late to worry about that now. Let's just get in there and get on with it.'

As Jackie urged her friend forward, herding her like a sheep reluctant to enter the dip, a petite, expensively dressed blonde in her thirties pushed straight past them, pulling off her linen coat as though she was in a hurry to be dealt with.

'See,' hissed Angie. 'She's like something out of a magazine.'

'A ten-year-old magazine,' sneered Jackie, giving Angie a shove. 'Now just get in there.'

As Jackie corralled her friend between her and the desk, she leaned forward – she hoped, casually – to listen to what the heavily made-up receptionist was saying to the haughty-looking blonde. It needed a bit of effort, as she was competing with the salon's sound system that was belting out Sandie Shaw's 'Long Live Love'.

'Welcome to Michaelton's,' she made out the receptionist growling, in a not altogether perfected version of the Mockney accent that had become quite the thing amongst nice young ladies from the Home Counties. 'I'm Dusty. Do you have an appointment?'

Angie, Jackie and 'Dusty' watched – respectively alarmed, fascinated and bored – as the woman's smile slipped from her lips as fast as raspberry sauce dripping off a 99 cornet in a summer heatwave and was replaced with a hard-faced scowl.

'Are you a Saturday girl?'

Dusty studied her blue-painted nails. 'Yeah.'

'I see. That's why you don't know me.'

Slowly, Dusty raised her glance to meet the woman's. 'Can't say as I do.'

'I'm Mrs Fuller. Sonia Fuller. Terry sees to me personally. I don't usually come in at the weekend, I—'

'You mean you haven't got an appointment.' It was a statement, not a question.

Sonia sucked in her cheeks, stared about her as if she were about to explode, then leaned close to Dusty and spat through her even white teeth: 'Call Terry. Tell him I'm here.' Then she straightened up, and flicked her hair over her shoulder. 'Now.'

'Sorry, Terry's in the New York salon all this week. I'm surprised you didn't know.' With that, she looked straight past Sonia and flashed a friendly smile at Jackie. Angie might as well have been invisible. 'Welcome to Michaelton's. I'm Dusty. Do you have an appointment?'

Before Angie could object, Dusty and Jackie had

whisked her past the now puce-faced blonde to the basins for her consultation with a stylist, who was described as a junior, but whose skills would have set her apart as positively senior in the place where Angie had her usual twice-yearly trim.

But this was Michaelton's, hairdressers to the trendy, the famous, and the absolutely gorgeous; the place where Dusty worked on Saturdays for a pittance – after a full week's slog in an office in the Tottenham Court Road – all in the hope that she would get spotted by a photographer collecting one of his girlfriends. And then she would start appearing in her rightful place: the front cover of every fashion magazine in Europe. It had happened to at least two girls already. Maybe three. Everyone knew that.

Dusty loved Michaelton's, and she loved having one over on rich, snooty old cows like *Sonia Fuller*, who couldn't cope with not being nineteen any more. And what a neat revenge this was: a little girl coming up to Kensington for the day from the suburbs being seen immediately, while she, *Sonia Fuller*, got a knock back. Dusty only wished she could have made a real show by taking the boring-looking kid straight over to Terry. That would have been perfect.

'Terry left a note that Miss Knight here was to be made a special fuss of,' Dusty had lied loudly over her shoulder in the direction of Marcie, the junior stylist, making sure that Sonia, who was struggling back into her linen coat, could hear every word. 'And do your very best to squeeze her friend in as well, will you? As a favour to Terry.'

That showed the old bag.

Unaware that Angie was at that very moment about to be shampooed, conditioned and set about with scissors by an expert in stylish shaping and cutting, Sarah Pearson was fretting about her family. Despite being in her fifties, she, Sarah, prided herself in keeping up a smart, clean appearance, and could only wonder about how her daughter and granddaughter lived.

They were both lovely, of course, but the last time Sarah had seen Violet, she was painting herself like a cheap tart and wearing skirts that showed most of what she had, and as for young Angie, she didn't seem interested in how she looked at all. It was such a shame. She could have really made something of herself.

Deep down, Sarah knew why Angie was the way she was: her thoughtless, self-regarding daughter, Violet, had knocked all the confidence out of the poor little love. She kept her as little more than a skivvy, so that she didn't have to soil her own lazy hands either doing stuff indoors or, God forbid, going out and finding a job somewhere.

Sarah just hoped that Vi hadn't conned Angie out of the ten pounds she'd given her for her birthday. She was such a soft touch. It made Sarah weep.

To take her mind off things, Sarah was popping along to see her friend Doris Barker for a chat. She only lived a few flats away, just along the balcony, but Sarah only saw her once or twice a week. Unlike many of the women in Lancaster Buildings, Sarah Pearson liked to keep herself to herself. She was friendly, of course, but she was a proud woman and liked her privacy, just as she liked to keep herself looking nice.

She rapped on the door, as she called through the letterbox. 'Only me, Doris.'

Going into Doris Barker's flat was like entering a department store. Apart from the kitchen, which was kept

60

'clean' for unexpected visitors, it was crammed with everything from lacy underwear to overcoats, all the things from the West End that she fenced for the group of hoisters – shoplifters – who lived on and around the estate.

Doris's was a profitable business, which she spoke of as if it were some kind of community service; her view being that it provided gainful employment for local women, who would otherwise not be able to care for their broods of kids, who, regardless of their mothers' circumstances, still needed new shoes and bigger-sized jackets for school.

Apart from her almost tangerine, dyed hair, which was teased and lacquered into a bouf of high, swirling curls, Doris was a plainly presented, middle-aged woman who opted for rather matronly Crimplene frocks in shades of muted blue or beige to cover her ample sideboard of a figure. She thought that her subdued wardrobe afforded her some sort of invisibility, the protection of anonymity, but she might just as well have dressed in pink lurex tops, leopardskin capri pants and matching stilettoes. Every-one in the area knew about Doris's entrepreneurial activities.

Not only did most of the neighbourhood do business with her – if they weren't selling, they were buying – but most of the older members of the local police force had, over the years, happily accepted 'gifts' for their wives and children from her. Their justification being that while the business was kept at a domestic level in Doris Barker's flat in Lancaster Buildings, then it was all OK. It wasn't as if she was involved in the rapidly escalating drugs business that was now taking a hold outside the once almost exclusively West End market, and that was the talk of police stations throughout the country. And, anyway, most of them had relatives, aunties, mothers even, who were as good as employed by the old girl.

The door was opened by a thin, pasty-faced woman in her sixties. 'Morning,' she said, letting Sarah into the hall. 'She's through in the kitchen.'

Doris was sitting at a blue Formica table dipping a Marie biscuit into her tea. 'Morning, Sarah. Nice out again,' she said, pulling out the chair next to her. 'Another cup before you go, Val?'

The woman who had opened the door shook her head. 'No thanks, Doris. I'm working this morning and I don't want to have to find a lav when I've got me drawers full of gear.'

The three women laughed at the vision of Val being caught short with her hoister's drawers, the specially designed shoplifter's underwear, stuffed full of swag.

'You'd better spend a penny before you go,' Doris said good-naturedly. 'Give the street door a good slam after you.'

'Will do. Bye, Sarah. Bye, Doris. I'll be round later.'

Doris raised her hand in a little wave. 'See you, love. Mind how you go.'

'Now, you'll have a cup won't you, Sal?'

'Please.' Sarah dipped into her apron pocket and pulled out the crocheted flying helmet that had so humiliated her poor little Angie. 'You ain't got these in a bigger size have you, Doris?'

'I told you they were knock-off copies for little ones.'

'I know, I just thought it might do her. She's been a bit . . . you know.'

'Sal.' She hesitated, knowing how touchy her old friend Sarah could be about her family. 'Have you

62

thought about going round to see your Violet about her?'

Sarah looked levelly at her neighbour. 'No business of your own to worry about, Doris?'

Mikey Tilson bashed on the door of the Canvas Club with the flat of his hand, and kept bashing until Jeff let him in. 'I want a word with you.'

Jeff had been expecting this particular visit. He stood well back and let Mikey in at arm's length. With his sore nose still bothering him, he was buggered if he was going to put himself in the range of any more slammed doors.

He ushered Mikey through, with a lift of his chin. 'Drink?'

Mikey settled himself at the bar. The Canvas Club was surprisingly stylish for a discothèque, even in the harsh reality of natural daylight. Unlike most similar clubs, that were little more than matt-black-painted spaces with tiny makeshift stages, this one had been decorated to an exceptionally high standard. It had imported, mosaic-style mirror tiles on the walls, a properly sprung dance floor, professional-grade sound systems, two bars with high stools and plenty of sofas and low tables. Before she had grown bored with it, Sonia had made the Canvas one of her projects and, for once, she had been right about spending so much money. The club raked in a weekly fortune. But the takings were suddenly down five per cent, and Mikey had the hump. It meant he wasn't able to rake his usual cream off the top – the cream that he had been emboldened to scoop since he had started seeing Sonia – without it all looking like it had gone boss-eyed, when it so obviously hadn't.

Mikey missed that cream; it had kept him in the manner to which he had recently become very agreeably accustomed. And Sonia wasn't a cheap hobby either.

'What's going on here? Eh?' He picked up the large vodka and ice that Jeff had pushed across the bar to him. 'I've been collecting five per cent less every night this week. How am I meant to rake me bit of bunce off that?' He tossed back almost the whole glassful, and continued with barely a pause. 'Have you been opening that big, ugly gob of yours? Or have you got yourself some little scheme going with one of your black bastard mates? I know how you lot stick together.'

Jeff pulled himself up to his full six foot three. He would take crap from David Fuller, he was his guvnor and he treated him a lot more fairly than anyone else he'd ever worked for. But being expected to take crap, especially crap like that, from a stupid prick like Mikey Tilson who kept his brains in his underpants?

'Do you want to think again about what you just said, Tilson?' Slowly, he took the long serrated knife from under the bar that, in a raid, could just about pass for a lemon slicer, and slapped it down – whack! – on the shiny wooden surface. 'I don't think I like your tone.'

Mikey drained the rest of his drink. 'Don't be so fucking touchy.'

Jeff raised the blade and touched it to Mikey's pale, smooth throat. 'Tell me, do you whiteys bleed the same colour as us *black bastards*?'

'Jeff.' Mikey put his hands up in surrender. 'Don't get aerated, mate. I'm upset, that's all. Take no notice of me.'

'No notice?'

'I'm sorry. All right?'

'You make me sick. Now clear off. If you've got any questions about the takings, you ask Mr Fuller.'

Mikey stood up to leave.

'Only I don't think you will ask him, will you, Mikey boy? And let's face it, you won't exactly be going without, will you? Knowing your past form, you've got some rich old tart keeping you. Paying you for your services.' Jeff stared at Mikey's groin. 'Ain't there a name for blokes who do that?'

Mikey shrugged down into his expensive tonic mohair jacket and sneered his derision. 'You want to mind your own business, then perhaps you won't get that nose of yours bashed in no more than it already is.' He swaggered over to the door. 'See you tonight.' He turned and looked the other man up and down with slow contempt. 'Jeffrey.'

Angie felt like a star as she stepped out of the hairdresser's with her glossy, conker-brown hair shaped into the very latest geometric cut.

Dusty's words were ringing in her ears. Her hair was a 'perfect frame for her lovely green eyes', and her 'really pretty face'. Pretty!

Jackie followed her out of the salon, with her shoulder-length fair wavy locks frosted to a pale, Nordic blonde and relaxed into a dead-straight, centre-parted style with a heavy fringe. Marcie's colleague, Mojo, had achieved the look with the help of up-to-the-minute smoothing tongs and a styling brush, a bit different from the iron-and-brown-paper job that Jackie used at home.

Mojo had insisted that it made her look just like Julie Christie.

Marcie, the bemused junior stylist, had taken real care with Angie, and had made sure that Jackie was fitted in as well – as a favour to Terry – and kept insisting that everything was absolutely 'no trouble at all'. Typical

Terry, she had thought, as she had smilingly asked Mojo to help her out, he was always meeting these little girls and promising them the earth. She just wished he could actually carry out the promises himself sometimes. Mind you, she'd been a bit shocked at first, when she'd seen the state of the dark-haired one, but once she'd taken a closer look she realized the potential that Terry had seen in her. With a bit of know-how, she could be quite a stunner, far more attractive than her more obviously pretty friend. Terry had taste all right. But then that was probably why he owned a string of top salons around the world and why she was only a junior stylist.

Jackie would never have admitted it to her friend, but she had been as terrified as Angie about going into the celebrated hairdresser's. She had never met people called Dusty, or Mojo, or Marcie before, and they scared the life out of her. It was only because she had casually tossed the name Michaelton around in their conversation in the Wimpy, when she and Angie were planning her transformation, that she hadn't been able to back out.

She just hoped her nerve held out, now that they were going clothes shopping in Kensington Church Street, and that she would find the courage to actually go inside the trendy boutiques she had been frantically reading up about since she had rashly made all these promises to Angie.

While Jackie took a deep breath, lifted her chin in the air, and prepared to hustle Angie into a terrifyingly trendy shop, with black-painted windows, a pulsating light show and throbbing music, Sonia was climbing into the taxi she had flagged down outside a boutique just a few doors away.

She had stood there, seething, while the driver – who was thinking that this arrogant mare had better come up with a decent tip – stuffed the back of his cab with all her glossy carrier bags. But despite having spent the entire morning venting her anger on the world, and on 'Dusty' in particular, by seeing just how much of David's money she could manage to get rid of before lunch-time, Sonia was still in a bad mood. A very bad mood indeed.

'Let's have a look, then.' Jackie emptied the bags on to her bed and held up a navy chiffon, A-line, sleeveless shift, covered with tiny white dots. 'See, it didn't matter we couldn't afford West End prices,' she said airily. 'This is smashing. Romford market's always got the latest styles. And you don't get taken on like a mug.'

'I think it's smashing too.' Angie held it against her and looked into the full-length mirror on Jackie's dressing unit. The dress finished a clear four inches above her knee. 'And I think it was definitely worth blowing all that on the haircut.'

'So do I, Ange. Now let's see. With the navy one you've got there.' She rubbed her hand thoughtfully over her chin. 'The two I got. A few of my other bits and pieces you can borrow. Then there's all the material we bought – I'll show you how to make that up later. Yeah, I reckon you'll be able to get by for a good couple of weeks. Till you've saved up enough to buy something else.'

'I'll have to get some shoes.'

Jackie jerked her thumb over her shoulder towards the see-through plastic racks hanging on the back of her door. 'There are more shoes in there, Ange, than there are in the

Oxford Street Dolcis. Everything from black patent Mary Janes to a purple suede tap style – thank you, Mum's catalogue – and I'm only half a size bigger than you.' She picked up the lime-green dress she had bought earlier. 'I might wear this tonight.' Then she picked up the other one, which was almost the same, but with a pattern of bold psychedelic swirls. 'Mind you, this is nice as well. What do you think?'

This was novel; Jackie never asked Angie's opinion about anything to do with fashion or appearance. 'I . . .' She hesitated.

'Yeah?'

Here goes, she thought. 'I think the bright colours in the patterned one show off your hair really well, and the lime-green one would look really good with my eyes.'

'Right. That's what we'll wear tonight.' She tossed the dresses on to the bed. 'Now, let's have a good look at that material we got.' Jackie studied the lengths of fake Pucci cloth bought from a remnants stall in Romford market. 'We'll have to use the pattern I had to make my maroon halter-neck. This'd look great in that style.'

'When shall we do it?'

'Tell you what, instead of us doing it, I'll be nice to Mum and get her to run it up for us.' She screwed up her nose. 'It'll be a bit of a nuisance. We'll have to re-sew the hems. She won't make anything shorter than mid-knee. But it doesn't matter what our sewing's like, we'll only wear them once or twice.'

Angie carefully folded the navy and lime-green dresses. 'I'd better get home now, Jack. By the time I have a bath it'll be almost time to go out. And you said you wouldn't mind—'

'—doing your make-up. Course I don't. I'm just

pleased you're actually coming out with me for once.'
She raised her shoulders and grinned. 'This is like
playing dressing up.' She gave Angie a big kiss on the
forehead. 'With a great big, real-life doll.'

Angie grinned back.

They were both still grinning as Jackie saw Angie to
the street door.

'Watcha, Squirt.'

Angie spun round to see Martin, with just a bath towel
wrapped around his waist and a smaller towel draped
round his neck, appearing from the bathroom.

'Hello, Martin.'

'Look at you,' he said appreciatively. 'With your
hair all pretty like that, you're going to make me
jealous.'

'You're right there, Martin.' It was Tilly Murray, red-
faced from doing yet another batch of baking. 'Doesn't
she look a picture? But it's a shame about your hair,
Jackie. If you're not careful you're really going to spoil
it. Other girls'd love having all them waves you keep
getting rid of.'

As Jackie rolled her eyes at Angie, sharing the
knowledge that Mrs Murray was *such a square*, Angie
could not remember feeling happier in her entire life,
until that was, Martin winked broadly at her, grabbed the
banister rail and raced up the stairs two at a time.

'See you, Squirt,' he called down to her. 'Or should I
say, see you, gorgeous?'

Almost swooning, Angie just about managed to find
her way down the front path and back along the terrace to
her own house.

Martin, who was whistling like a canary as he
considered his freshly shaved reflection from every angle

in his bedroom mirror, was almost as ecstatic. He was getting ready to go to Jill Walker's.

To Jill Walker's flat.

'And where do you think you've been?' Vi, still in her dressing gown despite it being nearly five o'clock in the afternoon, was sitting in the little back kitchen drinking a mug of coffee. 'And what have you done to your hair?'

'I've been out shopping with Jackie and I've been to the hairdresser's, and,' she added before she lost her nerve, 'now I'm going dancing.'

'What?'

'Me and Jackie. We're going to the Wyckham Hall. In Romford.'

'If you think you're going out till all hours . . .'

'No, Mum, I don't. Jackie has to be in by eleven, and we'll be together. Mrs Murray gives her the money for a minicab.'

'Typical of that Tilly, lets them kids get away with murder.'

Angie refused to be drawn. She had heard what her mum had said to Chas about her. She knew what she really thought of her, her own daughter. But she wouldn't let her mum spoil things. Not tonight. She wouldn't let her mum spoil anything for her ever again.

'You can't go out and leave this place like this.' She waved her cigarette about to indicate the supposed squalor she was sitting in. 'Chas is coming round later.'

'Why don't you do it?'

'I don't think I heard you right.'

'Yes you did, Mum. And I can't do it. I'm getting ready to go out.'

'You'd leave me to do all this with my condition?'

'Mum, I don't want to be unkind, but I don't think you've actually got a condition.'

'If only you knew what I went through when I had you.'

Angie stared down at her feet. 'Women have babies all the time. All over the world. And they don't make their kids feel guilty just for being born. Every single day of their lives.' She raised her eyes. 'You can be so cruel to me. Do you know that?'

Violet gulped. 'Don't be soft. I'm not cruel. You know how much I think of you.'

'I know exactly what you think of me. That I'm pathetic. A timid little rabbit. Well, I'm not. Not any more.'

'I don't understand how you can treat me like this, Angela. Not after all I've done for you. When your dad got killed down the Mile End Road . . .' She paused to sniff loudly. 'They tried to take you off me. But I wouldn't let them. I said to them, I said, you're not taking my baby.' She fussed around, digging out a hankie from her pocket. 'Any other woman would have let them. But me, I wouldn't. I kept you. Despite everything.'

Angie had heard it all so many times before, yet somehow it still worked.

'I'll do the kitchen, but you'll have to sort the rest out yourself.'

'Thanks, love, you know how much I appreciate it.'

'Yeah.' Angie walked over to the door. 'I'll just hang up my coat.'

'Wait a minute, darling. Just come up and help Mummy make the bed before you start in here.'

'Peter, I'd like you to meet my wife.' David grabbed Sonia's arm as she glided through the crowd of chattering

71

strangers who were filling her drawing-room. He held her arm so tightly that she couldn't do anything but meet her husband's fat, slimy-looking, business associate.

'Sonia, this is Peter.'

'Peter? Peter who?' she asked, the boredom clear in her voice.

'Peter Burman, but just Peter will be fine,' he replied graciously in a heavy, middle European accent. As he smiled, he showed a mouth almost full of gold teeth. He inclined his head in a short bow from the neck, and took Sonia's slim, manicured hand in his large, plump paw. 'Charmed,' he said, and touched her fingers to his lips.

She was about to mutter some further inane pleasantry, but Peter's interest in her was apparently at an end. He turned from her and continued his conversation with David as though she was no longer there.

Sonia was momentarily furious at such treatment. What was going on? First that little madam at Michaelton's this morning, then the cab driver acting as if he were doing her a favour carrying a few parcels into the flat, and now this boor. But she was glad not to have to make any more ridiculous small talk with such a dull person. Peter, whatever his name was, was obviously in charge and if he wanted to talk business, then that, apparently, was what they'd all do.

Blah blah blah blah blah.

Anyway, Sonia had other things on her mind. Well, one thing, and that was how many hours it would be before she would be back in Mikey Tilson's arms.

'I'll leave you to it then,' she said sarcastically, and disappeared into the corner where she feigned a solitary fascination with her husband's vulgar popular record collection.

Burman accepted a light for his cigar from a passing drinks waiter and, while he was taking a moment to appreciate the flavour, David signalled for Bobby to go and keep an eye on Sonia. As if nothing had happened, Burman continued: 'Going legit, as our American associates might say, it's the only way forward, David. The only way. There are too many complications nowadays with all these amateurs becoming involved. Do as I have suggested, expand the property side. I have no interest outside of west and south London, so you won't be treading on my toes.' He studied the glowing end of his cigar. 'And it would be comforting to know that east London is under the control of a friend and not one of these Maltese or West Indians who are trying to muscle in all over the place.' He pointed his finger directly at David's face, something not many men could get away with. 'You, I know I can trust. That is right, isn't it, David? I can trust you?'

'Of course, Peter.'

'Good. And property has a very useful side benefit. Perfect for, shall we say, *processing* all those lovely profits from any other enterprises you might be involved in. I understand that pharmaceuticals are becoming a very rewarding area of business in the clubs. And the wholesalers are doing particularly well.'

'Can't complain,' David answered bluntly. This bloke knew even more about him than David had realized.

'Good. We are leaving now, but we will talk again soon.' With a barely discernible gesture, Peter brought all his associates, and all their very young female companions, to attention.

'Still chilly out there of an evening,' David said, as one of the men draped a fine black cashmere topcoat over

73

Peter's shoulders. 'And we all thought it was nearly summer. Still, the weather should be improving soon, eh?'

Peter inclined his head and a humourless chuckle rose from somewhere deep in his chest. 'There is no such thing as bad weather, David.' He scanned the room until his gaze fell upon Sonia, who was standing stiffly by the records under the unblinking gaze of Bobby Sykes. 'Only unsuitable clothing.' He gave another of his strange little bows. 'I very much enjoyed meeting your beautiful wife. And I very much hope you will accept my invitation to have dinner with me one evening.'

'Of course.'

'Good. I would very much like to meet her again.' With that he turned and made his way to the door without another word.

When David returned to the drawing-room after seeing out his guests, and instructing Bobby to go home and fetch the dogs ready for work, he strode over to Sonia and jabbed his finger at her. 'You. In the spare room.'

'I'll join you in the *study*,' she said pointedly, 'after I have spoken to the caterers.'

'Fuck the caterers,' hollered David, glaring at the young waiter who, while clearing the buffet table, had foolishly raised his eyes to look at him. 'Get in there. Now.'

'How dare you show me up like that? You acted like you've never been to a cocktail party before.'

'A cocktail party? Is that what it was?' Sonia didn't even bother to answer his accusations.

'Why? Why act like that? Don't you know nothing

about . . .' He hesitated, looking for the right word. 'Fucking circulating?'

Sonia didn't blink. 'You know I hate meeting people like him.'

'*People like him*? Who do you think you are? Fucking Princess Margaret? That man is my passport to going legit.'

'I've no idea what you're talking about, David, and I won't be shouted at. I'm going to have a bath.'

David grabbed her by the shoulders. He was shaking with temper. He could so easily have given her a real slapping there and then, and have thrown her out on to the streets where she belonged, just as he could have arranged for Mikey Tilson to disappear like the piece of shit he was, but the days of him being the sort of man who hit out first and then thought things through were over. David was learning from Peter Burman, the most successful slum landlord in the whole of London, that the only way forward was to look respectable. To mix with the right types and be seen in the right places. All those little hoodlums setting up all over London, they had no style, no idea about how to act in public or how to carry on a business. He was going to get away from all that, he was too old to spend his days always having to look over his shoulder. He was going to deal with Mikey Tilson, of course, but he would do it right. With a bit of style. A bit of class. And he'd do Sonia as well if she didn't mind herself. For now, she was hanging on by the skin of her teeth. She should just think herself lucky she had impressed Burman.

He let go of her and snatched up the elegant pigskin briefcase that Peter Burman had given him as a present at their first meeting. It had contained press cuttings covering just about every scam and blag that David had ever been involved in, but for which there had never been even the slightest whiff of his involvement. David had been shocked, but impressed. It had shown he was mixing with the really big boys.

'I'm going to work.'

Angie shivered as she and Jackie shuffled forward in the queue of teenagers making their way towards the double doors of the slightly dilapidated hall that stood next to the church in Romford market. 'I wish I'd put a cardigan on.'

'What, and make yourself look like a schoolgirl?' Jackie inspected Angie's face under the single lamp that shone down from a bracket high on the wall, and smoothed a streak of the Sheer Genius foundation that she hadn't blended properly into her friend's jawbone. 'You're going to have to give me more than five minutes to make you up next time, Angela Knight. Good job it's so dark in there.'

'I'm sorry I was late.'

'It's not me you should be saying sorry to, it's yourself.'

'What?'

'You know what I mean.'

They filed forward, knowing they were being scrutinized by all the boys – the huddles of preening peacocks, dressed in their checked Ben Sherman shirts and mohair trousers, with short cropped, mod haircuts, or in high-collared, plain white shirts, under chain-store versions of collarless Beatles' suits, with thick, floppy, mop-top fringes.

'I'd better warn you, Ange, this place has got a bit of a reputation as a meat market.'

'How do you mean?'

'The fellers who are not actually dancing, they sort of, well, go round the floor trying their luck at pinching and touching up the girls.'

'They what?'

'You know, they try it on. Like when we were at school, and if the boys who fancied you were with their mates, when they saw you up the shops or at the bus stop. They used to punch you in the arm and call you names. A more grown-up version of that. They all try it on here, but it's so crowded they can't take too many liberties. And, if they do, just tell them you'll scream the place down. That'll soon stop them. The bouncers here are bigger and uglier than that old teddy boy up Gale Street.'

Angie didn't know exactly what Jackie was going on about. She had an idea, of course, but she had never been one of those popular girls who boys tried it on with at bus stops, so wasn't sure of all the details. It was different reading about stuff in magazines from actually experiencing them, no matter how carefully you studied them. Angie didn't say anything though. It would have spoiled things.

It was as if she was entering another world, a world she had previously been excluded from, and to which she was at last being granted entry. But, as she took the raffle ticket that proved she had paid her admission and stepped over the threshold into the pitch-dark, cave-like interior, with 'The Last Time', the latest Stones record, belting out at ear-splitting full volume, and a boy immediately brushed past her with a whispered 'Nice knockers', Angie wondered what on earth she was letting herself in for.

*

'Are those for me?' Jill smiled broadly, as she took the bunch of windswept, almost petal-free tulips, and let Martin into the flat.

'Sorry, I had them buckled on to the back of the scooter.'

'Don't apologize, they're lovely. And it was a very kind thought. Thank you.' She went over to the sink in the corner that officially made the little basement room into a 'kitchen-cum-diner' and put them on the draining board, while she rinsed out a scummy-looking milk bottle to use as a vase.

'Throw your jacket on the bed.' She looked over her shoulder and nodded towards a door. 'Through there. Loo's upstairs on the first landing if you need it. Ignore the biology students if they're wandering about up there. They're foul. Then you can open the wine while I sort out these flowers.'

Martin opened the door and nervously entered Jill's bedroom. It was a small, dingy room – there was less light at the back because of the high walls that surrounded the tiny yard – but she had made it as cosy as she could. Most of the miserable beige wallpaper had been hidden by LP covers and there were three pink-shaded lamps that added a warmish glow to the old, heavy furniture but clashed horribly with the yellow candlewick bedspread on the narrow, ancient-looking bed, and, on a shelf made from a plank and two piles of bricks, she had a Dansette record player and a wobbling stack of 45s.

As Martin put down his parka he noticed the pile of textbooks and a pad and pen on the rickety kitchen chair that served as her bedside table. He looked at the pages of closely written notes. Martin grinned to himself. She really had decided to catch up. She must be planning to stay.

'Not exactly swinging London, is it?'

He turned round to see Jill standing in the bedroom doorway with a straw-covered bottle in one hand and a corkscrew in the other.

'I was just looking,' he said guiltily, dropping the pad on to the books as though it were a hot coal.

'I didn't think there was much to look at.'

'At your books,' he explained. 'You're catching up. I'm glad.'

'Good. So am I.' She held out the wine. 'Here, open this. I'm about to serve the spaghetti.' She went back through to the other room. 'But don't expect too much, this gas ring thing is hopeless.'

'The records have finished,' Martin said.

Jill stood up. She looked decidedly unhappy. 'I'm really sorry, Martin.'

'You can always put on another one. My record changer's the same, only plays six at a time. And I have to use this special gadget and knock all the centres out.'

'It's not the records I'm sorry about. There's no room at this stupid little table. I should have cooked something not quite so messy.'

Martin didn't understand at first, then he looked down in the direction of Jill's gaze. It was then, mortified, that he realized he had managed to eat only slightly more of the food than he had dropped on to his lap and the table.

He rose clumsily to his feet, just stopping the stool on which he'd been perched from crashing back into one of the battered utility armchairs that stood either side of the little fireplace.

'I can't believe I've made all this mess. I'm so sorry.' It was then that it occurred to him: he had probably managed to cover his face with a good dollop of the bloody stuff as well. 'I've never had this sort of spaghetti before. I've only ever had it from tins. And that's sort of short.'

Jill bit hard on her bottom lip. She genuinely wasn't sure whether she was about to laugh or cry. 'Here,' she managed to splutter, and she advanced on him with her napkin. 'It's me who's sorry.' As she reached up to wipe his mouth, Martin put his hands on her shoulders and, instead of dabbing his lips with the gingham cloth, she kissed them instead.

The kiss was tentative at first, shy, with their lips pressed softly, almost innocently, together, but then it became more urgent, with their tongues deep and searching.

Martin held her tighter, pulling her towards him, his hands moving down her back, lower and lower. She could feel him hard against her, and heard his breathing quicken as he grasped the flesh of her buttocks.

She pulled away, and looked at him, directly, steadily, straight into his eyes. 'You taste great,' she said, wiping her finger on a smear of bolognese on his chin. She was panting slightly and her voice was huskier, lower than before. 'Really great. And I don't mean the sauce.'

'And?'

'Don't let's take things too quickly, Martin.'

He dropped his chin. 'I'm sorry.'

'I think we've said sorry too many times tonight.' She put her arms round his neck. 'Don't you?'

He looked at her, trying to understand what she wanted.

'I'd like this to go further, Martin. I really would. But not too soon. Not tonight.'

'Can I at least kiss you again?'

She pushed him gently backwards on to one of the armchairs. 'You don't have to ask me that,' she whispered as she fell on top of him.

Since Martin had seen a scratch on his precious scooter just two days after taking possession of it, he had never been quite so close to bursting into tears of frustration in all his young adult life, but he could no more have dragged himself away and made his excuses to leave than he could have tackled that plate of spaghetti without plastering himself with the stuff.

As Angie felt the boy's breath, warm and damp on her neck, and listened to the sweet Tamla Motown sounds of the Temptations' 'My Girl' wafting over her, she didn't notice Jackie manoeuvring herself and her own leech-like partner so that they were dancing right next to her. But she felt the tap on her shoulder.

'What?' she mouthed.

'All right, Ange?' she mouthed back, rolling her eyes and indicating, with a bored glance, the blond six-footer who was trying – unsuccessfully – to get his hand up her skirt.

Ange surprised herself by smiling and nodding.

She hadn't been sure about what to do at first, when the nice-enough-looking boy with the light brown hair had asked her to dance, but she had said yes when he had smiled at her so gently. Then, as he held her close to him in the dark, and the music filled her head, and it was obvious that every couple that shuffled by was snogging, Angie closed her eyes tight, lifted her chin, and let him kiss her.

It was strange, frightening in a way, kissing a stranger

– and she had had to be very clear that she would *not* let him touch her like that – but she liked being kissed. It felt good. And so very different from the chaste, lips-tight-together, experiences she had had when she was about thirteen, her only other experience of such things. Whether it was the music, the atmosphere, or just that she had grown up, this made her feel sort of buzzy and tingly. It was hard to describe, but it felt good. Really good.

But what felt best of all was, at last, being desired. Being desirable.

She was no longer an outsider, someone who just read about what it would be like to be held in someone's arms. She was now one of the in-crowd, one of those girls who boys wanted to try it on with.

And Angie was going to make the most of every single minute of it.

Chapter 4

'You two have got to eat something before you go out.' Tilly Murray stood in the door of her daughter's bedroom with sandwiches, fruit and two glasses of milk on a tray. 'No, Jackie, don't even try and interrupt me, I've got wise to you two shopping all day of a Saturday and running out again before you've had so much as a drop of soup inside you.'

'You can be so aggravating, Mum.'

'I'll cock a deaf ear to that sort of talk, Jacqueline Murray, and I'll turn a blind eye to you ironing that pretty hair of yours again. You'll ruin it, just you wait and see.' Tilly squeezed past the ironing board, where Jackie was pressing the waves from her hair between two sheets of brown paper, and put the tray on the dressing unit, where Angie was experimenting with the contents of Jackie's make-up bag.

'There you are, Angie. Tuck in, love, and make sure that girl of mine eats something, will you?' She smiled fondly at her wayward neighbour's lovely daughter. She'd really blossomed these past few weeks. It was lovely to see it.

'Course I will, Mrs Murray, and thanks very much. It's really kind of you.'

'It's a pity you're not a bit more like Angela, Jacqueline,' Tilly said as she let herself out of the bedroom.

Jackie waited for the sound of her mother's footsteps on the stairs. 'If she could see you later tonight, I don't think she'd say that.'

Angie pelted her with a crust, and they both giggled.

'How did your mum take you going out again?' asked Jackie, still stretched across the ironing board.

'I never told her,' she said, her mouth full of sandwich. 'Nice bread.'

'What?'

'I said, nice—'

'Angie . . .'

'I told her I was going over Nan's.'

'Lucky they don't talk to one another, or you'd really be for it.'

'She wouldn't care.'

'I bet your nan would.'

'I suppose.' She helped herself to an apple. 'I'll go over there in the week. After work.'

'Blimey. You're going mad, aren't you? You've been out the past four Saturdays on the trot, and now you're going out in the week as well?'

'I haven't seen Nan in ages. I've spoken to her on the phone from work, but I've never let it go this long without seeing her.'

'Who'll run round after your mum if you're out again?'

Angie shrugged and took a big slurp of milk. 'She'll just have to do things for herself or go without. Won't she?'

'Right, I'm off then. I'm going to the Canvas to check on things, then I'm meeting a few of the chaps there.' David was looking in the mirrored doors of the walk-in wardrobes, fixing his cuff-links. He could see the reflection of Sonia lounging amongst the heaps of pillows on their huge, satin-covered bed. 'I want to show off the place. Let them see how classy it is. Their wives are going to join them a bit later. I want you to be there.' He forced out a smile. 'You can brag about all the decorating you did.'

It killed David to almost beg her to go with him, but Peter Burman had specifically said they were taking the women along, and how much he had wanted to see Sonia again. David didn't want to look as if he had no control over her.

Sonia studied her nails. She really had to speak to that manicurist, the colour of the polish was totally passé, not the slightest hint of glitter. 'What time are you planning to be there?' She sounded bored.

'I'm having a word with Jeff, just before ten. Then meeting the others about quarter past, half past. Have a quick drink and—'

'Too late. It'll be packed with kids by then.'

'—and then,' he continued, barely keeping his temper, 'we're going to have a bit of supper at the Astor.'

'I don't feel like sitting in some stuffy night-club while you talk business.'

He closed his eyes, took a deep breath, then said lightly, 'You always love the Astor. Or how about the Pigalle?'

'Not tonight.'

He stared at her reflection in the glass. 'Are you saying you're not coming?'

'I've got a headache.' She dragged her hands dramatically down her face. 'I could', she said weakly, 'come along a bit later. Say, eleven? I could have a nice cool bath, take a few pills for this blasted head of mine, and then I'm sure I'll be right as rain. All smiley and fit to entertain your colleagues and their ghastly wives.'

He wanted to ask her what made her better than the other women, at least they knew their place, but instead he said grudgingly, through tightly stretched lips, 'I'd appreciate it. I'll tell Bobby to be here for you at half ten.'

'Don't forget your briefcase,' she called after him. 'Oh, and don't bother with Bobby. In case I decide to come a little earlier. I'll call a cab. OK?'

'OK.'

The moment she heard the door slam, Sonia snatched up the telephone.

'Mikey. It's me,' she breathed into the receiver.

'Me?'

'*Mikey.*'

'Sonia.'

'That's better.' She paused a moment, making him suffer. 'You didn't answer the phone right away. Busy?'

'Not too busy for you, doll. Fancy meeting down in the car park again? See if we can give the guard a thrill? Let him get a little peek at those pretty lace panties of yours, while I—'

'No, not tonight, Mikey,' she interrupted him.

'No?'

'No. I've got a much better idea.'

'Are you mad?' Mikey stared at Sonia as if she had taken leave of her senses. She had parked two doors along from the Canvas Club, and there, as clear as day, under the flashing, neon entrance sign, was her husband's dark-green Jaguar. 'How're you going to explain me being with you? Tell him we've been shopping this time of night? Even he won't swallow that one.'

Sonia licked the end of her finger and traced a wet line around his lips. 'We're not going inside,' she said, her

86

pupils dilating with desire. 'We're going round the back—'

Mikey gulped and took her finger in his mouth.

'—to the alley behind the club. And we're going to do it. Up against the wall. Apparently it can be quite a busy little spot.'

Mikey threw back his head and laughed. 'While your old man's inside?'

She nodded slowly.

'I love it. You are a dirty cow, Sonia. Do you know that?' He slipped his hand under her skirt, searching out the top of her thigh, and then the soft mound of curly hair. 'No knickers.' He laughed even harder. 'I like you, Sonia Fuller. I like you very much indeed.' He slipped two of his fingers inside her and closed his eyes as he felt her, warm and moist and ready for him. 'Now get out of this car,' he breathed, 'and let me give you a seeing-to you're never going to forget.'

Bobby stood there like a schoolboy, while his wife, Maureen, checked that his cuff-links were in properly, and that his tie and the handkerchief in his top pocket were knotted and folded, just so.

'When Dave tells you your jobs for next week, remember they're delivering the new carpet Monday morning, Bob.'

He tapped his temple. 'Got it in the diary, girl.'

'You will make sure you're here, won't you? You know I don't like strange blokes wandering all over the prefab when I'm by myself.'

Bobby squeezed her round her little waist. 'I won't let you down, babe.' He kissed her tenderly on top of her head. 'You know that.'

She twisted round, with his arms still encircling her. 'I'll be glad to see the back of this old carpet. Them dogs of Dave's have ruined it.'

'You love them dogs.'

'I know.' Maureen unpeeled his hands from her waist and walked over to the corner of the living-room, where Duke and Duchess were snoring in a contented tangle of paws and tails on Bobby's old sheepskin coat. 'But it was still a bit much being landed with two full-grown Alsatians, just because Lady Muck didn't want her place messed up.'

'Here, I meant to tell you, Maur.' Bobby patted his chest, making sure he had everything he needed in his inside pockets for a night out at work with David Fuller. 'You ought to see the mat she's made Dave have in their spare room.'

'What in his *study*, you mean?'

They both laughed at Sonia's pretensions.

'It's sodding horrible.'

'Language, Bob.'

'Sorry, babe. But you should see it. Right vile, it is.'

'I don't know why he puts up with her. He could have had his pick of anyone he fancied.'

'Not you though, eh, Maur?'

'No, not me.' She raised herself up on her toes and kissed her huge bear of a husband full and lingeringly on the lips.

'Here, watch it, girl, you're getting me all hot and bothered. I'll be wanting to play the hop if you carry on like that.'

'Just something to remind you to come home.'

'Eh?'

'After spending all night surrounded by pretty girls

dressed in frocks that show their knickers.'

Maureen flashed her eyebrows at him, then pulled away and busied herself plumping up the row of scatter cushions that she placed at even spaces along the back of the tan vinyl sofa. 'I can't understand how he tolerates her, Bob. Everyone knows he's loaded, but the money she spends. She acts like there's no tomorrow. I don't know how she gets away with it. Especially on that load of old rubbish no other person'd give house room to. And the way she acts. Like she's royalty or something.'

'I've always reckoned he only got hiked up with her because he liked having someone who wears posh clothes and talks proper and that. It's all this old nonsense he's got in his head about looking kosher.'

'We all know that, Bob, but there's plenty of girls around who could do what she does. And be a sight more convincing, if you ask me.' Maureen had now set her sights on giving the ashtrays a wipe round with the hem of her apron.

Bobby watched his wife admiringly.

'But what I don't understand is why he's still putting up with her.' Maureen cocked her head to one side to appraise her handiwork. 'After two years, he must have figured out what she's like by now. Everyone else has.'

'I was thinking that the other day.'

'Oh yeah?' Maureen spoke over her shoulder as she set about rubbing fingerprints off a heavy brass table lighter fashioned in the shape of an antique duelling pistol. 'Were you?'

'Yeah. See. I think she's playing away.'

Maureen just stopped herself from dropping the lighter on to the glass-topped coffee table. 'He'll kill her stone dead if he finds out.'

'He sort of knows.'

'You're kidding?'

'No. It's like he's playing some sort of a game with her. Beats me. If I ever found out that you—'

Maureen flung her arms as far round her enormous husband as she could reach, and rested her head on his great barrel chest. 'Bobby Sykes, that is not going to happen, now is it?'

'No, course not, babe. Take no notice of me. It's just, well, I can't imagine what's going to happen with them two. Something's got to blow.'

'She must be completely stupid.'

'You ought to have seen her the other night at the flat. When they had that party thing. No one said nothing, but I reckon she showed him right up.'

Maureen shook her head. 'I've changed my mind, Bob, she's not stupid, she's stark, raving bonkers. No one in their right mind would mess with Dave Fuller.'

'There's gonna be ructions tonight, I reckon. Dave and that Burman bloke – the one he's doing business with – are meeting up later on. At the Canvas. A crowd of them, there's gonna be. All with their old women and that. But I can't see Sonia trotting along and behaving like a good little girl. Not the way she's carrying on.'

'God help her. That's all I can say.'

Bobby stroked Maureen's cheek. 'Make sure the door's shut properly behind me, babe, and I'll tell you all about it in the morning.'

'Go on, get going, you big chump.' Maureen punched him playfully on his bulging arm. 'And make sure you clean them dog hairs out of the car when you get home.'

As Bobby carefully spread a tartan travelling rug over the back seat of the Humber, he smiled proudly to himself. He was a lucky man. There weren't many fellers who could say they had a little diamond like Maureen for a wife. Spotlessly clean; a good cook; never nagged him for money; and – he turned and winked at her as she stood, arms folded in the street doorway – she knew how to keep a man happy in more places than in the kitchen.

He felt sorry for Dave, stuck with Sonia.

'Chas,' Violet whined, 'why don't we ever go out?'

'We do.' He was lying on his back in Vi's rumpled double bed, smoking a cigarette. 'We go to the pub.'

'Yeah, that little place right out in the bloody sticks, full of yokels and their stinky dogs.'

'It's nice in the country. And we go for something to eat.'

'Yeah, the Chinese in Barking.' Her whining had turned to sarcasm. 'Great.'

'I took you out to Colchester last Sunday morning.'

'You had to go to Colchester to see that bloke about them pick-up trucks.'

'It was still out.'

Vi stroked her hand down his naked thigh, letting her bare breast brush against his chest. 'Why don't we go somewhere nice, Chas? Don't you like being seen with me?'

'Course I do. I just don't want me old woman seeing us.'

Vi slapped the flat of her palm down – smack! – on his stomach.

'Oi!'

'Well, don't be so horrible.'

'You know I'm married.'

'You don't have to keep reminding me.'

'And I don't have to put up with this either.' Chas looked at the chunky gold watch on his tanned wrist – the watch that had Vi picking Chas out for special treatment, above all the other clientele of the supposedly smart Chigwell pub, even before she had noticed his dark good looks.

'Don't be like that, Chas.'

'Sorry. Got a Masons' do tonight. A Ladies' Night. She'd kill me if I was late.' He threw back the covers, stood up on the bedside rug and stretched.

'But I'll be all by myself.' Vi ran the tip of her finger across his bare, taut behind. 'You wouldn't want that, would you, Chas?'

He stepped out of her reach and began getting dressed. 'Maybe if you was a bit nicer to people, that kid of yours for starters, a bit less selfish, you wouldn't be so lonely. I ain't seen her around in weeks.'

'Sod you.' Vi rolled over and closed her eyes. 'Don't think you're coming round here for a screw, then running out on me. You can go and bugger yourself.'

'That'd be a neat trick,' he said, pulling his sweater over his head. 'People'd buy tickets to see that.'

'You can't get round me by making me laugh.'

'Yes, I can.' Chas bent down and kissed her on the top of her head. 'See you.'

'When?'

'Not sure. In the week, probably.'

Vi sat bolt upright. 'That's not good enough, Chas.'

He looked at her sitting there. She was still a bit of all right – for her age – but she was getting demanding. And that got on his nerves. 'Like it or lump it, darling.'

She said nothing. She didn't want to burn her boats, not before she had found herself at least a temporary replacement. She smiled and shrugged. 'No choice, have I, lover?'

'No. Not really.'

He took out his wallet from his back pocket, took out two ten-pound notes and tossed them on to the bedside table. 'Get yourself a new dress.'

Vi looked up at him through her lashes and blew him a kiss. This was more like it. She'd have a nap, then she'd get up, get dressed and see if she could round up someone else to take her out for a drink and a bit of dinner.

Angie and Jackie sat at the table in the club, sipping their drinks which glowed peculiarly in the ultraviolet lighting.

'So, if that bloke sitting over there wants to meet you.' Jackie raised her chin to indicate a nearby table. 'All he has to do is pick up the phone in front of him, dial the number that's on our sign—' she pointed to the chrome-and-black number eleven by way of demonstration '—and our one rings and you pick it up.'

'I don't think so,' said Angie.

'I'm telling you, Ange. That's how it works. All the tables can ring one another.'

'No, I mean I wouldn't pick it up.' She paused and took another sip. 'Not if it was him ringing me. Look at him, he's like the old boy in *Steptoe and Son*.'

They both burst out laughing, and, as the disc jockey announced he was going to play 'She Loves You', a 'real golden oldie', Jackie snorted, 'Just like that bloke!'

As their laughter grew even louder, heads turned to see what was so funny.

At the sight of the pretty blonde and her lovely copper-haired friend, men around the room reached for their receivers. The girls' phone began ringing and didn't stop for the rest of the night.

They made a formidable pair in the unsophisticated atmosphere of Chadwell Heath.

Martin swallowed the last of his red wine – he was getting quite a taste for the stuff – and put the empty glass on the floor beside the armchair. 'Please, Jill.'

Jill was sitting on his lap, her arms around his neck. 'Martin, we've discussed this so many times. You know how much I like you. Really like you.' She paused to kiss him and he shifted urgently beneath her.

'Then why not?'

'Because I'm not ready yet.'

'It's not like I'm asking you to do anything you don't want to. I know you want to.'

'Of course I do, but . . .' Her cheeks reddened. 'Say we made a mistake and I got—'

'I'd be careful.'

'I can't.' She shook her head and stood up. 'Not yet. I need more time.'

'I suppose you want me to go.'

'It is late.'

'Yeah.' He got up from the chair, the ache in his body a mocking reminder of what he wanted to do with Jill, what he wanted to do so badly that he almost felt sick.

She fetched his coat from the bedroom, hurrying before he had time to follow her in there. 'Will you be in college tomorrow?'

'Course not. It's reading week.'

'I know, I just thought you might be popping in, that's all. Thought I might . . .'

'What? Get me all frustrated again?'

'I was going to say cook you something and then go through the notes for the next assignment.'

'I don't think so. You've cooked for me enough over the past weeks.'

'I like doing things for you.'

'Do you?'

'We could go to the pictures.'

'I'm doing a few extra shifts at the garage. To get some money for the weekend.'

'Planning something special?'

'Yeah, I'm going down to the coast on Saturday, but you wouldn't be interested. I'll probably be staying the night and that wouldn't suit you, would it? Who knows what I might try and do?'

'Martin, don't go like this. Please.'

'You can't keep leading me on, Jill. It's not fair.'

'Come on, Jackie. Make a bit of effort. We've got to get that middle bit right.'

'Sorry, Ange, I'm knackered.' Jackie let herself flop backwards on to her bed. 'I can't dance with blokes all night and then come home and start practising again.'

'But your mum and dad'll be back from your Aunt Mag's soon, and they'll make us turn the music off.'

Jackie rolled over on to her stomach. 'Getting a few dance steps right isn't what I call important. When I'm old, I don't know, when I'm thirty or something, I'm supposed to be able to look back on all this and say these were the best days of my life. I want something more, Ange. I've got bored with going to dances and that. Aren't you sick of seeing the same old faces?'

'I haven't been going anywhere long enough to get

sick of anything.' Angie stepped twice to the side, clapped, and spun round in time to the Supremes. 'Anyway, you seemed to like it well enough tonight when those blokes drove us home in their Triumph.'

'Yeah. That was all right.'

'All right? We were given a lift in a convertible.' She grinned wickedly. 'Here, do you think they're still waiting for us up on the corner?'

'I hope so. I told them we'd only be a minute while we nipped home and told our mums some lies about where we were off to next.'

'Good job you lied about which street we lived in and all. I'll bet they're searching Greenfield Road from top to bottom.'

The record finished and Angie bent down to put 'Stop in the Name of Love' back on the turntable for the fourth time. 'We've had a laugh tonight, haven't we, Jack? How about when you told that boy you were getting married and we were out on your hen night? Fancy him swallowing that!'

Jackie sighed grandly. 'I do look older than seventeen.'

'At least twenty.'

'Twenty-two, more like.' She picked absently at the pillowcase. 'Ange?'

'Mmmm?'

'D'you want to go somewhere special next Saturday?'

'I thought you already made plans for us.'

'I did. All the old gang from school are going to the Cubana in Ilford. Janice phoned and said she'd love to see you again. She heard all about your new look from someone who'd seen you getting on the train at Fenchurch Street.'

Angie snorted. 'She'd love to see me again? What, so

96

she can bully me like she used to when we were kids?'

'She wouldn't do that. Not now.'

'No, not now I look better than she ever could.'

Jackie said nothing, but it was true. Angie looked fantastic. With the new haircut, make-up and clothes – it was a complete transformation. Not like the ugly duckling or anything; Angie had never been ugly, and she wasn't exactly beautiful now. Not beautiful, but what she had was the look that every young woman was trying to achieve. Modern. Trendy. A dolly bird. The look that wasn't only envied by the girls, but which blokes all appreciated as well.

'Where do you fancy going then, Jack?'

'Anywhere that's not Chadwell Heath, Ilford, Romford or Tottenham. Not the Bird's Nest, the Cubana, the Wyckham, or the Royal. I want to go to somewhere really exciting. Like you read about. Up London. Where it's all happening. Somewhere like the Tiles. Or the Canvas Club.'

Angie stretched out on the bed next to her friend and they stared up at the ceiling. 'I'd like that as well. We might bump into Terence Stamp.' She elbowed her friend in the ribs. 'Here, Jack, say this is all there is? Say we stay in this street for the rest of our lives, living at home. Never getting married. Never having kids.'

Jackie sat up straight. 'And say we wound up looking like Miss Midgely?' She groaned. 'Looking like a geography teacher with your hair in a bun. Honestly, Ange, this can't be as good as it gets. There's got to be more.'

'Haven't you enjoyed me coming out with you these past weeks?'

'Don't sound hurt.'

'Well, I'm really grateful for everything you've done for me. I would never have known how to do my eyes or where to get my hair cut and everything. I don't want to think I'm tying you down, or holding you back from doing other things.'

'It's not you, Ange, it's just that all the magazines tell you this is the most exciting place in the world, Swinging London, the best place to be young. And what am I doing with my life? We might as well go back to the rotten youth club up St John's.'

Angie didn't much care for the direction which the conversation seemed to be taking. 'I never went to the youth club.'

'I asked you enough times. You always said no.'

'I said no to a lot of things.'

Jackie rolled over and stared hard at her friend. 'But you've changed now. And you're still changing. And so am I. I want to go places. Clubs where they have rhythm and blues. Modern jazz. Blue beat. Ska.'

'What's ska?'

'I don't know. That's the trouble. That's what I want to find out.'

'I'm sorry, Jack, I don't really fancy going up the West End. Not yet.'

Jackie returned to sullenly contemplating the ceiling. 'If you won't go up West, how about if we go to Clacton?'

'Why?'

'It's Whitsun next week. All the mods are going down their on their scooters. Hundreds of them, they reckon. For the whole Bank Holiday. Martin's not stopped going on about it.' She sat up again, her eyes shining. 'And we can go as well. We can get the train.'

Angie frowned. 'It's a long way.'

Jackie was now inspired. 'We could go Sunday afternoon and stay the night. Come back Monday evening. Sleep on the beach.'

'I don't think so.'

'Come on,' whined Jackie. 'We'd be mad to miss it. Martin says it's going to be the best weekend ever.'

'But say we get stuck and—'

'Don't be so wet, Ange. Come on. It'll be a right laugh.' She slipped off the bed and threw open her wardrobe door. 'You can borrow whatever you want. And just think: all them fellers . . .'

Chapter 5

'Let me look at you.'

Angie twirled round with her arms held wide.

Sarah Pearson could hardly believe her eyes. Here was her seventeen-year-old granddaughter, standing in front of her with her brand-new haircut, a trendy miniskirt, and cute, navy tartan knee socks with a row of gold buttons that she had sewn down the sides. She looked like a fashion plate come to life.

There was one thing, however, about Angie's new look, that Sarah wasn't so keen on. In her opinion, Angie was wearing far too much make-up. They all seemed to want to look like pandas nowadays; all the young girls were the same.

As she thought those words, Sarah's heart filled with pride. Angie was a fashionable young woman, just like all the other girls.

Sarah could have cried with happiness for her. 'Whatever do they make of you at work?'

Angie unhooked the Black Watch tartan bag from her shoulder, dropped it on the floor, and threw her arms around her grandmother's neck. 'They've put me in telephone ordering, Nan! Talking to the customers. Sorting out what they need. And "being charming", my supervisor said. And do you know what that means?'

Sarah shook her head; offices, and what went on in them, were a mystery to her.

'No more filing. No more tea-making. And no more

inking up that horrible old Gestetner machine and getting covered in it.'

Sarah had no idea what a Gestetner machine was, but if Angie didn't like them, then nor did she. 'That's great news, love. I'm so pleased for you. Just seems daft they never realized what you were capable of before.'

'I don't think I'd have thought I was capable of much myself. Not the way I used to mope about. But that doesn't matter. It's all in the past. This is me now.' She twirled round like a ballerina in a jewellery box. 'And it's fifteen shillings a week more!'

'I'm so pleased for you, sweetheart. You look just like one of them models.'

'Leave off, Nan. I've changed my hair and put on a bit of make-up, I've not performed a miracle.'

'If I can't be proud of my own granddaughter . . .' Sarah guided Angie gently towards the table. 'Now, you get stuck into that lot, while I fetch something from the bedroom. Don't wait for me. You must be starving after working hard all day.' Sarah was beaming with pleasure. 'Telephone ordering, eh?'

Angie settled down to tackle the heaped plate that Sarah had had ready for her. 'Smells lovely, Nan. I love your boiled bacon dinners.'

She had barely swallowed her first forkful of carrot and pease pudding, when Sarah was back by her side.

'I got these off Doris. She said they were all the go.' She held out a short, royal-blue, V-necked shift, with a long, white, pointed collar, and a pair of white plastic, mid-calf boots, with cut-out panels running round the top.

'Nan!' Angie was on her feet, touching the dress. 'It's exactly like the one me and Jackie saw in Kensington.

101

That we couldn't afford. And the go-go boots. They're fantastic.'

Knowing Doris's girls, it probably is the one you saw in Kensington, thought Sarah, but what she said was: 'Same as in the magazines, Doris reckons.'

'They are, and they're fab, Nan. Really fab.'

'I'm glad I picked the right things. And looking smart won't do you any harm in your new job.'

'They're much too good for work. I'm going to save them for going out at the weekend.'

'Well, sit back down and finish your tea, and you can tell me all about where you're going.' Sarah carefully draped the dress over one of the armchairs and sat at the table opposite her granddaughter. 'Anywhere special?'

Angie's enthusiasm seemed to wane momentarily, and she took a long moment cutting a slice from one of her boiled potatoes. 'Me and Jackie are probably staying round our friend Marilyn's. With a few of the others.' A stranger would have thought she was speaking matter-of-factly, but Sarah could hear the guilty hesitation in her granddaughter's voice. 'We're going out dancing. I'm not sure where yet.' She left the potato speared, uneaten, on her fork. 'Mum's driving me mad about going out again, and she said she hates me going out in short skirts.'

'You take no notice, babe, you look lovely. Really pretty.'

Angie dropped her chin. 'It's nothing to do with how I look, Nan. Not really. She just doesn't like the fact that I've started having a life of my own. That I'm not some little kid still. Not her slave any more. But I couldn't carry on like that, Nan. I couldn't.'

'Don't upset yourself, pet. I know how she gets.' She put down her knife and fork and reached out for Angie's

102

hand. 'And I also know what it means when you say you're staying round a friend's. I had it enough off your mum when she was a girl.'

'I am, Nan, I'm—'

'Listen to me, Angie. If you're going to a party, promise me you'll look after yourself.'

'Nan . . .'

'Promise me, Ange.' She went to pick up her fork again then changed her mind. 'And you know you can come and stay here any time you want. Doesn't matter how late. If you need somewhere, don't you dare think you can't just turn up. All right?'

As he eased the Humber into the kerb, Bobby Sykes ducked his head to get a good look at the decaying row of terraced houses in the Plaistow backstreet.

'Bloody hell, Dave.' He whistled softly. 'Fancy living in this shit-heap.'

'This shit-heap is near the underground, Bob.'

Bobby didn't know what sort of a reply he should give, so he said nothing and just watched as David shot his cuffs, pulling them just so, leaving an even half-inch of pure white Sea Island cotton showing under his dark grey, lightweight suit, making him look every bit the prosperous, urbane businessman.

David then felt around under the car seat until he located the length of lead piping he had stashed there, which he then wrapped in an anonymous, white hand towel.

'Get the dogs' leads on, Bob.'

As Duke and Duchess were transformed by their choke chains from snoozing teddy bears into snarling threats, Bobby took a closer look at the terrace and

103

wondered why the boss was worrying himself so much about a poxy row of houses. He knew he wasn't blessed with the most agile of brains, but he preferred it that way. He was quite content to provide the muscle. But this puzzled him. What was it all about?'

In the past, Bobby had managed to get his head round the niceties of running the protection racket – the core of Dave's business – the clubs and the snooker halls, well, as much as he needed to understand to do his job properly. And the way the money could be raked in from managing the girls, that was obvious, even to him, but this property lark his guvnor was getting into was well beyond his understanding.

Dave had tried to explain about buying houses at rock-bottom prices and then dividing them into flats, and Bobby had followed him that far, but then Dave had told him about getting bent mortgages on all the separate bits of the property or something, and that's when he had lost him. But apparently it all brought in a lot of dough. And, as long as it got him his wages to take home to Maureen of a Friday, that's all Bobby was interested in. He'd leave the big time and the figuring out to Dave.

David pulled on a pair of soft leather gloves and gestured, with a jerk of his head, for Bobby to follow him.

With the exception of number six, every house in the terrace had boarded-up windows and doors, and, with its little tub of pansies by the step, the clean, freshly painted woodwork, and the neat, lace curtains shading the windows, it stood out like a single, perfect tooth in a rotting skull.

David rapped on the polished brass knocker and waited.

He and Bobby heard a chain going on and bolts being

shot, then saw the door being opened the merest crack.

'Yes?' It was an elderly voice, probably a man's, but so frail they couldn't be certain.

'Cyril?' David asked. 'Cyril Watson?'

'Who's that? Is that you, Jim?'

'No, Mr Watson,' answered David. 'It's me, Mr Tennyson. Ronald Tennyson. From the council.'

'I don't know no Mr Tennyson.'

'I've come about the house. I've come to help you.'

'Show me your papers.' A parchment yellow hand appeared, palm outstretched. 'I'm not talking till I've seen your papers.'

Before the old man knew what was happening, David had grabbed his wrist, and had yanked him, hard, until he was pulled up tight against the door jamb.

'Now, Cyril,' David hissed at him through the narrow opening, 'you either slip that chain and let me in to talk to you, or I'm going to kick it down with you behind it, and snap your skinny arm right out of its socket.'

Bobby stood there impassively, with the dogs straining and whining for action.

'All right, all right. But let go. You're hurting me.'

'I'll let go when you undo that chain.'

As David listened to Cyril fumbling around and finally unhooking it, he kept hold of the old man's arm, twisting it round in an agonizing arc. 'Don't get no ideas, Granddad, I've got two dogs out here that haven't eaten since yesterday.'

The very slightest look of shame clouded Bobby's face for the very slightest of moments, as he followed his boss along the gleaming, polish-scented passage into the fragile old man's home.

*

'Hello, Nick,' Vi purred into the telephone. 'Yeah, long time no see. How are you?'

'I'm great, my love. Great. And all the better for hearing from you.'

Nick was an old flame of Vi's, who, while not nearly as attractive as Chas, and also a good fifteen years older, had been a very generous lover.

In financial terms at least.

For as many years as Vi could remember, Nick had been her saviour. And he didn't only have money, he had contacts. When Angie had been little more than a baby, it was Nick who had got Vi the council place on the Becontree housing estate in Dagenham. She had only mentioned how fed up she was living with her mum in Lancaster Buildings and, within a few weeks, she was moving.

It was also Nick who put the occasional fifty quid through the letterbox, even when she wasn't seeing him.

He had never been much good in bed, but Vi knew enough tricks and techniques to convince even someone as dull as Nick that he was a raging stud, a romeo of the very first order. His generosity had always made it more than worth the effort. Vi liked nice things, nice restaurants, nice clothes and an easy life, and Nick was the sort of bloke who made sure she had all those things. He was a really decent sort.

But that was the trouble. Who wanted decent? Vi was always attracted by excitement. That was why she was always leaving the poor sod in the lurch.

She had dropped him – this time – six weeks ago, when Chas had come on the scene. Going for the short-term benefit had always been a problem with Vi, and Nick had, at times, been more like a boomerang than a boyfriend.

But Vi just couldn't resist a handsome new face, even though she usually wound up paying the price for her impetuosity. This time, the price was having to make an extra special effort with Nick so she wouldn't be spending Saturday night all on her tod.

She'd have to get round him, get back in his good books, make him want her as much as she wanted his big fat wallet. And she had every confidence that she would do exactly that. After all, she'd done it plenty of times before.

But even though Vi prided herself on giving men what they wanted – their full money's worth, in fact – she would have been horrified if anyone had so much as suggested that what she was doing was prostituting herself. In Violet Knight's selfish, self-deluding world, there were her rules and there were rules for other people, and other people were the ones who led sordid, unpleasant lives. Vi merely had a good time; did things to stop herself being bored. She couldn't help it if she wasn't satisfied with the humdrum life that suited the likes of Tilly Murray and the other pathetic wives on the estate.

And a good time was what Vi intended to have tonight. Sod Chas and his bloody wife, and their stupid Masonic dinner dance. She'd make her own arrangements.

'What a lovely thing to say,' she cooed into the phone. 'I've missed you, you know, Nick. It's been hard looking after Mum while she's been so poorly. But you know I've got no choice.'

'You're a good girl, Violet. There's not many around who'd give up their time to look after their old mother, and to bring up their little sister all alone.'

Without missing a beat, Vi launched into an

elaboration of the tale that had served her so well over the years. 'Mum's no trouble, Nick, and let's face it, she gave up her life for me and young Angie when she was widowed. I just feel I owe her, that's all.' At least the old bag had some uses, even if it was only as an alibi.

'How's she doing?'

'Much better, thanks. And my cousin Susan's come down from Newcastle to give me a break. Sitting in with Mum for a few days. I don't like putting too much responsibility on Angie, she's only a kid after all.'

'You're kind, do you know that, Violet? There's not many young women about who'd bring up their kid sister and have her call them Mum. They'd be ashamed to have the neighbours putting two and two together and coming up with five. Really kind.'

Bloody kind, she thought, especially as I've not got a cousin Susan, Angie's obviously my own kid, and I've not talked to my old dragon of a mother since I can't even remember when. 'Don't be daft, Nick. But that's why I'm calling. Having this bit of time to myself, I wondered . . .'

'I'll be round to pick you up at eight. How's that?'

'Smashing.' She paused. 'What shall I wear?'

'Something really nice, darling. I'm going to give you a great big treat after all you've been through. I'm cancelling the do I was going to and I'm taking you up the West End for a meal and dancing. Then we are going to go back to your place for a little night cap, and . . .'

'Nick,' she giggled, rolling her eyes in anticipation of the big non-event, 'you are such a naughty boy. You'll have me blushing.'

Sonia closed her eyes and stretched out in the sweetly scented bath, with the bubbles right up to her chin. Her

108

hand stroked up and down her thigh as she pictured in her mind what Mikey had done to her in the alley behind the Canvas Club. Christ, he made her randy just thinking about him and the things he did to her. She had never known a man like him.

She slipped a finger inside herself and moaned softly. She wanted him so badly she couldn't wait until tonight.

But it was more than the excitement of the fantastic sex, Sonia had never felt so passionately about any man before, had never dared to take such risks, and had certainly never seriously considered leaving David for anyone. Even though she had been unfaithful to him since the day they had met, she had been discreet, careful, not wanting to gamble losing her very nice life, or, knowing David's temper and his fondness for violence, even losing her looks. But her feelings for Mikey were different; they had grown during these past few months into something she had barely recognized at first, then, when she had realized what was happening, they had completely surprised her, frightened her almost. She was helpless to do anything about it, and was no longer the one in control. Mikey was the man she wanted, wanted to be with for the rest of her life.

Wanted so badly . . .

She bit down hard on her bottom lip as she came to a fast, shuddering orgasm, picturing what Mikey would soon be doing to her again.

Aching for his touch, she took a deep breath and sank down under the foaming water.

Jackie and Angie walked towards the sea front from Clacton Station in the miserable dampness of a dull, misty twilight. They were supposed to have arrived early in the afternoon, but having completely misjudged how far away Clacton actually was, they had missed daylight completely. To make matters worse, now they had finally arrived, the place was practically empty.

'Hours we were on that train.' Angie stopped to rub her heel. Why had she worn her new go-go boots without breaking them in? She was already getting blisters; by the time they got to wherever it was Jackie was taking her they'd be rubbed up to the size of poached eggs. And the black-and-white, op-art mini dress, with its skimpy halter-neck and cut-out midriff that Jackie had helped her botch together on Saturday afternoon – *you'll only wear it once or twice, it doesn't matter if the machining's wonky* – was as good as useless against the chill of the evening air.

'I didn't think we were ever going to get here.' Angie shivered. 'And I'm sure it's going to start raining. I don't know why I ever said I'd—'

'Ange, don't go on. All right?' Jackie, in a red-and-green striped affair that looked more like a little boy's rugby shirt than a dress, was almost as cold as Angie, although she would never have admitted it. 'You're doing my head in, moaning all the time.'

'I'm not moaning, it's . . .' She waved her arms around in a pathetic show of disappointment. 'I don't know. After spending all that money on the ticket and coming all this way, I thought at least something would be happening.'

'Ten minutes ago. On that train,' snapped Jackie, marching forward with angry deliberation. 'You were worried that too much was going to be happening. That we'd be threatened by gangs of greasers. I wish you'd make up your flipping mind about what you want and what you don't want.'

'I'm sorry, I just wish—'

'What?'

'I don't know.'

'We'll be down the front in a minute.' Jackie could barely spit the words past her gritted teeth. 'You see. It'll be great. Wonderful. Where it's all flaming happening.'

At that precise moment, they found themselves passing the town hall. It was a stately brick building, set back behind a manicured lawn, and, stuck in the grass, was a notice-board which listed forthcoming events. Unfortunately, the highlights, as far as the month of May was concerned, seemed to be an over-60s tea dance, two whist drives, and a junior badminton competition. Not really what the girls had been hoping for.

Angie gestured at the notices in weary surrender. 'Did I really let you bully me into coming all this way for a tea dance? I know, maybe, if we hurry, we can get to a church in time for the evening service. Then we won't have wasted the entire day.'

Jackie took a deep breath and kept on walking in a straight, determined line, moving in what she could only hope was the direction in which the cosmopolitan attractions of Clacton sea front would soon be laid out, tantalizingly, before them. And if they weren't, she might just have to throttle her supposedly best friend, Angela Moaning Minnie Knight, because she was driving her right round the bloody twist. In fact, she almost wished she was really staying with Marilyn – as she had pretended to her mum – Marilyn, the girl who had moved away to East Ham in the second year, yet had still faithfully kept in touch with all her old school mates, and who had been so looking forward to seeing them all again at her birthday party. Shame Jackie had invented her on the spur of the moment – a birthday party was very tempting.

Jackie stepped into the road without a second glance, her lips and eyes contracting into tight, displeased circles. 'You are so ungrateful, Angie. I didn't have to ask you to come, you know. If it hadn't been for me, you'd have been sitting at home all by yourself tonight, and tomorrow. *Bank Holiday Monday*.' The gravity Jackie lent the words made it sound more like some arcane pagan ritual than a day off work.

'Oh, I am so sorry.' Angie broke into a begrudging trot to catch up with her – that'd be all she needed, getting lost in this place – her sore feet making her uncharacteristically sarcastic. 'I suppose I should be pleased you made me come with you. After all, you could have asked Marilyn. But, surprisingly, I am not absolutely flipping delighted that—'

Before Angie could finish her sentence, her words were drowned out by the roar of a pack of accelerating motorbikes that had appeared behind them from out of the dark.

Jackie spun round in alarm, and was confronted by a dozen, glaring headlights. She froze, a terrorized fawn in a hunter's sights.

Without a thought, Angie sprang forward and yanked her stunned friend out of their path.

They stood on the pavement, panting and staring, as the bikes sped past; the hollers of abuse from the foul-mouthed rockers, as to what slags everyone knew mod girls to be echoing in their ears.

'Exciting enough for you?' Jackie gasped, her chin almost touching her chest. 'They could have splattered me. All over that tarmac.'

'They said we were mod girls,' Angie gasped back incongruously.

Without warning, the first of the bikers did a screeching U-turn and began heading back towards them. 'Oi, slags!' he yelled.

Without further discussion, the girls broke into a run, their disagreement, and Angie's blisters, forgotten, as, with a single mind, they headed for a family, complete with suitcases, who were walking along about fifty yards ahead of them.

The girls, panting and wide-eyed, fell into step with the respectable-looking group.

'Mind if we walk along with you?' asked Jackie, in an ingratiating voice. 'Only we're trying to get away from those motorbike blokes.'

'They said horrible things to us,' explained Angie. 'Called us all sorts. Really scared us.'

The woman, a stern, matronly type, ushered her children to one side. 'You walk along with Daddy,' she said in a brisk, Yorkshire accent, then turned back to address the girls. 'Is it any wonder blokes are calling after you?' she challenged them. 'You', she pointed to Jackie's thigh-hugging dress, 'are practically showing your underclothes. And as for you.' This time she jabbed a finger in the direction of the circular cut-out that flashed a small patch of Angie's bare, pale midriff. 'You look like . . . Well, never mind what you look like. But you do.'

Angie hung her head, shame-faced at the woman's words, but Jackie was furious, her lips were pressed together so tightly her cheeks ached. Bloody old cow! What did she know, with her daft voice and her ugly perm? Jackie had a good mind to tell her where to get off,

113

and she would have done so as well, had the motorcyclist not just been joined by all his companions.

They were circling in the road alongside them, continuing to jeer, although in a more subdued way now that they were in earshot of grown-ups, especially as the man with the kids looked a bit fit and might well be the type to front them out if they pushed their luck.

The woman glared, narrow-eyed, at the bikers. She'd die if her Melvin grew up to be like one of those little tearaways, or, God forbid, if her Myra ever went out looking like these two. The make-up! They looked as if they'd had their eyes blacked for them in a fight. But they were still someone's daughters. Although the Lord alone knew where their mothers were, letting them out in such a state. 'Where're you heading?'

'Down the front,' said Jackie hurriedly, worried that Angie would ask for an escort back to the station and that she'd then have to come up with some bizarre explanation for her mum, to account for their abbreviated evening at Marilyn's. Bloody Marilyn. She was getting on her nerves almost as much as Angie. 'We're meeting my mum and dad down there.'

'You're in luck.' The woman relaxed a little at this slightly unexpected news. She took a map from her pocket and waved it in Jackie's face. 'We're going in that direction. We're off to the Waverley.' She paused, waiting for the name of the hotel her sister-in-law had recommended to register with the girls. Her efforts were wasted, there wasn't a flicker of recognition of the name. Obviously, it was far too decent for the likes of these two. 'I'll see you safely down there, but I'm warning you, if you so much as think of looking at my husband, I'll march right up to your mother and tell her exactly what I think of her. Allowing girls to go out with their private parts barely covered.'

Jackie resisted saying she'd rather poke her eyes out with a sharp stick than have to so much as take a single peek at her ugly old sod of a husband. Instead, smiling sweetly, she replied, 'That's really kind of you, thanks ever so much.'

The short, silent walk to the promenade brought them to a scene that couldn't have contrasted more with the sober, residential streets around the station. It wasn't only the bright lights and noise coming from all the typical seaside attractions that lined the front, it was the sheer numbers of young people milling about the place. Angie and Jackie had never seen anything like it. They were everywhere: on foot, on scooters and on motorbikes; parading up and down the front, jostling for space, swaggering and shouting; mods and rockers, male and female, divided only by tribal affiliations marked by choice of hairdo and clothes.

The atmosphere of youthful anticipation was so thick that the girls could almost taste it. It made their skin prickle with nervous excitement. And the underlying threat of conflict and violence that was bubbling up amongst the hordes of barely restrained young people wasn't lost either on the woman who had guided them into this maelstrom of hormone-propelled tension.

'I don't know, Arthur. What on earth was your sister suggesting, sending us here when we could have gone to the Lakes?' The woman scooped her children to her and shook her head. 'Trust you for listening to her. Trust you. I'm warning you, this Waverley place had better have clean sheets, acceptable lavatory arrangements and good

115

strong locks on all the doors. Or, Arthur Turpin, you'll have me to reckon with.'

Jackie and Angie scarcely acknowledged the Turpin family's sour-faced departure for their hotel, sparing them only a brief mumble and a half-hearted wave to see them on their way; they were also now oblivious of the cold, and their row was a distant memory. The girls were transfixed.

Youth, as it always had, and always will, was calling to youth.

'This is more like it, eh, Angie?' Jackie took her arm and they joined the packs of youngsters patrolling the promenade.

This was where it was all happening. And they were right in the middle of it.

Sonia walked across the car park and astonished the guard with a flickery wave and a cheery goodnight. It was the first time the stuck-up tart had even acknowledged his existence. Little did she know what he'd seen her getting up to with that dark-haired bloke the other night.

It made him flush, remembering the shape of the dirty cow's naked backside.

Bloody hell! She was coming over to the booth.

'Mr Fuller's not back yet, then,' she trilled, as she pointed to his empty parking space. 'These businessmen and their meetings.'

'No, he's, er, not back yet.' Had the woman gone mad? She hadn't said a word to him all the time he'd worked here and now she was practically flirting with him.

Perhaps she fancied him.

He'd read in the Sunday papers about these hoity-toity women liking a bit on the side with a man in a uniform.

And while he wasn't exactly a copper or a fireman . . .

He swallowed hard. What would he do if she made a grab for him? He had his lumbago to think of. Never mind his old woman. They didn't go in for all this modern stuff, all this wife-swapping and that, not round his way they didn't. Although he had heard stories that there were certain housewives who waited for their husbands to go out, then they put a packet of Omo washing powder in their front window – OMO: Old Man Out – as an invitation for blokes to come round and join them. It made him feel quite unnecessary just thinking about it.

But he needn't have worried; Sonia hadn't gone mad, she was not flirting, and she definitely had no intention of making a pass at him. Her odd behaviour had a simple explanation: for the first time in her life, Sonia Fuller was truly happy. She was in love.

It was almost eleven o'clock, and the girls, having spent the last of their money on an orgy of sugary, greasy junk that they had tucked into as if it was their last meal, were sitting on the sea wall, licking the final grainy remains of candy floss from round their mouths, watching the now booze- and pill-fuelled crowds from a safe distance.

'What now?' asked Angie, closing one eye and looking down her nose for any stray strands of pink sugar.

She had enjoyed, far more than she thought she would, being part of this youthful, simmering pot of turbulence; well, more of a witness than a participant really, but that hadn't been such a bad thing. A rocker had thrown a bottle that had narrowly missed Jackie and had shattered on the pavement in front of them. Rather than causing alarm amongst the crowd of mods it had been intended to strike, it had merely infuriated them. They spun round in

117

formation, like a shoal of short-haired, Ben Sherman-shirted fish, and started running after the gang who had attacked them.

It was then that Jackie and Angie had retreated with their goodies to the safety of the sea wall.

'Not sure,' said Jackie. 'But I know I wouldn't mind being indoors. It's getting flipping freezing out here.'

'I'm glad you said that. I really thought you wanted to sleep on the beach.'

Jackie swung her legs idly back and forward, knocking her heels against the rough sea wall. 'I imagine, somewhere, there's got to be . . .' She paused. 'Dancing.'

'Dancing?' yawned Angie.

'Yeah.'

'In a lovely warm club.'

'No. On the beach. By moonlight. More romantic.'

'Do you reckon crabs and shrimps do the Hitchhiker?' Angie shimmied and windmilled her arms. 'With all their little legs waving about.'

'Well they wouldn't get very far doing the Stomp, would they? They'd sink in the mud.'

'But they'd be good doing the Swim.'

They had collapsed into childish giggles, a combination of tiredness and a surfeit of sugar, when they heard the first screams. At first, they thought it was someone larking around, maybe getting up to a bit of hanky-panky on the sands behind them, but when the screaming continued and they saw a group of hobble-skirted mods with tears streaming down their heavily made-up faces, and one with blood gushing from her nose, being chased by a pack of leather-clad, chain-wielding rocker girls, they realized it was more serious than a bit of adolescent horseplay.

The next thing they heard was the defiantly aggressive sounds of male whooping and hollering, as a horde of blokes came barrelling out of a side-street towards the sea front, with another bellowing mob close behind.

They were heading straight for where the girls were sitting.

Angie grabbed her friend's arm. 'Bloody hell, Jack. Let's get out of here.'

They barely noticed the drop as they angled themselves round and plunged down into the darkness on to the damp sand below. With hearts racing, they crouched close to the wall, listening to the smashing and crashing of missiles being hurled between the roaring, shrieking gangs of rivals.

When a house brick came flying over the wall and thudded on to the seashore somewhere in the gloom behind them, they knew they had to get moving.

Jackie pulled off her red suede shoes. 'We can leg it along the beach. To the steps by the bus shelter. All right with your blisters?'

'Watch me.'

With the wail of police sirens and the crunching of heavy boots adding to the clamour and confusion above them, the girls fled from what was turning into a full-scale riot on just the other side of the wall.

They covered the four hundred yards to the shelter at adrenalin-fuelled speed, and hauled themselves up the steep steps back on to the promenade.

'I'll bet Arthur's getting what for,' said Jackie, in a creditable impersonation of the Yorkshire woman's accent.

'God help the poor sister-in-law,' panted Angie. 'All this'll be her fault.'

The girls carried on their act of composed nonchalance as they sat on the wall behind the shelter, in what they hoped were its impenetrable shadows, brushing the sand from their feet, but they were both shaking. The naked hatred they had just witnessed was like nothing they had ever seen before, and it had terrified them. And the sounds of chaotic, frenzied battle, still so close, were not dying away; if anything, they were growing louder and more angry.

'That girl. The one whose nose was bleeding. Do you think one of those other girls could really have done that to her?'

Jackie nodded, as she leaned on Angie, while she pulled her shoes back on. 'Definitely. Sandra, this girl at work, she told me about her mate. She's a mod. And this rocker girl, know what she did to her?'

'What?'

'The rocker called Sandra's mate a slut, and then she ripped the pierced earrings right out of Sandra's mate's ears.'

Angie clapped her hands protectively over the tiny gold sleepers she had only just been brave enough to have put in her own ears.

'A copper come up and grabbed them both. And, you won't believe this, the rocker girl only wore Sandra's mate's earrings to court. When she was in the stand being done for assault.'

'That is so disgusting.'

'I know.'

Angie swallowed hard. 'If you'd told me that before, I'd never have come.'

'Tell you the truth, Ange, I never really believed it. Not till I saw all this here tonight.'

'I think we should go home. I know we were going to stay overnight and everything, but this is getting dodgy.'

'Couldn't agree with you more, but how on earth are we going to get to the station without an armed guard?'

Angie rubbed her goose-pimpled arms. 'I am so cold.'

'Let's at least get out of the wind, while we wait for it to quieten down.'

They crept round into the shelter, huddled into the corner, and sat there in the dark, lost in thoughts of warm beds, sand-free feet, and nice places where you didn't have to look out for bottles being aimed at your head or chain-wielding greasers wanting to bust your nose.

At the sound of loud male voices accompanied by running footsteps, the girls grabbed on to each other and pressed themselves back against the slatted wood.

They watched, in dry-mouthed silence as two blokes stumbled into the shelter and leaned heavily on the wall for support.

'Did you see that?' asked the first voice, almost choking with laughter.

'How could I miss it?' asked a second, drink-slurred voice. 'Wonder he never got arrested.'

Jackie leaned forward. No. It couldn't be.

There was a sudden, huge roar of anger from outside, and then an amplified police demand for calm, booming through a megaphone.

'Bit of luck we left the scooters behind, eh?' It was the first voice again. 'Mind you, you're so pissed, Mart, I doubt you could even have balanced on yours.'

'Must have a piss,' the other one muttered.

'Martin! Shit!' The loud expletive had left Jackie's lips before she could do anything about it.

'Jackie?' the now drunk *and* shocked, second voice asked. 'What are you doing here?'

Jackie shook her head self-pityingly. Just her flaming luck. It was Martin. Her big, rotten brother. This was all she needed, him knowing she was here. Why, with all these people, did she have to bash into him? He'd never let her forget it. He'd have her running around after him for months if he had this to hold over her.

She'd have to strike first.

She took a deep breath, stood up and marched across to him. 'You've been drinking.'

Martin nodded happily, and grinned at his friend. 'You could say that.'

'Who's he?' She lifted her chin at his tall, rather good-looking companion. Unlike Martin, he appeared fairly sober, but, in all other ways, they looked very similar. Both of them wore gingham shirts, stone-coloured trousers, desert boots and parkas, and, as her vision adjusted to the dim, half-light, Jackie could see that, also like Martin, his friend had short, neat hair and, the sign of the true mod, *a swipe of blue eye shadow and mascara.*

Had she not wanted to attract any passing rockers, she would have whooped with pleasure. Mod style or not, she'd never let her brother live this one down. Not only half-cut, but *wearing eye make-up*. She would play this one for all it was worth.

'Jackie,' said Martin, enunciating with the pointed care of a drunk. 'This is my pal. Keith. From the petrol station.'

'I didn't think he was one of your stuck-up college friends. Not wearing make-up.'

'Keith.' Martin narrowed his eyes, and wagged a

122

finger in Jackie's face. 'This is my gobby little sister. Jacqueline.'

'She don't look so little to me, Mart.'

'Hello, Martin.' Angie stepped out of the shadows and smiled shyly. All the horrors that were taking place only a few hundred yards along the beach had melted away, dissolved by the radiant presence of Martin Murray.

'All right, Squirt?' He looked her up and down appreciatively. 'You're looking prettier every day.'

'You can say that again. You've been keeping these two a right secret.' Keith flashed his eyebrows in appreciation. 'Let's see what we've got hidden away in here, shall we?'

He mimed a kiss at Jackie and produced a pint lemonade bottle from a deep pocket inside his parka.

'Vodka and orange,' he said, gesturing with the bottle towards the interior of the green-painted shelter. 'Care to join us, ladies?'

Jackie smiled back at him. He was a bit of all right. Things were definitely looking up. 'Yeah, you can keep us warm. We were freezing our bits off in there.'

'And we can protect you from all them nasty rockers,' Keith leered.

Vodka and orange was something neither Jackie nor Angie had had before; their drinking was usually limited to halves of lager and lime and the occasional, sickly Snowball, but it slipped down surprisingly easily, and soon the bottle was empty.

'You said someone never got arrested. Who?' Jackie was sprawling tipsily on one of the three benches that ran round the walls of the shelter. She felt all mellow and restful, especially now that most of the noise outside had died down.

'The WOW man.' Martin hiccuped, folding his arm more tightly round Angie's shoulders. Angie wasn't cold any more but she liked being cuddled up to his soft green coat. Liked being cuddled up to him.

'He's got a "W" tattooed on each side of his bum,' chuckled Keith. 'So when he drops his pants and bends over . . .'

'That's terrible,' said Jackie, feigning disapproval.

'Give us a kiss.' Keith suddenly pounced on her. 'You're gorgeous.'

Angie felt embarrassed sitting so close to her friend while she snogged Keith with all the subtlety of a blocked vacuum cleaner, but she didn't dare move in case Martin took his arm away.

With some difficulty, Jackie untwined herself from Keith's clutches. 'Let's go round the back of the shelter,' she whispered, dragging him up from the bench. 'I can't snog in front of my brother.'

Jackie needn't have been so dainty, Martin was now too drunk to notice anyone other than Angie, over whom he had draped himself like a wet towel.

'Why isn't Jill like you?' Martin breathed into her hair.

'Sorry?'

'You like me, don't you, Squirt? You wouldn't try and push me away if I kissed you.'

Angie could barely speak. 'No,' she rasped, turning to look up into his eyes. 'I wouldn't push you away.'

'Or if I touched you?'

She went to shake her head, but Martin already had his mouth pressed hard against hers, his tongue forcing and searching its way between her lips. He tasted of booze

124

and cigarettes, but Angie didn't care, her head was swimming and her body was buzzing.

Martin was kissing her, and he was running his hand up and down her thigh, closer and closer . . .

Suddenly he pulled away from her, staggered to his feet, tore off his parka and, with a bit of effort, spread it out on the narrow bench seat. 'Lay on that,' he muttered.

Angie stared at the coat. Her head was muzzy from the vodka.

'So you don't hurt yourself. When I take down your lovely white lacy tights. And lick that daisy.' Martin closed one eye so that he could focus on the black and white felt flower that Angie had so carefully cut out and stuck on to her thigh with eyelash glue. 'Then I'll lay on top of you and—'

'Do you mean you want to . . .' She couldn't say it.

He held her close to him and nuzzled her neck. 'I like you, Squirt, d'you know that?' he slurred into her ear. 'I really like you.'

'And I like you,' she whispered back.

'Lay down then.'

Angie closed her eyes. Martin wanted to *do it*. With her. She hadn't thought she would ever do it with anybody, not so quickly. She wasn't that sort of girl.

But this was Martin.

Her Martin.

Her mouth was now completely dry, and she felt almost sober, as she stretched out on the bench and held out her arms to him.

Martin squeezed clumsily on to the bench alongside her, stuck his hand straight up her dress and began an inept search for the waistband of her tights.

'Taking you to a party.' His head felt strange. 'Next Saturday. Party.'

Angie's heart was racing so fast, she thought she might faint. 'I'd like that,' she panted, as she felt and heard her new tights rip. 'I really would.'

'So would I. I would like that. I would . . .'

The bus shelter began to spin, and Martin passed out cold on top of her.

Chapter 6

Angie was sitting on the sofa in the front room, with her legs tucked up under her, watching Cathy McGowan on the television, introducing *Ready, Steady, Go!* with an excitable squeal: *the weekend starts here.*

'I told you Jackie's mum would get fed up with you hanging around there all the time.' Vi sounded like she looked – sullen – as she dragged viciously on the cigarette she had just lit from the stub of her previous one. 'She's all on top, that Tilly. A right toffee merchant. Pretends she's so bloody perfect.'

'If you must know, Mum, she's not fed up with me. She said I'm always more than welcome.'

'Eeuuh!' sneered Vi in a mocking voice. '*More than welcome.* So why did you get ready to go out in here then?'

'I didn't want to take liberties, that's all. It's bad enough Jackie and Martin fighting over the bathroom, without me being under her feet as well.'

'Pity you don't worry about your own mother for once.'

Angie turned, disbelievingly, to face her. 'Are you really going to start all that hard-done-by act again?'

'Well, what am I meant to do? Look at this place.'

'Looks all right.'

'It's a mess. And Nick's coming round in a couple of hours. There's tights hanging over the bath, the sink's full, and . . . Aw, I don't know.'

Angie returned her gaze to the television, tapping her

foot agitatedly to the Kinks' latest. 'You know none of that mess is mine. I've cleared up after myself all week. Even though I've been working. While you've sat around all day and done nothing. You figure out whose fault it is.'

'You are so ungrateful. Who walked all the way up the shops and got the fish and chips you've just eaten?'

'Big deal.'

'I am not saying all this for fun, young lady. It is not some sort of game. I am being serious.'

'Am I laughing?'

Vi clapped her hand dramatically to her forehead, spraying the carpet with ash from her cigarette. 'I don't know what's got into you, Angela.'

Angie didn't take her eyes off the television. 'I've grown up, Mum, that's what.'

'Too grown-up, if you ask me. You can wipe all that stuff off your face, for a start.'

'Leave off, Mum. Please. I don't want to argue with you.'

Vi pouted pathetically. 'Why aren't you my sweet little Angie Wangie any more?'

'You're not getting round me. Not this time.'

Pathetic Violet suddenly turned into Furious Mother. 'I won't have it, young lady. If this is your attitude. Then you're not going out tonight.'

'Don't be silly, Mum.'

'How dare you speak to me like that?' Violet leaped from her chair, her nylon housecoat flapping about her like quilted, lavender wings, and snapped off the television. 'If that's your attitude. You can get out. Go on. Leave. See how you manage without me.'

Angie sighed. 'You don't mean that.'

'Just try me. Go on.' She pointed dramatically to the

window. 'You go out tonight and I'll lock the door on you.'

'Who'll do all that ironing? You won't have a thing to wear.'

Vi said nothing for a long moment, she just pursed her lips tightly and snorted down her nose. Then she turned her back on Angie and flounced out of the room.

'I'm having a bath,' she shouted, slamming the door so hard it rattled on its hinges.

Sitting in the tiny, partitioned-off area that served as the office – profit-making space for the paying customers was at a premium in Soho clubs like the Canvas – David rocked back in his chair and clasped his hands across his muscled belly. 'So, Jeff, tell me, what you've—' he paused for effect, picking at imaginary debris between his teeth with his little fingernail, '—observed these past weeks?'

Jeff looked uncomfortable, but he owed his boss too much to mug him off like some gormless punter in off the street. When Jeff had arrived in London from Jamaica, and the so-called 'colour-bar' had seen him not only without a job but without even a roof over his head, David had given him a chance. He had treated Jeff as just another bloke looking for work as hired brawn, and, when David had realized that he had a brain as well, he had promoted him, trusted him. So Jeff owed David Fuller, even if it meant crossing that piece of shit, Mikey Tilson. Jeff wasn't a man who scared easily, but he knew Tilson could be a really nasty bastard. When something stood between him and what he wanted, he went after it with a childlike greed and cunning that was never predictable, but was always spiteful.

'He came in that first night, Dave, after you told me to hold back the five per cent, and he got all confused. Counted the takings three times. Then he stared at me, hard like, but he never said nothing. When it was the same the next night, he accused me – me – of helping myself.' Jeff allowed himself a wry grin. 'Threatened to grass me up. To you.'

'He's got more sodding front than Brighton.' David shook his head. 'Then what?'

'I acted the innocent for the rest of the week.' Jeff hesitated, considering whether he had overstepped the mark. 'Then I kind of, you know, used my initiative.'

David showed no signs of emotion, he simply nodded for Jeff to continue.

'I told him it was a management decision. To hold back the five per cent.'

'Management decision? What did he say to that? Long words ain't exactly Mikey's strong point.' Another thing that made it so aggravating that Sonia was so impressed with the little arsehole.

'You're right there, Dave. I had to explain it was because the dough had been disappearing before it reached you. The boss. He wasn't happy about it.'

Still David's expression gave no hint of what he was thinking. 'Then what?'

'I thought he was going to burst a blood vessel. He went all red and lunged across this table at me. Grabbed me by the collar. Saucy fucker. Told me I was a liar, and if I thought I was getting away with it, he'd kill me.'

'He did, did he?'

'Yeah. Flash little git.' Jeff curled his lip into a disgusted sneer. 'I'd like to see him try. I'd rip his stupid head right off his shoulders.'

David stood up and straightened the handkerchief in his top pocket. 'Jean and the family all right, are they?'

'Yes thanks, Dave. They're fine.'

Sonia was sitting, naked, in the back seat of Mikey's dark-blue Ford Zodiac, repairing the damage that Mikey's passion had wreaked on her make-up. She had felt a bit let down when he had driven them to High Beech again. Epping Forest was all very well, but Sonia had fancied trying somewhere new, and then, despite the gloriously sunny start to the early June day, the heavens had opened. Looking up through the car window, as Mikey spreadeagled her along the car seat, was like trying to peer through a curtain of grey steel stair rods. It had actually made her feel quite depressed. It wasn't what she had wanted for today at all. Today was meant to have been special. She had had it all planned. But, after her initial disappointment, Mikey's fingers, insinuating their way between the silk of her underwear and her eager, moist body, soon had her forgetting that she had ever wanted anything else to happen that afternoon than what Mikey was doing to her right there and then, in the thunderous, pouring rain. The sound of it sheeting down on the car roof had suddenly sounded thrilling, and she had helped him to tear off her clothes that were now discarded in a heap on the floor. After half an hour of Mikey's attentions, Sonia had relaxed into a mellow, receptive state in which nothing could have been better.

She licked her freshly painted lips, and pouted at her lover. 'Will I do?' she breathed girlishly, angling her chin towards him and running her fingers through her tousled blonde hair.

As usual, Mikey wasn't in the mood to talk after sex,

let alone pay compliments, and he just ignored her, concentrating instead on tidying himself up ready for the journey back into town.

'Mikey. Look at me.' Sonia took his hand away from re-zipping his fly, and put it on her bare breast. 'Please.'

He did so bad-naturedly. Bloody women. Why couldn't they just let him do the business and be done with it?

'Mikey . . .'

In a grudging gesture of goodwill he squeezed her breast hard and flicked his thumb backwards and forwards across her nipple. He didn't want to spoil her, but then again he didn't want to risk upsetting her too much either; say what you like about Sonia, she was no prude, and he thoroughly enjoyed her very willingness to do the sorts of things that most women called him a pervert for even suggesting.

'I think I'm too tired for another go,' he mumbled into her neck.

'Try. For me.'

Mikey moved slowly down her body, running his tongue over the salty film of sweat on her naked belly. She caught her breath as he moved lower still.

'Mikey,' she gasped, her head tilted back. 'I think I've fallen in love with you.'

Mikey's head popped up like a Jack-in-the-box. 'I don't know about that, Son.'

She held his head in her hands, drawing him to her, then touched her lips tenderly against his. 'I mean it, Mikey. I know this started out as just a game.' She kissed him again, harder this time. 'But I'll do anything to make you happy. Anything.' As Mikey lay on top of her, staring into her eyes, she ran her hand up and down his arm. 'Anything at all.'

132

A slow smile spread across his face, crinkling his eyes, and making little creases appear by the sides of his nose.

Sonia wanted to almost cry with pleasure. She had made him happy.

'You mean that?' he asked.

'You know I do. You can ask me to do anything.'

He wriggled his trousers and underpants down to his ankles, and stroked her cheek. 'Anything at all?'

She wrapped her legs round his waist and stared into his eyes. 'Name it.'

'The keys to the Canvas Club would be a good start,' he said, and pushed himself into her, his passion re-ignited by the thought of what he was about to do to David Flash Boy Fuller, and it wasn't just screwing his wife.

'Are you sure this is the right place?' Shielding her eyes from the glare of the lamp-post, Angie stepped back to get a better look at the imposing, four-storey house in the narrow street close to Tower Bridge. 'Not that I've ever seen any before, Jack, but don't you think this looks a bit posh to be student digs?'

'Posh? Take a closer look.' Jackie pointed to the weed- and litter-strewn, cracked stone steps, which led up to the broad, but peeling, front door. 'Try to imagine it in daylight. And remember, it's all fellers living in there.'

'I suppose it does look a bit run-down.'

'You're not kidding. When Martin told me how to get here, he said to look for the really grotty one next to the lamp-post.'

At the mention of Martin's name, Angie's stomach contracted as a rush of elation surged through her. She had relived those moments, when he had kissed and touched her, over and over again. And now she was going to a party with him. She hadn't set eyes on him since the weekend – not since he had staggered off with Keith, groaning that he wanted to be sick, leaving her and Jackie to weave their drunken way back to the station, where they had waited half the night for the milk train – and she couldn't wait to see him, and to be back in his arms.

'He reckons there's about fifteen of them living here,' Jackie went on. 'Maybe more. All sharing the place. There's only meant to be half a dozen, but they all bunk in and split the rent. He reckons the whole street's what they call short-let housing. A developer's bought up the lot. Can you imagine having that much money, to buy a street? And he's renting them out to students till he's ready to demolish them. Then he's going to put up luxury places for rich people who work in the City.' She snorted sceptically. 'Can't see anyone *wanting* to live in an area like this, can you? He'll go broke, I reckon. City types'll never put up with this dump.'

'Do you think we're dressed right? We're not exactly student types, are we? I'm going to hate it if they all stare at me.'

Jackie rolled her eyes. 'You've not listened to a flipping word I've said.' She steered Angie up the steps and knocked on the door.

She was about to rattle the knocker for a second time when a serious-looking girl, dressed in a man's shirt tied in a knot around her waist and purple satin hipsters, threw open the door. As Jackie opened her mouth to introduce herself, the girl turned her back on them and walked off down the hall.

'Great sounds,' Jackie shouted above the throbbing

beat of Eric Burdon belting out 'Don't Let Me Be Misunderstood'. 'Let's go and see if we can find Martin.'

A dim, bare bulb, hanging down from the ceiling barely illuminated the musty-smelling, moth-eaten hallway, but, in the girls' eyes, a place lived in solely by young people could appear nothing but exotically glamorous. The few bits of wall which could be seen, between the posters declaring solidarity with the North Vietnamese and gigs for the Yardbirds, were painted a matt, deep red.

They passed an open door on the left and peeked in, but all they could make out in the dark were moving shapes that looked as if they were snogging couples swaying to the earthy, pulsating rhythms of the Animals.

'He's here somewhere,' mouthed Jackie with a falsely jolly expression. She felt completely out of place, just as Angie had feared they would, although the problem wasn't that they were being stared at. Not one of the scruffily dressed young people who were sitting or squatting on the floor took a blind bit of notice of them, as they picked their way along the passageway towards the door at the end.

The door opened on to the kitchen, a big, wide room, which took up the whole of the back of the house. Angie, as if she was connected to him by some invisible radar system, immediately spotted Martin. He had a paper cup of beer in one hand and a cigarette in the other, and was talking animatedly to a boy, who could, in the dingy red light of the scarf-shaded bulb, have been a double for John Lennon, right down to his forward combed hair and collarless Beatles jacket.

'Martin!' Jackie called to her brother, waving as if she were a desert-island castaway who had sighted a ship.

Before he looked round, Martin closed his eyes for a moment longer than a blink. They'd turned up. Christ. His little sister and Squirt, his little sister's bloody friend. The seventeen-year-old he had very nearly screwed . . .

As the shameful, drunken memories had gradually come back to him during the week, they had made Martin feel sicker than the vodka and orange.

He slapped on a smile and turned round. 'Hiya, Jack.'

'Great place, Mart.' Jackie punched her brother playfully on the shoulder. 'How about getting us a drink then?'

'Yeah. Course.'

'Not vodka and orange though.'

'Not vodka and orange.' He lifted his chin, sheepishly, at Angie. 'You all right?'

She nodded shyly, hoping he'd notice the trouble she had taken to look nice for him. 'Yeah. You?'

'Great.' He gulped anxiously at his drink. 'Just great.'

John Lennon smiled at Jackie. 'Hello,' he drawled. 'Where's young Martin been keeping you?' He certainly didn't sound like his Liverpudlian double, more like Prince Charles.

Jackie looked at him steadily. Despite her nerves at being in such unaccustomed territory as a student party, she knew she could still turn it on at will as far as individual blokes were concerned. 'At home, of course.'

'Oh.' Deflated, he turned to Martin. 'You're a darker horse than I thought. I never knew you were living with someone.'

Martin snorted, horrified, into his beer.

Jackie laughed girlishly. 'I'm Jackie, Martin's sister.'

'Really? What good news. I'm Richard. How about a dance?'

Without further discussion, Jackie left Angie, with no more than a flash of her eyebrows and a wink over her shoulder, and allowed herself to be led away to whatever was going on in the front room.

'I'll get you that drink.' Martin beckoned, with an urgent jerk of his head, to a slim, blond boy, who was standing by the open back door, narrowing his eyes against the smoke, as he drew long and deeply on a hand-rolled cigarette.

'Steve. Come over and meet Angie, while I get her a drink.'

Despite knowing Steve's reputation for getting through girls as if they were of no more value than the disposable paper cup in which he had his beer, Martin was more than willing to abandon her, while he escaped to the safety of the draining-board bar.

This was a bloody nightmare. What was he going to do? Here he was, waiting for Jill to turn up, and now he was stuck with his little sister's mate, a kid with a major crush on him. He felt bad about kissing her, really bad, but he'd been as drunk as a rat. So it wasn't his fault. And she hadn't exactly objected . . .

He took a moment to compose himself, then took her her drink.

'Lager and lime.'

'Thanks.'

Angie sipped her drink. 'Great sounds,' she said, imitating Jackie and hoping she sounded smart and sophisticated.

'You like the Who?' Steve nodded his approval. 'I've got loads of their stuff. Upstairs. In my room.'

Martin took a moment for his conscience to kick in. 'Oi. Watch it.' He stared pointedly at Steve's arm that had somehow found its way round Angie's shoulders.

Angie, unaware that Martin's motives were fuelled by guilt rather than concern, smiled ecstatically. She was Martin's girl!

Steve put up his hands in mock surrender. 'Sorry.' And wandered off.

Martin and Angie stood in silence, Martin wondering how he had let himself be suckered in to such a ridiculous situation, and Angie wondering when Martin was going to kiss her. She had made up her mind that, when he did, she was going to tell him that she wasn't ready – yet – to go all the way, but, once they had started seeing each other properly for a while, then she would be.

'You've been busy all week, Jackie said.'

Martin swigged at his drink. Shit. Now she wanted a bloody conversation. 'That's right. Loads of work to finish. For college.'

'Been spending all your time in the library.'

'Yeah. You know how it is. Work, work, work.'

'So,' a voice said from behind her, 'that's where you've been, in the library.'

Martin looked over Angie's shoulder. 'Jill.'

'Aren't you going to introduce us?' she asked flatly, looking Angie up and down. She hadn't seen this one around college. Martin must have brought her with him. She was quite pretty. In a vulgar sort of way.

'Jill, this is my little sister's friend. Squirt.'

Jill's face softened into a smile and she held out her hand to Angie, but Angie didn't notice. She was staring at Martin.

Squirt? How could he? How could he show her up like

this? Making her sound like a little kid. Especially in front of this tall, dark-haired girl, who looked so together and mature, standing there all in black, in her velvet skirt and skinny rib roll neck. Angie felt like ripping off her own lime-green bloody dress and throwing her rotten white go-go boots in the bin.

'Squirt. What a funny name. Sweet.' Jill was amused. Relieved. 'Hi.'

Angie said nothing. Who was this Jill? This stuck-up cow who was staring into Martin's eyes?

'I've really missed you, Martin,' she cooed in fluting, cut-glass tones that sliced through Angie like a shard of broken crystal. 'Really missed you.'

Angie could do nothing. She was powerless as she watched this Jill making herself into a couple with Martin right there in front of her.

'I wondered if you'd like to come back to my flat later,' Jill was saying to him, as she straightened his collar, and stroked the side of his neck with the back of her finger. 'You could stay if you like.'

'Jill,' Angie heard him murmur. 'You know how much I've wanted that.'

It was as if everyone else at the party except Angie, Martin and Jill had disappeared, melted away to some other place. There was no music. No laughter. No talking. Just the gut-wrenching sight of Martin taking Jill in his arms and kissing her.

Angie turned slowly away.

When Angie woke the next morning, it took her a few moments to figure out that she was in Jackie's bed. It took only a few more to remember the humiliation of the previous night.

When Jackie came into the bedroom with a tray of tea and toast, two glasses of water and a bottle of aspirins, tears were rolling down Angie's cheeks.

'That bad, is it? I thought you'd need some of these,' Jackie said, offering her two of the tablets. 'This hangover lark's getting a bit of a habit with us.'

Angie took the aspirin and Jackie plonked down on the bed beside her.

'That Richard said he wants to see me again. What do you think? Bit too gormless? And I think he's a bit of a snob.'

Angie ignored her question. 'It's not a hangover,' she said, rubbing away her tears with the back of her hand. 'I'm angry. That's all.'

'No puzzles, eh, Ange?' Jackie pleaded, holding her head. 'I can hardly remember getting home last night, let alone working out what you're going on about.' She closed her eyes self-pityingly. 'I just hope Mum never finds out we came home in that bloke's van.'

Angie wasn't listening to her. 'I might not be going to college,' she sniffed. 'I might not even have a single O level to my name. But I'll show them. I'll show everyone. I'm going to make something of myself. I'm going to live life more than that lot ever will.'

Chapter 7

Jackie sat back, tongue clamped between her teeth and an eyeliner brush held aloft, and admired her handiwork. 'That looks fantastic, Ange. If I say so myself. I reckon I'm a bit of an artist.'

Jackie had spent nearly half an hour making up Angie's face as a mirror image of her own: she had covered her friend's face and neck with the palest Sheer Genius foundation, then had dotted white Mary Quant highlighter on to her cheekbones, between her eyes, and on the point of her chin, and then she had stuck false eyelashes on to her top lids. Next, she had painted an exaggerated line of matching lashes, with stark black eyeliner, along Angie's bottom lids, and then dotted a sprinkling of light-brown freckles over her cheeks and the bridge of her nose. Jackie had then finished off the whole, sooty-eyed, child-woman face with the palest of pink lipsticks.

'Get those rollers out,' she said, lifting Angie's chin with the back of her hand, 'and I'll back-comb the top for you, then you can iron my fringe.'

Finally, satisfied with their make-up and hair, the girls took off their housecoats and got dressed.

They had chosen identical outfits: bottom-skimming, black PVC miniskirts with matching braces that crossed over their black and white polka dot shirts, and white mid-calf boots over white, lacy tights.

The girls stared admiringly at themselves in the mirror.

Jackie's hair hung to her shoulders in a straight blonde

curtain, with the thick, heavy fringe almost touching her spidery, artificial lashes, while Angie's chestnut hair swung in a glossy, geometric bob that tapered away to points which brushed against her carefully highlighted cheekbones.

Angie turned her head to one side, trying to get a glimpse of her profile.

'Nice work, Jack.'

'Not bad, is it?' Jackie turned round and looked over her shoulder, checking out the back view. 'Are you still sure about this? It's not going to be cheap, you know.'

'I told you, after that party, I'm going to start doing things with my life. Going to start living a bit. And it was you who said you wanted to go somewhere like the Tiles or the Canvas Club.'

'Yeah, but the cost.' Jackie reached under her skirt and hitched her tights up a bit higher – uncomfortable, but it showed off the lace pattern to the best effect.

'I can afford it, with all the commission I'm earning. And after everything you've done for me, I want to take you out to say thank you.'

Jackie shoved her in the side. 'Good job really, who else would be good-looking enough to go out with a beautiful girl like you?'

Angie thought for a moment. 'Marilyn?'

'I'm not joking.'

'No?' Angie was preoccupied, inspecting her teeth in the mirror for stray streaks of lipstick.

'Seriously, Ange.' Jackie took a deep breath. 'The girls from school. They never really used to want you to go out with us.'

Angie straightened up and affected a look of shock. 'Never?'

Jackie shook her head. 'Never.'

'I'm not an idiot, Jack. I know you used to pretend they all wanted me to go along.'

Jackie shrugged. 'It's different now. Now they wouldn't dare.'

'Really?'

'Really. They couldn't compete.' Jackie pointed at their reflection. 'With either of us. We're flaming gorgeous.'

'You're right. I reckon if we set our sights on a bloke, we could have anyone we fancied.'

'Paul McCartney?'

'No trouble.'

'Roger Daltrey?'

'Easy.'

'That bloke who wears the teddy boy clothes up the shops?'

'Even I'm not that adorable, Jack.'

'I can't believe they charged you that for just two drinks.' Jackie sipped at the watery glass of gin and tonic that Angie had just handed to her, trying to hide the involuntary shudder at the horrible taste. 'And that barman. He looked like he was doing you a flipping favour serving you.'

Both of them had sworn that they would never let a drop of vodka and orange, or lager and lime, anywhere near their lips ever again, and had had to wrack their brains for suitably sophisticated drinks that they could order without making themselves look like clueless kids from out of town. The barman's weary attitude, as they dithered and considered, hadn't helped.

'And the entry price. We could have bought the new

Stones album, all the top five, and still have had enough left over for a Wimpy each.'

'It would have been even dearer if we'd come later, when it gets busy. But when you think what they're charging for.' Angie pointed to her lap, and lowered her voice. 'We are sitting on bar stools in the Canvas Club in Soho. The stools you see in photographs in the Sunday papers and all the magazines.'

Usually Jackie would have made some sort of smart comment, but she was as impressed as her friend.

'Just think, Jack.' Angie gestured at the mirrored walls with a lift of her chin. 'Pop stars have sat here looking at themselves.'

'It is amazing.' Jackie stared, wide-eyed over the rim of her glass. 'Shall we go and have a dance, do you think?'

'Let's wait a bit. Till it gets busier, so we're not on show.'

'Good idea. We can have a look round first. See what the others get up to. So we can act like we're used to it.'

The girls studied the people in the club as closely as explorers trying to fathom the behaviour of a previously undiscovered tribe: noting the steps of the first tentative dancers; listening to the casual laughter of the coolly jaded; and watching the approaches of peacock males fluttering around their cruelly judgemental female targets.

Jackie jerked her head towards a crop-haired boy of about nineteen, who was standing by the door to the men's lavatory. 'Over there,' she spluttered into her drink, her attempts at subtlety completely failing.

'What?'

'He's just handed', she leaned forward and breathed

out the words, 'something to that red-haired bloke with the glasses. And taken money off him.' She sat up again and added authoritatively, 'They'll be French Blues he's selling. Or Black Bombers. I've read all about them. All the mods take them. To get blocked.'

'I bet Martin doesn't,' Angie snapped nastily. 'Your mum'd kill her precious little boy if he did.'

'What's got into you?'

'Nothing.'

Jackie grabbed her hand. 'Don't look, Ange.'

'What?'

'This might be the last drink you'll have to buy tonight.'

'Why?'

'Look – slowly – in the mirror. Them blokes over there. They're watching us.'

'Which ones?'

'The cross-eyed one with the wooden leg and the green teeth, and his mate with the bag over his head. Which ones do you think? The fab-looking one with the suit who's walking your way, and his friend in the mohair jacket. Quick, look all pleased with yourself.' Jackie gulped back what little of her drink she hadn't managed to spray all over the place and jabbed Angie in the shoulder. 'Angie, you are so funny, you always say things that make me laugh so much.'

Without a beat Angie let out what she hoped was a tinkling, charming giggle. 'You know me, Jackie, always know all the latest jokes.'

'Any clean enough to tell me?' The one with the suit checked the bar top for any signs of wetness, then, satisfied it was up to his standards, he rested his arm between the two girls.

145

Angie dropped her chin and looked up at him through her long, false lashes. 'I don't think so.'

'If you won't tell me a joke, how about a dance?'

Angie glanced at Jackie, who swivelled her eyes at his friend, and nodded encouragingly.

'I'd love to.'

'Ray,' he said, holding out his hand to help her down from the bar stool.

'Angie,' she replied, letting him lead her on to the floor, where just two other couples and a few huddles of girls were dancing.

'I like the record,' she mouthed.

'Spencer David Group,' Ray mouthed back. 'It's nearly finished. Fancy another drink instead?'

Angie looked over at Jackie, who was being chatted up by his friend, and smiled her agreement.

Ray bought the drinks and then steered her to the other end of the bar from where Jackie and his friend were now both sitting.

'Not much goes on in here till about half nine,' he said, leaning close to her. 'So why don't we go outside for a while?'

'Outside?'

'You know, round the back.'

Angie didn't actually know what he meant but she had a good idea.

'I don't think so.'

'Come on. Your mate's all right.' Jackie, who had just got up and was now on the floor dancing with his friend, was giving every impression that she was really enjoying herself. 'And you don't have to worry. I've got a rubber.'

Angie didn't want to seem juvenile, or silly, but she

146

knew she definitely didn't want this – rubber or not. She also knew she had no idea how to handle the situation. 'Let's have a dance,' she suggested, more in panic than through any logical reasoning.

Ray looked at her, weighing up the chances of being able to wear her down.

On balance, he thought it was worth spending a bit more time and flattery on her. Maybe even shelling out for another over-priced drink. She looked very tasty, and he liked being seen with girls who dressed right. It was good for his image.

'OK,' he said. 'Let's show them how it's done.'

Bobby stopped the Jaguar outside a coffee bar, close to the entrance of the club. There would be no complaints. Local tradesmen knew better than to protest if David Fuller took their parking spaces.

David, who was sitting in the front passenger seat, twisted the rear-view mirror round and checked his tie. 'I'm just popping in to see to a bit of business. Won't be long.'

'Make sure you're not.' Sonia snapped from behind him.

Bobby sat impassively in the driver's seat. He was as deaf, dumb and blind as the three wise monkeys – until David addressed him personally.

'Who's on duty tonight, Bob? Jeff?'

Bobby thought for a moment. 'Half-a-lung Cassidy.'

'Lovely. Having him coughing all over me.'

The far wall of the Canvas Club's office, even though it was only a few feet from the door, was almost obscured by a thick fug of smoke. Cassidy, who stood in for Jeff on his one night off in ten, was choking and spluttering on one of his ever-present Senior Service cigarettes.

'Blimey, Half-a-lung, are you sure?' David gestured with a nod towards the cash box. 'Open it up, and open that window and all while you're about it.'

Half-a-lung fiddled around with the window catch, slipping his big meaty hand through the narrow space between the security bars, and then held the open box out for David's inspection.

'Still full. Mikey not been in yet?'

'I've not seen him, Dave. Not tonight. Mind you, according to Jeff, he's been getting like a right blister lately.'

Half-a-lung's jokes and puns drove David barmy, but he'd been a loyal worker, even once having taken a stabbing protecting his boss, so he tolerated his nonsense more than most people would have credited. 'Like a what?'

'A blister. Only shows up when the work's finished.'

David smiled automatically. 'Yeah. Very funny. Nice one. Jeff told you what to do, did he?'

'Yeah. And, like the famous Memory Man, I have it all tucked away for future reference.' He stopped speaking in order to choke a bit more, then, having lit a fresh cigarette, he went on. 'I know exactly what to do, Dave.'

'Good.'

David was about to leave when the unmistakable sound of breaking glass – something every club owner dreaded: fights were bad for business, they brought the sort of publicity that kept celebrities away – crashed through from the other side of the wall.

David threw open the door and scanned the room. 'What's going on out there?' he demanded from Cassidy. 'Where's the poxy doormen?'

What was going on was that Ray had lost his temper with Angie for daring to reject his advances again, and Jackie had started shouting at Ray for upsetting her friend, Ray's friend having disappeared, more interested in what the young man by the lavatory had to sell. The row, on the now-crowded dance floor, was beginning to reach boiling-point – the glass had been thrown by someone who fancied a bit of action, something more serious than a dreary little ruck between a bloke and his bird.

As for Jim and Graham, the bouncers, they were round the back in the alley, taking advantage of Jeff's absence, and enjoying the 'hospitality' of two young women who had been promised, in return for their willingness to have a quick knee-trembler up against the wall, free passes for the whole of the next month.

'You were quick enough to take that second drink off me.' Ray was now hollering, jabbing his finger at Angie's face. 'You are a prick teaser.'

Jackie was incensed. Not only had this idiot made her friend cry, but now he was showing them up. Both of them. In the middle of the Canvas Club, the place that Jackie had dreamed of going to. She wasn't having this, some thick git spoiling her big night out.

'Oi, you. She told you, she doesn't care what other girls do, she doesn't *go round the back* with strange blokes. She's not like that. And especially not with stupid buggers like you.'

'So why's she dressed like that?'

'Did you hear what he said?' gasped a miniskirted girl to her boyfriend. 'Bloody cheek. Who does he think he is? Thinking he can tell girls what to wear. Hit him, Paul. Go on.'

149

Paul wasn't so keen. 'Let's go. This is daft.'

Jackie, on the other hand, was ready for action. She was ready to scratch Ray's eyes out.

Just as she was about to make a lunge for his sneering, pasty face, someone grabbed her arm.

She twisted round, set to attack, but quickly changed her mind.

A very grown-up, very well-built, smartly dressed man was holding her arm, but he was pointing very firmly at Ray.

'Oi! Mouthy!' he yelled.

Ray looked shocked. This bloke was built like a number-nine bus, and his presence had coincided with the music stopping and all the lights being turned up full pelt. Ray, like most other people in the club, was blinking and wondering what was going on. He was also almost wetting himself. Being forceful with girls was one thing, but having a row with a great big bloke was quite another.

'What?' Ray asked, holding out his hands in the submissive, palms-up gesture of an innocent, injured party.

'Are you going to leave quietly, sonny?'

'What have I done?'

David let go of Jackie and grabbed Ray by the hair. He immediately let go again. 'Blimey. What's that muck on your hair? Surely it ain't Brylcreem?'

Ray, now tight-lipped with embarrassment, but still ridiculously cocky, started dancing around on the spot like an abandoned sparring partner. 'Hair conditioner, if you must know.'

David raised a single, shapely eyebrow – 'Hair conditioner? Aw, sorry, ducks' – then grabbed him firmly by the collar. 'You. Out.' He dragged Ray to the exit and shoved him hard, giving him an actually gentle, but thoroughly insulting, kick up the backside to see him on his way.

David went back over to Jackie and Angie, who were still standing, equally as shocked as they were embarrassed, in the middle of the dance floor.

'OK, everyone,' said David, guiding the girls towards the bar, and nodding for the disc jockey to get the music back on and the lights dimmed, 'the rubbish has been cleared away. Let's all get back to enjoying ourselves.'

The disc jockey, used to conducting a nightly form of crowd control, knew exactly what to play: as Sam the Sham and the Pharaohs blasted out 'Woolly Bully', practically the whole club was back dancing on the floor.

'Now, girls,' said David. 'First my apologies for that uncouth little twerp, and secondly, are you both all right?'

'Yes, thanks.' The girls spoke in unison as if they had been rehearsing.

'Good.' David raised a finger and the barman was immediately there. 'Rick. These young ladies are princesses for the night. Got it?'

Angie watched, impressed, as this big, tough man transformed the previously intimidating barman into Rick, their new best friend.

'Got it, Mr Fuller.'

'Anything they want. OK?'

'Got it.'

'Good.'

'Thanks, Mr Fuller,' said Angie.

'It's David, sweetheart.' He winked and chucked her under the chin. 'To a pretty girl like you, that is.'

As David swept out of the club, planning what he

would do when he got hold of the bouncers – something involving a pair of fucking pliers, he was so wild – two men were looking first at him, then at the girls, then at him, then at the girls again.

'I'm telling you, Matthew. That bird over there, it's that Violet's kid.'

'Who?'

'You know that old ripper I was giving one to.'

'What the bird over in Dagenham?'

'That's her. Violet. And that's her kid. Angie.'

'Don't be stupid, Chas. That girl over there's gorgeous. A right sort. You must need your eyes testing.'

'Yeah, I suppose you're right.' Chas chuckled to himself.

'What's so funny?'

'Violet was worried that you were after her.'

'What? Violet?'

'No. Her kid.'

'Christ, Chas, she wasn't only old, she must have been bloody senile.'

Wiping his hands on his handkerchief, with a look of disgust – hair conditioner, what was wrong with young blokes nowadays? – David got back into the passenger seat of his Jaguar.

'You took long enough,' sniped Sonia from the back of the car. Not only had she been left like a child, but she had been trying for weeks to get the keys for the club and had completely failed. Only David and Jeff had sets, and that awful Cassidy man on his one night in ten, and she couldn't think of a way to get the damn things off any one of them. Why couldn't he leave them around like a normal man? Throw them on the table, with his loose change when he came in at night? Anyone would think he didn't trust her.

Bobby stared straight ahead as though he hadn't heard a thing.

David shifted his leg so that he could stuff the handkerchief into his trouser pocket, then, changing his mind, he wound down the window and tossed it into the gutter. He didn't look at his wife as he spoke to her.

'You're not gonna start, are you, Sonia?'

'Start? You leave me sitting out here with this moron for company while you go inside and—'

'I ain't having this. Bobby, where's your motor?'

'I left it at the Blue Moon, Dave.'

David rolled his eyes. 'Why?'

'When you said you needed me to drive the Jag, that's where I was. I got Terry to bring me over in case I couldn't park and had to keep you waiting.'

'All right, Bob, don't give me earache.'

'But it's Saturday. You know what it's like. Parking round here and that. I didn't—'

'What's up with you? It's either feast or flaming famine. You swallowed a dictionary or something?'

'Sorry, Dave.'

'Don't worry, mate. She makes me nervous and all.'

Sonia sneered from the back seat. 'How touching, the organ grinder worrying about his monkey.'

'Just take us back over there, Bob. Pick up your motor. Then take Mrs Fuller home to the flat. I've got business to see to.' David thought for a moment, angled the rear-view mirror until he could see his wife, then said: 'Tell you what, while you're there, you can kill two birds with one stone. Pop in the Moon and tell the girls that, if they know what's good for them, they'll think twice about doing any business on the side. Right? Tell 'em I've heard some rumours. Just to keep 'em on their toes.'

Bobby nodded.

'It doesn't do them any harm, reminding them who's boss now and again.'

Sonia sighed dramatically. 'So I'll be left outside again, will I? While this cretin gives your tarts a pep talk. Saturday night on the town. Oh, such sophistication. I know, why don't Bobby and I tour all your most sordid little clubs? It would be such fun. I could report the evening's festivities for the social pages.'

David gestured for Bobby to pull away. 'Shut your gob, Sonia. You're really beginning to get on me nerves.'

David stopped his car at the back of the hospital in a space marked 'Doctors Only' and reached behind him to get his coat and a brown paper bag off the back seat.

It was a quarter to ten and could still have been quite light, but, from how dark it was, it looked more like midnight. The sky was heavy with the purple grey clouds of a summer thunderstorm, and the raindrops were coming down in fat, sploshing coins on the bonnet of the car.

David opened the door, pulled his overcoat collar up to his ears, took a deep breath and made a run for the entrance.

'Bloody pouring down out there,' he said, flashing his eyebrows at the nurse who had held the door open for him.

She smiled. At first sight, she had thought the big, well-dressed man might be a new doctor she hadn't yet come across, but his voice had immediately given him away. No doctor, even at the London, spoke with a broad cockney accent.

'Where can I find Lenny Tawse, darling? He's in Turner ward.'

'Second floor,' she directed him in a singsong Caribbean lilt, and with an even broader smile. He really was handsome. 'It's a bit late for visitors, but tell sister up there that Nurse Bradley sent you. Nurse Coral Bradley. The one who gets off at half ten tonight, and who isn't doing anything other than going home by herself to curl up with a good book.'

David winked. 'If I wasn't a married man, Nurse Coral Bradley . . .'

'Pity,' she said to herself as she watched him stride away with as much confidence as if he were the chief consultant himself.

'Hello, Len.'

Lenny opened his eyes and stared up at the man hovering above him. 'Dave.'

'Don't shift yourself, Len, I know how much you must be hurting.' David flicked the back of his hand over the bedside armchair to remove any unwelcome fluff, and sat down, his immaculately cut navy overcoat draping in elegant folds about him. 'So, how's tricks?'

'You know, Dave, fair to middling.'

'Glad to hear it.' Remembering the brown paper bag, David put it on Lenny's locker. 'Few grapes for you. Any idea when you'll be out?'

'Soon as the collar-bone sets. They're still a bit worried.'

'Yeah, I heard. Nasty that, the bone shattering in so many places.'

Lenny said nothing.

'Still, that's the price. If you want to be on the firm,

Lenny, old son, you have to behave yourself.'

Lenny nodded, shame-faced. 'I know, Dave.'

'You're silly to yourself. You could have been really hurt.'

At that moment a woman with over-bright blonde hair covered with a luminous pink chiffon headscarf tottered into the ward on high, spiky patent leather heels. 'Dave,' she said coldly and sat on the chair that he vacated for her. 'How's Sonia? Busy, is she?'

David didn't flinch. 'Sonia's fine, thanks, Sylvie.'

'Good. Me on the other hand, I'm knackered. I'm having to do extra shifts in the pub to make ends meet. Cos Len's not working. Then I have to get over here to visit him. Then get home again. Nearly midnight it is when I get to bed. Good job they let me visit this late. As a favour. Or I'd never see my Len. Would I?'

'I've been meaning to drop round and see you.' David stuck his hand inside his jacket and pulled out his wallet. 'Here,' he said, handing her a wad of notes. 'To help you get by till Lenny gets better.'

'Thanks.' She didn't take it from him immediately, instead, she took her time, taking off the scarf and shaking the raindrops on to the dark green tiled floor, then opening the chrome clasp of her pink, pearlized-plastic handbag. Only then did she take the money and snap it safely away into her bag. 'The kids could do with some new shoes. They cost a fortune.'

David laughed at her cheek. She was a gobby cow, but she was loyal to Lenny. David approved of that. 'You're a one, Sylve.' This time he took money from his trouser pocket, a thick roll, secured with an elastic band. 'Here. Treat yourself and all.'

'Thanks.'

He gave the thumbs up to Lenny. 'Get well soon, mate, and we'll see you back at work when you're ready.' With that he bowled out of the ward, knowing that, as in most places he found himself, all eyes were on him.

As soon as he judged David to be out of earshot, Lenny, despite the pain from his cracked ribs and busted collar-bone, rolled over and turned angrily on his wife.

'Why did you do that, you big-mouthed mare?' he hissed under his breath.

'Do what?' Sylvie asked, making no attempt to keep her words private from the others in the ward.

'Ask him about Sonia?'

'I was being polite.' She picked over the grapes, selecting the plumpest.

'No you weren't, you stupid bitch. You were winding him up.'

Sylvie, ignoring her husband's abuse, took out the two wads of money and, shielding what she was doing from the other patients within the folds of her beige raincoat, began counting out the notes with accompanying breathy commentary. 'Ten, fifteen, twenty—'

'Sylvie!' Lenny snatched the money from her hand. 'Have you taken leave of your senses? You can't talk like that to David Fuller.'

'Leave off, Len.' She snatched the money back. 'Everyone knows that stuck-up tart of his is schtupping Mikey Tilson.'

'And everyone knows he had Mad Albert put me in here just because I forgot to lock up his bloody Jag.'

Calmly and coldly, Sylvie leaned closer to her husband and spat the words into his face. 'Well, why don't he have Mad Albert put fucking Mikey in here and all?'

Lenny flopped back on to the pillow and closed his

eyes, trying to block out the pain and the aggravation of being married to a loud-mouthed simpleton like Sylvie.

'Because David Fuller is a sadistic bastard who likes playing games.' He almost laughed. 'And when the games are played for stakes that include people's lives and happiness, he likes them even better.'

'What are we going to do?' Angie popped her head out of the shop doorway and stared along the rain-slicked Soho street. There was no sign of a cab, not a vacant one anyway. And it was pouring down.

'I don't know, Ange. I just wish we'd have gone to the Cubana. At least we could have walked home from Ilford.'

'I don't think we're ever going to get a cab in this rain.'

'I hope Mum don't wake up. She'll kill me.'

'At least she cares about you.' Angie stared at the tawdry neon lights reflected in the puddled pavement, the same lights that had, a few hours earlier, held so much promise.

'Too flipping much.'

'I might start smoking,' Angie said, watching a tarty-looking middle-aged woman in the doorway opposite drawing on a long slim cigarette.

'What?'

'I think it looks good.' She was thinking of Martin and his ultra-cool girlfriend.

'Looks good? Leave off, Ange. I'm too wet and cold to start arguing with you.'

David dropped down into third gear. Here he was, supposedly one of the most powerful blokes in the manor, and what was he doing? Driving round the poxy streets by himself, while his old woman was who knew where, carrying on with fucking Mikey Tilson. He'd really thought he had been on to something, that he'd let their pathetic little affair go on for long enough for the pair of them not only to hang themselves but to provide their own sodding rope for the bloody execution. But, truth be told, he had lost interest in what they were getting up to. Sonia was still glossy enough when he needed a bit of arm-candy to show off to the likes of Burman, and she'd be bored with Mikey Tilson sooner rather than later – if he didn't lose his temper with him first – but what had started as a game was beginning to bore him.

But then that was David's trouble. He had a low boredom threshold. Always had. And it was that, along with his miserable, poverty-stricken childhood, that had driven him, had made him the ambitious man that he was. And ambition in Bethnal Green didn't have many outlets, other than boxing or crime, and David had never fancied getting his nose flattened or a cauliflower earhole. He was too proud of his looks.

He looked up at the façade of yet another trendy club that had recently opened in Wardour Street. Despite all this new gloss moving into the area, Soho was still a seedy, bloody hole of a place. He laughed mirthlessly to himself. A bit like Sonia really.

God he was pissed off.

And look at them in that shop doorway by the Canvas. If regular girls saw amateurs on their pitch they'd have their knives out for them. Literally.

He slowed down even more, to get a closer look.

There was something familiar about the dark-haired one. The one who looked ready to burst into tears. She'd get herself into right trouble if she did. Even the amateurs didn't dare show any weakness round these parts.

Hang on. Wasn't it? Yeah. It was that girl from the club. The one he'd rescued from that oily-haired little shit.

David braked, sending a splash of water up from the gutter.

'Great!' Jackie held up her arms and stared down at her legs. 'Mud! Just what I needed. I have had enough, Ange. I have really and truly had enough.'

Angie gnawed at the inside of her mouth, refusing to release the tears that were making her nose prickle and her eyes sting. 'So have I.'

David wound down the window. 'All right, girls. Need a lift?'

'We're fine thanks,' said Jackie sharply, refusing to make eye contact.

'What, in this rain?'

'Yes.' Jackie looked away into the middle distance, hoping that she was giving a convincing impression of someone waiting for her six-foot-six boyfriend to come along in the car he had gone to collect so that she wouldn't get wet.

'Got any money?'

Angie flashed a look at Jackie. She didn't understand what he was talking about. Was he begging? Not in that car, surely. 'Sorry?'

'For a cab.'

'Yes, thanks,' said Jackie, forgetting the conscientious boyfriend.

David took a fiver from his inside pocket and held it out of the car window. 'Here. Take this. Get yourselves a cab. These streets are no place for two little princesses.'

'Thanks ever so much.' Angie took the money and brightened. It was the man from the club. Mr Fuller. David. 'Can you tell us where we can get one, please?'

'Hold on.'

David got out of the car and trotted across the street to the doorway, where the tarty woman was still standing smoking. He said something to her, she nodded, and then followed him through the door.

Angie noticed that the woman had laughed easily, as if they were friends.

He returned almost immediately. 'Christina over there. She's called you a cab. It'll be here in less than five minutes.' He paused. 'Or you can have a lift with me if you like.'

'That's really kind.' Angie smiled. What a nice man.

Jackie mouthed at Angie to *shut up*, then addressed the man, still without looking at him. She snatched the money off Angie and held it out at arm's length. 'Thanks for offering us the fiver. But we don't need it.'

Angie looked at the man's kind, smiling face, and at his big shiny car, and wondered how long a student would have to save up to buy a car like that. How long a student would have to stop drinking vodka and orange to be able to afford to give a fiver away to a girl, just because he wanted to make sure she had the fare home.

'You're ever so kind,' she said, stepping out of the doorway into the rain. 'You won't remember me but—'

'Course I remember you. We met in the Canvas.'

'That's right. I think it's fab.'

'Glad you approve. I own it.'

Jackie tapped Angie on the shoulder. 'There's a cab coming.' Then she waved and the taxi drew into the kerb.

The driver got out and went immediately to the

driver's door of the Jaguar. 'You wanted a cab, Mr Fuller?'

David handed him the fiver and raised an eyebrow at Angie. 'Do I?'

Angie turned to Jackie. 'Does he?'

'I'm not getting in that car with him.'

'I am.'

Angie ran round to the passenger's door and jumped in.

She lowered her head and spoke past David's chest at her horrified friend. 'See you later, Jack.' Then looked up at David. 'And the cab's paid for.'

Before Jackie could say another word, David had the car in gear and had pulled away.

'What's your name?'

'Sacha.'

'Your real name?'

'Angela Sarah Patricia Knight.'

'Blimey, that's a bit of a mouthful.'

'Sorry. People call me Angie.'

'Angie. Angela. Tell you what, I'm going to call you Angel.'

David surprised himself. This wasn't like him, messing around with a girl of – what was she? Nineteen? Twenty? – but what the hell? He hadn't had a bit of stray for months. Too busy being good to that whore Sonia. He could just imagine the look on her face if she knew she had to compete with this tasty little bit. It would have her rushing to her pots and potions and creams faster than finding another grey hair. And it'd make her fling with Tilson seem just a little bit boring. Schtupping your old man's hired help, well, it was beneath contempt.

This could turn into quite an interesting little adventure.

'So, where's home then, Angel?'

'I'm staying with a friend.'

'But where?' He laughed. 'I can't keep driving round Trafalgar Square all night. We'll get dizzy.'

'Poplar.' Angie just hoped she wouldn't wake her nan, or she'd have all sorts of explaining to do about where she'd been till this time of night.

'My family's originally from Bethnal Green,' he said, peeling off along Northumberland Avenue and heading for the Embankment. 'I've not lived there for years though. Since I was about your age. I took a look round the West End, and I thought to myself, that'll do for me. I'll have some of that, thank you very much.'

He stopped smoothly at a red light. 'What street does this friend of yours live in?'

She ran through the possibilities. The last thing she wanted was this man driving up to Lancaster Buildings in his big flash car. Her nan had a sixth sense about these sort of things and she'd be out on the landing wagging her finger and shouting the odds about young girls getting into strange blokes' cars, and what was a man of his age thinking, before she had even put a foot on the pavement. Angie felt herself blushing at the thought of it.

'If you wouldn't mind, could you just drop me off on the corner of Burdett Road? The East India Dock end.' That should do it, she could double back and get to the flats over the back railings.

David roared with laughter. 'I might have known it. You're all the same, pretty girls like you. This friend's a feller.'

'No, she is not.' Angie was offended. 'Actually, it's

163

my nan I'm staying with, and I don't want to disturb her.'
Or have you knowing where she lives, Angie thought for
no other reason than that her nan had always warned her
to be careful what she told strangers about herself.

If her nan could see her now . . .

When the lights turned green, David didn't move the
car, instead, he turned to look at her. He reached out and
touched her cheek. 'You're a strange little thing. You'd
rather walk in all this rain than disturb your nan?'

Angie knew she'd made a fool of herself. 'She's
special to me.'

'Glad to hear it, sweetheart. Now, this is my card. I'm
going to give it to you so you can phone me. I'll take you
out for a nice meal. How about that? A bit of dinner and
maybe a show?' He could hardly believe the words were
coming out of his mouth. *Dinner and a show?* Who did
he think he was? Fucking Noel Coward?

Angie took the card and tilted it towards the light from
a nearby lamppost. It had his name, David Fuller, an
address in Greek Street, and a telephone number. The
lettering was in black, and was all shiny and raised as if it
had been carved out of the thick white paper. 'Thanks.'

David turned back to the steering-wheel and shrugged
the creases from his jacket. 'Now, how close can I drop
you to your nan's without you getting yourself in
schtook?'

164

Chapter 8

Jackie stomped up the steps of Fenchurch Street station, aware of the grief she was doling out to the already grumpy Monday-morning commuters as she pushed and shoved her way past them to reach the exit, but not caring.

'You were so stupid getting in that car, Angie, I can't believe you did it. And I never knew you were staying round your nan's. I was worried sick till you came round for me for work. Then all you wanted to know was why Martin had had to leave so early. Nothing about me, how upset I was. You are so selfish.'

'For goodness' sake, Jack, that was a sodding week ago! Change the record, can't you?' Angie stopped and held out her arms, scattering commuters off into tutting, complaining eddies all about her. 'Look at me. I'm here. I'm safe. All right? What more do you want?' She paused, searching for words. 'Know your trouble? You never take a chance. Never do anything exciting.'

Jackie grabbed her by the elbow and pulled her along. 'Exciting? Are you mad? You're bloody lucky to be alive. Bloody lucky. Haven't you read about blokes taking young girls away?'

Jackie continued carrying on about safety and luck and selfishness – just as she had done every day for a week – until she left Angie on the corner of Lime Street, where, as usual, they parted to go off to their respective offices. But, this morning, Angie wasn't actually planning to go in to work. Not to stay, anyway.

She walked into the reception area of the company

where she was now a telephone ordering clerk, plonked herself down on the big leather sofa, and buried her head in her hands.

'Marge, could you do me a favour?' she asked the sleek, thirtyish brunette, who was all but obscured by a massive vase of pale yellow lilies.

Marge skipped round her desk and sat down beside her. 'Are you all right, poppet?' She took Angie's hand.

'Could you tell Miss Shanks I don't feel well? I tried my best. But the train journey. It's made me feel even worse.'

'You should have stayed in bed.'

Angie nodded miserably. 'I know, but I've been so pleased with my new job, I didn't want to let anyone down.'

Marge put a hand on Angie's forehead. 'You do feel a bit warm.'

That was news to Angie, who felt just fine, but she nodded in agreement. 'I'm burning up.'

'I'll call a cab. And get you home.'

'No. Please. I'll be all right.'

'I'll put it on the company account.'

'No, honestly, Marge. I'll only get car sick. I'd rather go by train.'

'Wait there.' She went back to her desk and dialled through to Janet Shanks.

'I feel terrible about letting you down, Miss Shanks.' Angie smiled weakly at her supervisor. 'I know how busy Monday mornings are.'

Janet Shanks smiled back with a caring, pleasant expression, knowing that, if she wasn't careful, Angela Knight would be off looking for a new job. Somehow, from being a totally innocuous little junior run-around, she had suddenly become Miss Telephone Sales Woman of the Century. It was driving Janet Shanks mad, but Angie's enthusiasm for her new job, along with her bizarre desire to please and to work really hard, rather than to compete, had seen the sales figures soar.

At least being the supervisor meant that she was taking most of the credit.

'You nip off home and get yourself better,' she smarmed brightly. 'Your figures were fabulous last week, Angela. Just fabulous. You have a good rest and let us all have a chance to catch up with you.'

'She won't let me call her a cab,' twittered Marge, who thrived on other people's dramas.

'I'm sure Angela knows what she's doing,' Janet said, asserting her authority over the receptionist.

And she was right. Angie knew exactly what she was doing. By the time Miss Shanks was back in the department, fretting about sales figures and unanswered telephones, Angie was running down Gracechurch Street towards Monument underground station as if she were the sole competitor in the City of London's very own version of the hundred yards dash.

Angie stood by the revolving doors, trying hard to find the courage to enter the intimidating building, and wishing she hadn't dressed quite so brightly that morning. Her pale lilac, moygashel minisuit might have been just the confident sort of outfit to wear for her new job, but it made her stand out from all the young people who were milling about in the sunshine outside Queen Mary College in the Mile End Road like a white feather in a crow's wing.

Taking a deep breath, she plunged in.

'Yes?' The bored-sounding woman, sitting behind the sliding glass panel, spoke without looking up.

'How can I find Martin Murray, please?'

'Course? Year?'

'Economics, I think. Yes. Economics. First year.'

'First year's easy. Common courses.' She still hadn't looked up, but was now studying a colourful chart mapped out on graph paper. 'Lecture theatre 3.'

Astonished, but gratified by the woman's lack of any concern regarding security, or even curiosity as to who she was, Angie, now with a genuine feeling of nausea, set off to find Martin.

She cracked open the door just wide enough to see inside and was surprised to see that the lecture theatre was exactly that. She had been expecting something more like a classroom, but this was a massive, tiered room full of people. She'd never be able to find him in there, it would be like trying to find someone in the pictures after the main film had started. She would just have to wait until it was over.

She waited for forty-five minutes, increasingly embarrassed by the interest she was arousing: superior sneers from many of the young women, appreciative glances from most of the young men.

'Hello, Martin.' Angie spoke before she noticed Jill was standing next to him.

Martin looked shocked. 'Squirt? Is everything all right? Is Jackie in trouble?'

'Jackie's fine. It's me. I need to talk to you.'

His mind was racing; whatever this was all about, he

was sure he wouldn't want Jill hearing it. 'Jill, you remember Squirt. My little sister Jackie's friend.'

Angie and Jill both noted how he had stressed *little sister's friend*.

'I introduced you at Steve's party?'

'I remember.' Jill's smile was icy. 'Hello, Squirt.'

'My name's Angie actually.'

Jill looked at Martin. 'Are you coming to the library, or are you too busy?'

'I'll see you there in about . . .' He looked at his watch, then at Angie, then at Jill again. 'Fifteen minutes?'

'Fine. I'll see you then.' Jill hauled her bag up on her shoulder and nodded at Angie. 'Bye. Give my regards to Martin's little sister.'

'I think she's upset,' Angie said, watching her walk away along the corridor. She was secretly pleased at the effect she had had on the conceited cow, but didn't want Martin to see her being spiteful. 'I hope it wasn't something I said.'

'More like something you've done.'

'Sorry?'

'Squirt, what are you doing here?'

'Can we get some coffee somewhere?' Anything to play for a bit of time.

Martin managed to scrape up enough coppers from the bottom of his bag to buy them drinks in the college refectory. It was a big noisy room full of scruffy-looking students, all with piles of books, folders and files, and Angie felt even more out of place than she had in the corridor outside the lecture theatre.

He set down two disposable plastic cups of hot brown, almost coffee-smelling liquid on the table, and sat opposite her on one of the ugly, dull red plastic chairs that, apart from Angie's suit, provided the only splash of colour in the room. Black, dark grey, and sludge green seemed to be the predominant shades in students' wardrobes.

'What's this all about?'

'Have you been avoiding me, Martin? I need to know. After what happened at Clacton, I . . .' She had run out words, the words that she hadn't even been able to run through and practise in her head before she got here, because, in all truth, she didn't know what she wanted to say. She knew she wanted to be sure there was no hope of Martin feeling anything for her, before she made the telephone call. The call she had already half made up her mind she was going to make anyway. But there was still hope, that wild hope, no matter how small, that Martin was interested in her, that he had sort of slipped up, made a mistake, and that he would like to start all over again. But, if she was wrong, how could she say all that without making herself look even more pathetic?

So she sipped at her drink instead.

Martin felt the sweat begin to bead on his top lip. 'But nothing happened at Clacton. Nothing.'

'All right. What almost happened. I need to know, Martin. Did it mean anything to you?'

'Squirt, I was drunk. You know I was.'

'That's all I wanted to know.'

'And when you asked me to the party?'

'Angie, I don't mean to be unkind . . .'

'It's all right. I'm not some soppy lovesick kid.'

'No, you're not. You're lovely. And I—'

'Save it, Martin. I've made a fool of myself. Let's leave it at that.'

As Angie stood in the telephone box, her hands were shaking. Not only because she was about to make the call that part of her said was just about one of the stupidest things she had ever done, but because she had allowed herself to be humiliated all over again.

But she had had to go to see Martin; had had to be sure that he really didn't care about her. Because say he had cared about her all along, and she hadn't done anything about it?

And say she got home tonight and her mum had wall-papered her bedroom for her, had baked a cake and was wearing an apron and a great, big welcoming smile?

Angie took the card from her bag and rang the number in Greek Street.

'Mr Fuller, please,' she said. 'Tell him it's Angel calling.'

'Angie.' Jackie hissed into the receiver, she wanted to shout, but didn't want to cause a scene at work. 'It's nearly four o'clock in the afternoon. Where the bloody hell are you calling from? I called you at twelve. To meet up. And they said they'd sent you home not well.'

'They did.'

'So what's wrong with you?'

'Nothing. I've taken the day off.'

'You've what?'

'I'm out. With a friend.'

Jackie took a deep breath. 'Angie. Where are you? What are you up to? And who are you with?'

'I'm with David.'

'That old bloke in the car? Are you barmy?'

Angie hoped David couldn't hear Jackie shrieking.

'That's right,' she said casually. 'And we're at . . .' She put her hand over the mouthpiece. 'Where are we, David?'

'Westbourne Grove,' he said. He looked amused for some reason.

Angie looked at him and shrugged, not understanding.

'West London.'

'West London,' she repeated to Jackie. 'I didn't want you hanging about for me at the station tonight.'

'Very thoughtful.'

'And, Jack. I need a favour.'

Jackie sighed and shook her head, resigned now to the fact she had been coming to terms with during the past few weeks: she was no longer top dog in her friendship with Angie. 'Tell me.'

'I told Mum I was going out with you tonight. All right?'

'Course.'

'Thanks. Bye.'

Jackie jumped in before Angie had a chance to hang up. 'Wait. Before you go. There's something—'

'I know what I'm doing, Jack.'

'I know. I only wanted to say that I wish I wanted something so badly I just had to do it. There's nothing I want that much. Nothing. And it's a bit depressing.'

'Don't be put off by this place, Angel. It might look divey, but I've got to meet this bloke here. It shouldn't take too long.' David nodded at the doorman who waved them past the peeling, rusting railings, and on to the cracked path.

It reminded Angie, far too closely for comfort, of the students' house where she had been so shown up; right down to the booming music that was so loud she could feel it through her feet.

'They all come here. All the stars. All the ones that David Bailey bloke photographs. This is the proper business, this is.'

As they slowly went down the steep, metal stairs to the basement, clinging on to the greasy handrail, Angie wasn't so sure.

'Slumming, you see,' he went on. 'They like going to West End places like mine, the places to be seen in. But they come over this way, to Bayswater and Notting Hill and that, for a bit of excitement. They love this sort of thing. These West Indian clubs. All the famous stars and actors.'

Despite what she had said to Jackie, Angie wasn't convinced she knew what she was doing at all. Not any more. She was about to go with David Fuller, a man she knew nothing about – well, nothing except that he seemed to have loads of money, that he drove a big, shiny car, and he was probably at least fifteen years older than she was – into a club he had described as a dive, in the middle of the afternoon, in an unfamiliar part of London.

When he had driven her to her nan's he had said about taking her for a meal and to see a show. Some show this was turning out to be. She must have taken leave of her senses.

To cover up her nerves, Angie said the first thing that came into her head. 'Anyone ever told you, you look like that actor?'

Had she really just said that?

David held open the tatty, flaking door and gestured for her to go inside.

'Don't tell me. Michael Caine.' He laughed, a warm,

173

easy laugh, and winked at her, making her feel more good than gauche. Safe rather than quite so scared. 'A lot of people say it. I'll have to get together with him one day. Have a beer or two. So he can see who this Fuller bloke is, who everyone keeps telling him he looks like.'

As they left the bright afternoon sunshine behind them and entered the dark, pulsating cave of the club, Angie found herself joining in with his laughter.

'This is good music,' Angie said. She was sitting stiffly, on a grubby chair, by a shabby, splintered table, worried about her new suit and holding the strong-smelling drink David had ordered for her at arm's length, sure it would choke her.

'It's ska.'

So, this was ska. 'It's good.' Angie nodded as if she knew what he was talking about, and strained to make out the words so she could remember them for Jackie. Although she thought she probably wouldn't tell her much about the club itself. David must have made it up, about famous people going there, because, for the life of her, she couldn't see why anyone, let along a star, would go there. It was horrible. It would make Wyckham Hall in Romford look glamorous.

When she thought about it, maybe David wasn't as sophisticated as she'd thought. Maybe he only worked at the Canvas Club, for someone else, and he was borrowing his boss's car. And a man of his age was probably married anyway.

'See that black girl over there, by the bar?'

Angie peered through the gloom. 'The one in the red dress?'

'That's the one. She's going to be a top singing

star, that girl. Fantastic voice. Georgie Fame introduced her to me. I might ask her to do a spot at my next party.'

Angie's uneasiness about the strange situation in which she had somehow found herself was instantly forgotten. 'You know Georgie Fame?'

'Yeah, really nice feller.'

'I love his music. Especially "Yeh Yeh".'

'You'll have to meet him.' Suddenly distracted, David stood up. 'Hang on a minute, Angel. That bloke I've got to see. He's turned up. Won't be long.'

Angie was only a little disappointed to see that it wasn't Georgie Fame.

Jackie jumped on to the tube just as the doors were closing.

'No Angie tonight?' asked a voice from somewhere inside a huddle of bored-looking strap-hangers.

Jackie peered round a man, who was trying, not very successfully, to read the *Evening Standard*. 'Rita!' She was pleased to see it was one of the old schoolfriends she used to knock around with – before Angie's transformation into a bloody dolly bird. One of the old friends she might well need again if Angie insisted on going through yet another transformation – into a flipping night-club queen. Despite Angie's generosity, going up to the West End still hadn't been a cheap night out: the fare alone would have bought a couple of pairs of tights, and the journey home had been a nightmare. Then, to top that, despite her elaborate tale about getting separated from all her mates, her mum had led off alarming when she had rolled in, soaking wet, after midnight. It was an experience Jackie wasn't in a hurry to repeat.

'Excuse me.' She shoved her way past the now tutting

Evening Standard reader to join her. 'They sent her home from work. Not well.'

'That's a shame,' said Rita with a knowing look. 'Sure it wasn't a hangover?'

'Actually,' lied Jackie, coming over all protective – it was all right for her to have a go at Angie, but it was nothing to do with Rita – 'it was her monthly.'

Rita put on a sad face. 'Poor thing.' Then, without a pause, she added, 'I heard you went to the Canvas Club.'

'Blimey, news travels fast.'

'What was it like? Fab?'

'Better than fab. A bloke nearly caused a fight over Angie and the boss gave us free drinks all night. And Angie . . .'

'Yeah?'

'Er . . . Really enjoyed it as well. We thought we might go again some time. Going anywhere this weekend?'

'All right then, Peter. If they're the terms, then the answer's yes. You've got yourself a deal. The distribution in that area is now my responsibility.' David held out his hand to Burman and they shook on it.

'Is Sonia with you?'

'What, here? What do you think?'

Burman laughed. 'Silly of me. But as you're alone, please, join us, we're having a few drinks. Then supper.' He smiled, showing his gold teeth. 'Not here, of course. In St James's.'

David flashed his eyebrows and lifted his chin towards the corner table where Angie was sitting, tapping her feet and shrugging her shoulders to the insistent, hypnotic beat of the music. 'Who said I was alone?'

Burman studied her for a moment. 'Not a brass?'

'No.'

'You have good taste, David.'

'Especially in business associates.'

'I think so.' Burman gave one of his stiff-necked little bows. 'If you will excuse me.'

David waited for Burman to leave with his entourage, who had reappeared from the shadows of the club as if summoned by a silent dog whistle, and then went over to Angie.

'I have made, Angel, what is going to be a very satisfactory business deal. You brought me luck. I'm taking you somewhere nice to celebrate.' He gave her one of his winks. 'I've got to make a couple of quick calls first.'

The barman lifted the flap and let David behind the bar to use the telephone.

David called Bobby, to organize cover for the evening, then he spoke to Sonia.

'Son, it's me. I'm going to be back late.'

'How very attentive of you to let me know,' she sneered sarcastically. 'But it makes no difference to me. I won't be here.'

'I want you to wait in. Till Bobby comes round.'

'David, this is so inconvenient. You know Barbara's having a bridge evening.'

David knew no such thing. What he did know was that Sonia could barely play Snap, never mind keep up with this supposed new best friend, and the rest of her fictitious, card-playing mates, at the contract bridge evenings that had suddenly started to figure so centrally in Sonia's busier than ever social life.

'Sonia. I'm not messing about. Bobby's coming over for my keys for the Canvas. I'm going to drop them back to the flat in about half an hour. He's got to have them because I'm too busy to do the rounds tonight, and Half-a-lung's got Jeff's set. Understand? Or am I speaking too fast for you?'

Sonia wanted to laugh out loud – the keys! – but, instead, she sighed wearily. 'If I must. But I'm going to the hairdresser's now, and I won't be back until six. And remember, I've got to be at Barbara's by nine.'

'I'll tell him to come round at eight o'clock.'

'He'd better be here by eight.'

'He'll be there.'

As Sonia dialled Mikey's number, she was shaking with excitement. He would be so pleased with her.

'Darling. I have a surprise for you.'

'Aw yeah?'

'I have no idea how one does these things, but if you come here after six, I will have a set of keys for you to copy.'

'Keys?'

'For the Canvas. You have them for two full hours to do your worst.'

Detective Constable Jameson was sitting alone in the canteen, drinking a cup of foul, stewed tea, working his way through a greasy fry-up. He'd have to watch it, he'd only been at the station for a week and his trousers were already feeling a bit snug. Much more of this and he'd have to think about buying a new suit.

On a table nearby, two older, uniformed officers were discussing the new arrival.

'See the college boy picking about with his food?'

'Surprised he's not got them making prawn cocktails and chocolate gateau for him.'

'It makes me laugh. What do these kids know about police work?'

'It's a piss-take, if you ask me. Straight from college and they're on them wages. Disgusting.'

'I heard how he reckons he's read all the files on all the gangs. It's going to be his *special interest*. Going to start at the beginning. Bring in all the old faces to answer for business from years back. Then start on the new stuff. Going to clean up the place.'

'Oh yeah? Read all of them, has he? And cleaning up. That's nice. That's going to go down very well. The Old Man's going to have that little git for breakfast.'

Jameson heard the two uniforms laughing – woodentops was more than an appropriate nickname for fat buffoons like them – and knew it was at his expense. But their mockery didn't rile him, it merely strengthened his resolve to show everyone that a good brain and a college education was just as valuable, no, more valuable, in police work than sitting around for hours in smoke-filled pubs mixing with villains.

Not only would he prove them all wrong, he'd prove them so wrong they'd all be wetting themselves. He already had his eye on one old lag, Mad Albert Roper, who was due for release next week.

The Old Man – Detective Chief Inspector Gerald Marshall – was far too preoccupied to think about eating graduate-entry officers, for breakfast or otherwise; he was sitting in a club in St James's, where, in a couple of hours, he would be starting on the first course of what he knew would be a very impressive dinner.

Marshall was the guest of Peter Burman, and was

listening attentively as his host told him about his new business arrangement with David Fuller.

'I would very much appreciate it, Gerald, if Mr Fuller isn't bothered. While he gets this new enterprise off the ground.'

'You know me, Peter,' oozed the Chief Inspector. 'Always glad to oblige a friend.'

'And we are friends, aren't we, Gerald?'

Marshall raised his glass. 'Very good friends, Peter.'

David released the handbrake, but before he pulled away he looked at his watch: nearly four o'clock. 'I've just got to drop something off at my flat first, but then we'll go to this restaurant I know. They'll do us either a nice late lunch, or an early dinner. Whatever you fancy. All right?'

Angie nodded. 'Sounds smashing.' This was more like she had been expecting.

He drove fast, confidently, and Angie enjoyed seeing people stare at the smart, sleek car as it pulled away, always first, from the traffic lights.

All the time he drove, he was speaking to her, making her laugh, telling her stories about the restaurant they were going to, about Stefano, the man who owned it, and the evenings he had spent there.

He didn't mention who had spent the evenings with him.

'Here we are. I won't bother to go into the car park.' David had stopped opposite a big block of flats in yet another area of London that was new to Angie. 'Won't be a minute.'

'I'll be fine.'

David smiled. She was an easy-going kid. He liked that. It made a nice change not being moaned at every time he opened his mouth. And she was a real little looker. He could imagine what Sonia would have to say if she looked out of the window and saw he had a passenger who wasn't Bobby, and who certainly didn't weigh sixteen stone, or have a broken nose and a cauliflower ear.

He ran across the street and pushed the buzzer. No reply. He checked his watch again. Half four. Of course, she was at the hairdresser's. Till six.

Sod it. Why not? He felt lucky today. And he liked the idea of marking his own patch, like a tom cat proving his virility.

He trotted back over to the car.

'Come up with me. In case it takes me a bit longer than I thought.'

Angie had to stop her mouth falling open as he led her across the impressive, communal hallway to the ornate brass lift that took them up, with a subtle *ssshhhhhh*, to the top floor.

Thank goodness she had put on the lilac suit after all.

She barely heard what he was saying to her as he let her into the flat. If the rest of it was like the entrance hall, then it was massive.

The sitting-room was more the size of a dance hall, with pictures on all the walls. Not of kittens and cottage gardens and green oriental ladies like her Nan had, but big, bold paintings – Modern Art – like you saw in the films.

'Sit down,' he said, pointing to one of the big white sofas, thoroughly enjoying the feeling of having one over on Sonia. 'Fancy a drink?'

Angie shook her head. 'No thanks.' She couldn't say

yes – say she spilled it on the carpet? 'Do you' – how could she ask him? – 'live here? Alone?'

'I've always thought it was a bit on the big side.'

He hadn't answered her. 'So you don't share with anyone then?'

'No.' He took a set of keys from his jacket pocket and put them on a glass-topped coffee table by one of the room's many vases full of exotic blooms and strangely contorted foliage.

'Who puts all these flowers everywhere?'

'Sonia.' Shit!

'Who?'

'My housekeeper.' *She'd love that.* He walked over to the complicated-looking sound system and selected a record. 'Dance, Angel.' It was more of an instruction than a question.

He was grinning and holding out his hand.

Angie, dry-mouthed, stood up and let him put his arms around her.

But they didn't dance.

As the Hollies started singing 'I'm Alive', David Fuller pulled Angie to him and kissed her in a way that made her realize she had never been kissed, not properly, before.

Chapter 9

'I'm really sorry we couldn't stay up in the flat a bit longer.' He was lying. Lying was easy for David. This time it was to cover up the fact that, despite feeling as randy as hell, he hadn't wanted to hang around and have to confront Sonia. Not yet, anyway. The game he'd been playing with her was getting interesting. All over again. Thanks to the arrival of Angel. 'But we'd never have got this table otherwise.' He flashed her one of his smiles. 'Everything all right?'

'It's lovely.' Angie nodded, eager to please, although she couldn't imagine how anyone could have found it anything other than all right. This was a lot more than all right. It was fantastic. Here they were, in a romantic booth by the window, in a West End restaurant, with everyone who walked by looking in and wishing they were sitting there instead. It made her feel like a celebrity, a pop star or someone.

The fact that when they had arrived at Stefano's they had been the only customers and so would hardly have been fighting for a table – the owner had opened up early after David had called him – hadn't occurred to Angie. All she knew was that David was amazing. He was rich, suave – suave! she would never have believed she'd have met anyone she could use *that* word about – and, at the flat, he had been really nice to her. He hadn't tried to push her into doing anything. Not to get his hand up her skirt as Martin had done, not to maul or grapple with her. He had just kissed her.

Just.

That was a bit like saying the Beatles were *just* a pop group. And he had apologized for almost getting carried away, and had said they had better leave soon or he couldn't be held responsible for his actions. Then he had told her how really attractive she was, how difficult it was for a man to resist her . . .

Angie wriggled in her seat as the tingling sensations in her body came flooding back.

If anything, and this was confusing to admit even to herself, she would have liked David to have gone further. A lot further. And not just to please him, as she had been willing to do with Martin, but because her body was telling her that it was what she wanted more than anything. More than she had ever thought possible.

She felt herself blush.

'I've got stuff to see to later.' David looked at his watch and smiled. 'But don't worry, I'll drop you off first. Staying at your nan's?'

She became suddenly interested in the bowl of pale yellow roses that stood between them. 'No, not tonight. I've got work in the morning, so I'm going straight home.'

'To your mum and dad's?'

'Mum's.' She raised her eyes for a brief moment then returned to her study of the flowers. 'I've not got a dad.'

'I lost my mum and my dad, both of them, by the time I was twenty. Still miss them. I sometimes wonder what would have happened if they were still around.' He rolled his eyes and tutted at himself. 'Hark at me going on like an old woman. So, Angel, where do you and your mum live?'

Angie didn't much like the idea of telling this man,

who lived in such grandeur, that she came from a sprawling housing estate in Essex; an estate full of displaced cockneys who couldn't wait for Saturday to come, so they could get away from the place and go shopping 'up home' in the Roman Road street market, or to the terraces at Upton Park to cheer on their team, West Ham. Where wouldn't sound too horrible?

David said his own roots were in the East End.

'Poplar. I live in Poplar. Not far from Nan's. Walking distance.'

'So I can drop you off where I dropped you the other night. Is that what you're saying?'

It was as if he could read her mind. Was she that obvious? 'Yeah. If you don't mind.'

'How could I mind? It just means we've got plenty of time to enjoy a nice glass of bubbly and some of Stefano's grub before we have to go. You'll love his food. Top notch, it is. Now, let's see what we can have.'

Angie sat silently, watching, as David chatted easily with Stefano: asking him first about his wife and children, then about what champagne they might like, then they discussed things that were listed in the menu, and finally Stefano explained to David a selection of what he called the 'specials'.

By the time Stefano left them to think about what they fancied eating, Angie was panicking so badly, she was seriously considering replaying the nausea scene she had acted out that morning for Janet Shanks. Especially as the restaurant was now filling up with early, pre-theatre diners, who were so confident and loud, so full of themselves and their own importance, that they terrified her.

Angie might have looked all grown-up in her

fashionable suit, she might even be acting all grown-up, sitting in a restaurant opposite a sophisticated, older man, but she didn't feel grown-up. She felt like the scared little girl who used to spend all that time alone, curled up in her bed, knowing her mum had gone out yet again and wouldn't be back for hours.

'David,' she began, not quite knowing how she would finish the sentence.

He looked up from the menu with a ready smile. God, this made him feel good. Almost like a kid again. 'Decided yet?'

She dropped her chin, unable to face him. 'I don't really understand what the food is.' Her voice was about to crack, but she had to carry on. 'I've not been anywhere like this before. And all these people. They're so, you know . . .'

He reached across the table and lifted her chin with his finger. *There were tears in her eyes*. He could hardly credit it. The birds he usually came across were so slick, so composed, so ready to grab whatever was on offer, and here he was with a genuine innocent. It was bloody marvellous. Made him feel all protective. Something he hadn't felt for years.

'What do you like eating?' he asked. 'You can have anything you like. Stefano'll be only too pleased to make it for you.'

'What do you think?'

'How about steak and chips? That always goes down well.'

She nodded.

'I'll get him to make it a bit special for us, eh? Few mushrooms and that.'

She nodded again. 'And will you help me with these,

186

please?' She pointed tentatively at the array of cutlery set out before her.

'Angel.' He swept all the knives and forks and spoons to one side and took her hand. 'Let me tell you something. Till I was twenty-three years of age I had never been inside a gaff like this. Wouldn't have known a bottle of wine from a bottle of light ale. I used to pass these places and think to myself – one day. Then a mate of mine said to me – I don't understand you, Dave, you've got just as much money as all them in there, don't you think your dough's as good as theirs or something? So, you know what I did?'

She shook her head.

'I came in here and said – I want to speak to the owner. Stefano came over to me, and I said to him – Here's thirty quid. Me and Bobby here want a meal. We don't know nothing about grub like your'n, so we need you to help us. And he did. And I've been coming here ever since. Plenty of other places as well, of course. Places that think they're *chic*' – he said the word with such contempt that, for a moment, Angie flinched – 'Well, let me tell you something else. You, Angel, are as good as anyone in here. Better, because you're not a phoney. You don't pretend. You are who you are. Got it?'

Angie stared down at the pure white cloth. She wanted to say, but I'm not. I'm no dolly bird, I'm just Squirt, a frightened kid from Dagenham, who wishes she could get up and run away. But he was being so kind. 'Yeah. I've got it.'

'Good. Now I'm going to make you a promise, Angel. I like you. I like you a lot. And I'm going to teach you all the things that Stefano taught me.' He squeezed her hand harder. 'And lots of other things as well.'

Angie didn't know why but somehow he had made everything seem all right again. Just like he had when they had gone into the club in Westbourne Grove.

'I'd like that,' she said, lifting her chin and meeting his gaze. 'I know I've got a lot to learn.'

'All the better, Angel. All the better. Self-knowledge, see.'

He turned her hand over and looked at the marcasite watch her grandmother had given her for her birthday.

She gazed down at it. Was it really only six weeks ago?

'That's a nice watch. A boyfriend get it for you, did he?'

'Yeah. That's right.' Why had she lied? She knew why: to come over as all experienced. 'A boyfriend.'

'I'm not surprised. I fancy spoiling you myself. That's why I'm taking you shopping.'

'Shopping?'

'Yeah. Tomorrow.'

'I can't. I've already taken today off. I've got to go to work or I'll get in trouble.'

David snorted loudly. 'This is a first. A bird preferring to go to work rather than be taken out shopping? You really get to me, do you know that, Angel? You're a real one-off.'

'I didn't mean to be rude.'

'Don't get all upset.' There was laughter in his voice, but it wasn't cruel. 'I don't think you're rude. I think you're a really nice girl. And it doesn't matter. We can go on Saturday.'

Vi pulled back her bedroom curtains and watched Angie stride easily along the front path. Then, as her daughter bent forward to open the gate, Vi saw her already short

188

skirt ride up to show almost the full length of her firm, young legs.

Vi raked her fingers through her unbrushed hair. If only she was seventeen again. It wasn't fair.

She let go of the curtain, plonked down on the bed, and lit her first cigarette of the day, drawing the smoke deep into her lungs.

She had heard Angie come in last night, it was gone eleven – a good quarter of an hour after Nick had left – and yet there she was this morning as fresh as a bloody daisy.

God, she hated getting old.

Angie stood waiting for someone to open the Murrays' front door. Unsurprisingly, it was Tilly. She was holding a fork in her hand as if it were a magic wand and she was the good fairy in the pantomime.

'Morning, Mrs Murray. Don't suppose Jackie's ready yet?'

'You're a bit early for that, love. But come in.'

'It's such a lovely morning, I woke up all raring to go.'

'Good to hear you so cheerful. Let's just hope it's catching. Go up and see if you can make that girl of mine get a move on.'

Angie pointed to the little paved area of the garden under the front room window, where Martin's scooter was usually parked.

'Martin up and out all early as well?'

'No,' said Tilly, heading down the passage towards the kitchen, where she was frying enough bacon and sausages to feed half the street, but which was intended solely for Stan, her defiantly slim husband. 'He phoned last night. Tea-time it was. To say he was staying with a

189

friend of his from college. Had to get some work done. I just hope he gets a decent breakfast down him. I know what you youngsters are like.'

What Tilly didn't know about her own particular youngster was that his breakfast that morning consisted of nothing more than sex with Jill Walker, followed by a cigarette and a cup of black, instant coffee.

Remembering to buy milk hadn't been the first thing on either Jill's or Martin's mind.

With only a little coaxing and cajoling, Angie had Jackie out of the house and on the way to the station a good ten minutes before they really needed to leave. Not only was Angie bursting with all the things she had to say about her day playing hooky from work with David Fuller, Jackie was as eager to hear them.

'So you didn't think it was as good as the Canvas Club then?'

'Good? It was a total grot hole. Terrible. But David said all the stars go there. Can you imagine?' She shielded her mouth with her hand as though the streets of Dagenham were teeming with spies, and dropped her voice to a low whisper. 'Apparently, even a member of the Royal Family goes there.'

Jackie had no such concerns. 'No!' she shrieked.

'Yes,' Angie continued, all wide-eyed and breathy. 'And – you won't credit this, Jack, I'm telling you – she, *she* likes girls. If you know what I mean.'

Jackie was momentarily lost for words, then she gasped, 'No! What, like that Kay at school?'

If it hadn't been for Angie wrenching her backwards, Jackie, completely distracted by such juicy gossip, would have stepped straight into the Woodward Road, right in the path of a passing 62 bus.

'Not exactly like Kay,' Angie said, looking for a gap in the traffic. 'She likes blokes as well.'

'I don't know what to say.'

'Nor did I when he told me. But the music was brilliant. Ska.' Angie shoved Jackie across the road to the safety of the far pavement, and they began climbing the little hill up to Becontree station.

'Sing us one of the songs then,' Jackie demanded, her old bossiness with Angie not quite forgotten. 'Go on. How did they go?'

Angie pulled a face. 'I knew you'd say that. I did try to learn one for you, but they're sort of hard to understand. You must have to be used to the accents. But they're great for dancing to. Honest, Jack, you wouldn't be able to sit still if you heard one.'

Ordinarily, Jackie would have felt more than a touch narked, being excluded from something as important as the music that the magazines were saying was going to be the Next Big Thing, but this morning there were too many other things for her to hear about for her to start throwing tantrums.

'What else did you do? Where did you go after he'd had the meeting with the bloke?'

Angie shrugged up her shoulders and sucked in her lips in anticipation. She had been saving this bit. 'He took me to his flat. In Mayfair.'

This time Jackie stopped dead without any need for any arm dragging on Angie's part. 'Angela Knight. You went to his flat? Don't tell me you and him . . .'

Angie pushed Jackie towards the ticket barrier, while doing a very passable impression of looking absolutely mortified. 'No we did not, thank you very much. What do

191

you take me for? He had to drop something off. Some keys. For his housekeeper. Then we went to Stefano's.'

They both began fumbling around in their bags for their season tickets.

'What's that then?' The casual reference to 'housekeepers' and 'Mayfair' would, ordinarily, have supplied enough material to have kept Jackie questioning Angie closely for hours on end, but this was all so appetizing, she hardly knew where to start. 'This Stefano's? Another club is it?'

'No. It's an Italian restaurant.' Angie smiled pleasantly at the ticket inspector. 'We had champagne. He's taking me there again. On Saturday. For . . .' She hesitated, wondering what the word would sound like coming out of her mouth. '. . . lunch.'

Instead of the mocking reaction she had expected from her friend – *hark at you, lunch* – Jackie blinked slowly, like a cheap ventriloquist's dummy, and said simply, 'So you won't be coming shopping with me on Saturday?' She had kind of assumed that Angie's big day out, her mad adventure with an older man, was going to be a one-off. OK, they'd probably go to the Canvas Club again some time, in a few months maybe, but as for Angie seeing that bloke again . . .

'You don't mind do you, Jack?'

'And how about Saturday night?'

'I'm not sure yet. I've got to phone him.'

'Angie—'

'Angel.'

'What?'

'That's what he calls me: Angel. Good, eh?'

'Yeah,' Jackie said flatly. 'Great.'

*

192

Angie walked over to the changing-rooms in Solar, a King's Road boutique that she and Jackie wouldn't have been brave enough even to enter a matter of weeks ago, with a pile of dresses slung over her arm, a cerise floppy hat with holes punched in the brim perched on her head, and a turquoise feather boa draped round her neck. David had insisted she try them all on. He was very persuasive.

As the curtain fell behind her, Angie's eyes widened. Instead of the individual cubicles she had been expecting, what she saw was a communal changing area.

Communal.

She had heard they existed, of course, but she had never actually been in one. And she wasn't sure she liked it. No. Wrong. She knew she didn't like it at all.

The room was full of young women, all in varying stages of undress, and all totally uninhibited. She buried herself away in the corner and turned her back on them, as if her not seeing them would somehow make her invisible, would spare her blushes.

It was a vain hope.

Slowly, she slipped out of her dusty-pink minidress, folding it and putting it on top of her shoes – anything to avoid eye contact with the other girls – then pulled on the simple white shift.

'That looks absolutely gear. Really fabulous on you,' yipped a plummy-voiced, rather sturdy brunette, who Angie hadn't even noticed in the crowd. 'You are so lucky.' She brayed a whinnying, horse-like laugh. 'Wish I had a figure like yours, I'd buy up the whole ruddy shop.'

Angie raised her eyes and looked at herself in the mirror. Her nan had always said she had a good figure. And Martin had certainly seemed to have approved of her. And that student – that horrible student – and now David.

Maybe she was OK.

Maybe she was better than OK.

She turned to the girl and looked directly at her. 'Thanks,' she said. 'But do you think it's short enough?'

'How are you doing, Angel?' David, standing outside Solar, with his arms filled with bags and packages, had spotted a cab at the traffic lights.

Angie didn't hesitate. 'I'm so tired. After that really nice . . .' she paused for just a beat '. . . lunch. Then doing all this shopping. I don't know if I've got the energy to try on anything else.'

He looked relieved. 'I'm glad you said that. Look, it's nearly five. How about if we go and have a drink?'

'Smashing.'

'I know a nice little hotel. Not far from here. We could have an early dinner.' He shoved half the bags under one arm, put two fingers in his mouth, gave a piercing whistle and showed out to the cab driver.

'A hotel,' said Angie softly, panicking about how she would handle being in yet another new, and no doubt scary, type of place. 'That'll be nice.'

Sonia strolled aimlessly along Kensington High Street, deep in thought, barely registering the existence of the regular crowd of Saturday browsers, window shoppers and tourists who moved around her in shoals, like small fry avoiding predators.

She didn't notice any of them, that is, until she saw one particular young woman – a uniformed nanny who was pushing a high-wheeled, coach-built Silver Cross pram in the direction of Kensington Gardens.

It was as if a light suddenly came on in Sonia's head, as if she now knew what she had always wanted to do with her life, but had simply never realized it before. Up until now she had been happy – well, driven, more than happy – to have nice things, to go to nice places, and to live the life she had believed, truly believed, she had wanted. But now she knew she had just been passing the time, playing around, living half a life.

What Sonia really wanted, what she *had* to have, was Mikey's baby.

She lay back on the rumpled pillows, her sweat-covered body tangled in the sheets, with a smile of blissful satisfaction. Not only sex in the afternoon with Mikey, but in the flat, when David could turn up at any moment. And she hadn't put in her cap.

It couldn't get a lot better than this.

Mikey stroked his hand over her taut, flat belly. 'Sonia, you are—'

'Insatiable?' She stretched lazily.

'I think that's the word.'

'That's a big word,' she purred suggestively.

He raised an eyebrow, patted her belly as if it was a pet dog, and rolled over on to his back. 'You don't just love me for the size of the words I know, do you, darling? Cos I don't know very many.'

'Mikey, I just love you.' She opened her eyes and propped herself up on her elbows. 'And I want to have your baby.'

He turned on to his side so his back was to her and yawned. Here we go. 'Course you do.'

'I mean it, Mikey. I want us to go away together.'

195

'Yeah. So do I, darling.'

'You did like my little present?'

Mikey frowned. 'Present?'

'The keys.'

'Oh yeah. Lovely.'

'Did it work? Pressing them into the Plasticine?'

'It had better.'

'And will . . .' She gently pulled him round by the shoulder until he was looking at her. 'Will having those keys mean we'll be able to get enough money to go away?'

Mikey looked at her blankly.

'You said you wanted to. You do, don't you, Mikey?'

'Course I do.' Mikey blasted her with a smile. 'Come here.' He put his arms around her and pulled her on top of him.

As he closed his eyes, he could see his future: him on a white, sandy beach, a glass of bubbles in one hand, and the little blonde sort who worked in the Coffee Bongo in Greek Street in the other. And that's exactly what he would have, just as soon as he'd creamed off enough of Sonia's old man's takings.

Within a quarter of an hour, Mikey was up, washed and gone. He had work to do, he had explained to a blissful-looking Sonia. What he hadn't explained was that he wanted to be out of there before Fuller turned up, which he might well do at any minute, to get ready for his usual Saturday-night tour round his businesses.

Sonia, all smiles and pecky little kisses, had assured Mikey that she understood how busy he was, how she knew he was only doing it all for their sake, and that she had to make some telephone calls anyway.

196

It had made Mikey feel a bit queasy, a woman of her age acting all lovey-dovey. She was probably going to call her mates, to tell them what she'd been doing all afternoon. Just like a bloody teenager. But he hadn't said anything. It wouldn't have been right: being honest after schtupping a bird. Mikey considered himself a gentleman like that.

She picked up the telephone twice before she actually dialled, and had almost finished the cigarette she had lit before she eventually allowed the connection to be made.

Then, when the number answered, Sonia had to swallow hard before she could speak, and, when she did so, it was in a broad, Dudley accent.

'Sorry I've not called, Mum. I've been really busy. You know how it is. Did you get the money I sent you?'

She paused while her mother answered.

'Good. Look, Mum, I wanted you to know I might be going away for a while, but I'll be in touch.'

Another pause.

'No, nothing to worry about. Honest. Bye, Mum.'

She put down the receiver and closed her eyes. Nothing to worry about.

Not so long as David didn't find out.

When the taxi had dropped them outside the hotel in the discreet side-street, it looked so pretty that Angie forgot to be scared. Instead, she was enchanted by the window boxes full of scarlet flowers and glossy green leaves that glowed against the white stucco walls in the bright summer afternoon sunlight.

'They do a nice little meal in here,' said David, bumping her back to reality.

Angie looked crestfallen. 'If it's all right with you,'

she still felt shy about using his name, 'I'm still really full.'

'I suppose it is a bit early to eat. And we did have plenty at lunch-time.' This was good. Exactly how it was meant to go. 'We could just have a drink.'

'Please.'

David nodded for her to go in through the revolving doors that were being steadied by a uniformed man with grey handlebar moustaches, and stepped in after her.

'Don't much fancy sitting listening to all them old crows over there,' he said, raising his chin at the tables of middle-aged and elderly women who were tucking into the hotel's lavish afternoon teas. 'How about somewhere private?'

Angie could have clapped with relief. The hotel might have been very pretty, but the women who were patronizing it, groomed to within an inch of their glittering lives, looked terrifying. 'I'd like that.'

'Hang on, I'll see what I can do.'

Within moments, Angie had been escorted to the lift and whisked up to the fourth floor, and was now standing outside a door marked 405.

'Private room,' said David with a wink.

'Show me what you look like in some of that new gear,' said David, handing her a glass of champagne, and one of the bags from Solar. He was enjoying himself. It was a long time since he had had to be so encouraging with a bird. They usually saw his motor, or his wallet, or realized who he was, and they had their drawers off before he was even ready for them.

'Where can I get changed?' Angie asked, looking around. Not having been in a hotel before, she had no idea that she was standing in what was described in the tastefully glossy brochure as a 'well-appointed suite, complete with dressing-room and two full bathrooms'.

'Not shy, are you?' David stood up and took the glass and bag from her. Then he turned her slowly round so that her back was to him, and, even more slowly, began to lower the zip on her dress.

Angie closed her eyes. She wanted this.

But she didn't.

She didn't know what she wanted.

He bent his head and breathed into her neck, then whispered into her ear, 'You are so beautiful. My little Angel.'

It was what she wanted. Exactly what she wanted.

She turned to face him, closed her eyes and stood on tip toes.

He kissed her, just as he had kissed her when they had been in his flat, then he lifted her into his arms as if she weighed nothing and carried her over to the bed.

As he undressed her, he kissed her again, gently, pressing his lips against her mouth, her throat, her shoulders, then – she could hardly breathe – her breasts.

She was naked, and he was looking down at her, smiling with approval. 'You're lovely,' he said, pulling off his clothes and tossing them on the floor.

Angie knew she was blushing, but she didn't care. This man's approval was what she wanted. Although she couldn't bring herself to look anywhere other than at his face.

Not yet. She was still far too shy for that.

But, as he stretched out on the bed beside her, and ran his hand up and down her thigh, she knew there was something she had to be really brave about.

'There's something I've got to say,' she whispered.

'Not your prayers, I hope, Angel.'

Unable to face him, Angie turned over, only to see herself staring back from the huge dressing table mirror. Come on, Angie, tell him. Tell him now.

'David,' she began. 'You remember what I said when you took me to the restaurant?'

He frowned. Christ, what had she said? She wasn't hinting she had a dose, was she? 'You told me lots of things,' he said cautiously.

'About it being new to me, and me not knowing what I was supposed to be doing.'

'Yeah.'

'Well, this is sort of new as well.'

'New?'

'Yeah. I've never . . .'

A look of realization slowly spread over David's face. 'You mean you've never?' His words came out in a mixture of disbelief, spluttering and amazement. 'With anyone?'

She nodded, embarrassed by her own innocence.

'I don't suppose you're on the Pill then?'

She shook her head. 'No.'

David twisted round and was on his feet and pulling on his trousers in a single, fluid movement. 'Get dressed,' he said firmly.

She turned over and faced him, forgetting her embarrassment. 'David, please. I didn't mean to spoil everything. Don't let's go yet. It's only early.' She glanced desperately at her watch. 'Five o'clock. That's all. And I want to. I really want to.'

He angled his head so that he was looking at her over his shoulder. 'You've not spoiled anything, Angel.

Nothing at all. You get yourself dressed and I'll drop you round your nan's.'

Resigned to her own stupidity, Angie did as she was told.

'I'm going to make an appointment for you to see a friend of mine. Get you sorted out.' He winked. 'And don't you worry yourself. We can continue with this education of yours at our leisure.'

And what leisure it was going to be. It was almost unbelievable. David could hardly keep the grin off his chops. He had found himself a real-life, genuine virgin.

Just wait till he told Bobby.

'Here,' he said, handing her one of the two cigarettes he had just lit from a single match. 'Calm your nerves.'

Angie took it from him and began to smoke. She didn't like to mention that was something else she had never done before.

David had just stepped inside one of his East End snooker clubs, off Shoreditch High Street, where he was meeting Bobby and Mad Albert Roper. The plan being that the three of them were going to collect a very large interest payment on a loan that Lukey Gold, a more than averagely stupid, mug punter had actually thought he could get away with not handing over.

Despite it being almost twenty minutes since he had left Angel in Poplar, David was still grinning – she was a virgin! – but when he saw the expression on Bobby's face, as he stood alone, by one of the tables, filling a thick, fisherman's sock with billiard balls – a favoured weapon of his – thoughts of Angel couldn't have been further from David's mind.

He stepped into the low pool of yellow light

illuminating the green baize table and spoke to Bobby in a low, guarded voice. 'What is it?'

Bobby looked over his shoulder, making sure no one could hear. 'Albert's had a tug.'

'Not already?'

'Yeah. Whole crowd of coppers burst in on him. When he was doing the business with a brass.'

'They what?'

'There was murders apparently. Did him for a list of charges long as your arm. Not even one or two, just to hold him. Some of them went back years. Tried to collar him for the lot.'

'Fuck me, Bob, he's only just got out. Where they holding him?'

'They ain't. He was lucky. The bird he was with, that Christina—'

'The old tom who works the pitch opposite the Canvas?'

'That's her.'

David was taken aback. 'Lucky? You sure?'

'I know. She's almost as potty as Albert. And pissed as a fart as usual. Can't see how even Mad Albert could fancy—'

'Yeah, all right, Bob. Get on with it.'

'Well, she's grabbed this box of matches and she's only set light to the net curtains.'

David couldn't help himself. He started laughing. 'She what?'

'Truth. Then she threw a bottle of Scotch on it and the whole lot went up. Heavy curtains and all. Like bonfire night. Then they've fell down, on the bed like, and the eiderdown's gone up. Bloody nuthouse by the sound of it. And while they're all fannying around trying to put the flames out, Mad Albert's gone and jumped out the window.'

'But she's . . . What? Two floors up?'

'Three. But he was so pissed, he was sort-of relaxed. Landed with hardly a scratch, and had it away on his toes like a fucking greyhound.'

'How about the tom?'

'Down the nick.'

'I'll get hold of Marshall. He'll sort her out. Where's Albert now?'

'He turned up at the Blue Moon. And, as luck would have it, I was over there checking the drink stocks.'

'And now?'

'I took him over my brother's and he drove him down his caravan. In Suffolk it is. Right hole. So fucking quiet. But it's safe. For now, anyway.'

'You did well, Bob.' David thought for a moment, then took the sock from Bobby's hand and poured the billiard balls out on to the green baize. He picked one up and sent it spinning into the far pocket. 'I'd better go and see Marshall right away. Sooner Christina's out the better. Don't know what Mad Albert might have said to her.'

'You can trust Albert, Dave.'

'Bob, he's only been out a few weeks after eight years. And if Christina was pouring Scotch down both their throats, who knows what's been said?'

'See what you mean.'

David jerked his head for Bobby to follow him. 'Come on. Lukey Gold's in luck tonight.'

'You ain't gonna let him get away with it, are you, Dave?'

'Don't be silly, Bob.'

'You want me to take someone else over there with me?'

'And have me missing out on all the fun? No. I'll pay him a visit another night.'

Chapter 10

It was Monday evening, and Jackie, with fat, plastic rollers bristling from her hair, was struggling along the street after Angie, who was sprinting towards the Murrays' house.

'Hang on, Ange,' gasped Jackie, clinging to the privet hedge. 'I'm getting a stitch. Your nan's flat's not on fire. She only wants to speak to you.'

'Nan'd never phone me at yours unless it was urgent.'

Tilly Murray was fretting, theatrically, on her door-step. Incidents such as unusual telephone calls from grandmothers brought Tilly far closer to hysteria than any air-raid warnings of her girlhood had ever managed. Bombs were one thing, but family problems were quite another.

'Angie, love,' she wailed, 'you've got to give your nan a ring. Quick. She's so upset. Gawd knows what's the matter.'

Angie nodded her thanks and made straight for the phone on the black, wrought-iron stand just inside the front door.

When she finally managed to get her fingers into the right numbers on the dial, she drummed impatiently until Sarah Pearson answered.

'Nan, it's me, Angie. What's wrong? Are you ill?'

'Sorry to bother you, love. I'm just being a silly old woman. I had to talk to someone, and I—'

'Fifty-one is not old, Nan, and you are not being silly.'

'I wondered if you fancied coming round tomorrow.'

'Nan. Tell me. Please. What's happened?'

'I feel so useless, Ange. I don't know where to turn. It's Lily. She's being chucked out.'

'Who?' asked Angie.

'Lily Patterson.'

'Lily Patterson?'

'That'll be Doris's old pal,' hissed Jackie's mum, throwing her bit into the conversation.

'We'll be out the back,' mouthed Jackie, ushering her mother into the kitchen.

'Mrs Murray says she's a friend of Doris's,' Angie said with a nod to her friend. 'Is that right?'

'Yeah. It's terrible. Something to do with slum clearance.'

'Nan, calm down, eh?'

'They say they're not doing up the terraces. Not like they did the Buildings. Instead of making them nice and letting people stay in them, some bloke's bought them all up.' Sarah started crying again.

'And?'

'He's going to make all them little houses into flats. Right expensive they're gonna be. No place for the likes of Lily. It'll kill her if she has to move away, Ange. She's got her life here. Her daughters round the corner. And her little job with Doris. And say I'm next? Say this bloke buys up the Buildings? Where would I go then? Who'd have me?'

'Don't cry, Nan. No one's going to make you leave. I promise. I'll come over tomorrow and see you. All right?'

'You can't miss work for me.'

'Don't worry about that, I'll be over. I'm not sure when, but I'll be there.'

'Your poor nan.' Tilly Murray, who had hovered in the kitchen doorway until she had heard Angie replace the receiver, was standing by the phone table, holding her face in despair. 'And that poor Lily. She wouldn't move to Dagenham when we all came, you know. Wouldn't hear of it. Always said it'd kill her if she had to leave that house. Born there, she was.'

'So Nan said.'

'Stay and have a cup of coffee, love. You and Jackie go in the front room. I'll bring it in to you. I'll make it with nice hot milk and put in plenty of sugar for the shock.'

Angie didn't actually feel so much shocked as saddened. She had never heard her nan so upset before. She had always been strong. She blew out her cheeks and pushed open the front-room door.

Jackie plonked down on the sofa next to Martin, who was watching a television programme that featured a man's not very impressive efforts to make his voice come from out of a suitcase.

'Your nan all right, Squirt?' asked Martin pleasantly, twisting round so he could see her.

'Yes thanks.' Angie gripped the back of the sofa and stared, unseeing, at the black-and-white images flickering on the screen. 'Just a bit worried about something, that's all.'

'Never mind all that, Angela Knight,' bossed Jackie, without looking round. 'You tell Martin what you told me on the way to work this morning.'

'About what?'

Jackie turned her head and opened her eyes wide in exasperation. 'About what? About your job.'

'He won't be interested.'

He twisted round to face her again. 'I will.'

'I'm thinking of giving in my notice.'

'What? Got something better?'

'Not yet.'

'Tell him,' demanded Jackie.

'Someone I was talking to said I could do a lot better for myself than working in an office for slave wages.'

'Actually,' said Jackie to her brother, 'she's just got a rise and is earning very good money.' Then she turned her attention back to Angie. 'And tell him who that someone is who's giving you all this good advice.'

'Jackie. You promised.'

Jackie shrugged and said nothing, knowing that, in almost mentioning David Fuller, she had very nearly gone too far. 'You try and talk some sense into her, Martin,' she said airily to her brother. 'While I go and fetch the coffee. Mum'll be fiddling about with biscuits on saucers for bloody hours if I leave it to her.'

Once Jackie was safely out of the room, Martin patted the now empty seat beside him on the sofa. 'Everything all right, Squirt? I won't say anything to anyone.'

Angie just shrugged. 'It's nothing. You know Jackie. Doesn't like to think she's not got me under her thumb any more.'

'So long as you're sure I can't do anything.'

'I'm sure.'

He touched her gently on the shoulder, and Angie felt the same flutter that could almost have had her giving away her virginity in a grotty bus shelter in Clacton.

She closed her eyes, half-wanting Martin to pull her hard towards him, and half-repulsed at herself for being such a tart. She was already seeing David, for goodness' sake, and was actually going with him tomorrow to see this 'friend' of his. So, how many blokes did she want?

It wasn't easy being this new, trendy person.

'I'm glad you're not in trouble,' said Martin briskly, and patted her as if she were a puppy. 'You're like another little sister to me. Do you know that?'

Angie's eyes flicked open. Little sister? That wasn't the right reaction.

'Sorry I can't stop and chat, Squirt. I'm meant to be meeting someone and I've not even had my bath yet. But if you need to talk about anything some other time . . .'

Angie did her best to smile brightly. 'Thanks, that's kind. Enjoy yourself, won't you? Have a good time.'

He waggled his eyebrows to try and make her laugh. 'I will. But, if not, I'll be careful, eh?'

Angie giggled dutifully, and Martin almost knocked into Jackie coming back into the room. She set down a tray of coffee and the inevitable biscuits on the low table in front of the sofa.

'He's off to meet some girl from college,' said Jackie.

Angie helped herself to a biscuit but made no attempt to eat it. 'Is he?'

'Do you care?'

'Why should I?'

'You cared in that bus shelter.'

'We were all drunk. And, anyway, I've got a boy-friend.'

Jackie spooned sugar into her coffee. 'Don't you think he's a bit old to be called a boyfriend, Ange? And you've only seen him a couple of times. That's hardly a boyfriend, is it?'

'Jealous?'

Jackie dropped her teaspoon on to the tray with a metallic clatter. 'Angie!'

Angie stood up. 'I'm not going in to work tomorrow.'

'If you take another day off, you won't have to worry about leaving, they'll sack you.'

'I can't help that.'

'Sit down, Angie. Please.'

Angie did so. 'I've got to go out somewhere.'

'Where?'

'Just somewhere.'

'Why won't you tell me?'

'It's private.'

Angie's words deflated Jackie as surely as a pin bursting a toy balloon. 'I didn't mean to interfere.'

'That's OK.' Angie stood up again. 'Look, I'd better get back home. I want an early night.'

Jackie followed her to the front door. 'Is it your nan's you're going to? I could go with you if you like.'

'Thanks, but I'm not going there till later. I've got something to do first.'

'Is it an interview?' Jackie was scratching around for a clue. She was hurt.

'Sort of.'

'You can tell me.'

'You wouldn't approve.'

'Why not? What sort of job is it?'

'Look, Jack, I can't tell you. Not now.' Angie flicked a glance towards the kitchen where Tilly Murray was trilling away like a songbird as she cleared up. 'I'll tell you later.' With that, she let herself out and shut the Murrays' street door behind her.

'I wouldn't bet on it,' said Jackie to the door.

'Talking to yourself?' asked Martin, brushing past her

on his way from the bathroom to the stairs.

'I might as well be,' said Jackie.

'So, what was the big emergency?' asked Vi, jiggling one crossed leg up and down on the other. 'Lost her false teeth?'

'Nan doesn't need false teeth.' Angie was standing in the doorway to the front room, looking at her mother's make-up-clogged face and stained, fag-burned house-coat. 'You'd know, if you ever went to see her.'

Vi lit herself another cigarette after adding the remains of her last one to the pile of butts in the ashtray on the arm of her chair. 'Why would I want to do that?'

'Because she's your mum?'

'And I'm yours, but you care far more for her than you've ever done for me.'

'Don't be selfish, Mum. She's really upset.'

'She's a manipulative old cow is what she is. If only you could . . .' Vi's words trailed away as the Tom Jones record she had been playing on the radiogram came to an end. 'Put that on again, Ange.'

'I'm going to bed.'

'Bed? But it's only nine o'clock. What am I meant to do for the rest of the evening?'

'Phone one of your blokes to take you out. I'm sure one of them will oblige.'

'You little—'

'Save it, Mum.'

'If that's your attitude, I don't know why you don't just get out. Find somewhere else to live if I'm so terrible.'

Angie shook her head at her mother's childishness. 'You know you don't mean that.'

'Don't I? Try me. Go on. Leave.'

'Goodnight, Mum.' She closed the front-room door quietly behind her and went upstairs to bed.

'Sleep tight,' Angie said to herself, as she climbed between the sheets. 'See you in the morning.'

Detective Constable Jameson had parked his beaten-up, dull-grey Morris Minor opposite the staff entrance to the Canvas Club. Slumped as he was, low in his seat, he could get a clear view of the doorway without being seen.

He'd come straight from work and it was way past midnight, but he wasn't tired, he was too revved up to be bothered about sleep, too angry with his boss, Detective Chief Inspector Gerald Marshall. Boss or not, Jameson couldn't believe the man's cheek. How could he have the bare-faced front to tell him, not even wrapped in some sort of nicety, but straight out, that he was releasing that raddled old tart from custody, and that he should leave David Fuller and his businesses, and all his associates, alone. *As a favour.* Jameson would show him favour. He was compiling a private file on every part of that thug's enterprise he could trace, and he didn't care how long it took. And he was going to show up the corruption in that station if it was the last thing he did.

Tonight, Jameson's patience was rewarded. Within the hour, the man he knew to be Mikey Tilson had arrived. Jameson jotted down the time on his pad, and watched as the man first checked over his shoulder to see if he was being followed, then let himself in to the staff entrance of the club.

'Hello, Jeff.'

Jeff, shocked at hearing a voice in the little office, spun

round to find Mikey Tilson standing behind him. 'How the hell did you get in here?'

'Never you mind yourself about that, Jeffy boy.' Tilson pointed at four thick piles of used notes and nodded approvingly. 'Tonight's takings? This place is doing well. And on a week night. With all them little pill-heads in buying gear of a Friday and Saturday, it must be like a bloody harvest.'

'Don't try anything stupid, Mikey.' Jeff put down his glass of milk – he considered it a weakness to drink anything else when he was working: leave the booze and the pills to the punters – and scratched uneasily at his neck. He didn't like Mikey Tilson, didn't like him one bit, but he particularly didn't like being surprised by the slimy, arrogant, little arsehole.

'Who said I was trying anything?'

'No one said anything about you collecting tonight. How did you get them keys?'

'Never you mind that. That ain't your business. I just come in to tell you that I'm going to be collecting every night over the next few weeks. A little tax. The five per cent you've been putting in your bin is going to stay in the safe till I turn up. And it's going straight in my bin, not yours. Got it?'

'Mikey. Don't do this. It'll lead to all sorts of trouble, mate.'

'Mate? I'm not your mate, you black bastard.' Mikey reached into his jacket and pulled out a Luger, one of the many souvenirs that were still to be bought all over London a full twenty years after the war had ended. 'See this? This means you don't start getting lairy. You just leave the five per cent in, and we'll say no more about it.' He held out his hand.

Reluctantly, Jeff counted out the minimum number of notes he thought he could get away with – he suspected, rightly, that Mikey wasn't the brightest when it came to maths – and handed them over. He not only hated giving it to Tilson, he hated letting Dave down.

Mikey fanned out the money, waved it, sniffed at it, and smiled greedily. 'Lovely. See you tomorrow.' He put the notes away in his inside pocket, turned on his heel and walked over to the door. He took hold of the handle, then looked over his shoulder at Jeff. 'Aw, and by the way, I'm also going to be collecting a nice big bagful or two of gear off you. French Blues and some Black Bombers'll do for now. So, if you'll have them ready bagged up for me.' He smiled coldly. 'See you.'

Bobby sat opposite David in the Greek Street office, with a glass of Scotch in his hand and a wide grin on his big, broad face. 'No kidding, Dave? She's really a virgin?'

David grinned back. 'No kidding.'

'Blimey, who'd have thought you'd have found one of them in a club nowadays?'

'Not me, Bob, I'm telling you. And I nearly wasted the chance to savour it. If you know what I mean.'

Bobby's grin wilted a little. He could talk about birds with the best of them, but nothing in too much detail.

'All right, Bob, don't go all shy on me. I'm getting her sorted out. Taking her to see that quack up Marylebone tomorrow morning.'

Bobby frowned. 'What, the one who took the bullet out of Bill's arm that time?'

'That's the feller. He'll do anything for a few quid.'

Bobby really didn't get it. 'What's she need to see him for?'

'He's gonna give her the once-over and stick her on the Pill for me.'

Bobby hid his embarrassment by taking a big swig of whisky. Too big. He started choking.

'Calm down, Bob.'

'I leave that sort of thing to my Maureen,' he spluttered, his eyes streaming.

'Good thing too, by the look of it.'

'Why're you getting involved with all this women's lark?'

'I'm not sure how old she is.'

'So?'

'Look, if she's under age, I don't want her getting up the duff and having her mother causing trouble for me, now do I? I know you can usually pay someone off, but it'd be my luck her old girl's some sort of nutty church-goer or something. I mean, why else would she be a virgin at her age?'

'How old d'you reckon she is?'

'Dunno. And I don't much care, to tell you the truth. But I'm telling you, she's got a body on her . . .'

They sat, finishing their drinks, each lost in his own thoughts.

Then David said: 'Marshall did his job for Christina. She was back working tonight.'

Bob grimaced. 'Don't know for how much longer. She's looking a right state.'

'You're right there, Bob. Still, as long as she pays her full whack every week. How's Albert getting on in the caravan? All right?'

'Sort of. But it's making him a bit stir crazy. And all that countryside makes him nervous. I think we're gonna have to move him.'

'Time for a quick one?' David stated, rather than asked, filling the other man's glass almost to the brim.

'Ta.' Bobby sipped at the whisky – his fourth very large one in a row – and it began loosening his tongue. 'Dave?'

'Yeah?'

'This Mikey Tilson business,' he began, then added quickly, so that his boss would know he wasn't talking about Tilson and Sonia. 'What Jeff just said on the phone. About him binning that five per cent from the Canvas, I mean.'

'What about it?'

'No disrespect, Dave, and you know I'd never interfere, but, out of interest, why are you letting him do it?'

David's face creased into a wide, handsome smile. 'Bobby, my old son, it amuses me to see that idiot thinking he's having me over, when all I'm doing is setting up the little prick for a really hard fall.' He swallowed a drop more Scotch and winked. 'Saves me from getting bored, you see, Bob. You know how much I hate getting bored.'

Bobby nodded, hoping he looked as if he understood. But, even though his boss had just given him the same sort of explanation he himself had tried to give to Maureen about Tilson, Bobby, in truth, didn't have the slightest understanding of what Dave actually meant. But that's why he was the boss.

Thank gawd.

'Tell you what, Bob. Talking about being bored, how about a ride down Ernie's spieler for a few hands of cards? I'm not tired yet. Are you?'

Bobby knew what his answer had to be.

'Bob, get me Mikey on the blower.' David Fuller didn't look up as he spoke, he was too engrossed in the column of figures that he was checking off with a pencil. Despite their previous late night, David still looked immaculate, as if he'd had not only his full eight hours but had also had a soothing lullaby thrown in for good measure.

Bobby, on the other hand, despite Maureen's best efforts, looked even rougher than usual. With his chin unevenly shaved, his tie askew and one of his shirt collar peaks standing up at an angle, he had a slightly comical, less menacing look about him than usual. But mistaking Bobby for anything other than the tough, bull-necked thug he actually was would have been a bad mistake.

It took Bobby some considerable effort to focus on the dial, then as soon as the number began ringing, he handed the receiver, gratefully, over to David.

'Mikey? It's Dave here.'

'Right. Dave.' Mikey's voice was thick with sleep. He screwed up his eyes and stared in disbelief at his bedside clock.

Half past eight? Half past fucking eight?

He didn't even think of waking up until noon. What was the bastard playing at?

'You owe me some money, son.'

Mikey was suddenly wide awake. His heart and mind were racing. He'd been collecting his 'tax' from the Canvas for just one night and he'd really thought it had all gone so smoothly. He'd kill that bastard Jeff when he got hold of him.

'You there, Mikey?' David's voice sounded soft, concerned.

'Yeah. Yeah, I'm here.'

'So, how about my money?'

'Money, Dave? How d'you mean?'

David was enjoying the fear in the little runt's voice, but he had too much to do to string his pleasure out for too long. 'You had a sub on your wages a couple of weeks ago. Remember? Said you needed a new suit or something?'

'Right. Yeah. Course. The sub. I'll drop it round the office. End of the week, all right?'

'Good. And, Mikey.'

'Yeah?'

'Did you know the takings went down at the Canvas last night? Five per cent or so, I'd say.'

'Did they?'

'They did. Why do you think that was?'

'Dunno, Dave, but I'll make sure I keep a special eye on that Jeff for you.'

'Good kid.'

Kid? Mikey's lips twisted into a sneer. He'd not only kill Jeff if he didn't keep his mouth shut, he'd kill David fucking Fuller as well – once he'd creamed off enough to make a break for it. He was sick of all this. Sick of the lot of them. Jeff. Fuller. Sonia moaning on about babies. And even the little blonde sort in the coffee bar, who'd started whining on about not seeing enough of him. It was all doing his head in.

'You still there, Mikey?'

'What? Yeah. I'm here.'

'Good. I mean, we wouldn't want nothing happening to you, now would we?'

David replaced the receiver and shook his head in wonder at how someone as thick as Tilson could actually think he'd ever get one over on him, David Fuller. If the challenge was going to be this pathetic, then Mikey Tilson would soon begin to bore him again. And this particular game would have to be brought to an end.

As Mikey lay on his bed, smoking furiously and plotting revenge on just about everybody he knew, Angie was sitting at the kitchen table with her transistor playing softly, so as not to wake her mum, making up her face, transforming herself into Angel.

She was taking even more care than usual, doing her best to cover up the fact that, despite her early night, she had hardly slept. She had tossed and turned, fretting about what might be happening to her nan and to Doris's friend Lily, and going over and over what was going to happen to her. This morning. When she went to see David's friend.

As she looked down her nose into her magnifying mirror, painstakingly sticking on individual false eyelashes to her top lids, Vi suddenly appeared in the reflection behind her.

Angie, tweezers in hand, turned round to see her mum dragging across the kitchen to the other side of the Formica table with a cigarette dangling from her lips, her housecoat undone, revealing a sheer, black, baby-doll nightie and her hair scragged up in a nylon leopardskin scarf.

'Why haven't you gone to work?' she asked, dropping on to the chair facing Angie.

'Day off.' Angie returned to her lashes.

'Then why are you getting all done up?'

'Interview.'

'Liar.'

'No, I'm not.'

Vi reached across the table and pinched her daughter's cheek. 'Angie darling, give me some credit. You can't kid a kidder. You're just hopping off. Being a lazy mare.'

'Shame you don't get a job.'

'You nasty, ungrateful little madam.'

Angie tossed the tweezer aside and gave up. She would have to do. 'If you weren't so lazy, Mum, maybe you wouldn't be putting on so much weight.'

Violet ran her hands down over her hips. She wasn't putting on weight. Not at all. 'I can tell you've been talking to your bloody grandmother again. I'll have her one day. Poisoning my own daughter's mind against me. It's not right.'

'Nan never says a word against you. Never. Only ever asks how you are.'

Violet snorted scornfully.

'Anyway, what are you doing up so early?'

'I went to bed at bloody nine o'clock. Remember? Because I had nothing to do.'

'It's not my fault you can't entertain yourself for more than five minutes.'

'You are getting such a mouth on you, Angela.'

Angie gathered up her things and shoved them into her make-up bag. 'I'm just standing up for myself. And it's about time, I reckon.'

'It's about time you learned some manners.'

'I'll see you later.'

'Aren't you even going to make me a cuppa tea?'

'No, Mum. You can manage that yourself.'

Vi stayed at the kitchen table until Angie had left the house – there was always the hope that she might have given in and made her some. But she hadn't.

Defeated, Vi made herself a cup and stomped grumpily back up the stairs to her bedroom. She pulled back the curtains, flooding the room with bright July sunshine, and sat at her dressing-table.

She leaned on her elbows, propped her chin on her hands and examined the dark rings under her eyes and the ever-increasing number of grey hairs that were threatening to dull her once-glowing chestnut tint to a miserable, muddy brown.

What had happened to her? How had she got to be like this? Her, a bright, beautiful woman, who had had everybody in the palm of her hand, and now she couldn't even control her spiteful bloody scrap of a kid. It was all her mother's doing.

'Well,' she vowed to her reflection, 'if that little mare can change, then I certainly can. I can change anything I like. Be anyone I want to be. I'll bloody show her. I'll show bloody all of them.'

She stubbed out her cigarette in the slops in her saucer and stood up.

'First things first,' she announced brightly, and began to make the bed. Her interest, and efforts, soon waned and she merely threw the satin counterpane over the rumpled sheets.

She could finish that later. After she had been to the shops. She'd get in something for tea. Some ham. Then she'd get some chips later from the fish shop to go with it. That'd give her something to tell her precious grandmother.

Twenty-five minutes later, Violet was fit to face the world. Her hair was lacquered into place and her tired complexion had been brightened with make-up that she'd suddenly decided was looking just a little out of date

221

compared to what her daughter Angie was wearing. She would have a word with her about all the stuff she used; go out and get herself a few new bits maybe. It wouldn't do any harm to update her look a bit. Pep up her appeal.

But the first item on Violet's shopping list wasn't lipstick or mascara, it was cigarettes. She couldn't even begin to think, let alone make plans, without knowing she had at least a spare packet of twenty in hand.

Vi sauntered along the street towards the small, local parade of shops, knowing that her short, tightly belted, floral print dress showed off her wiggle, her curves and her legs to perfection. Her earlier lack of confidence had immediately been dispelled the moment she had stepped outside the house and Reg, the man across the street, who was polishing his beloved car – he was a shift worker at Ford's and was usually around during the day while his wife was at work in Peark's the grocers – gave her his customary long, low whistle of approval.

'Reg!' she had chided him. 'Good job your Betty's not around. She'd have your guts for garters.'

'It'd be worth it,' Reg had growled in reply, blowing her a kiss.

She had then rewarded him with a flirtatious glance over her shoulder, a cheeky wave, and a pouting reply of: 'Sauce pot.'

By the time she reached the shops, Vi was singing 'It's Not Unusual' happily to herself, and swinging her handbag in time to the beat. As always, she had a quick glance at the postcards in the tobacconist's window before she went inside. She had once, on a whim, bought a portable sewing-machine advertised there and, although she had never actually used it, it had been a real bargain and she didn't like the thought that she might miss another such opportunity.

Today, one card stood out.

'Smart lady assistant required. Afternoons only. Apply within.'

Vi had done little bits of part-time work before; she'd had to whenever there wasn't a bloke on the scene, and before Angie had got herself a job. And the idea of being a 'smart lady assistant' was quite appealing, especially to the new, dynamic Violet who was changing her life for the better. A job. That'd rub all their noses right in it.

'Twenty of my usual, please, Sam.' She sparkled brightly, turning on the charm for the balding man behind the counter. 'And, now what else was it? I know! How much are you paying the assistant?'

The man took down a packet of cigarettes from the shelf behind him, then leaned over the counter and looked at her legs. 'Three hours a day, at five bob an hour. Seeing as it's you, Vi.'

She slapped her hand on her chest, knowing that Sam's eyes would follow its every movement. 'Five bob? I'd need at least twice that to make it worth my while.'

'Don't suppose it does seem much compared to what she can earn laying on her back,' muttered a woman in a dull serge coat, who was picking bad-temperedly through the racks of greetings cards.

Vi spun round. 'What did you say?'

'Nothing.'

Vi snatched up the cigarettes. 'Never mind no jobs, Sam. If you go letting sour old bags like her in here, I might have to take my custom elsewhere. Put these on my bill.' With that she stuck her nose in the air and marched out of the shop.

Sam followed her on to the street. 'We could come to an arrangement.'

Vi stopped, plastered on a suitably friendly smile, turned and directed it straight at the hapless tobacconist. God, he looked exactly like a pudding with no currants. But he had a few bob.

'Sam,' she beamed. 'I'd love that.'

Sam puffed up like a turkey cock. 'Would you?'

'Not half.' She took a step closer and ran a finger up and down his chest. 'You know, Sam, I think I know your wife. Cissie, isn't it?' Vi didn't actually know her personally, but, like everyone else in the neighbourhood, she knew all about her. It was a good story. Cissie had married Sam years ago, when she'd been left a destitute young widow, and had taken him on as her husband not out of love but out of desperation. And now they owned a whole chain of shops all the way from the East End right out to Romford. What everyone else knew was that, despite the money they must have earned over the years, Cissie still made sure they both worked every hour God sent. Most people agreed it was because she couldn't stand the sight of the man and wanted him out of the way, and that she had only ever loved her first husband, who, those in the know reckoned, had turned out to be some sort of crook, something to do with the underworld.

'Runs one of your other shops, doesn't she?'

'That's right.' Sam took a step back. He looked far less pleased with himself. Where was all this leading? Was she trying to set him up or something?

Vi put her head on one side and looked up at Sam through her lashes. 'Shame she works all them hours. You must get ever so lonely.'

This was more like it. 'I do, Violet. Very lonely.'

'Well, Sam, perhaps I wouldn't exactly have to work for you. But be more like a sort of companion. Keep you company. You know. Stop you feeling lonely.'

Sam gulped. 'A companion?'

'Yeah. You'd like that, wouldn't you, Sam?'

Sam nodded.

'And a few quid would come in more than handy. And not having to worry about paying off my cigarette bill, that would be such a relief—' She leaned forward, shrugged her shoulders prettily and smiled excitedly. 'I'd be even better company than usual.'

Angie stared at the blanket-covered leather couch on which the doctor had just examined her. Even though she was now dressed and was shielded by the green cotton screen from his and David's gaze, her cheeks still burned red. She had never been touched or looked at so intimately before, even by a doctor, and now she was listening as the very same doctor – who had introduced himself, charmingly, as the director of the clinic – discussed her with David.

She could just picture them on the other side of the screen, sitting in the grand, wood-panelled consulting room, facing one another across the gleaming partner's desk, two successful, confident men. And they were talking about her, Angie Knight, as if she couldn't hear them.

'In normal circumstances, Mr Fuller, your niece would need to wait a full two weeks after beginning the first packet of pills.'

'Wait?'

'Before engaging in unprotected sexual acts, Mr Fuller. If she were taking them for contraceptive purposes, that is.'

'If,' she heard David reply.

'Quite. But as your niece is merely taking them to harmonize her, let us say, her particular ladies' problem, then that need not concern anyone.'

So that was it then. In two weeks' time she could engage in 'unprotected sexual acts'. It was all so, well, clinical. So unromantic. Part of her longed for the spontaneity of the bus shelter and a lemonade bottle full of vodka and orange, but David had explained how it was all for the best, that he really liked her a lot and that if she really liked him, if she trusted him, she would know he was only doing this to protect her. For her own good.

It was just all so new to her. Frightening.

But she was sure he was right.

'You've gone quiet, Angel.' David eased away from the traffic lights on the Commercial Road, knowing that the drivers of the cars he had so easily left behind were staring enviously after his big, shiny Jaguar. He liked that feeling. 'Bit rough with you, was he, that doctor? I know they can be.'

'No.' Angie felt the flush return to her cheeks as she pictured the doctor standing over her, while David sat just the other side of the screen, knowing what the other man was doing to her. He might have been a doctor, the director of the clinic, but he was still a man.

But it wasn't her experience on the blanket-covered couch that was upsetting her, that was all over with, thank goodness. As they gradually got closer to Poplar, all Angie could think about was the contrast between the elegant mansion block, where the clinic was sited, and the little terraces in Poplar that, despite their cramped rooms and outside lavs, meant so much to people like

Doris's friend Lily.

Angie could feel the tears. She turned towards the window and buried her face in her hands.

David pulled the car into the kerb outside the Star of the East, lit two cigarettes for them, then put an arm round Angie's shoulders. 'What's up, Angel?' He sounded concerned, and he was. This was the last thing he wanted, a bloody hysteric.

'My nan.' Angie puffed on the cigarette, then sniffed pitifully, as she scrabbled through her bag for her hankie.

'She ill or something?'

'No. It's her friend, Doris. And her friend, Lily—'

'Ssshhh. Now blow your nose and tell me all about it.' David didn't think he really needed all this, but at least she wasn't throwing one over seeing the quack. She'd have been right out the door if that had been the case.

Angie did as she was told, took a deep lungful of smoke and then spilled out all her worries. 'Someone my nan knows is getting thrown out of her house. It's been her home for years and she won't have anywhere to go. And Nan's worried she'll be next. Everyone's really scared, and I'm going round there now and I don't know how to help her. I can't stand her being so sad.'

David rubbed his hand over his chin, and sighed inwardly. Why couldn't he have found himself one of his usual hard-faced little whores, who didn't give a shit about anything other than what they could grab off him? Because he was bored with them, that's why.

'This friend, Angel.'

'It's Doris's friend. Lily Patterson.'

He took a moment to study the glowing tip of his cigarette. 'Do you know where she lives?' He sounded thoughtful, as if he were working something out.

'Burton Street. Poplar.' Angie was no longer crying; she was looking at him, a man, who – she didn't know why or how – would be able to help her. 'Only a little way from here.'

'I know it.' He turned on the engine and pulled away into the light afternoon traffic. 'Know it well, in fact.'

'Do you?'

'Very.' He paused briefly. 'Yeah, I, er, had an aunt who lived there. When I was a kid.'

Angie nibbled at her lip. Please be able to help. 'They're doing them up, you see, David,' she used his name, forgetting her usual shyness about doing so, 'but not so the people can stay in them. This bloke has bought the whole terrace, and he's splitting them up into flats. The rent's going to be so much money that Lily won't be able to afford to live there. It'll kill her if she has to move away, Nan said. She's got her life round there.'

David wound down his window and threw his barely smoked cigarette into the gutter. 'I'll see what I can do.'

'Would you?'

'Leave it to me.'

'But how?'

'Let me worry about that.'

'It wouldn't be too much trouble, would it?' Angie realized David had powerful friends, who could probably do all sorts of things to help people, but, as much as she wanted to help Lily, she didn't want to spoil things between her and David by making a nuisance of herself. She liked being Angel. It was the best thing that had ever happened to her.

'Because if it did . . .'

'I told you. Leave it to me.' He drew the car to a halt at what had become the usual place where he dropped her

228

off, chucked her under the chin, and reached across her to open the car door. 'Now, don't you worry. I'll see you soon. OK?'

Angie stopped, half in, half out of the car. Soon? 'When?'

'In a fortnight.'

She felt her lip begin to tremble, remembering what the doctor had said. 'Right. In a fortnight.'

David grinned. 'Only joking, Angel. See you at the weekend. There's a special party on.'

Angie felt her heart lighten. 'That'd be great.'

'And tell you what. Phone me at about half nine tonight. On the Greek Street number. And I'll let you know what I've been able to do for your nan's friend.'

'It's weird, Bob, how long this Mikey and Sonia business has been going on.' Maureen draped the shirt she had just finished ironing over the clothes horse that stood in front of the coal-effect electric fire and took the next one from the pile in the plastic basket by her feet.

Bobby swallowed down the last of the bacon sandwich that Maureen had rustled up for him when he had turned up between jobs for a quick bite to eat – Maureen didn't approve of him eating greasy café food, not if she could help it – and took a gulp of tea. 'I reckon Dave's going to out her soon, you know, Maur. Just like he done all the others.'

'Yeah, but he never married any of the others, did he? And everyone knows he picked her out because she went with this new businessman image he's gone mad on.'

The contempt in Maureen's voice was echoed in Bobby's thoughts, but his monotone never changed, although, for him, he was being astonishingly indiscreet.

'Well, you should have heard the phone call he made this morning. Honest, Maur, he put the right shi . . . put the right fear of beejesus up Mikey.'

Maureen concentrated on pressing the creases from the shirt collar. 'It's got to end in tears.'

'You're right, babe. As usual.' Bobby rubbed his hands over his big, shiny bald head, then got up and stood behind her. He put his arms round her waist and kissed her tenderly on the neck. 'Thank gawd we're normal, eh?'

'Thank gawd.'

'Here, and you'll never guess this one. Some old girl he heard about in one of the terraces he's just bought up. In Poplar. He told the boys this afternoon that they ain't to upset her or nothing. He said she's got to be allowed to stay there. Just as she is. Well, for three months. But it's still three whole months' rent you're talking about.'

Maureen put down her iron and turned round to face her husband. 'But I thought the idea was to drive everyone out of them places. To put the frighteners on 'em.'

'So did I. But like I say, babe, don't ask me what goes on, I'm just a normal bloke.'

Tilly Murray was going like the clappers at the oven with a Brillo pad and a good shake of Vim, while Jackie sat at the kitchen table watching her listlessly.

'No phone calls for me today, Mum?'

'No, love. Not today.' Tilly stood back and stared at the gas rings through half-closed eyes, daring one more spot of dirt to show itself. 'Were you expecting any?'

'Not really.' Jackie had, in fact, been expecting, well, hoping, that Angie might be in touch, that she had been bursting to tell Jackie where she had been and what she was up to. It didn't seem right travelling to and from work without her again. And it didn't seem right not seeing her.

Jackie was beginning to feel as she knew Angie had once done: that everyone else was out enjoying themselves, while she was sitting at home by herself. Jackie could still see all her old mates, of course, the ones she used to go out with before Angie became 'Angel' or whatever it was she said that bloke called her, but it wasn't the same any more. Nothing was. Not now she knew that Angie was going to places that she, Jackie, had never even dreamed of going to. It was as if the shine had been rubbed off everything.

Jackie sighed, wondering if she would ever have a boyfriend who would take her to a restaurant.

Tilly, satisfied with her triumph over the mucky cooker, put her cleaning materials away under the sink and put the kettle on. She knew how to cheer up her daughter: a nice milky coffee and a slice of cake.

'Apart from popping in last night to 'phone her nan, we've not seen much of Angie lately.' Tilly spoke cautiously, not wanting to put her foot in it. 'She courting, is she, love?'

Jackie slumped forward over the table, resting her head on her folded arms. 'Don't really know.'

'She'll be going out with you on Saturday, won't she? For your birthday.'

'Doubt if she'll remember.'

'Course she will.' Tilly took down the cake tin from the shelf over the table and inspected the contents with a frown. She'd have to do some baking tomorrow. 'She wouldn't forget an important day like that.'

Jackie felt so choked she could have cried. Everything

was changing and she didn't like it. 'I think she might, Mum.'

'Never mind, love. You've got that nice Marilyn to go out with. You'll have to bring her home for tea one night. You know I like to meet your friends.'

At half past nine that same evening, Angie was standing in the telephone box near Becontree tube station. She hadn't needed to explain to her mum where she was going, as Vi had already gone out. She had gone with Sam to an Italian restaurant in the Leytonstone High Road, to discuss what he had called her 'terms and conditions of employment', and what Vi simply thought of as 'a fair rate of pay for services rendered'. Although neither of them had any illusions about what they were really discussing, and, as they sat at the corner table, tucking into Veal Milanese, rosemary potatoes and a second bottle of Mateus Rosé, they were soon talking openly about the most convenient times and places for them both, and just how much Vi needed to get by these days, what with everything being so expensive.

Angie, on the other hand, was far more circumspect, and about a conversation she wasn't even having yet.

While she had only had a glimpse of it, Angie realized that David was from a very different world from hers, and that she didn't really know what sort of a person he actually was. And she wasn't entirely sure she would like everything she discovered when, or if, she did know.

In simple terms, Angie was scared.

Things were all moving so fast: Angela Knight, an ordinary little seventeen-year-old girl from Dagenham, had transformed herself into a dolly bird; had gone on the

Pill; had told all sorts of lies; was thinking about throwing in a perfectly good job that she would have killed for just a few months ago; and was seeing a man who was years older than she was – a man who had the power to fix things.

But, although it was a truly worrying idea that he might have such power, and that she was rapidly getting out of her depth, it also meant that he might be able to do something for her nan . . .

Angie picked up the receiver with one hand and crossed the fingers on her other, as though she were a ten-year-old making a wish that she might be picked to play in a game of Bulldog. She dialled the number quickly, before she lost her nerve.

'Yeah'llo.' It was him.

'It's me, Angel.'

'Hello, sweetheart. Glad you called. Good news. The old girl in Burton Street's all sorted.'

'You mean she can stay?'

'Sure. Now about Saturday.'

Angie was so flustered – could it really have been solved as easily as that? – she could hardly gather her thoughts. 'Saturday. Errr. Right.'

'Problem?'

'No.'

'Not got something better to do than go to a party with me, have you?' David sounded amused by the idea.

'No. Nothing better. Of course not. Saturday's fine.' As she caught a glimpse of her reflection in the mirror above the coin box, it suddenly occurred to her. *Saturday.* It had been in the back of her mind for days. Jackie's birthday. But it couldn't be helped. 'I'm really looking forward to it. What time?'

'Earlyish. Around seven. But I'll be over your way about five, so I'll come round yours and pick you up.'

'Right.' How was she going to explain to him that he couldn't come to her house, because she didn't live where she'd said she did? Because she'd lied to him. 'David. I've just remembered.'

'Yeah?' He sounded preoccupied. Angie could hear someone talking to him in the background.

'I'll be out all day.'

That got his attention. David laughed. 'Here. Not trying to elbow me, are you, Angel?'

'No. Honestly. It's my friend. Marilyn. I promised to see her. I can come and meet you. If that's OK.'

'Fine. Chelsea'll do.'

'Right. What shall I wear?'

'Anything would look good on you, Angel. Phone me Friday and I'll tell you where I'll see you.'

With that, David put down the phone. He smiled to himself. It was nice, keeping her happy. Made her grateful. And it was no skin off his nose, leaving some old girl in her house for an extra few weeks before he outed her. Plus he needed to grease a few more palms, so the work wouldn't be starting for a month or so, anyway. And he'd probably be bored with the kid by then.

Immediately dismissing Angie from his thoughts, David picked up a plastic bag full of white powder that the man who had come in the office while he was talking on the phone had put down on the desk in front of him.

'Right,' David said, 'let's discuss price and quality.'

Chapter 11

It was seven o'clock on Saturday night, and when David drove up to collect her, Angie had been standing on the corner of Tite Street in Chelsea since five to six. She had been too nervous about being late to let a little thing like an hour-long wait bother her.

She smiled hesitantly as he leaned across from the driver's seat and opened the passenger door.

'You look terrific, Angel,' he said, appraising her slowly, taking in every part of her. 'Pretty as a picture. But sophisticated with it.'

And possibly young enough to get me sent to jail, if that quack at the clinic was even close about your age.

Angie's smile broadened. She'd been right: the simple, black chiffon minidress, with its doll-like elasticated bodice, had been exactly the right choice. She'd felt rotten at first, asking Jackie to help her decide what to wear, especially as it was her birthday, and all she was doing for her Saturday night was going to the Lotus, a fading dance hall over the shops in Forest Gate, hoping to be sized up by the local yobs. But it wasn't all bad. When Angie had given her her present – a tiny pink handbag, covered in shilling-sized sequins – and explained she was going to a party in Chelsea, Jackie had become almost as excited as Angie. That really was Swinging London. No more messing about like a kid. Angie was part of the real thing.

'Whose flat is it?' Angie took David's hand as he helped her from the car.

'Mine.'

'But don't you live in that place in Mayfair?'

'I've got a few places.' He said it simply, not bragging, just fact.

The old girl in Burton Street can stay. I've got a few places. This was all getting a bit overwhelming. 'Is it going to be a big party?'

'Not really. About fifty, sixty people. Few more maybe.'

Angie hoped David didn't notice her gulp back her fear.

Once they had entered the flat, Angie was placed in the care of a bulky, shaven-headed man called Bobby, with a glass of champagne and a smiling 'Won't be a minute' from David. But she didn't mind. As she watched him working his way round the room, greeting his diverse collection of guests, she felt relieved that she didn't have to accompany him. But, unused to events anything like as smart as what she was witnessing, Angie found herself nervously compelled to make conversation.

'What's going on at the table over there?' She had been introduced to Bobby by name, but couldn't bring herself to use it. Using such familiarity with a man of his age would have felt impudent.

Bobby ran his finger round his thick, bull neck, loosening his collar. This was all he needed, a bird bloody chatting to him. 'Scalectrix.'

'What? The kids' game?'

'Mmmm . . . Scalectrix . . .' he began again.

As if on cue, David appeared at their side, flashing another of his smiles and saving them both.

'With a bit of a difference, eh, Bob?'

Bobby nodded. Thank gawd for that.

'Fancy a go, Angel?'

Angie smiled back at him, still apprehensive about all the people, yet captivated to be back in his orbit, the orbit of the most handsome man in the room, the Michael Caine lookalike, who seemed almost telepathic in understanding her fears, and who knew how to sort everything out.

'Yes, please.'

She took David's offered hand and walked off with him as if Bobby no longer existed. Even with her lack of experience in such matters, Angie had grasped the pecking order in the room, having placed David very near the top and Bobby a very long way below him. And that, as host of the evening, David was important, but maybe not as important as several of his slightly older, male guests – if his attitude to them was anything to go by.

As David led her to the whooping, laughing, crowd huddled round the table, anyone who looked over their shoulder to see who was trying to squeeze to a place at the front of the action automatically made room for him.

And Angie.

With their position secured, Angie, finally, could see what was going on, and it wasn't like any Scalectrix game she had ever seen.

At one end of the table stood a beautiful blonde woman, who, Angie guessed, was around her mother's age. She was wearing an elegant, black velvet cocktail dress and was taking bets, very professionally, from the men and their young female companions; big bets, that were being placed on which of the two little cars would cross the line first. But, instead of the toys being steered by eager ten-year-olds – like Jackie's spoiled, squabbling cousins had done last Christmas on the Murrays' front-room floor – these ones were being operated by two girls, who were equally as beautiful as the croupier but who were a good fifteen years younger, much closer to her own age, in fact.

Even more incongruously, they were wearing PVC Artful Dodger-style caps and minute PVC bikinis, all colour co-ordinated to match the cars they were operating, and, tucked inside their skimpy bras and pants were fans of bank notes.

'Tips from grateful punters,' explained David, as a puce-faced man slapped his victorious driver hard on the backside before rewarding her with a couple of notes stuffed firmly down her heaving cleavage. 'How about you having a go at driving?'

Angie looked horrified.

'Don't worry, Angel, you haven't got to strip off. They only have to, because they're . . .' He thought for a moment then laughed. 'The pros.'

'I'd rather watch.'

'Fine.' He took some money from his inside pocket and handed it to her. 'Here. Bring me luck. What colour do you fancy?'

'I think I'll try the red car this time.' Angie, excited by her beginner's luck, handed over five pounds to the blonde woman at the end of the table.

'I'll have a pony on that as well, darling,' said a short, squat man standing by Angie's side. 'Your little lady's got luck on her side tonight, Dave.'

'Course she has,' he grinned. 'She's with me. She's—' Suddenly distracted, David's expression hardened, then, having scanned the crowd, he began to ease away from

238

the table. 'You all right here a minute, Angel? I won't be long.'

'Yeah. I'm fine.' Angie, absorbed in the fate of her five pounds, was happy to keep watching the little cars whizzing round.

He made his way, with copious nods and smiles for his guests, over to Bobby, who was standing in the corner, with his hands clasped in front of him, apparently silently observing the goings-on in the room. Only David had noticed him signalling to him.

'What is it, Bob?'

Bobby stretched his lips wide over his strong, even teeth. How best to put it? 'It's Marshall, Dave. He was keen to get off. Wanted one of his, you know, special treats. Terry took him to get fixed up.'

'Where to? One of the flats?'

'No. Said he fancied going over to the Missy Me.' Bobby stared down at his highly polished shoes. 'You know how he likes being seen.'

'Shit, Bob. He was pissed as a pudden when he got here. Never mind all the gear he's taken since.'

Bobby looked sheepish. 'He was mouthing off a bit.'

David ran his fingers wearily through his hair. 'Tell me.'

'About being untouchable. About how rich he's gonna be when he retires. And something about how he's gonna be the first copper ever to need a Swiss bank account.'

'Bloody hell, Bob. Let's hope Terry keeps him a bit quieter in the Missy Me.'

'Shall I go after them? Make sure?'

'Yeah, maybe you should. That club's got itself a name already. Gawd alone knows who might be in there. How long they been gone?'

'About half an hour.'

'Fucking hell, Bob!'

'I tried to tell you. But you were busy.'

'Just get moving.'

'That damned train. Now we're going to be late for supper.' Jill Walker checked her watch. 'Daddy hates being kept waiting. And I know Mummy will have made something special.'

'Will we be sharing a room?' Martin was speaking to Jill, but he had his head ducked down so that he could get a full view of the big Georgian house as the taxi made its way along the tree-lined gravel drive.

Jill caught the taxi driver's eye in the rear-view mirror and giggled girlishly; it was a small village and she had known the man all her life, and she knew what a gossip he was. 'You are funny, Martin. Always joking.' Jill pecked Martin on the cheek and said softly into his ear, 'You'll just have to creep along the corridor when everyone's asleep.'

Martin smiled with his lips pressed close together. He was as nervous as a kitten, as nervous as he had been on the first day at university. No, far more nervous than that. At least when he had started his course, he'd known there would be a few students he could relate to, students who, like him, had gone to their local grammar. Coming here, to Sussex, to spend the weekend with Jill's family, Martin knew he would be out of place, no matter how Jill tried to persuade him otherwise. But he had still agreed to come. Jill was the best thing that had ever happened to him – it was miraculous, she was actually as keen on having sex as he was – so if spending a few nights with her family was the cost of keeping her happy, then Martin thought it a small price to pay. That's what he was telling himself, anyway. Actually he would have been happier, and more at ease, standing naked on the college steps, balancing his text books on his head.

As the taxi scrunched to a halt by a sweep of stone steps leading up to a blood-red front door, Jill squeezed Martin's hand excitedly. 'You'll love Mummy and Daddy,' she said, 'and I know they're going to adore you.'

Missing the straight-through train from Victoria certainly had made Martin and Jill late, and Mr Walker, Jill's father, was annoyed. He simply could not understand why Martin hadn't planned better, why he had not insisted on them catching the earlier train and why he hadn't consulted the timetables more closely. Jill seemed exempt from any criticism, and Martin was beginning to wish that instead of coming down to Sussex, he had come down with some horrible, possibly fatal, disease, which would at least have prevented him from travelling.

But eventually Mrs Walker came to the rescue, first showing Martin to his room – the most distant from Jill's own, he noticed – and then smoothing everything over with kind words, excellent food and a steady supply of wine.

'A little more duck, Martin?'

'Thanks, Mrs Walker, I'd love some.' Well-apprenticed in praising mothers and the food they produced, Martin had earlier said yes to a second helping of the rich, coarse pâté with which they had started the meal, and was now on to his third helping of duck. His experience of home-cooking might have been rather more prosaic than the dishes Jill's mother was serving up, and the kitchen

241

table in Becontree might have been about a tenth the size of the dining-table in Twycehurst, but the effects of an appreciative eater were just the same on the cook.

Jill smiled happily as her mother topped up Martin's plate. 'Mum's a great cook, isn't she?'

'Terrific,' said Martin. 'I love this sauce.'

'What? That? It's nothing.' Mrs Walker brushed away the compliments, but she was glowing with pleasure. 'Just a few cherries, that's all.' She held up her glass to her husband. 'Darling, how about some more wine? That one looks almost empty.'

Mr Walker grumped a grudging reply, but, Martin noticed, he seemed quick enough to go to fetch another bottle.

'We're so pleased you could come, Martin.' Mrs Walker looked on admiringly as Martin worked his way through his duck. 'And it's such a pleasure to cook for someone who enjoys his food. Jill has always had the appetite of a bird, and Mr Walker doesn't seem to notice what he's eating.'

'More interested in the wine, eh, Mummy?'

Jill's mother shot her a warning look. 'You'll be giving Martin the wrong impression, dear.'

Martin carried on eating as though he hadn't heard the slightly pointed exchange.

'I hope you've brought something pretty to wear, Jill. We're having people over tomorrow.'

'Oh? Who's coming?'

'Everyone. You know the village. They're all desperate to hear your news from London. And to meet Martin, of course. It'll be such fun.' She looked up as her husband came back into the dining-room. 'You'll have to keep an eye on him, Jill. Having a handsome young man

242

like Martin around will turn a few Twycehurst heads.'

Jill giggled.

Mr Walker hurrumphed.

And Martin swallowed what was left in his glass of the wine that tasted to his unaccustomed palate as if it was just this side of paint stripper.

Everyone. Everyone from the village wanted to meet him. Martin felt his appetite shrivel like a plucked cherry left out in the summer sun.

'Sorry I was so long, Angel. Bit of business to sort out.'

'Can I ask you something?'

'Sure.'

'Those girls.' Angie, who had drifted away from the table when the short, squat man who had placed twenty-five pounds on her choice of car had become a little too familiar, was standing where she had earlier been parked with Bobby.

'What?' David pointed with his whisky glass at one of the smart but scantily dressed young women who were circulating with trays laden with drinks and little silver bowls. 'The hostesses?'

Angie nodded. 'The stuff in those bowls. Is it . . .' She tried to come up with a word that wouldn't offend David, and that wouldn't make her look like an inexperienced kid. 'Pep pills?'

'Some of it.' He stopped a passing hostess and took a glass of champagne from her tray and gave it to Angie along with a lighted cigarette. 'They give my guests whatever they fancy. Some go for speed. Others like a bit of pot. Amyl nitrate. One or two are going for acid. Me, I stick to a good malt, or a drop of fizz.'

'How can you be so . . . easy-going about it?' Angie

243

was whispering, glancing nervously about her for eavesdroppers. 'What if the police found out? You could go to prison.'

David smiled to himself at the thought of the amount, and variety, of gear that Chief Inspector Gerald Marshall had just consumed. 'The police wouldn't bother us, Angel. Private party, see. And they're only having a laugh.'

'But—'

'Look, the difference between the Purple Hearts and the Black Bombers on the streets and what's going on here is that these are all adults. They all know what they're doing. Relaxing after a hard week at work. That's all. No different from you enjoying that glass of bubbly and your cigarette.'

Angie sipped automatically at her drink. David was so calm about it all. So persuasive. She looked around the room, listening to the buzz of conversation and the occasional eruptions of pleased laughter. It all looked so beautiful. Like a film set. The clothes, the jewellery, the people. She thought about the girls with their bikinis stuffed full of cash. More money than she earned in a month sitting behind a boring desk.

It was a different world from the one she knew. Maybe the rules were different for people like these.

'How about giving the cars another go? Or roulette? I've got a table set up in the other room.'

Glad of the distraction from her thoughts, Angie was about to say she'd like to try roulette, if that was OK with him, when Bobby appeared.

'Sorry to bother you again, Dave.'

David looked displeased. 'I thought you were going over the Missy Me.'

'I got held up. By a phone call.' Bobby leaned close to

David and said quietly into his ear. 'It was Terry. Something needs sorting out.'

'Give Angel some money and take her through to the roulette, then see me in the back bedroom.'

When Bobby came into the room, David's muscular frame was perched on a delicate pink-and-gold brocade bedroom chair; he was puffing angrily on a panatella, his broad legs splayed wide. Had anyone not known David Fuller's reputation, they might have been inclined to have laughed.

'That Terry needs a fucking good hiding. He knew he had to keep an eye on Marshall.'

Bobby agreed, but said nothing.

'How bad is it?'

'It was a set-up, Dave. The papers were there.'

He threw up his hands. 'Well, that's it. I can't do anything for him now. I don't think even Burman could get the silly bastard out of this one.' David stubbed out his cigar in a porcelain dish on the dressing-table, stood up and adjusted his tie in the mirror. He closed his eyes and shook his head in wonder. 'Fucking stupid idiot. Still, can't be helped. Might as well get back to the party, eh, Bob?'

It was the early hours of Sunday morning and Detective Constable Jameson was sitting in the canteen, working his way methodically through Saturday's *Guardian* crossword, while he ate the cheese-and-salad sandwich he had eventually persuaded the woman behind the counter to make for him. He was drinking tea from his flask, having given up on the foul, dark brown brew that the rest of the station seemed immune to.

As usual he was alone, but a table close to him was occupied by two female constables. Jameson closed his ears to their inane chatter, not wishing to know about their sex lives and the various preferences of their boyfriends, but suddenly his attention was grabbed.

'At least he doesn't get up to tricks like the Old Man,' said the red-haired one.

'What tricks?'

'You haven't heard?' She grinned knowingly.

'Sandie . . .'

Sandie leaned forward for the sake of privacy, but she still spoke loudly enough for Jameson to catch her every word. 'Know that new club over in King's Cross? The Missy Me.'

'Can't say I do. Gambling, is it?'

'No. It's for people who like to take their pleasures rather seriously. The type who enjoy a bit of S and M, but with an audience thrown in for an extra thrill. The right hardcore, really extreme lot, I'm talking about.'

'Are you saying the Old Man . . .'

Sandie leaned back, folded her arms across her chest and opened her eyes wide. 'Yep. He got caught in there last night.' She could barely keep a straight face. '*Sadomasochistic practices*, according to Barbara down on the desk.'

'No . . .'

'That's right. All dressed up in this rubber women's corset thing and stockings. With long, pink rubber gloves.' Now she was sniggering helplessly. 'Doing horrible things with surgical appliances. The whole three-ring circus. With a few extra trick ponies thrown in for good measure.'

'Never!'

'I'm telling you. He's finished.' Tears of laughter were pouring down her cheeks. 'The papers're only going to be able to show them photographs from the waist up.'

She handed Sandie a glass of water. 'Is this kosher?'

Sandie sipped the water, wiped her eyes with the back of her hand, and did her best to control herself. 'Wait till you see the papers in the morning. It was the *Clarion* that set him up. It's going to make the front page. And', the sniggers exploded again, 'you know how quiet Monday is for news.'

Jameson calmly folded his newspaper, wiped out his cup with a paper napkin and screwed it back on his flask. He stood up and tidied his empty plate on to a plastic tray, which he returned to the counter, then walked out of the canteen towards the car park.

When he reached his Morris Minor, Jameson slapped the bonnet hard with the flat of his hand.

DCI Marshall was finished. Well and truly finished.

He unlocked the car and got in. 'Right, Fuller,' he said in a low, steady voice. 'Your protection's gone. I'm ready for you now.'

Jameson hummed tunelessly to himself as he drove towards Greek Street. With a bit of luck, Fuller and his cronies would still be there, going over the day's business, and, with a bit of patience, Jameson would get a glimpse of them when they left, and would see if they looked worried.

But, much as he would have enjoyed such a sight, Jameson doubted if they would look even slightly concerned.

Those men had a mentality, lived a life, that thrived on risk and notoriety as much as it did on financial gain; you only had to see them swanking about to know that. It

247

drove Jameson mad, how so many ordinary, supposedly decent, men and women had such an appetite for reading all about the villains' so-called glamorous lives, with their night-clubs, their tarts and their showbiz friends.

The public encouraged it. Encouraged it, that was, until they were touched by it. Until it was their kid found out of his head on acid, or caught selling it on to even younger kids to finance their kicks. Then they weren't so impressed by the likes of David Fuller.

Jameson was going to have him. Show him that his glamorous life also had its costs, and that being banged up in the Scrubs wasn't glamorous at all.

'I didn't know whether to expect you or not this morning, Ange.' Jackie closed the street door behind her. 'You've not exactly been a regular at work lately, have you?'

'Don't start, Jack.'

Jackie managed to keep quiet until they had almost reached the station, then it all just spilled over. 'Martin's been away for the whole weekend. At his girlfriend's. He phoned late last night to say he was going straight in to college today, and wouldn't be home till tonight. Big posh house in the country, they live in. He says her family are loaded. Her dad drinks too much, her mum seems lonely and he wouldn't live in the country if you paid him.' She glanced sideways at Angie, then added, 'I think he's sleeping with her.'

'What?' Angie sounded preoccupied, as if she hadn't been listening.

'Martin. Sleeping with Jill. His girlfriend.'

'Why shouldn't he?'

'Angie!'

'Well, don't be so square.'

'Pardon me for breathing.' Jackie linked her arm roughly through Angie's, punishment for not being interested. Or pretending not to be interested. 'Mum would kill him if he got her pregnant.'

'Jackie, I couldn't care less about your brother's sex life. Can we talk about something else? Please?'

'You've changed.'

'What, because I've got a boyfriend?'

'Boyfriend.' Jackie snorted. 'Angie, he is a man. Not a boy. A much older man. And I think you should be careful.'

'Not jealous, are you?'

'All right. If you must know, I am.'

Angie looked at her. 'Are you?'

'Course I am. You go off to some party in bloody Chelsea with a bloke in a Jag, and I wind up in a dance hall over the shops in Forest Gate with a gang of girls from school. And it was my birthday.'

'Sorry, Jack. Did you have a good time?'

Jackie smiled. 'Yeah. I did actually.'

'Did you?'

'I met someone.'

'Yeah?'

'Andrew. Really nice. Works in the City. And he's nearly as mod as Martin.'

Angie narrowed her eyes.

'All right, I won't mention him again.'

They pushed their way through the crowd down the station steps.

'Know what would be nice, Ange? If we could go on a double date some time.'

'I don't think so, do you, Jack? David's not exactly the sort to go dancing at the Lotus.'

249

'Pardon me for breathing. But I didn't mean with David, I meant with one of Andrew's friends.'

'Don't be silly, Jack.'

'Too good for going out with the likes of me now, are you?'

'No. You know I don't mean that. I just like the life David's shown me. The places he takes me.'

Jackie had it on the tip of her tongue to say – you mean, the things David gets for me, and that Angie was sounding a bit too much like her mum – but she didn't want to cause a row.

Angie stepped back from the edge of the platform as the train came into sight. 'By the way, Jack, I've decided I'm giving up my job.'

It was almost lunchtime, and Vi was walking back from Sam's shop, where she had been 'helping' him in the stock-room. She was reading the headlines of the *Daily Clarion*, laughing out loud.

'Morning.' It was Tilly Murray coming towards her. She addressed her neighbour through pursed lips. 'Something's tickling your funny bone, Violet.'

Vi held out the paper. 'It's this dirty old sod,' she said, pointing to the front page that was almost entirely taken up with a flash photograph of a startled-looking Detective Chief Inspector Gerald Marshall. 'Strange what gets some fellers going.'

Tilly tutted and adjusted her headscarf. 'Disgusting. Ought not be allowed.'

Vi smiled craftily. Baiting her saintly neighbour was one of her little pleasures. 'Don't you and your Stan ever fancy something a little bit . . . you know, kinky, to put the lead in that old pencil of his?'

Tilly's face went an unflattering, pale mauve. 'Jackie tells me you're seeing that Nick again.'

Vi folded the paper and tucked it into her gondola-shaped straw basket. 'I'm flattered you've been discussing my private life, Tilly. Delighted, in fact. And, as you're so interested, you might as well know the real story. I've not seen Nick for a while. He's been busy.' The part of the truth she didn't mention was that she'd left Nick high and dry, just as she had so many times before, to chase what she saw as a temporarily better prospect. Sam. He might have been even less physically attractive than Nick – he had the looks of a spanked arse and the manners of a monkey – but he had a chain of shops and he worked a lot, giving her the chance to indulge herself with the very handsome, if far less dependable prospect, Craig.

Craig was Vi's latest passion: slightly younger, better-looking by miles than Nick, Scottish, and more than a touch unreliable. He wasn't entirely new on the scene – she had first met him about a year ago – but he was always being called away, always having to go back north of the border. It had annoyed Vi then, not because he was married – she couldn't care less about that – but because at the time he had been the only one on the firm and she hadn't liked not having a back-up. But now it suited her perfectly. When Craig wasn't around, it gave her a bit of time to spoil Sam, to keep him sweet, to 'help him out' in the stock-room, and to enjoy first-rate dinners and some lovely little presents, all at pudding-faced Sam's expense.

The arrangement was all rather neat; it would be neater still if she could guarantee the times that Angie would be out of the house everyday. She didn't know what had got

251

into the girl. When she wanted her at home to help, she was out, and now, when she wanted her to piss off to work or somewhere, she was always under her feet. It didn't actually bother Vi, Angie being there, it was that she was looking so . . . well . . . sodding good. Too good. It was bloody infuriating.

Tilly folded her arms. 'Must be lonely on your own.'

Vi raised a heavily pencilled eyebrow. 'Who said I was on my own?'

Tilly's lips became even thinner. 'My Martin's courting. Lovely girl. Comes from a really good family. Rich and all.'

'That's nice.' The boredom in Vi's voice was as apparent as the look of tedium on her face.

'And I reckon your Angie's seeing someone as well.'

'News to me.'

Before she could stop herself, Tilly snapped, 'Don't you care about that girl, Violet?'

Vi took her cigarettes out of her trenchcoat pocket and took her time lighting one. 'Not as much as you do, obviously.' She smiled nastily. 'Better get on, Tilly, some of us can't spend all day gossiping. Things to do. People to see.' She inhaled deeply and blew the smoke out slowly. 'Ta ta for now.'

With that, she tightened the belt of her mac, slung her basket further up her arm and wiggled off on her high heels.

Chapter 12

It was almost a fortnight since Tilly had had the exchange with Violet about Angie and now, a chance meeting with Pauline Thompson – the biggest gossip on the whole estate – had only served to confirm Tilly's worst fears about the girl's welfare.

'Stan,' she gasped, standing over her husband as he sat in his armchair in the front room, puffing on his pipe and reading the *Daily Mirror*, digesting the enormous bacon-and-onion suet roll he had had for his tea. 'You'll never guess what Pauline Thompson just told me.'

Stan Murray didn't respond. It was Friday night, he'd had a long, hard week at work, and listening to some old nonsense passed on to his wife by Pauline Thompson, who could talk a glass eye to sleep, wasn't very high on his list of priorities. So he just cocked a deaf one, and let her carry on.

'Stan. Are you listening to me?'

'Yes, dear.'

'I was outside sweeping the front path – you wouldn't believe the rubbish that gets blown under that gate from the street of an evening. But I know who the kids are, the ones who drop all them sweet wrappers. They're out there, hanging around by the lamppost. I've a good mind to go and see their mothers.'

Stan, more interested in an article on the evil threat of drug-pushers moving in on the housing estates than in the provenance of discarded Jamboree Bags, kept on reading. But, knowing his wife's persistence when it came to putting the world to rights, he kept up the pretence of having a conversation with her.

'Really?' he offered non-committally.

'Anyway, according to Pauline Thompson, Violet Knight is having *an affair*.' As she said the last two words, she banged her broom down twice for added drama. 'Affair' wasn't part of Tilly's usual vocabulary and her using such a word, along with the broom banging, had the effect of getting Stan's full attention.

He let the paper drop to his lap and took the pipe from his mouth. 'An affair, Tilly? Are you sure?'

'Positive. And with Sam Clarke, if you don't mind. Whatever would that poor wife of his have to say if she found out? There's her working all hours and there's that hussy, Violet Knight, flashing around the presents he's buying her and bragging about all the fancy places they go to. No better than a Cable Street trollop, if you want my opinion. No wonder her Angie's running loose. Our Jackie said she's never in of a night. Never. And you won't believe this, she's handed in her notice. And her with that good job and all. A disgrace. That's what it is.'

The conversation, or rather his wife's monologue, had lost its sparkle for Stan. Affairs were one thing, any man would be interested in the idea of Violet Knight . . . well, of Violet Knight, full stop. She was a fine-looking woman. But what some kid was getting up to at work? Stan could easily get by without knowing the details of that, thank you very much.

'You know, Stan, I feel like going up to Poplar and having a word with Sarah Pearson. That girl's nan would be shocked if she knew what was going on.'

Stan picked up his paper and began searching for his place in the article.

'Don't get involved, Tilly,' he said, knocking out his pipe in the ashtray. 'It's none of your business.'

'But poor little Angie. She's like one of our own.'

'You're too good, love,' Stan said, closing his part in the proceedings. Then added ambiguously, 'That's your trouble.'

At the other end of the terrace, there was rather more than a bit of sweeping, gossiping and reading going on. Angie was watching television in the front room, singing along with the Byrds' 'Mr Tambourine Man'; Vi was in the kitchen, fresh from the bath, with just a towel wrapped round her, checking her hair in the small mirror over the sink and looking forward to a Friday night on the town; and Craig was standing behind her, running his hands up and down her hips.

'Don't jog me, Craig,' Vi said, batting at him playfully, 'or I'll never get these flick-ups right.'

'Don't bother with your hair, Vi,' he murmured in his soft, Scottish drawl, nuzzling into her damp neck, and breathing in the scent of talc and hair lacquer. 'We don't have to go out.'

'Oh yes we do.' Vi twisted round in his arm and pecked him on the lips. 'I want a very large gin and tonic, followed by a slap-up meal and a bottle of wine. Then we'll come back here and I'll show you how grateful I am for such a smashing night out.'

Resigned to paying for his pleasures, Craig slumped down on to the kitchen chair. 'You win. As usual.'

Vi used one hand to trace his lovely, sculpted mouth and the other to tuck in her towel more securely. 'Of course I win. Now I'll just go up and get dressed. I'll be five minutes.'

Craig looked sceptical.

'OK, ten. Fifteen at the most.'

Craig rolled his eyes and slapped her on the backside. 'I know you, Vi. I'll see you in about half an hour. When you've tried on every frock in your wardrobe.'

As she ran giggling up the stairs, Vi called out to Angie, 'Make some coffee, Angie. The kettle's almost boiled.'

Rather than going through the rigmarole of having yet another row – her not going in to work every day was becoming almost an obsession with her mum – Angie did as she was told.

Still singing at the top of her voice, Angie stopped dead in the kitchen doorway. 'Oh, you're here.' She gave Craig nothing more than a passing glance as she went over to the cooker where the kettle was whistling loudly. She turned off the gas and took a moment to compose herself. She couldn't stand the cocky so-and-so. He was so full of himself. And the way her mum swooned over his every word. It turned Angie's stomach. Why she was going out with him again was beyond Angie.

No it wasn't.

He was good-looking, at least five years younger than her mum, and he earned good money. What more could she want?

Angie gritted her teeth. He was acting just like he used to: as if he owned the place – feet stretched out under the table, flicking through her mum's copy of *Weekend* and waiting for her to make him coffee.

And she was sure he was ogling her. Even with her back to him. It made her flesh creep.

Angie was right, he was.

Craig hadn't seen Vi's daughter for months, and he

was, to say the least, very pleasantly surprised. She looked sensational. He tossed the magazine on to the kitchen table and looked her slowly up and down.

'Very tasty, darling. Very tasty indeed. I have to say, it is a very striking improvement. Been to the beauty parlour, have you?'

When she ignored him, he tried another tack. 'Smoke?'

Angie would have loved to have said yes to a cigarette, she was gasping for one, but she wouldn't dare risk smoking in front of her mum, it would just give her another excuse to have a go at her. 'No. I don't.'

She bit on her lip and spooned Nescafé, crossly, into two mugs, one for her mum and, grudgingly, one for him. 'I can't remember, do you take sugar?'

Craig stood up and moved so close to her, she could feel his breath on the back of her hair.

'No. No sugar. But I like my girls sweet, Angie. Just like you.'

She could hardly believe the cheek of him. *The creep was actually touching her leg.*

Angie spun round to confront him. 'What the hell do you think you're—'

Before she could finish, Craig's mouth was covering hers and his hand was grabbing at her breast.

Angie struggled and kicked out at him, but it was useless, he was too strong for her; he had her pinned against him and was forcing his tongue between her lips.

He might have been strong, but his timing was lousy. He had just torn two of the buttons off Angie's top, in a fumbled attempt to get inside her bra, when Vi came back into the kitchen.

'Angela! Stop that! Stop it now!' Vi grabbed Angie's arm and wrenched her out of Craig's grip.

'Me?' Angie staggered back, stunned, against the table. Not only had her mum's boyfriend just attacked her, she was being blamed for it. She rubbed the back of her hand roughly across her mouth, trying to get rid of the taste of him. 'You should ask that . . . that *thing* what he thinks he's doing. Not me.'

Vi poked Craig in the chest. 'Well?'

'Don't get excited, Vi.'

'Don't get excited?' Vi's hands trembled as she snatched up her cigarettes from the window ledge. 'I come in the kitchen—'

'Just look at her. Throwing herself at me, she was. Begging for it. Dirty little slut.'

'Mum,' Angie pleaded. 'He ripped my shirt open.'

'For Christ sake!' Vi, having just noticed that her daughter's nipples were showing through her exposed, lacy bra, was becoming almost hysterical. 'Cover yourself up.'

Angie, with tears spilling down her cheeks, pulled the torn blouse around her.

Craig curled his lip. 'If my daughter—'

'Your daughter?' screamed Angie. 'How old's she then? Can't be more than, what, five or six? Because, let's face it, Craig, you're not much older than me.'

'Angela,' Vi's voice was now low and menacing, 'if you think you can carry on like this under my roof.'

'Like what?' This was so ridiculous it was almost funny. It was like watching a farce on the telly, when everything gets confused and people pop in and out of the wrong doors and girls' dresses just fall off and men run around in their underpants. 'Mum . . .'

Vi dragged on her cigarette. 'Get out.'

'Me?'

'Get out of my sight.'

Angie suddenly felt very calm. 'You've said that too many times.'

'Well, I mean it this time.'

'All right then. I will.'

Vi blinked rapidly. 'It's not as easy as that, young lady.'

'Let go of my arm, Mum.' Angie pulled away and ran out of the room.

Vi caught her at the bottom of the stairs. 'Angie, I'm warning you.'

Craig joined them in the hall. 'I don't need all this bloody drama.'

Angie started up the stairs. 'What? Get enough of that in Scotland, do you, Craig? From your wife and kids?'

'I'm going back to my hotel,' he said, puffing out his cheeks and shaking his head. 'I'll see you sometime, Vi.' He undid the front door, turned, smiled up at Angie and winked. 'And I hope to see you again too, sweetheart.'

Vi's eyes were blazing. She had spent nearly two hours getting ready to go out and now she was being elbowed. 'Don't think you can come running back here any time you like!' she shrieked.

Craig stepped outside and closed the door quietly behind him.

'Good riddance,' shouted Angie, running up the stairs.

'How could you do that to me?' Vi wailed. 'Chucking yourself at him. It's disgusting. You're meant to be my daughter.'

Angie stopped on the landing. 'And you're meant to be my mother.'

'I just don't understand you any more.'

'No, you don't, do you, Mum?' She held on to the

banister, leaned forward and stared down into her mother's face. 'You know this was nothing to do with me. It was your snake of a rotten boyfriend. He could have raped me. But you couldn't care less. So long as you get what you want. And you have, yet again. I'm leaving. Satisfied?'

Vi slapped Angie, hard, across her tear-stained face. 'You spiteful cow. I'll be glad to see the back of you. And don't think you can go running along the street to Tilly Murray. Cos I'll tell the old bag exactly what you're like.'

'What I'm like?'

'Yeah. A bloody Lolita. That's what you are. Nothing more than a grubby little whore.'

Angie said nothing more. She turned round, went into her bedroom, shut the door behind her and pulled out all the glossy carrier bags from her shopping trips with David. She stuffed as many of her things into them as she could carry and left the house to the sound of Vi screaming that she never wanted to set eyes on her, ever again.

When she heard David's voice, Angie took a deep breath and pressed the sixpenny bit down into the slot; she could barely move for all the bags packed around her in the phone box. 'It's me, Angel.'

'Everything OK?' He sounded busy, distracted.

'Fine. I know it's late, but—'

'Angel, I'm a bit tied up at the minute.'

'Sorry, I know we're not meeting till tomorrow, but I wanted to tell you those two weeks are up. The two weeks the doctor said I would have to wait, if I . . .'

'So they are.' David motioned for Bobby to close the door to the outer office so that he could hear her better.

260

'Now, what are we going to do about that then?'

Angie could hear the smile in his voice. She only hoped he would be as happy when he heard what she had to say next. 'You know the other week, when you told me you had more than one flat?'

She thought she heard a slight pause before he said 'Yeah.'

'Well, I've sort of fallen out with my mum. And I need to ask a favour.'

'Go on.'

'Would it be a real cheek if I asked to stay in one of them? Just for a day or two. Until I sort something out. I wouldn't need much space, and I'm really tidy.'

'Angel, don't say anything else.'

She closed her eyes. She had gone too far. Asked too much. Why had she chucked in her job? At least she would have had some money. Where could she go now? Her mum wouldn't think twice about telling Tilly Murray all sorts of lies. And that would mean getting Jackie caught up in the whole rotten mess. And if she went to stay with her nan, how would she explain being out with David till all hours and not going in to work any more? Angie almost laughed. Shame she didn't have Marilyn's number on her.

'Angel? You there?'

'Sorry. I was miles away.'

'I said, have you got a pen?'

'I think so. Somewhere.'

'Well, find it. I'm going to give you an address. It's the top floor of a nice little house. You jump in a cab and you can move in tonight. I'll meet you there in about an hour.'

While Angie was writing down the address, Vi was

banging on the door of Sam's shop. It was all shut up and the main lights were off, but she could see him through the glass door, in the pale light of the desk lamp that stood by the till. She banged harder. She was buggered if she was going to spend another evening by herself.

After much sliding of bolts and turning of locks, the door was eventually opened.

'Violet, what a lovely surprise.' Sam was almost drooling at the sight of his unexpected visitor, as if he was a big, pink, hungry baby and she was his next feed. 'I was thinking about you, while I was cashing up.'

'Were you, Sam?' Vi lifted her chin and looked into his watery, almost colourless eyes.

He nodded eagerly. 'I was. Come in. Please.' His mouth was so dry he could barely spit out the words.

'Thanks,' she said sweetly, following him through to the back of the shop.

He wasn't Craig, but any port in a storm.

It took Sam a lot less time to get her out of her clothes than it had taken Vi to get into them. Within moments they were writhing around on the sofa he had installed in the stock-room – her naked, him with his trousers round his ankles – and it took Sam even less time to reach a gasping, breathless climax.

Sam's always speedy achievement of sexual gratification – his own, not hers – was not a problem for Vi, it was a relief. She preferred to have as little contact with his flabby, sweaty body as possible.

Now Craig on the other hand, with his firm, taut belly, and his big, muscled thighs, she could have had him pumping away at her for hours, have had him touching her and . . .

She could kill that ungrateful little cow. Making a pass at him like that. Her own daughter.

'Violet.' Sam was panting into her ear. 'There's something I have to tell you.'

'What's that then?' she asked, looking up at him through the curtain of greasy grey hair that had fallen over his pudgy face.

'I've decided to tell Cissie. About us.'

With surprising force, Vi pushed him off her, shoving him to one side like an unwanted portion of overboiled cabbage, and then levered herself up on to her elbows. 'Don't be hasty, Sam.' Christ, if he left his old woman, he'd want to be hanging around her morning, noon and night.

'Don't you want to be with me?' He looked like a kid whose lolly had melted.

'Of course I do, darling.' With a bit of difficulty, Vi rolled him back on top of her, knowing that the feel of her flesh against his would soften his brain as surely as it would harden his penis. 'I just don't want you losing everything in the divorce courts. Not when you've worked so hard for it all.'

Sam smiled happily. 'You're so good, Violet. Always worrying about me. Most women would only be after what they could get.'

'I know, Sam,' she said, running a fingernail over his fluff-covered buttock. 'Some women are just selfish.'

'Craig.' With one eye on the light shining from under the lavatory door, Vi whispered urgently into the phone that was mounted on the stock-room wall. Sam had only just gone into the loo, and she knew from experience that he would be in there a good few minutes. 'I had to call you.

I can't get you out of my mind. I promise, nothing like what happened tonight will ever happen again. Honestly, Craig. It was all so stupid. She was just showing off. I don't know what's got into that girl lately. Please, let's be friends again.'

Craig took a long moment as he considered what to do, and eventually came to the conclusion that he was at a loose end for the night, Vi was always willing, and, what the hell . . .

'I'll be round in about an hour,' he said.

Gratified as she was to be back in Craig's good books, this wasn't what she had expected. She'd thought he would punish her. Make her wait at least a couple of days.

'An hour?' she said brightly, then jumped at the sound of Sam pulling the chain. She'd better get a move on.

'Tell you what, Vi. As I'm already in bed, come over to the hotel. I'll tell reception to expect you.'

She was already half-dressed when Sam appeared in the doorway of the loo, wearing a pair of voluminous white Y-fronts and a look of profound disappointment.

'Not going already are you, Violet?'

Vi put on an appropriately pained expression. 'I've got to, Sam. I was enjoying myself so much I lost all track of time.'

He wobbled towards her, his amorous intentions clearly showing in his underpants. 'Can't you stay for a little bit longer?'

'I'd love to. You know that. But I promised I'd go and stay with my mum. She's not been well and the neighbour who usually looks in on her has had to go away for the night. I can't leave her by herself. Not when she's been poorly.'

Sam smiled a benevolent, understanding yet disappointed sort of a smile, and kissed her chastely on the forehead. Then he led her through to the shop.

'Here,' he said, taking two five-pound notes from the still not cashed-up till. 'Take this for a cab, and get a few flowers for your mum in the morning.'

Vi looked suitably surprised and grateful. 'You are such a generous man,' she said, tucking away the money in her bag.

It was almost half past nine, and Sonia was driving at speed through the back streets of Chelsea, trying to avoid the worst of the Friday evening traffic. She was going to meet Mikey in a pub in the King's Road and she couldn't wait to be with him. She hadn't seen him for four whole days – David had been working him ridiculously hard – and all she could think about was being in his arms, making love with him and then discussing their future together, the family they would have and the life they would share for ever.

Sonia had just negotiated the left-hand turn into Flood Street – where she could only hope she would find a parking place – when she screeched to a sudden, tyre-burning halt.

There, across the road, outside a pretty, flower-bedecked house, was someone who looked exactly like David.

She frowned, screwing up her eyes for a better focus.

It was him. There was his Jag, parked behind a taxi, and there he was, unloading parcels from the back seat of a cab and chatting to a girl. A young, pretty girl.

Now he was carrying the parcels into the house. David, who never did anything that he could pay someone else to do for him, was carrying some kid's shopping.

And he was bloody smiling.

Smiling like a lovestruck teenager.

And – she didn't believe this – there was Bobby Sykes, coming out of the house and walking down the path, carrying a parrot in a cage.

A bloody parrot?

And he was sodding smiling as well.

Sonia, forgetting her carefully achieved reinvention of herself into a charming, sophisticated wife, slapped the steering-wheel angrily and hissed nastily under her breath, 'What the fuck is going on here, David Fuller?'

It took her only a few minutes more to work it out. The bastard was setting up some cheap little tramp in a cute little house off the King's Road, a place that she herself would have loved as a pied-à-terre. Some rotten bitch who looked barely old enough to have left school and, worst of all, looked almost young enough to be her daughter.

Sonia reversed into the kerb and did a careful U-turn. She didn't want to draw attention to herself, didn't want him to see her, didn't want him to know what she knew. Not yet. Not until she worked out what she was going to do next.

As she turned back on to the King's Road, Sonia took a last look at the sickening sight of the love birds in her rear-view mirror. 'Two can play at that game, David Fuller.'

'If I get off right now, Angel, I can sort things out and be back in an hour. Two hours, top whack.' He put his hands on her shoulders and looked into her eyes. 'OK?'

'OK. And, David. Thank you.'

He pulled a mock stern face. 'What for?'

'Everything. I can't believe you've done all this for me. You've been so kind and generous. And I am so lucky.'

He chucked her under the chin and winked. What a little doll. And a virgin! 'You make yourself at home. All right?'

'Thanks.'

'And don't keep thanking me.' He walked along the parquet-floored hall towards the door. 'You can show me your appreciation later.'

Angie smiled, but, as David closed the door behind him, her stomach was tying itself into knots. To distract herself from thinking about what was going to happen later – that something she had been longing for so badly, but which still absolutely terrified her – Angie wandered around the flat, trying to take it all in.

It was small, compared to David's other places she had seen, but it was incredible, fantastic, just like the fashionable pads featured in magazine articles about trendy, busy young women living in London.

There was a main, L-shaped room divided into sitting and dining areas, a neat little kitchen, fitted out with all the latest equipment, a smallish single bedroom, and, best of all, a big, bright, airy double bedroom with French doors that opened out on to a tiled terrace, with a table and chairs and pots and tubs spilling over with all sorts of plants and greenery.

Angie roamed through the rooms, imagining herself to be a character in some groovy film like *Darling*, or *The Knack*, or *A Hard Day's Night*, or something – with David co-starring as Michael Caine, of course – then, more prosaically, wondering how this had all happened to her. How such good fortune had smiled on mousy little

267

Angie Knight from Dagenham. How she had met this wonderful, exciting, powerful, generous, handsome man; had gone on the Pill; had got groped by that revolting Craig and thrown out by her mum – that had definitely been what her nan would call a blessing in disguise; and had then moved into a flat in Chelsea.

A flat.

In Chelsea.

Jackie was going to go green with envy, completely bottle green. No, she wasn't, she was actually going to pass out cold when she saw it. Flat as a mat.

If she saw it.

Angie started tidying all her bags and parcels into the wardrobe – she wanted it to look nice for when David came back, but wouldn't take the liberty of hanging anything up – and thought about Jackie. Angie really missed the closeness of their old friendship. Since she had become Angel, things just weren't the same any more; it was as if they were from different worlds.

Angie looked at her watch to see how much longer she had to wait for David. The watch her nan had given her.

She missed her too.

Angie wandered into the white-carpeted living-room and looked at the telephone on the smoked-glass coffee table.

David had told her to make herself at home. If she was quick, surely he wouldn't mind, and she could always offer to pay for the call.

She settled herself gingerly into the basket chair that was suspended on a chain from the ceiling, lit a cigarette and picked up the phone. It took her a moment to get used to the press-button dialling, but then she was through.

*

'Honestly, Nan, I'm fine. Marilyn's mum said I can stay as long as I like. I'm in Marilyn's brother's room. He doesn't need it because he's away at college. It's funny, he's at exactly the same place as Jackie's brother, Martin. And East Ham's really convenient for work. Much nearer than Becontree. The fares'll be so much cheaper.'

Sarah wanted to say, *Don't strong it too much, Angie, I'm no fool.* Instead she just asked her granddaughter, 'Are you sure you're all right, babe? You would tell me if you were in trouble?'

Angie put on her brightest, happiest voice, and set about changing the subject. 'I'm fine. Really. I promise. Here, how's Doris's friend Lily? Pleased she can stay in her house?'

'I wanted to ask you about that, Angie.'

Annoyed with herself for choosing such an unwise diversion as Lily Patterson and Burton Street – she didn't want to get drawn into discussing David, however indirectly – Angie butted in. 'Mum was ever so angry, Nan.'

Sarah Pearson let the subject of Burton Street drop. For the time being, at least. 'Does she know where you're staying?'

'No. I'm going to write to her. Let her know I'm all right.' Angie hesitated. 'I worry about her, you know, Nan.'

Sarah sighed. Poor little love, it should be Violet, the mother, worrying about her daughter, not the other way round. 'I know you do, lovely. Just like I worry about you.'

'There's no need, Nan.' Angie looked around the room at the impressive pictures, expensive furnishings and exotic plants and closed her eyes tightly. She hated lying to her. 'I told you, I'm fine here at Marilyn's. Just fine.'

'Come and stay with me.'

Not only would her nan never approve of David, *say she found her Pill packet* . . .

'I'm fine, Nan. You know Mum. It'll all have blown over in a day or two and I'll be back home.'

'If you're sure.'

'I'm sure.' And I'm sure I want to be with David as much as I want to be away from my spiteful, selfish mother and her disgusting boyfriends.

'Are you sure about this, Sonia?' Mikey definitely wasn't sure. After spending the past four days amongst the missing – he'd been busy schtupping the little blonde waitress from the Coffee Bongo, who he had generously decided to give a second chance – Mikey had expected Sonia to rip off his clothes the moment she saw him, not insist they go to bloody Plaistow to watch the boxing.

It wasn't as if he had even wanted to see her tonight. The novelty of fucking Fuller's wife, regardless of her very appealing adventurous streak, had worn thin. He preferred younger birds. Then, when she had mentioned the boxing, he had given her a knock back at first, not fancying being with her in full view of any face in London who fancied a bit of sport that night. But Sonia, much to his surprise, had started making threats about talking to her old man about the keys and the club. They were veiled threats, admittedly, but still threats. Then she had gone all soft and lovely again and had talked some girlie bollocks about how much she loved him.

Anyway, he was here now and he might as well enjoy himself, have a few drinks and earn a few quid – he'd already heard who was going to win the first bout from a bloke he knew, Dodgy Pete.

'I'm putting a ton on the Irish kid in the first,' he told Sonia, as they filed through an anonymous-looking, black-painted door. 'Same for you?'

Sonia nodded, took the money from her gold mesh evening bag and handed it to him. 'I'll be sitting over there.' She gestured with a lift of her chin, and smiled seductively at him. 'I'll make sure I save you a seat.'

The seating, set round a central boxing ring, made the room look like a miniature version of a professional sports arena, which it was – except for the large, well-stocked bar that ran all along one wall – but outsiders would never have guessed. The building was a brick-built, single-storey affair on a parcel of waste ground at the back of a pub near Balaam Street. It had been built to look like a storage facility, a small warehouse, but had never served any other purpose than staging unlicensed boxing bouts, and was known to those privy to such matters as one of the premier illegal venues in East London.

The crowd tonight were typical: men of all ages from youthful to quite elderly, mostly smartly dressed and prosperous-looking, with the occasional individual, attached to one or other of the fighters, in more casual clothes. The women, on the other hand, were generally much younger and, regardless of age, were dressed to the nines in outfits that would have graced a cocktail party – had they been the types to attend such functions. As for accessories, fur stoles seemed to be the favourite choice amongst the women, while the men sported large cigars; showy gold and diamond jewellery was favoured by both sexes.

As Sonia made her way to one of the simple, straight-backed chairs closest to the ring, she took note of all the familiar faces, making sure she was on full view. She'd show David what indiscretion was all about and, with a bit of luck, she would force Mikey's hand to go away with her sooner rather than later.

As she sat down, she was a bit disappointed to see that David himself wasn't there – that really would have got things going – but, if she was honest, she was also relieved. Mikey wouldn't have had the bottle to stay if David was around. She shouldn't have really expected him to be there anyway, not when he had his fancy piece to play with. But she was gratified to see that there were plenty of other people around who knew her, including Peter Burman and his entourage, and Jeff from the Canvas Club with his dozy, loyal little wife, Jean.

As he made his way over to Sonia with their drinks, Mikey wasn't sharing her pleasure at seeing so many blokes who were friends of Fuller's, and was feeling increasingly uncomfortable about being on show. Then he saw Jeff and his stomach flipped over. It was all very well Sonia saying that everyone would just think he was minding her while they were waiting for her old man to turn up, but that bastard Jeff had it in for him, and could cause him all sorts of trouble.

Mikey edged his way along the row, and a slow smile spread across his lips. What was he worrying about? If Jeff grassed him up, he would tell Fuller that the lying bastard was just covering up for his own little private enterprise – all the pills he was knocking off from the club and selling on the side, and the five per cent he was pocketing every night.

*

At the sound of the key in the lock, and David calling out that it was OK, it was him, Angie jumped up from the sofa where she had been curled up listening to the radio. She didn't want him to think she was taking advantage.

She heard him throw his keys on to the table in the hall, then his footsteps moving towards her.

He was smiling broadly as he came into the room, and was holding a magnum of champagne and a bunch of flowers. He was enjoying himself. He hadn't bought flowers for a bird in years. It was like starting courting again.

'Hello, Angel.'

'Hope it's all right, I used the phone. To call my nan.'

'No need to ask. You help yourself to whatever you want.' He put the bottle on the table, went over to the long, low teak sideboard, took out two glasses and set about pouring them drinks.

'Thanks. You're ever so kind.' Angie jumped as he popped the cork. 'And this place is smashing.'

'Shame you didn't like the parrot.'

'But I did. I loved it. Didn't Bobby tell you? I was worried I wouldn't be able to look after it properly, that was all. I'm going to be out most of the time during the day. Looking for a new job.'

'Bobby's a man of very few words, darling.' He handed her a brimming, foaming glass, picked up the bottle, and led her through to the bedroom. 'And I told you: you don't have to work.'

Angie took a small sip, smiled nervously, then knocked back the rest of it. 'I'll have to get something that does night shifts,' she said, gasping as the bubbles prickled their way down her throat. 'I'll need double time

273

if I'm going to find the rent for this place. Even if it is only for a few days.'

David put down his own glass on the bedside table and then took Angie's empty one from her. 'Don't you worry about rent, about work, about anything, Angel.' He pulled her towards him, all the while looking into her eyes. 'You're my girl now and I'm going to look after you. You can stay here as long as you like. Right?'

Angie swallowed hard. This was going to be it. 'Can I have another drink?'

David refilled her glass.

'Bobby will look after the parrot, won't he?' she asked, backing towards the bed. She took two big gulps of wine, and coughed.

David nodded. He took the empty glass off her again, then scooped her up in his arms. 'His Maureen's nuts about animals.' He placed her gently on the purple satin covers, smoothing her hair on to the pillows. 'They've got two dogs already.'

Angie closed her eyes and David began the lesson.

The young Irish fighter stood panting over his pummelled and bloodied opponent, who was trying, and failing, to rise to his knees; the crowd was on its feet roaring for him to finish off the job.

With supreme effort, the already defeated boxer managed to stand up and then stagger sideways. Calmly, the Irishman stepped forward, jerked his head sharply, and butted his dazed opponent squarely between the eyes, then, before he had a chance to crumple to the ground, the Irishman loosed a massive haymaker which sent the now-unconscious man crashing against the ropes, his blood and sweat spraying the whooping, yelling crowd.

Sonia clapped excitedly. 'We won! We won!' Then without warning, she threw her arms round Mikey's neck and kissed him full on the lips, raising her leg so that her thigh rubbed against his.

Mikey, all too aware of being on full view, unpeeled her hands from his neck. 'All right, Son, it's only a few hundred quid you've won.'

'*We* won.' She pressed hard against him and kissed him again.

A small, wiry man in a brown suit and matching suede pork-pie hat who was sitting next to them, grinned broadly. 'The sight of blood gets you tarts going, don't it, girl?' he shouted over the roar of the crowd, giving his slightly tipsy, female companion's waist a hard squeeze. Then he added, at full volume, and with a raucous, smoker's laugh, 'And us blokes and all. Go on, moosh, do her a favour. Take her out to the car park and give her one. Look at her. She's gagging for it.'

'Sex in the car park!' cried Sonia in a loud, even posher voice than usual. 'What a fab idea!'

Much of the crowd were now as interested in the Sonia and Mikey show as they were in the victorious Irishman, and offered their own ribald suggestions about what exactly Sonia 'could do with' and how Mikey might oblige her, and, if not, who would volunteer to do it for him.

Then, much to the amusement of everyone around them, Sonia clambered along the row, her already short skirt up around her thighs, leading Mikey by the hand towards the exit.

He didn't bother to resist. It was too late for that now, anyway, what the hell? With the extra dough he'd made from selling the pills, he had enough money to piss off any time he liked. And that bloke was right, watching the fight had got him going. He might as well give Sonia one last treat before he left.

At the sound of the street door opening, Maureen almost dropped the kettle.

'Bob?' she called out. 'Is that you?'

'Yes, Maur.'

She wiped her hands on her apron and hurried through to the hall. 'Everything all right? What are you doing home so early? And what the hell's that?'

Bobby beamed at his wife and held up the parrot's cage. 'I got you a surprise.'

'Surprise? I'll say it's a surprise. Whatever will the dogs make of it?'

Bobby, still grinning, carried the cage through to the kitchen and put it on the draining board. 'They just travelled with it in the car all the way from Chelsea, and they didn't seem to mind it. Sniffed at it a few times and that, but nothing really. Pretty thing, innit, Maur? Lovely blue feathers.'

'Bobby, it's a parrot, and this is a prefab, not the flaming zoo.'

'Don't you like it?'

Maureen eyed the bird suspiciously. 'Where did you get it?'

This was the bit he had been practising. 'Dave bought it and—'

'I might have known. Another of madam's castoffs.'

'No, it wasn't Sonia's. Dave got it for that kid he's seeing.'

'Very nice. We have to have her rejects and all now, do we?'

'No. She liked it. But she can't look after it cos she's got to go out and find a job. Up the City or something.'

Maureen, still staring at the bird, folded her arms tightly across her chest. 'A bird of his looking for a job? That'll be a first.'

'She's all right, Maur. You'd like her.'

'D'you reckon?' She shook her head. 'You've got to learn to say no to him, Bob.'

Bobby was still trying to think of something to say that would make the peace, when the phone rang in the sitting-room.

'Go on, go and answer it and I'll stay here with this thing to make sure it doesn't start pecking the wallpaper.'

'Bob, it's me, Jeff. I don't know how to put this, but I'm down at the boxing in Plaistow. I'm in Jim's office. He's let me use the phone.'

'Very nice to hear it, Jeff. He's a generous man. But what're you telling me for?'

'Sonia's here.'

'Sonia? She hates boxing.'

'It's not the boxing she was interested in. It was Tilson. She practically had his dick in her mouth.'

'Not at it in the car again?'

'No, Bob, in front of everyone. Including Burman. It was a right show-up. She was all over him. You should have heard the cheye-eyeking. I was going to call Greek Street and tell Dave, but I bottled out. I didn't know what to say.'

'Dave's not there anyway.' Bobby rubbed his hand over his shaven head. 'Leave it with me, Jeff. I'll sort it out.'

*

When he went back into the kitchen, Maureen was feeding an appreciative Denise, as the bird was now apparently called, with chocolate digestives, but Bobby didn't even notice her change of heart.

'Whatever's wrong, Bob? You look like you've seen a ghost.'

'Make us a cuppa tea, Maur. Sonia's just done something very silly, and I've got to think of a way of telling Dave.'

Angie pulled the sheet up to her chin and took the glass of champagne – her fourth – from David who was sitting up in bed next to her.

'Happy, Angel?'

'More than I thought I ever could be.' And she was. David was an experienced, skilled lover who had made her feel that she was the most important, wonderful, beautiful girl in the world.

'Here's to a very successful first lesson,' he said, toasting her.

'Was I all right?' Angie asked softly, her cheeks and throat blushing scarlet from a combination of modesty, love-making and alcohol.

David's broad smile of satisfaction spread even further. 'Angel, you are a genuine one-off.' He put his arm round her shoulders and drew her to him. 'A real breath of fresh air. And you were fantastic.' As he kissed her, and she responded – still shy but less nervous – he felt himself stirring again.

'Give me that glass,' he breathed into her ear. 'And we'll start lesson number two.'

David was about to pull her on top of him when the phone rang on the bedside table. He was immediately alert. Only Bobby knew he was there, and only Bobby had the number. Something must be wrong.

'Hang on, Angel,' he said snatching up the receiver. 'Yeah'llo?'

Angie watched as David listened. The look on his face, and the way the colour drained from his skin as though his blood had been siphoned away, frightened her. She had been so elated just a moment ago and now something awful had happened.

David clenched his jaw and a vein in his neck began to throb.

Angie had no idea what the person on the other end had said, but it must have been the most terrible news. He had put the phone down without another word.

'Can I do anything?'

He threw back the covers and swung his legs out of the bed, making her spill the dregs of her drink that she had been sipping absent-mindedly. Then he grabbed his trousers from the floor and started getting dressed.

'I've got a problem. I've got to go.'

'When will you be back?'

He pulled on his socks. 'Don't know.'

Angie didn't know what else to say.

Still buttoning his shirt, he hurried out into the hall. As Angie heard him pick up his bunch of keys from the hall table, then open the front door, she sprang out of bed, and stumbled tipsily after him. 'David?'

The door slammed shut. Something must be really wrong. She had to see if she could help him.

She flung on her yellow oilskin coat, grabbed a pair of shoes and her bag and rushed out of the flat. Just as she stepped on to the pavement, David pulled away in the Jag without even noticing she was there.

'David . . .' Her shoulders drooped with disappointment. Then, as if on cue, just to make matters worse, a distant rumble of thunder announced the start of a heavy, drenching, summer downpour.

Angie, balancing drunkenly first on one leg, then the other, pulled her shoes on to her bare feet, then opened her bag to look for her keys.

Her mounting panic, as she realized that all she had in her bag was a couple of tissues, half a packet of cigarettes, and a few pounds' worth of silver, meant that she didn't give a first, let alone a second, thought, to the rather battered, dull-grey Morris Minor that pulled away at the same time as David. Neither did she register just how fast David had accelerated away, nor the look on the Morris driver's face as he cursed furiously at the disappearing Jaguar when he stalled his motor at the lights.

Angie wrenched her coat round her more tightly and shivered. How bad did a problem have to be to have made David run out like that?

And what was she going to do now?

She had no choice. She'd have to go to Jackie's.

'Hello, Squirt.' Martin looked at the damp, slightly dishevelled girl standing on his doorstep and smiled – she looked terrific, if a bit pissed. 'Everything all right? It's nearly eleven o'clock.'

Over his shoulder, at the top of the stairs, Angie spotted Tilly's bare legs and carpet-slippered feet. 'Is that you, Jackie?' she called.

Angie signalled urgently for Martin not to say she was there.

'It's no one, Mum. I just thought I heard someone messing around with my scooter that's all. Go back to bed. I'll wait up to let Jackie in.'

Tilly Murray didn't approve of youngsters having keys, it encouraged them to take liberties. 'All right, love. Night, night. Don't study too hard.'

Angie mouthed her thanks and followed Martin into the front room.

She sat on the sofa, carefully pulling her coat down as she did so. 'Didn't expect to see you in of a Friday night, Martin.'

'My girlfriend's gone to see her parents in the country. I couldn't make it. Term's over but I've still got college work to finish.'

Despite her predicament and the befuddling effect of the booze, Angie managed a smile. 'Jackie told me you didn't like it down there.'

'Understatement,' he said flatly. 'So, what's your story?'

Angie gave him a censored version of events, that left him with the correct impression that she had left home and had moved into a flat, but which made no mention of the champagne, David, or his unceremonious exit almost immediately after she had made love for the very first time.

'Chelsea, eh? You must be earning plenty.'

She shrugged non-committally. She was feeling a bit sick.

Martin thought about the two more years he had at university before he would even begin earning proper wages. 'How did you get locked out?'

'Went down to the milk machine on the corner,' she lied. 'So I could make some coffee. Must have left my keys on the table.'

'I'm not thinking. Fancy a cup now?'

'Martin,' she put her head in her hands. 'I could murder one.'

He stood up. 'Want me to take your coat?'

Angie looked up at him through her tear-dampened lashes. 'Better not, Mart. Me coat and shoes are all I'm wearing.'

The thought of Angie travelling on the tube all the way from Chelsea, surrounded by other passengers, with nothing on but a short oilskin coat, made Martin gulp. No wonder she hadn't wanted his mum to know she was there.

He was still staring at Angie, and was seriously considering whether she would respond as favourably as, according to Jackie, she had apparently done in the bus shelter at Clacton, when there was a knock at the door.

'Must be Jackie,' he said, dry-mouthed.

'You'd better let her in.'

He nodded dumbly.

While Martin went in to the kitchen to pull himself together and to make the coffee, Jackie and Angie sat in the front room, whispering so that they didn't disturb Tilly who, now her daughter was safely home, had allowed herself to go to sleep and was snoring loudly above them.

'So, this Andrew you've been out with.' Angie's head felt as if it had been stuffed with cotton wool, and she was having a bit of trouble concentrating. 'He's the bloke you met at the Lotus on your birthday?'

'Yes and he's very nice, but never mind him. I'm worried about you, Angie.'

Angie, who had been rather more explicit with Jackie

than she had with Martin, shrugged. 'Not heard of free love?' She hoped she looked and sounded more casual than she felt about the situation. With everything that had happened, she'd not been able to stop worrying about whether it was true what they said: that once you let a bloke have his way with you, he lost interest and cleared off, dumping you like used goods.

'Angie—'

'It's all right, I'm on the Pill.'

'*The Pill?*'

'So? I said I'm on the Pill, not that I'm an axe murderer.' She took her cigarettes from her bag and held them up. 'Mind if I have one?'

Jackie shook her head. 'Since when have you been smoking?'

'A while.'

'Put them away and don't be so stupid. Mum'd be down here faster than a fire engine if she smells smoke. And you've been drinking.'

Angie snorted. 'Like you never have.'

'Angie, I'm serious. Travelling all that way by yourself in that state. Anything could have happened to you.'

'Don't look at me like that, Jack. I'm too knackered for a row. Let's just go to bed, eh?' Angie smiled self-pityingly, undid her coat, and flashed her naked body at her friend. 'Lend us a nightie?'

Jameson sat in his Morris Minor watching Sonia, David Fuller's wife, who was sitting in the driver's seat of her scarlet Mini Cooper, kissing Mikey Tilson as if she were a kid in the back row of the pictures, in the full glare of the street lights.

The detective constable was always amazed when a man let himself be driven by his prick rather than his brains – not that Tilson gave any evidence of being in possession of much in the way of grey matter – but to be so blatant about carrying on with David Fuller's wife. That took a particularly spectacular brand of stupidity.

After five minutes or so of passion, Sonia got out of the car, and Tilson clambered over into the driver's seat. She stood and waved and blew kisses as he drove away, then crossed the road and let herself into the mansion block where she lived with her husband. The mansion block where all the lights in her flat had been burning for the past couple of hours, and where the back-lit silhouette of a large man, who looked very like David Fuller, could be seen standing by one of the windows.

From what Jameson knew about Fuller, his wife was either as stupid as Mikey Tilson, or she had a very advanced case of death wish.

As Sonia opened the flat door, David was waiting for her in the hall.

'What do you think you're up to?'

'Me? How about you and your little scrubber?'

David grabbed her by the wrist. 'I asked you a question.'

She looked contemptuously at him. 'Grow up, David. You don't own me. I do what I want.'

'No, you don't.'

'Yes I do. And, I'm afraid, that includes falling in love.'

'You what?'

'Mikey and I are going away together. I'm going to have his baby.'

David let go of her wrist and raised his hand above his head.

'Go on, big shot, hit me. Show me what a pathetic creature you really are. No wonder you have to go with little girls. That's all you're fit for.'

David shoved her out of the way and stormed out of the door. 'I'll show you, you bitch.'

Chapter 13

It was three hours since David had driven away from the flat, oblivious of having abandoned Angie on the pavement in the rain, and less than twenty minutes since he had stormed out on Sonia. He was now parking his Jaguar behind a dark-blue Ford Zodiac, close to the staff entrance of the Canvas Club. It was a spot which suited David's purposes very well, as it was outside the patisserie, one of the few local shops which was never open at this early hour, and one which would stay locked and silent until the bakers arrived to begin their day in about an hour's time.

He scanned the rain-slicked street in his rear-view mirror. The few people he saw seemed to be paying more attention to keeping dry and getting home before daybreak than in bothering with the bloke in the expensive motor. Of the two who did afford him more than a passing glance, one had him down as a worried father, probably up from the Surrey stockbroker belt, waiting for his spoiled, drug-using child to eventually condescend to leave some club or discothèque, and the other dismissed him as one of the upper-crust types who came slumming in Soho, looking for a bit of sleazy action in the small hours.

If the latter had been the case, David wouldn't have had much luck, the toms were all indoors, either too lazy or too averse to getting a soaking to be working the almost empty streets.

David turned off the engine, and the wipers *shwooped*

to a stop; the windscreen was immediately pitted with rain drops the size of shilling bits.

He took a pair of tan leather gloves from his briefcase on the passenger seat and eased them on, unhurriedly, checking each finger for a perfect fit, then leaned forward and felt around under his seat. Pulling out two heavy, empty cola bottles and a copy of the final edition of the *London Evening News*, David smiled to himself. That bastard Mikey Tilson would be in the papers himself before too long.

He wrapped one of the bottles in a few sheets of the newspaper and slipped the other into the pocket of his rain coat. Checking that no one was watching, he opened the car door, stepped out on to the pavement, walked up to the bonnet of the Zodiac, and placed the paper-wrapped parcel in the gutter by the front wheel. With another brief glimpse along the almost deserted street, he brought down his heel in a swift, hard movement, smashing the glass in the now soggy paper, then placed the jagged shards around each of the front tyres, just so, making sure each shattered piece was clearly visible.

David then melted into the shadows of the cake-shop doorway, wrapped the other empty bottle in the rest of the newspaper, took out a cigarette, shielded it behind his hand and lit it. He figured he had ten minutes or so to wait.

In fact, he had to wait just five.

As Mikey came out of the staff entrance to the Canvas, head well down against the sheeting rain, he was grinning like a prize candidate for the Happy Olympics. He had plenty to be happy about.

He had laid Fuller's old woman for the very last time

– thank Christ – he was well shot of that one, she had gone bloody baby bonkers these past few weeks and had been getting right up his pipe; he had enough dough stashed away not to have to worry, as he stretched out on a Spanish beach, thinking about which of the bars he fancied buying; and, the icing on the cake, the tasty, young blonde from Coffee Bongo had turned out to be a genuinely hard-nosed and very experienced little pill-pusher. She would come in more than handy on the Costas, if Mikey ever ran short of a few quid.

He patted the pocket that contained his final instalment from the club and his grin broadened. He had more than had one over on David fucking Fuller.

But Mikey's happiness was as short-lived as a pint of cold lager on a hot summer's day. When he saw the jagged chunks of broken glass that had obviously been placed deliberately by his front wheels, his expression hardened into a thin-lipped, angry scowl.

'What rotten little bastard's done that?' He bent down and, gingerly, began picking up the thick, transparent remains of the soft-drink bottle from the slick of unidentifiable muck in the wet gutter. 'Fucking kids.'

He never had time to straighten up again.

David stepped forward, brought the paper-wrapped bottle up over his head, then brought it down – *thwack!* – in a single blow to the back of Mikey's skull.

As Mikey crumpled like a deflated balloon, David dropped the empty bottle and paper into the gutter, alongside the broken glass and other old news stories – just a bit more litter for the bin-men to smash and crash into their truck in the pre-dawn hours – hooked the unconscious Mikey neatly under the arms, and dragged him back to his car like some mug-punter who had overindulged in overpriced mock champagne in one of David's clip joints.

He would finish off the job somewhere a little more private.

All the while this was going on, Christina, the tom who was increasingly too drink-raddled to be doing much business – regardless of the weather – except with the likes of Mad Albert Roper, sat in her dingy, unpleasant-smelling, fire-scorched and blackened room, looking down at the scene from behind the safety of her incongruously new net curtains.

David Fuller. What was he up to?

He might have got her out of trouble with the law, but that still didn't mean she was very happy with him. Bringing all these kids into the area, with these new discothèques of his; it was completely ruining her pitch. A Friday night and what had she earned? Bugger all, that's what. Her sort of punters weren't interested in dance halls, they wanted strip joints and dirty book shops. Something to get them going. The proper trade of Soho.

And he had the cheek to complain if she didn't get his bloody rent together on time. Threatened to throw her out on her arse.

It was a right bloody liberty, the way he was treating the working girls round here. They'd brought him a good living over the years, a right good living, but now he had no respect for any of them. It wasn't good enough.

She took a swig of whisky straight from the bottle.

Hang on. Whatever was he up to now?

When Tilly Murray took her daughter's usual morning cup of tea and biscuits into her bedroom – at ten o'clock rather than seven thirty, it being a Saturday – she had been pleased, if a bit surprised, to find that Angie was in there too. She was, after all, another customer for breakfast. And even if Jackie had claimed she was going out with Andrew, a very nice young man by all accounts, and Tilly's hopes of her daughter maybe settling down and thus ceasing to be a worry to her had been falsely raised, she still liked the idea of Jackie going out with her friend and having a good time. There was still a year or two for engagements of the non-desperate kind to be announced, when all was said and done.

But when Angie had sat up, claiming that she wasn't hungry and couldn't possibly face a fry-up, Tilly had seen the state of the child, and had changed her mind. She looked terrible. Maybe some of the rumours she had been hearing about Angie – and, up until now, always loyally refuting – were actually true. And maybe she didn't want her Jackie mixing with the likes of Violet Knight's daughter. Not if she really was following in her tramp of a mother's footsteps.

She would have a quiet word with Jackie later, when Angie had gone home. Get a few things straight.

It was a good job Tilly was patient. It was nearly midday by the time Angie eventually managed to drag herself out of Jackie's bed and then to make her way unsteadily down the stairs to the bathroom.

She was now sitting at Jackie's white melamine dressing unit staring at herself in the mirror. She looked as miserable as she felt.

'Can I borrow some make-up, Jack?'

Jackie was still flat out, staring up at the ceiling. 'Help yourself.'

'Thanks. I look like a real freak.' Angie sorted through

290

the drawer full of cosmetics, selected a few tubes and bottles and set about her face.

Jackie propped herself up against the headboard and mouthed and squinted along with her friend as she shaded a grey banana shape into the crease of her lid and then drew a deft, subtle line along her lashes and topped it off with two layers of mascara.

'You've been practising. That looks good.'

'I went up to Selfridges. Had a make-up lesson.'

'Why didn't you ask me?'

'You were at work.'

'Course.' Jackie dropped back down on to the pillows. 'Want to borrow a dress?'

'Please.'

'Don't know if I've got any good enough for you.'

'Jackie.'

'Just take what you like.'

'Thanks. Then I'd better be off.'

Jackie turned over and faced the wall. 'All right. See you.'

Angie lifted the curtain and looked out at the sky. The storm clouds had cleared and the sun was shining brightly again. She pulled on a pair of Jackie's tiny, lacy knickers, then took a daffodil-yellow linen shift from the wardrobe and slipped it on over her head. 'Jack.'

'What?'

'You couldn't lend me the tube fare, could you?'

'In my bag.'

'Any plans for tonight?' Angie asked, rummaging through her friend's bag for her purse.

Jackie rolled over to face her. 'Not sure. How about you?'

Angie held up a pound note to show Jackie what she

was borrowing, then leaned over the bed and hugged her. 'How about meeting up with Marilyn?'

'I miss this, you know, Ange. I miss you.'

'Me too.'

'You will be careful?'

'I told you, I'm on the Pill.'

'I'm not talking about you getting up the spout.'

Angie stiffened. 'So what are you talking about?'

'This David bloke. He's so much older than you. And where did he rush off to like that? What do you really know about him?'

'I know that he's kind, generous, good-looking, and that he cares about me.'

'If he cares so much about you, how comes he let you get so drunk last night?'

Angie turned away from her friend and looked in the mirror again, smoothing and primping her hair. She laughed carelessly. 'Drunk? I was practically sober by the time I got here. You should have seen me a few hours earlier. The trouble is, champagne goes right to my head. It's all those bubbles. You should try it some time.'

'It's not funny, Ange. And just because it's champagne, it doesn't make it any better.'

'You are such a hypocrite.'

'I'm not.'

'Yes you are.' Angie folded her arms and stared levelly at her friend. 'Are you saying you wouldn't jump at the chance of doing what I'm doing?'

After a moment, Jackie said, 'Yeah, you're right. Course I would.' She sounded as if she meant it.

Angie pulled on her shoes and her oilskin. 'Fancy coming over to the flat? You can try some champagne.'

'Won't he mind?'

'No. Course he won't.' She paused, then added lightly, 'I'll ask him.'

David and Bobby were driving along in stony-faced silence – their practised ability to deal calmly and practically with events having proved a life-saver on more than one occasion – even though Bobby had been closer to panicking than David had ever seen him when he had arrived at the Greek Street office and had found Bobby waiting anxiously for him to turn up.

That wasn't usual either, him being at Greek Street on a Saturday morning. Bobby always took his wife out in the car to do her weekly grocery shopping, and only showed up at the office for the racing on the telly some time in the afternoon. And then, when Bobby had flashed a nervous, sideways glance at Bill and George, who were taking bets over the phones in the outer office, and had said in a low voice that he needed to speak to David urgently, somewhere more private, David knew something was really up. So, at David's suggestion, they were driving over to the flat that Angie had moved in to the night before.

He needed a bath and a change of clothes, anyway.

David went through the flat calling for Angel, but the place was empty and the bed was still unmade.

'She must be out shopping or something.' David ushered Bobby into the main room and gestured for him to sit at the table. David remained standing, leaning on the back of one of the dining chairs. 'What's all this about then, Bob?'

Bobby gnawed at the inside of his lip, giving his speech one final rehearsal in his head, then said, 'I don't know if someone's trying to send you a message, Dave, but the word is, Mikey's been done in. Right outside the Canvas. Last night.'

David's expression was blank, but his mind was working overtime. How the hell had it got out already? Then he said flatly, 'I know. It was me. I got rid of the slimy little cowson.'

'You?'

'Yup.'

'Dave, tell me you mean you got someone else to get rid of him.'

'No. I did it. Knocked him out cold, then used the stupid bastard's own Luger on him. Didn't even have to use my own tool.' For the first time that morning, David unbuttoned his raincoat. His shirt was spattered with blood.

Bobby drew in a deep breath. 'Where is he?'

'You just drove over from Greek Street with him. He's downstairs. In the boot of the Jag. I drove him down to the marshes earlier, but it was still too wet, didn't want to leave no tyre marks, did I? Then we had a trip down to a pig farm in Black Notley. Same story. Been all over the place, that boy has, this morning.'

Bobby stood up and went over to the phone. 'I'll call Toby.'

As Angie neared the house, she was thrilled to see David's car parked outside. She had been fretting all the way back on the tube from Becontree to Sloane Square and all the time she was walking along the King's Road to Flood Street that David would simply have locked up the place and disappeared, bored and with no further use for her now that they had actually 'done it'. At least she'd have the chance to explain where she had been all night.

The door opened and she was just about to fling herself into his arms, but it wasn't David standing in the hallway, it was Bobby.

'Hello, Bob,' she said sheepishly. 'Can I come in?'

Bobby opened the door wider and stepped back. 'Course. He's in—'

'It's OK.' Without waiting for him to finish, Angie dashed down the hall to the main room where she saw David sitting at the table with a skinny, mopey-looking man dressed in an ancient black suit. There was a Scotch bottle and three, almost empty, glasses between them.

She stood in the doorway and smiled happily. 'Hello, David.'

He looked up as if she were interrupting him. 'I'm a bit busy at the minute, Angel.'

Bobby squeezed past her and went and joined the other two men at the table.

'Right,' she said, feeling hurt, like a child being dismissed by the grown-ups. 'Sorry.' Hadn't he even realized she'd been out all night? She had to get his attention somehow. She couldn't leave it like this. 'I was wondering if I could have a friend over.' The moment the words had left her lips, she regretted coming out with such a genuinely childish question. Talk about botching things up.

The dark-suited man made a noise that was probably a laugh but could as easily have been a hacking, tubercular cough. 'Not a boyfriend, I hope?'

'No.' Angie was offended. 'My friend, Jackie. Jacqueline.'

'Ignore Toby,' David said kindly. 'Course you can have her over.'

'When?'

Toby rolled his eyes. 'For gawd's sake. Look, sweetheart, we're trying to do business here. Birds keep their traps shut, right? They don't ask questions and they don't butt in.'

David said nothing to the man about being so rude to her, he just poured three more drinks and said, 'Go through to the kitchen, Angel, and make yourself some coffee or something. I won't be long. Me and you'll shoot out later.'

Without a word, Angie did as she was told.

As she opened the cupboards to look for the cups, she could hear David saying that there was some rubbish that had to be got rid of, and while it was obvious he wasn't talking about dusting round the flat, she couldn't really figure out what he did mean. It was as if he was talking in secret code.

But even if she didn't understand the details of what David was going on about, it was obvious from his tone that it was serious. Very serious.

She was just revving herself up to go through to them, to ask if they fancied a cup of coffee or some tea maybe – anything that might cheer up that miserable Toby – when Bobby came into the kitchen.

He strode over to the transistor on the window ledge and snapped it on at full volume, drowning out David saying something about Toby remembering he owed him a favour.

As the Yardbirds exploded into the opening lines of 'For Your Love', Angie grabbed him by the sleeve and wailed, 'Bobby, what are you doing? You're rattling the windows.'

Bobby said nothing, he just frowned and stared down

296

at her fingers that were still gripping his jacket – they looked pathetically small against his big, meaty arms – and waited until she had let go and had backed away from him. Then, with a disappointed shake of his head, he left, slamming the kitchen door firmly behind him.

If Angie had not been frozen into wide-eyed shock by Bobby's mute belligerence, she might have had the courage to have lowered the volume, then she would probably have understood the rest of the men's conversation quite easily, as it was, in its own macabre way, relatively straightforward. David was negotiating with Toby, who was an undertaker, the rate for what he was referring to as a double burial, in order to rid himself of potentially incriminating evidence: the mortal remains of Mikey Tilson. The exchange between them would further have revealed that, in his final resting place, Mikey Tilson would be sharing a coffin with Arthur Cedric Baker, the late, not-much-liked, landlord of the Nag's Head in Canning Town.

'Make sure you don't let Mr Baker's family know nothing about all these arrangements, Toby,' David had said, with a wink, as he let the undertaker and Bobby out of the flat, 'or they'll be expecting me to go halves, and I ain't laying out for no boiled ham tea for people I don't even know.'

Within moments of Bobby and Toby leaving the flat, Angie's and David's bodies were entwined on the big, still-unmade, double bed, and all Angie's fears about David no longer being interested in her were completely forgotten, and Bobby's behaviour was not even a vague worry somewhere in the back of her mind.

When they eventually emerged from the bedroom, David wouldn't let Angie tidy up, but instead had taken her shopping for something to wear that evening, while a team of caterers and cleaners he had hired organized the little Flood Street flat for the party that Angie and he were apparently throwing there that evening.

'So, you are Angel.' The olive-skinned man, with the slightly lisping, foreign accent, who had introduced himself as Salvo, smiled winningly at Angie as he took her hand and shook it gently.

'That's right. I'm a friend of David's.'

'Aren't we all?'

Angie wasn't sure what to say next. She was getting a bit better at speaking to strangers at parties, but it was still really hard, especially when they were as sophisticated and stylish as this lot. She was on the verge of fleeing to the lavatory when a magazine article she had read recently – had read particularly carefully – popped into her head. *Ten things to keep your man interested. Number three: smile and ask him about his work.*

'Do you work with David?' she asked brightly.

Salvo raised his eyebrows and looked at her with ill-concealed surprise at being asked such a question. 'I am involved with the import-export side of commerce, so I work with many people.'

Another silence loomed. 'David persuaded me to give up my job.'

Salvo inclined his head to show interest.

'But I think it's a bit boring doing nothing. You can only do so much shopping, can't you?' She forced out a tinkly laugh. 'He was so surprised earlier, when I started clearing up the flat. He said that Sonia, you know, his housekeeper, could learn some things from me. Although she does do lovely flower arrangements.'

'I see! Your English sense of humour.' Salvo was now laughing heartily. 'Asking about my work. And Sonia being David's housekeeper. You are very funny.'

Angie thought he was probably a bit bonkers, but at least she'd amused him.

'No wife would care to be described as her man's housekeeper. But one with Sonia's looks? Very funny. How angry she would be.'

'Wife? No, Sonia's not his wife. David's not married. She's his housekeeper. Honest.'

Salvo smiled coolly. 'David is a fortunate man to have a friend as lovely as you. Now, if you will excuse me.'

Angie managed a tiny smile in return. He must have misunderstood. He was foreign, after all. And a loony. The way he'd laughed like that.

'You all right, Angel? Enjoying yourself?' It was David.

She nodded, looking up into his handsome face made her feel the usual flutter of excitement, but, this time, it also made her feel queasy. Say that Salvo was right? Say David really was married? 'I'm fine,' she said quietly.

'You don't look it. Salvo not upset you, has he? I know what them Italians are like.'

She felt the tears begin to prickle. 'No. It's not Salvo. Well, not him exactly. I'm still not used to people like this. That's all.' She was babbling, but she didn't care what she was saying.

'Like what?'

Had she really been had by one of the oldest tricks in the book? A bloke pretending he was single? 'You know,' she said, distractedly. 'Posh people.'

David threw back his head and laughed. 'So that's it. I

told you before. You're special. And you're certainly better than any of this lot, darling. Miles better.'

Angie sipped at her champagne, but the glass was empty.

David took it from her and replaced it with a full one from a passing waiter.

She knocked back a big swig, noticing, incongruously, that it no longer seemed to make her cough or tickle her nose as it had once done. She must be getting used to it.

'I'm going to introduce you to each and every person in this room, Angel, and they're all going to love you. But, before I do, I'm going to teach you another lesson. A very important lesson. OK?'

'OK.' Her hands were shaking, it was all she could do to stop spilling her drink.

'Look around this room. There's all types. And, one way or another, they all fit into this crap you hear about the so-called London scene, where duchesses mix with dustmen, and they all go to the same clubs and parties, sharing their drugs and beds. But, when you get down to it, it's just a load of old bollocks.'

Angie was too preoccupied to even wince at, let alone be surprised by, David's foul-mouthed hostility.

'Sure they might meet, they might even have a dance, might even have a screw. But they all still know their place. This trendy, swinging scene, Angel, is as unfair and as unequal as the rest of the world. You can change the way you speak and dress, but the really posh ones, they know the difference. They might pretend they're your friend – to do business with you, or to lay you – but really they despise you. But knowing that means you can use it to your advantage. It's when you start believing the lies that you're in trouble.'

She was barely listening to him now, all she could focus on was that she had to say something. She had to.

'Take my Sonia.'

That had her listening again.

'She comes from Birmingham. Dudley.'

'What, your housekeeper?'

'Yeah. That's right.' He took a gulp of whisky. Nearly, you silly sod.

This was it. Her opportunity. 'Your friend, Salvo.'

'Yeah.'

'He said.' She paused, finding it hard to say the name. 'Sonia was your wife.'

David puffed out his cheeks, picked up a bottle of champagne from a side table and led Angie through to the main bedroom and out on to the balcony.

'So you really are divorced?' Angie was standing among the flower pots and troughs, holding on to the white-painted railing, staring unseeingly at the pretty Chelsea street down below.

'Yup. I really am.' He lit two cigarettes and handed her one.

Angie no longer held a cigarette as if she were an actress playing the part of a smoker, but did so automatically, drawing the smoke deep into her lungs.

'And it's all over. At last. But for a long time she just wouldn't give up hope. Kept thinking we had a chance to get back together. It was a bit pathetic. She'd turn up at the Mayfair gaff at all hours, fill the vases and that. Do what she could to try and make it all homely. Act like she was still my wife. She was a liar even to herself. Pitiful really.'

'That's sad. How did you finally persuade her?'

David took her by the shoulders, turned her to face him and kissed the tip of her nose. 'I told her all about you, Angel, and she knew she had no chance. Poor old Sonia's not very attractive, see.'

Angie remembered Salvo mentioning something about her looks, and how angry she would be about being mistaken for a housekeeper. She felt almost sorry for her. 'Is she all right?'

'I've looked after her as far as money's concerned, but she hated giving up all this. The parties and that. She loved all this. That's what was hardest for her, losing the people she'd thought were her friends. But, of course, they were here because of me, not her.'

Angie dropped her chin. 'Whatever must they think of me?'

'You? They think you're great. You act yourself. Natural. But you have to remember, in the end, they're just amusing themselves, mixing with the likes of us. They think going to the Krays' gaffs or the West Indian clubs is all one big laugh, and that when they've had their fun, or done their bit of business, they can go back to their *better* lives and leave the likes of me behind. But – and this is another lesson for you – the truth of the matter is, they are no different from anyone else. No one. They can set themselves up as being better, but I know the truth. In fact,' he raised his glass at the French doors, 'I know more about the people in that room than you'd credit. Kinky or crooked, or both, most of them.' He pointed to a man, familiar to Angie from the television news. 'Politician, right?'

Angie nodded.

'I went to a party over at his drum once. Coked out of his brain, he was.'

'Sorry?'

'Cocaine.'

'Oh.'

'Anyway, he had this one-way mirror where you could see him having it away with—'

'What? *See* him?'

'Yeah. See everything, you could. He was going with this young girl.'

'But he must be at least fifty.'

'Nearer sixty. And the kid was no more than what, fourteen, fifteen.'

'That's—'

'The way of the world. So don't you ever feel inferior to anyone. They probably act a lot worse than you ever would, and, if you knew the truth of it, with a lot less scruples than you would ever dream of, in all their so-called superior lives. Here, see that bloke just coming in?'

Angie turned round and found herself staring through the glass doors at a bronzed, muscle-bound actor, famed for his good works in his foundation for deprived children. Up until now, he had been no more to Angie than an heroic image on one of the posters given away with *My Guy* that had adorned her bedroom wall in Dagenham. Now she was practically in the same room with him.

As David, in a tone more suited to discussing whether it was getting a bit nippy for her out on the balcony, gave Angie details of the hunky actor's very particular private interests – involving being treated like a baby, with nappy-changing and regular feeding thrown in – her mouth gaped open like the entrance to the Blackwall Tunnel. She really did have a lot to learn about the world.

'Before I forget, Angel,' David added casually, draining the last of the champagne into her glass. 'A good friend of mine, Albert; he's going to be staying in the spare room here for a few days. He won't be no trouble.'

Vi reached under the table and squeezed Craig's thigh. God he was sexy. 'I've had a lovely time,' she purred at him. 'The hotel was lovely, and this restaurant is just beautiful.'

'I'm glad.'

And that Scottish accent! It made Vi's toes curl.

'I've been thinking about moving down south.'

'Have you?' Vi's mind started whirring. 'Any reason?'

'Most of my business is down here now, so why not?'

She considered her words carefully. 'How about your family? Won't you miss them?'

Craig clicked his tongue at her. 'Very subtle, Vi.'

'What d'you mean?'

'My wife, who I believe you are referring to, has decided that what she wants from life is a house in the country – somewhere full of children, dogs and home-cooking – and a husband who never leaves her side. I'm afraid it's not how I see myself.'

'So . . .'

'So she's found someone who does.'

'See himself in the country, with . . .'

'Exactly.'

'Well.' Vi fiddled with her wine glass. 'Fancy that.'

'And you know I enjoy your company.'

'Thank you, Craig,' she breathed, thrusting her bosom across the table at him. 'And I enjoy yours.' Where was all this leading?

'You're so uncomplicated.'

That didn't sound so good. 'Am I?'

'Yes. And I'd like to think we'll be spending more time together.'

This was better. 'So would I.'

'But—'

Definitely not good. 'There's a but?' There's always a but.

'I don't want you seeing anyone else.'

Vi lit up as if someone had put a shilling in her meter. 'Craig, you are so sweet.'

'Not really. I just don't fancy getting the clap. And if I'm going to be seeing more of you, I don't want to push my luck.'

Rather than being put out by such bluntness, Vi simply nodded. 'Right, fair enough, Craig. You're on. And there's no time like the present, as they say. So I'm going to let you order me a glass of brandy to have with my coffee, while I go to make a phone call.'

Rather than using the restaurant phone – she wasn't keen on being within earshot of Craig as she wasn't sure how the call was going to go – Vi dashed out of the restaurant and ducked into the greasy spoon along the road, which had a payphone hanging on the grimy, tiled wall by the serving hatch.

She dialled the number of the shop, knowing that Sam would be cashing up for the night, standing there in his overalls, hoping that she might pay him an unexpected evening visit to give him the only thrill he had to look forward to in life.

The phone began ringing.

This really couldn't have come at a better time. She

was past letting a bloke she didn't fancy have it away with her on a grotty sofa in a box-filled store-room, just for the sake of a steak dinner and a few gin and tonics. Even if he had been good to her.

God, what a terrible thought. She had been going with someone because he was *good to her*. Not because he was handsome, or exciting, or just because he was a bloody good lay like Craig. But because he was *good to her*. Christ, that made her feel old.

The connection was made. 'Hello. Sam Clarke here.'

'Sammy, it's me.' The sob Vi managed to catch in her voice, made her sound pitiful – overcome with emotion. 'I've got something to tell you.'

'Violet. My dear. Whatever is it?'

'Sam, it's . . . I . . . I don't think I can see you any more. My conscience won't let me.'

'But I've told you,' Sam sounded desperate, 'I'll leave her. You've only got to say the word and—'

'No. I can't do this to you, Sam. Or to Cissie. It's going to break my heart, but this is goodbye.'

With that, Vi slammed down the receiver, gave the grubby-looking man serving in the café a wink of thanks for the use of his phone – he had stumped up the sixpence when, surprise, she had not had the right change – and hurried back along the street to her coffee and brandy, thinking about what she and Craig could get up to in his big hotel bed by way of celebration.

No more than a few stairs up from the greasy spoon, Christina, the overripe tom, sat on her bed staring forlornly out of the window.

'Look at them,' she muttered spitefully, her dark lipstick bleeding into the spider-web cracks around her dry, thin lips. 'Bloody kids. No more than twenty years of age, most of them.'

She watched as they queued in the street below, in a long, winding snake, laughing and joking, waiting to get in to the Canvas Club.

Discothèques. What use were they to her? She blamed the likes of David Fuller. Why couldn't he stick to the businesses he had always been in? The snooker halls, the spielers, the strip shows, the clip joints, the all-day private drinking clubs. They made sense to Christina. They brought in decent trade, the genuine punters with a few quid to put in her direction, not kids rushing to spend every penny they had on pills and all that other crap they took.

Christina and her friend Marie had been talking about it all that very afternoon, after Christina had told her about what she saw happen outside the Canvas last night.

Marie had agreed with her, of course: it was a disgrace what was happening in Soho. The place was going downhill fast. And the working girls were losing money because of it. But then so were the likes of Dave Fuller, in the long run, because brasses like her and Christina wouldn't be able to find his bloody rent for him, would they? Then what would they all do? It didn't make sense to Marie. None of it.

As Christina remembered their increasingly agitated conversation, an idea slowly formed in her drink-sozzled brain. Maybe Dave Fuller could earn her a few bob after all. Maybe if she told someone other than Marie about what she had seen outside the Canvas . . .

Despite the warm evening, Christina pulled on her astrakhan swagger coat – she couldn't seem to get warm lately, it was as if her bones themselves were frozen – and tottered down the rickety stairway to the payphone in the greasy spoon downstairs.

'Mr Jameson,' she said, shielding the mouthpiece with her hand, 'it's gonna cost, mind, but I think I might have a bit of information that might interest you.'

Chapter 14

Doris Barker folded her arms as far as they would reach across her substantial shelf of a bosom, and moved back – just a little – to let the man into her flat.

'Not so quick,' she said to him, blocking the hallway. 'In the kitchen, if you don't mind. The front room's kept for best.'

The man did as he was told. He knew full well the other rooms in the flat would be full of knocked-off gear, but he wasn't interested in the old bat's fencing, not this morning he wasn't. He could pop round another day to sort all that out, or he might just file the thought away and fetch it out when he needed to. Storing useful information was, after all, a mainstay of Detective Constable Jameson's policing methods.

'And you are?' Jameson asked a middle-aged woman, who was sitting on a high stool at the breakfast bar, in the tidy, spotlessly clean kitchen. He knew very well who she was, but he liked to play his hand carefully.

'This is Mrs Pearson. My neighbour.' Doris waved at a chair, indicating he could sit at the little fold-down table.

'Pearson? That would be Sarah Pearson, would it?'

Doris and Sarah flashed a look at one another.

'That's right,' said Doris, speaking for her stunned-looking friend.

'I thought so.'

'At the door, you said you were based up the West End,' Doris went on.

'I am.'

'So what are you doing round here then? Wasting our Monday morning. You might not have anything better to do, young man, but me and Mrs Pearson have got washing and ironing to get done. Laundry don't do itself, you know.'

Jameson looked cynically at the two mugs of tea and the plate of biscuits that the women had obviously been enjoying before he arrived. 'I can see for myself how busy you are, ladies. We learn to sniff out those sorts of clues during basic training.'

Doris bristled. 'If you're going to get sarcastic . . .'

'My apologies, Mrs Barker.' His tone was as arrogant as his sneering expression. 'But I'm here to follow up a lead.'

Doris narrowed her eyes. 'Down from the West End? And by yourself? That's not very usual, is it? Not that I'd know very much about police comings and goings, of course.'

Jameson allowed himself the pleasure of a mocking smile. 'Let's call this a courtesy visit. I tell you a few things, and you – I hope – tell me a few.' He studied his fastidiously clean nails, before concluding smugly: 'That's fair, isn't it?'

Doris went over to the stove, looked over her shoulder at the police officer, and lifted up the kettle by way of a question. She didn't like this one little bit, but she had to keep steady. Not do or say anything silly.

'Thank you, Mrs Barker,' Jameson said very formally. 'Two and a half sugars, not too strong, and just a splash of milk. And I prefer a cup and saucer to a mug, if you don't mind.'

Usually, Doris would have laughed at such affectation,

especially in a so-called man, but today she didn't feel like laughing. This pale, insipid weasel with his watery, colourless eyes and his sparse, mousy hair was obviously a right nasty little bastard.

'So, like I was telling you, Sal' – as she set about making the tea, Doris addressed Sarah as if their conversation had never been interrupted, and certainly not by the arrival of a policeman – 'when I was down the market on Saturday, I said to Ginger Freddy: "I can't get through here," I said, "not between them stalls. That gap's far too narrow for the likes of me." And he said, "Well, turn sideways then, girl." And I said to him: "Darling, I ain't got no sideways."'

Despite her churning stomach, Sarah managed a fair imitation of tickled amusement.

'Anyway, all the stall-holders are laughing and cheye-eyeking. You should have heard them.' Doris spooned tea into the warmed pot. 'So I turned to Ginger Freddy and said, "But it's worth sticking with big girls like me, you know, Fred. We keep you warm in the winter, and throw out shade in the summer."'

The women laughed – an apparent vision of relaxed, self-assured pleasure.

Jameson didn't register so much as a smile.

'Now, Mr Jameson.' Doris handed him his tea in a delicate bone china cup. 'Seeing as you're not in uniform, I presume you really are a copper.'

'Mrs Barker, I showed you my warrant card.'

'I'm sure I wouldn't know what one looked like. So I'll just have to take your word for it that it was genuine.'

Jameson was growing bored with this innocent act. 'It's genuine.'

311

'Then perhaps you'll tell us why you're here.'

'Before I start' – he made a great show of sampling his tea, considering if it was to his liking, then dabbing the corners of his mouth on his very white handkerchief – 'I think you should know that I am fully aware of the blind eyes that are being turned on this estate.'

'Blind eyes, Mr Jameson?' Doris looked suitably puzzled.

'Regarding the, shall we say, *informal economic activities* being carried on.'

Doris hoiked herself up on a stool next to Sarah at the breakfast bar, leaving Jameson to look up at them from his much lower chair by the fold-down table. 'I haven't got a single idea what you're talking about. And I thought you said you was from the West End. Why should you care about the estate?'

'I make it my business to know what's going on in all kinds of places, Mrs Barker. Poplar included.'

'That's nice,' said Doris, catching Sarah's eye, silently urging her neighbour to keep calm. 'Makes you feel safe knowing the law's looking out for you.'

'And one of the things I know about this place is that there are plans to start pushing drugs round here. They're big plans. And for very bad drugs.'

'All drugs are bad,' said Doris through pursed lips. 'I don't even approve of drinking. Not after what it did to my Harry, God rest his soul. And, anyway, I can't see people round here putting up with drug-dealers.'

Sarah just listened, taking it all in.

'The drugs are coming, Mrs Barker. Believe me. The club and dance hall trade's at saturation point, so the pushers are looking for new markets and willing new customers. They start by selling it at cut-down prices to

312

your children and grandchildren, and before you know what's—'

'They won't be selling that rubbish to my grandchild,' Sarah broke in. It was the first time she had spoken.

'How can you be so sure, Mrs Pearson?'

'Because she's a good girl, that's how.'

'Is she? Are you sure?'

'I beg your pardon?'

'Don't you wonder what she's been up to lately? Where she's been? What her new boyfriend's like? How he's got so much—'

Sarah stood up. 'You,' she pointed at him, 'outside in the hall, if you don't mind. I want a private word. You will excuse us, won't you, Doris? No offence.'

'None taken, Sal. You go ahead. I'll wait in here.'

With that, Doris closed the kitchen door on them, topped up her mug of tea, selected a biscuit, and sat down to wait until Sarah had finished.

She admired Sarah Pearson, just as she admired many women on the estate. They hadn't had easy lives, most of them, but they had done what they needed to do, in order to get by, and they would do whatever was in their power to protect the ones they loved. Even if it meant someone as quiet as Sarah Pearson standing up to a snotty-nosed copper like DC Jameson.

She took her cigarettes from her apron pocket and lit one. Not that any of poor Sal's efforts had served any purpose as far as her tart of a daughter Violet was concerned. Still, she'd have more luck with Angie, she was a good kid. A nice kid. Sensible too.

It was almost noon, and Angie, having struggled with the idea of forcing down a late breakfast, abandoned the toast

313

she had made to the bin and was making do with a pot of weak tea and a cigarette; the sight of the butter melting and dripping off the grilled bread had made her feel physically ill.

Angie was no stranger to hangovers, in fact, she had had more than her share of them lately, but having one on a Monday morning seemed worse somehow. It made her feel guilty. It was such a shabby way to start the week. She also felt stupid, as she genuinely hadn't realized just how much booze she had actually swallowed.

They had only intended to pop out for a couple of hours, going round to visit half a dozen or so clubs owned by friends of David's, who all seemed to owe him money. But while David was collecting what was due to him, they had all insisted on pressing drinks on her. The club owners probably wanted to repay David's generosity, as she noted that he was allowing them to pay by instalments, as he promised every one of them that he would be back the same time next week for their next payment. When she saw David so clearly approving of the welcome they were extending to her, she hadn't liked to refuse, and they had wound up staying at each of the clubs far longer than David had originally intended.

The drinks had just slipped down so easily.

But it wasn't only the hangover, or the feeling of guilt, or even her own stupidity, that was putting her off eating anything, it was the table, no, the whole kitchen. It looked, and smelled, disgusting.

When they'd pulled up outside the flat last night, David had told her that his friend Albert had moved in earlier that evening, while they were out, but, by then, it was so late, and David was so keen to get her to bed – he'd been turned on by the way the club owners had all so obviously fancied her, he'd said – plus she had had so much to drink, she hadn't noticed the mess. But she noticed now all right. It was a complete tip. And he'd only been in the flat for a few hours.

She knotted the belt of her turquoise towelling bathrobe, lit another cigarette, stuck her elbows on the table and buried her face in her hands. Maybe she should go back to bed for a couple of hours. Then she would feel all fresh and be able to sort out the place before David came home.

She was just wavering between whether she should close her eyes for five minutes at the table, or actually try to find the energy to haul herself back to her bed, when she heard the spare bedroom door being swung back violently on its hinges, then whacking against the wall with a hangover-amplified crash.

Angie's head snapped up from her hands and she staggered out into the hallway to find out what was going on. She was confronted by a heavily made-up woman with a dated, platinum-blonde beehive and a far too youthful minidress hopping out of the spare room, pulling on her shoe.

'You weird fucker,' she was hollering at a man, who was standing in the bedroom doorway in baggy, off-white underpants, grinning broadly at her. 'You're fucking sick in the head. Do you know that? Sick.'

'And I thought you loved me,' he said amiably.

'Get stuffed.'

'That'd be nice. Maybe you'd be prepared to oblige me again in that department, darling. How about tonight?'

'I wouldn't come back here tonight for all the tea in fucking China.' The woman, suddenly noticing Angie, shot her a sympathetic glance and strode off down the hallway. 'Rather you than me, sweetheart,' Angie heard her call as she let herself out of the flat.

'I hope you don't kiss no one with that filthy mouth of your'n,' he shouted after her, then turned his attentions to Angie. He leaned against the door jamb, and rubbed distractedly at his crotch, as he slowly assessed her.

'Beautiful,' he said, levering himself towards her. 'Just my type and all. Mind you, there ain't many that ain't my type. Albert's the name.'

Angie nodded abruptly, backing away from him and into the kitchen. He might have been good-looking, in a swarthy, gypsyish sort of way, but he had the manners of a pig. Touching himself like that. It was revolting. David couldn't know he'd be so horrible, or he'd never have let him stay. She'd have to phone the office. Get rid of him.

She was about to pick up the red wall phone by the Fridgedair, when she heard Albert come into the kitchen. She turned to face him. Why hadn't she gone back into her bedroom? She could have locked the door while she phoned.

He was so close she could smell him. He reeked of staleness and must, and something she didn't even want to try to identify. It made her want to choke.

'How about a little kiss? Just to be social. To welcome me to your lovely home.'

'Your girlfriend wouldn't be very impressed,' Angie said to the floor – anything to avoid looking at him playing with himself.

'Girlfriend?' He didn't understand. Then he laughed. 'She was a brass, darling. Girlfriends have to be better-looking than that old what's-it. Girls like you, now you're girlfriend material. A man could have dreams about having the likes of you.'

Slowly, Angie raised her eyes, and stared at him. 'Don't even think about it,' she said through gritted teeth. 'Or I'll tell David.'

Albert let go of his genitals and raised his hands in mock surrender. 'Only having a laugh, darling. What can you expect when a man's been away for an eight stretch?'

Angie pushed past him and ran into the bathroom.

She opened all the taps and flushed the lavatory, praying that he couldn't hear her vomiting over all the noise, and that he wouldn't realize just how much he terrified her.

Martin sat in the college refectory, staring blindly over Jill Walker's expensively clad shoulder into the middle distance. He felt as if he had been pole-axed.

Jill was holding his hand across the Formica table, beaming at him like an evangelist intent on sharing her vision of the light and the one true path.

Whatever else Martin had expected this morning, it certainly wasn't this. He had come along to college to see his personal tutor, to hand in his final piece of work before the long vacation, and to put up with the embarrassing rollicking he actually knew he deserved for being so late with the essay. But, as humiliating as that had been – he had felt like a naughty schoolboy – it was nothing compared to this bombshell.

'It'll be fine, Martin. Truly. You can still finish your degree. Mummy and Daddy have promised to help. And', she squeezed his hand, 'guess what? Daddy says there's a place for you in the partnership.' She laughed happily. 'Not as a partner, of course. Well, not yet. But sons-in-law do get special treatment in the City, especially when their father-in-law is the senior partner

317

in the firm. And there's this sweet little cottage in the village . . .'

This was going too fast for Martin. A job all set up for him in an accountancy firm? He'd only just finished his bloody first year at university. Say he wanted to travel the world? Be a pop star? Screw as many girls as he could get his leg over? Just be a drunken twenty-year-old in the student union bar? Be the sort of person who had opportunities in life, not someone chained to a bloody drudge-filled life, day in, day out, for the rest of his natural. Visions of his parents, and their silent evenings in front of the telly, swam before his eyes. He didn't want this.

'When did you find out?' He sounded as if he had a mouth full of wadding.

'I suppose I've known for a couple of weeks. I'm never late.'

'Have you been to a doctor?'

She nodded. 'Mummy took me to her gynaecologist. He said I'm nearly three months.' She touched Martin lovingly on the cheek. 'I can't believe you didn't realize, when I kept being sick in the mornings.'

Sick? Martin was the one who felt sick. 'But how did it happen?'

Jill dipped her chin and smiled coyly. 'I thought I was meant to be the virgin, Martin.'

Martin screwed his eyes shut and pressed his lips hard together; he hadn't cried since Elvis, his tortoise, had gone missing when he was ten years old.

'You know what I mean,' he managed to say. 'Why didn't you take precautions?'

Jill stiffened. 'How was I meant to go to the doctor or the family planning clinic? I haven't even got an

318

engagement ring to show them, never mind a marriage certificate. And if you were so bothered, couldn't you have used something?'

Martin rubbed his hands over his face. 'I don't know what to say.'

'You don't have to say anything. I'll sort it all out and it'll be fine. I promise. I'm so happy, Martin, please, don't spoil it by worrying.'

He said nothing.

She took his hand again. 'You're happy too, aren't you?'

He pulled away from her and stood up. 'Bloody delirious,' he said, and strode away.

Jill sighed contentedly. 'Don't worry, baby,' she cooed, gently stroking her middle. 'Daddy's just in shock. Everything's going to be wonderful. And you are going to be the happiest, prettiest little baby in the whole, wide world.'

As Angie waited for Bobby to open the back door of the Jaguar to let her out, she leaned across the front seat and whispered to David, 'I don't know how you didn't get my messages. I left them for you all over the place.'

David spoke to her reflection in the rear-view mirror. 'Angel, you know I've been busy all day.' He turned and flashed her a blistering smile. 'That's why we're going to the Canvas, to have a few hours' break away from it all.'

When he had turned up at the flat thirty minutes ago and had told her to hurry up and get ready to go out, Angie had almost wanted to protest that she would much prefer staying in with a cup of tea and the telly, and a nice cuddle on the sofa. She was so exhausted. But at the sight of Albert dragging his disgusting carcass from the spare room to the kitchen, she was grateful for the chance to get away for a few hours. And for the chance to tell David how horrible Albert was. But when they had gone downstairs to the car, Bobby had been sitting in the driver's seat, and, knowing David's obsession with privacy, she'd thought it better to wait until they were alone to discuss her unpleasant flatmate and his even more unpleasant suggestions. So, now they were in the Canvas Club and Bobby had disappeared into the office, she had her chance.

'David. I need to talk to you about Albert.'

'Yeah, hang on, Angel.' David nodded at Rick, the head barman, for him to fetch them a couple of bar stools. 'Let's get some drinks in first. Relax and have a good time.'

'Right, but this Albert. He's really—'

'Dave, sorry to interrupt.' It was Bobby, he had appeared at David's elbow. 'Jeff said Half-a-lung thinks he's got a lead on Lukey Gold.'

David stood up and began walking to the exit, with Bobby close behind. 'Look after Angel, Rick,' he said. 'Be back later.'

'Certainly, boss.' The chief barman smiled at Angie. 'Busy man, David Fuller. Now, what can I get you?'

'Rick?' Angie mumbled. She had been sitting at the bar for almost two hours, waiting for David to return, and had managed to get through almost a whole packet of cigarettes and was already on to her second bottle of champagne. She beckoned floppily at him, trying to focus through red-rimmed eyes. 'Over here.'

320

Rick gestured for one of the other barmen to take over serving his customers.

'Yes, darling?' Christ almighty. The boss had told him to look after her and she'd gone and got pissed. What idiot had let her drink this much?

Before he could find the culprit amongst his stupid, unthinking morons of bar staff, Angie had reached across the bar and was flicking him – very annoyingly – under the chin. 'Do you want to have sex with me?'

'What?'

'Albert does.' She smiled in what she thought was a provocative, sex-kittenish sort of way, but which actually made her look as if she had toothache.

'Right.'

'He's staying with me. At the flat. Horrible.' She folded her arms on the bar and rested her head on them. 'Do I look sexy?' she mumbled into her sleeve. 'Like a tart? Like my mum?'

Shit. What was the answer to that little lot? 'Course not,' he ventured. He'd have to get some water down her. 'Here. Drink this. You must be really thirsty.'

She lifted her head. 'Thanks. You looked after me before. Remember? David told you I was a princess. Am I a princess, Rick? Am I your own, special princess?'

'Yeah. That's right. Finish your water, eh, Angel?'

She sipped at the pint glass. 'Rick. What's an eight stretch?'

Blimey, she really was well and truly rat-arsed. 'It's when someone gets sent down. For eight years.'

'Prison?'

'That's right.'

'I thought it was something like that. That's what

321

Albert said. Eight stretch.' She rubbed her forehead. 'My head aches.'

'I'll get you something.' Rick searched around under the bar until he found a brown pill bottle. 'Try a couple of these,' he said shaking two white tablets into the palm of his hand.

When Angie eventually focused on what he was offering her, she threw up her hands in disgust, knocking her water all over her lap. 'I don't use that junk,' she slurred.

Rick sighed wearily. 'They're aspirins.'

She shook her head, and wished she hadn't. 'Just more water. Please.'

She swallowed two glasses straight down. 'You got a phone, Rick?'

'You're not calling Dave, are you?'

'No.'

'Sure?'

'Mmmm.'

Rick brought out the phone from under the counter.

'Can't see. Too dark in here. Can you dial?'

At least he'd know if she was calling the boss, and could pretend he couldn't get through.

'Sure.'

'Dominion 5483.'

A Dagenham number. Definitely not Dave.

'There you are. It's ringing.'

'Jack? It's me.'

'Who?'

'Angel. Angie. Angela Sarah Patricia Knight.'

'What's up with you, Angie? Have you been drinking again?'

'Why're you whispering?' Suddenly, she sat up very

straight. 'You don't want to talk to me, do you. You don't want to be my best friend any more.'

'Angie, I'm whispering because it's half past eleven. I've only just got in. And the phone started ringing as I was creeping up to bed. Do you want me to get in trouble with Mum?'

'Sorry.' Her shoulders slumped again. 'Ever so sorry. You still my friend?'

'You're drunk, aren't you?'

'No.'

'Well, you sound it.'

'It's the Canvas. It's noisy.'

'Right.'

'Jack. Will you come to see me tomorrow?'

'I can't. I've got to go to work.'

Angie started snivelling. 'You've got to, Jack. I don't want to be by myself.'

'Are you in trouble?'

'There's a horrible man.'

'Someone's bothering you?'

'No. It's nothing. Jack?'

'What?'

'Please. Come over.'

'I've got to go. I can hear Mum. I'll try and get over tomorrow morning some time.'

With Angie safely out of his way – draped across the back seat of a cab on her way back to Flood Street – Rick set about dialling some phone numbers of his own. He eventually tracked down his boss in a cubicle-sized office at the Starlight Rooms, a coyly romantic name for what was considered, even by Soho standards, to be far and away one of David Fuller's more squalid clubs.

'This had better be important, Rick.'

David, in his search for Half-a-lung Cassidy and his lead on Lukey Gold's whereabouts, had been side-tracked at the Starlight, where interviews for potential 'performers' were being conducted. He wasn't carrying out the interviews personally – he was too mindful of his health and far too fussy about matters of hygiene for that – but he had been watching the selection process, which consisted of two young women being put through their paces by four of his less fussy employees, most appreciatively.

Until Rick had called.

'It's Angel, boss.'

'What about her?'

'I'm not saying you can't trust the girl, Dave, but Albert seems to have been a bit indiscreet. Mentioning his form and that. I think she was a bit freaked by it all.' He considered mentioning how pissed she was, but was worried Dave would think it was his fault. 'Thought you'd want to know. Sorry again about interrupting you.'

'Don't worry. You did well. I'll arrange something. And Rick.'

'Yeah?' *Please don't ask how drunk I let your stupid little whore of a bird get tonight.*

'I like it when my staff use their brains. I'll make sure there's a nice drink in this for you.'

'Thanks, Dave.' Rick closed his eyes, gave silent thanks, and put down the phone.

When Angie woke up the next morning, David had already left.

She groaned pathetically, closed her eyes tight and covered them with her hands, trying to block out the shaft of sunlight that had found its way through the bedroom blinds. Her head was pounding.

She had a vague recollection of being in bed with David the night before, but it slipped out of her reach as she tried to focus it more clearly. And she remembered something about her annoying him, when she had wanted to talk about . . . Something or other. And all he had wanted to do was . . .

What had she wanted to talk about?

As she slowly gathered together the slippery strands of her wayward thoughts, she groaned again.

She'd wanted to talk to him about Albert. That was it. Getting rid of Albert. But all David had wanted to do was tell her about what he'd seen two girls doing at some club, and how he really fancied the idea of her . . .

She flushed scarlet at the memory of his words, and rolled over into the pillow with a wail of self-pity.

How had she let herself get in this state again? She couldn't even remember what she and David had wound up actually doing.

Was she turning into a tart? Was she just like her mum?

The sound of the doorbell blasted through those distressing thoughts. All she could hope was that Albert hadn't invited anyone over.

Invited?

She sat bolt upright and stared at the bedside clock. Half past eleven. She had invited Jackie to the flat. And she hadn't even had a wash.

'Jackie. You didn't have to do all this.' Angie, showered and freshly made-up, looked round the neat and tidy kitchen.

'I know I didn't, but what are friends for? And you didn't look fit enough to lift a dishcloth, let alone clear up this lot.' She held up two carrier bags. 'Do you know how many empty bottles and fag ends are in here?'

Angie gingerly took the bags from her and, holding them at arm's length, stowed them out of sight behind the door. 'I don't want to even guess.' She smiled weakly and checked the kettle for water. 'I'll make us some coffee, and then I'll show you the rest of the flat.'

'Lovely.'

'You're not kidding,' said a gruff male voice.

Jackie looked round to see a dishevelled-looking man, wearing nothing but a pair of dingy, greying underpants. He fiddled uninhibitedly with himself as he leered at them from the kitchen doorway.

'Two of you today. This is getting better and better. My own private harem. David Fuller is a very generous feller.' He laughed coarsely. 'Just going to the bog. But don't worry, I won't be long, girls.'

'Explain the mess?' Angie asked, getting on with making the coffee to stop herself from screaming.

'Who the bloody hell's that?'

'Sort of friend of David's.'

'Right.'

Loud, unpleasant noises started coming from the bathroom.

Angie handed Jackie a mug. 'I'll just get my fags.'

While Angie was in the bedroom looking for her cigarettes, she heard the kitchen phone ringing. Before she could get back to stop her, Jackie had answered it.

Angie hadn't mentioned to David that Jackie was coming over and – she didn't know why – she thought he wouldn't be very happy about having guests he didn't know about. And especially not with Albert there.

Jackie had her hand over the receiver, and was trying not to laugh. 'Some nutcase says he wants to talk to,' she went cross-eyed and pulled what she thought was a scary, loony-scientist face, and said in a horror film, cod-German accent, '*Mad Albert.*'

'Put it down,' hissed Angie. 'Now!'

Jackie's smile disappeared and she dropped the phone as if it were on fire.

'Let's go into the other room and drink our coffee, eh?'

Jackie followed her through to the sitting-room, and Angie shut the door and turned on the radio to drown out the sounds from the bathroom.

The Rolling Stones were singing 'Play With Fire'.

'Angie?' Jackie was speaking to her friend but she was looking anxiously at the door, as if it might burst open at any moment.

'What?'

'That bloke in the bathroom. His name's Albert, isn't it?'

Angie nodded.

'And that phone call wasn't a joke. That's Mad Albert Roper. It's been all over the papers.'

'Don't be silly, Jack.' Angie's hands shook as she lit a cigarette. 'I'm glad you came over. Do you like the flat?'

'Angie!'

Angie started crying. 'Jack, I want to come and stay with you. Just for a while. Just till he goes.'

Jackie put her arm round Angie's shoulders. 'How about your mum?'

'I can't go back there.'

'No. I mean it'd be awkward. Her being just a few doors away.'

'It'd be fine.' Angie's voice cracked. She was sounding desperate. 'With the hours she keeps, she'd never see me. Never even know I was there.'

'How about your nan's?'

'She wouldn't understand about me and David. She's old.'

Jackie wanted to say that *she* wasn't old, but she didn't understand either. Why would Angie put up with a bloke, no matter how much money he had, who expected her to stay in a flat with a nutter like Albert Roper?

'And I don't want to upset her.' She puffed on her cigarette. 'Honestly, Jack, it won't be for long. As soon as David knows how he's been behaving, he'll get rid of him.'

Jackie stared into her coffee. How would anyone *expect* a bloke called Mad Albert to act? 'I'm sorry, Ange. You can't. Mum's heard some things. Off Pauline Thompson.'

'What things?'

'You know what she's like.'

'No. Tell me.'

'Look, Ange, Mum's already said it might be better if we don't see each other for a while.'

'So what are you doing here?'

'She thinks I'm at work. But I pulled your old trick and told my supervisor I had a bilious attack.' She paused. 'Sorry.'

Angie rubbed away her tears with the back of her hand. 'That's all right,' she said a bit too brightly. 'Tell you what, let's go out. Let's go shopping.'

'I think going out is a very good idea,' Jackie said as they heard the sound of the lavatory flushing. 'But it'll have to be window shopping. I'm skint till the end of the month.'

'Don't worry about money, Jack. I've got plenty. David's really generous.'

They were standing outside Sloane Square station, without a single carrier bag or shoe box between them. No matter how hard Angie had tried to persuade her otherwise, Jackie had turned down all her attempts to buy anything. Angie had guessed, rightly, that she didn't want to explain to her mum how she could afford to buy stuff this close to pay day. But she hadn't mentioned it. She hadn't wanted to start a row, hadn't wanted Jackie to get angry and go off and leave her. But now she was insisting it was time to go anyway.

'Sure you don't want to go to the Canvas later? Rick, you remember him, the chief barman, he's a really nice bloke. And he really likes me. We'd get VIP treatment all night.'

'I told you, Ange. I can't. I'm due in from work at six. And it's gone four already.'

'Let's go and get some coffee. You won't be late. I'll pay for a cab for you.'

'No. It's all right. I've got my season ticket.' Jackie nibbled at her lip. 'I really have got to be going.'

'Course.' Angie managed a weak smile. 'And give my love to Marilyn, eh?'

'Yeah. I will. She misses you.' Jackie pecked her on the cheek. 'And so do I.'

Angie stood by the tube station for nearly an hour, watching the commuters buying magazines and the early evening papers for their journeys home. Their journeys

329

back to nice ordinary, boring, homes like the Murrays'. Homes that didn't have a resident madman in them. She couldn't stand the idea of going back to the flat, not with that pig still there. She'd have to tell David about him. Tell him how he'd acted, and the things he'd said. Her head still ached and she felt so tired. But she had to do something.

She gathered up the last of her energy and dragged herself into the phone box outside the theatre just along the street and called the office in Greek Street.

'Bobby, it's me, Angel. I need to speak to David.'

'He's busy.'

'But I—'

'Look. I said, he's busy.'

'But it's serious. There's something bothering me. I've got to talk to him.'

'He can't come to the phone.'

'What time will he be finished?'

'How do I know?'

'It's nearly five o'clock now. Can't you ask him?'

'Not really.'

'OK, I'll come round to the office then,' she said, but Bobby didn't hear her. He had already put down the phone.

'So, Lukey. We've caught up with you at last.'

Lukey Gold, who now owed David Fuller a lot of money, was unable to speak because of the filthy rag that Bobby had rammed into his mouth, and unable to move because of the leather straps that Bobby had used to bind him to the chair. All he could do was stare, wild-eyed, at the long, slim blade that David was heating up in the gas fire.

David tutted and smiled pleasantly. 'But I know what a rascal you are, Lukey. And I just know you're gonna say you ain't got the money. The money you owe me.' He moved closer to the chair. 'But I ain't a fucking bank. And I don't like being mugged off. Got it?'

Despite the gag, Lukey managed to let out quite a scream as David touched the white hot blade to his throat.

David grinned. 'Now, now, Lukey. Just think yourself lucky Mad Albert's otherwise disposed.'

'I'm telling you, Bill, he knows I'm coming. I phoned and spoke to Bobby. Less than twenty minutes ago.' Angie was standing at the top of the stairs, in the shabby hallway outside the outer office at Greek Street, totally frustrated in her attempts to get in to see David.

'George,' she pleaded, standing on tiptoes and peering over Bill's shoulder. 'You'll let me go through, won't you?'

'Look, darling. We're working ten phones between us in here. And if we don't do it right, we're going to have some very unhappy punters. Now, do as Bill says and go home. I'll give Dave a message for you later.'

'Can't you tell him I'm here?'

Bill rolled his eyes. 'For Christ sake, George, stick a note under Dave's door. Anything to stop her giving me this flaming earache.'

'I'm trying to settle bets here, Bill.'

'George.'

Within seconds of George doing as he was told, the door to the inner office opened, and Bobby appeared.

Angie's smile of relief was short-lived. It was now Bobby who was determined to bar her way.

'Dave's busy.'

'Tell him I'll meet him.'

'Yeah.'

'At the Canvas.'

'No. He's gonna be a while. He said you was to get back to the flat.'

'But I can't. It's Albert.'

'He's gone.'

'But—'

'This afternoon.'

'But how do you know—'

Angie shut up abruptly as she was sure she heard a cry, or a scream, coming from the inner office.

'David?' she called, trying to push her way past Bobby and into the office.

But he wouldn't move. 'Leave. Now.'

As another scream, and it was definitely a scream, tore the air, Bobby slammed the door in Angie's face.

She turned and ran down the stairs and out into the street as fast as her kitten heels would let her.

Chapter 15

David stood in front of the wardrobe mirror adjusting his tie, and watching Angie's reflection as she sat up in bed smoking.

'You don't look very happy, Angel.'

'I want to ask you something.'

'This is about Albert.' David turned round and held out his hands in supplication. 'It was all a misunderstanding. I didn't know he'd upset you. If I had, I'd never have let him stay here. Soon as I realized, I moved him out.' He lied easily.

Angie dropped her chin. 'I heard something yesterday. At the office.'

'How d'you mean?'

'In Greek Street. It sounded like someone being hurt.'

David frowned as if trying to work out what she could possibly be talking about. Then, slowly, he smiled. 'That must have been Bobby.'

'No. Bobby shut me out of the office. There was nothing wrong with him.'

'Daft. I don't mean Bobby was hollering. I mean it was his fault. It was the telly. He kept it on after we'd finished watching the racing results. He's like a little kid, that feller. Loves his telly. It was some old gangster film or other. Edward G., George Raft. You know.'

'Humphrey Bogart?' she said flatly.

'Yeah, that's right, Angel. Humphrey Bogart.' He kneeled down on the bed, pulled her to him and kissed her.

'I don't have to go to the office right away, now do I?' he said, throwing his jacket on the floor, ripping off his tie, and then pushing Angie back on to the pillows. 'I am the boss, after all.'

A few hours later, Sonia was standing in the outer office in Greek Street, surprised to hear David's voice coming from the other side of the door – surprised because there had been no sign of his car outside – but totally dumbfounded when she heard what he was actually saying. She couldn't believe he was telling all these things to a moron like Bobby Sykes.

Still it was no skin off her nose if he was being so reckless. He could rot in hell for all she cared. And all his disgusting thugs along with him.

Growing bored with David's talk about Lukey Gold, Albert Roper, and the market for tabs of LSD, Sonia stared down at her nails. She really had to get a manicure, her hands were looking as if they belonged to a washerwoman.

But suddenly she lost all interest in her beauty regime. Did she really hear him say that?

She pressed her ear flat to the door that connected the inner and outer offices, oblivious to the rough, splintered paint.

'And according to Jeff, when he came to do his check on the premises – this was in the early hours of this morning, mind, Dave – the copper was hanging around here again. It must have been him who pulled out all that stuff on Mad Albert. Good job we got him out of the way again.'

David wasn't usually one to show if anything was getting to him, he knew it made you vulnerable, but

Bobby distinctly saw him flinch. He was getting through to him at last, making him take this seriously.

'The same copper who turned up at Bill and George's places yesterday afternoon. Jameson. He's a young DC. Right nosy bastard.'

David's chest was rising and falling with the effort of keeping his temper. Bobby who hardly ever opened his trap was going on like some bloody old woman. He'd give him two more minutes . . .

'It was all right when Marshall was still about.' Bobby was desperate to get him to see sense. 'He looked out for you. But now he's gone, this little berk's off the lead. Thinks he's the flipping Masked Avenger or someone. Asking all sorts of questions, he is. George's wife went potty, him going through their house. Nosing at everything. She was on the blower to my Maureen leading off alarming that he'd spoiled her Sunday dinner he was there that long.'

Despite it being only midday, David reached for the whisky bottle and two glasses that he kept on top of the tatty filing cabinet in the corner of the office. He poured two large measures.

'I don't want to talk out of hand, Dave, but why didn't you contract it out? There would have been no link between you then. No trail. Nothing. Why the amateur bit?'

'Bob, you've been my mate since we was at school together. So don't make me lose my temper with you, eh?' David threw the whole measure of Scotch down his throat and then refilled his glass to the brim. 'I killed the little fucker because he pushed me too far. Got it?'

Sonia's eyebrows shot up. That was why he had his car tucked away out of sight. He was lying low. He'd done a

335

sodding murder, and the police were on to him.

She walked over to the grotty partner's desk where Bill and George did whatever it was they did in the outer office, and picked up one of the bank of telephones. She could only hear the low drone of conversation now from the other side of the door, but she had heard more than enough for her purposes.

When Sonia had finished on the telephone, she took her mirror from her handbag, checked her lipstick and hair, then stood up, smoothed the creases from her skirt, lifted her chin, and marched boldly into David's office.

'What the fuck are you doing here?'

David's shocked expression gladdened Sonia's heart. 'Really, David, your mouth is exactly like a sewer. And drinking whisky at this time of day.' She shook her head disapprovingly. 'If you're not careful you'll end up—'

'Cut the shit, Sonia. What do you want?'

'I was looking for Mikey, but when I heard what you two had to say for yourselves, it was far more interesting standing out there listening.'

David leaped to his feet. 'Bob, where's Bill and George?'

Sonia perched on the edge of the table that served as her husband's desk. 'I mentioned – in jest you understand – that there was a police car downstairs, and they should get lost if they knew what was good for them.' She smiled coldly. 'It seemed to work. They shot down that fire escape—'

'Sonia, don't start winding me up. Just spit out what you've got to say.'

'I heard it all, David. Everything. And I thought I'd let you know that I've called the police and passed it all on.'

David sneered. 'Yeah, course you did. I can see how heartbroken you are.'

'Why should I be heartbroken? It's you that's in trouble, darling.'

Bobby was getting worried. This could all go very wrong.

'Sonia, why don't you piss off?'

'What? And miss all the fun?'

'If listening to us talking business is fun, then stay. If not, go and find yourself another bloke. Another little toe-rag like that ponce, Mikey. If one exists. And when you do, I'll have him as well.'

Bobby ran his hand over his bald head. 'Dave, she's probably bluffing about what she heard.'

Sonia twisted round to Bobby. 'Shut up you.' Then back to David. 'You'll *have* him?'

David laughed. 'Yeah. I'll have him all right.'

'Mikey.' She lunged at David's face with her nails. 'You've killed Mikey.'

He swatted her away. 'For Christ sake, woman.'

Completely thrown off balance, Sonia somehow managed to launch herself forward, and began pummelling David's chest with her fists. 'I loved him, you animal.' Tears were spilling down her no-longer immaculately made-up face. 'Really loved him.'

David for a fleeting moment actually looked concerned. 'Don't carry on.'

'I have grassed you.' She was shrieking, out of control. 'I told them all about David Fuller and his respectable business interests.'

'Don't be stupid, Son.'

'They'll be here soon. Then you'll see who's stupid.'

David grabbed her by the wrists, and held her still,

trying to work out what to do next. If she was telling the truth, where would he be most exposed?

'Bob, call Angel, tell her to disappear, in case they turn up at the flat.'

As Bobby dialled Flood Street, Sonia writhed around in David's grasp, frantically trying to break away from him, but he was too strong, he held on to her as if she was no more than a bothersome child.

'No reply, Dave.'

'Sonia, you are beginning to annoy me.' He let go of one of her wrists and smacked her, hard, around the side of her head. 'Will you just keep fucking still?'

Sonia felt as if she had been hit by a train. Her head lolled back, her ears rang and her eyes rolled.

Bobby stepped forward, this was all they needed, him losing it and doing her in as well.

'Dave, sit down and finish your drink, mate. Let me take her.'

David handed her over like an unwanted parcel.

Still stunned from the blow and wanting only for the pain in her head to stop, Sonia had no choice but to let Bobby sit her down on a chair by the filing cabinet.

'Don't worry, Dave. You're too careful. There's nothing around here that can tell them anything.'

'Depends what this silly whore's told them.' David took another gulp of Scotch, all the while staring at Sonia slumped in the corner. 'Better check Jeff didn't leave any pills around over the weekend.'

'He knows the place has to be cleaned up after Saturday nights.'

'Bob. Just do it, will you? Just phone him.'

Bobby was about to do as he was told, when they heard the door to the outer office opening. Both men's heads jerked up as if obeying the instructions of a starting pistol.

'Fuck it. Sonia must have left it open. I'm gonna kill her.'

Bobby, with surprising agility for his size, sprang across the room and grabbed David by the arm.

What neither of the men expected to see next was Angie, in a bright red trouser suit, walking in from the outer office, with a broad smile on her face, a basket over one arm, and a tartan travelling rug over the other, looking for all the world like a sexy Red Riding Hood about to go down to the woods.

She stood in the doorway, the threshold between the two offices.

'I'm sorry if I'm interrupting you, David, but,' she held up the basket and the rug, 'I know I was a bit silly this morning. I thought I could make it up to you. And to thank you for moving Albert. We could go into Soho Square for a picnic. I've got all sorts of nice stuff.'

Sonia, her fury at this latest development somehow giving her the strength to rise from the chair, staggered unsteadily to her feet.

Leaning against the filing cabinet, she pointed accusingly at Angie. 'You've got all sorts of nice stuff have you, sweetheart? How very touching.'

Angie blinked disbelievingly at the tear- and make-up-streaked face of the woman who was spitting such venom at her. Who was she? Why was she so familiar?

'Sonia. Shut your mouth.' David's voice was low, angry. If Bobby hadn't still been holding him back he'd have shut it for her.

Now Angie was really confused. *Sonia*? But they were divorced. Why should she care? And she had expected someone older. Much older.

Sonia moved slowly towards her. 'Does she know that I know all about her, David? And about all your other women? And do they know about her? Do you' – she jabbed Angie in the chest – 'know I'm David's wife?'

'David's divorced.'

'Is he now?' She stuck out her left hand, flashing a massive platinum and diamond ring. 'That's news to me.'

'I said, shut it!' David finally erupted. Shoving Bobby out of his way, he threw himself at Sonia, sending her crashing back into the heavy wooden filing cabinet.

Angie stared at Sonia crumpled to the floor, with blood pouring from her mouth and one of her ears. 'A boyfriend didn't buy me my watch,' she whispered.

David touched Sonia with the toe of his shoe. She didn't move.

'My nan did. For my birthday.'

David turned to Angie as if he had never set eyes on her before. 'What?'

'You're my first boyfriend, David. I didn't know you were married when I slept with you. Then you said you were divorced. You are divorced, aren't you?'

'Bob, get her out of here. Stick her in a cab or something.'

Bobby took Angie, too dazed to resist, by the arm, and began steering her towards the door, but the sound of police sirens and tyres screeching to a halt in the street below, stopped him in his tracks.

'Shit, she really did call the law. Come on, Dave, move yourself.' Bobby looked about him for inspiration. 'Through the back and along the alley. We can get to the motors that way.'

David said nothing, he just gave Sonia a departing, vicious kick in the side, and followed Bobby, as he dragged Angie, now sobbing pitifully, through to the fire escape.

David jumped into his Jaguar and sped off, without a glance or a word in Angie's direction. Bobby pushed her, sprawling, into the back seat of his Humber, and, after a squealing U-turn, drove off in the opposite direction to his boss.

As soon as she stopped carrying on and drawing attention to herself, he would get rid of the kid, drop her off somewhere – anywhere – then get himself home and make sure Maureen was all right.

It was almost three o'clock in the afternoon before Bobby finally thought it was safe to let Angie out of his car. He had been driving round for two and a half bloody hours since they'd bolted down the fire escape, when all he wanted to do was get home to check on Maureen. But he couldn't have risked letting an hysterical bird loose on the streets.

He could only hope that no one had got hold of Dave.

'Honestly, Bobby.' Angie was doing her best to appear calm, unperturbed by what she had seen. What she had seen the man she had thought she was in love with do to a woman. To his wife.

'I'm fine. Please. Leave me here.'

'Where'll you go?'

'My nan's. She only lives—' She could have bitten off her tongue. '—nearby.'

Bobby had to hand it to her, she was looking out for herself better than he would have credited. 'Don't worry, I ain't gonna follow you. I've got plans of me own.' He pulled into the kerb. 'Need any money?'

Angie shook her head, but Bobby pressed a fiver into her hand anyway. She wasn't a bad kid. Just a bit too innocent for her own good. 'Go on, clear off. And, Angel.'

'Yeah?'

'Mind you keep your trap shut.'

Angie banged on her nan's front door for a good five minutes before a kitchen window along the balcony was pushed open, and Doris Barker stuck out her head.

'What's all that sodding row?' she hollered.

Angie stepped back from the door so Doris could see her. 'It's only me, Mrs Barker.'

'Hello, love. I thought it was them bloody kids from downstairs again.'

'Have you seen Nan?'

Doris considered her words. 'She had to nip out.'

'Do you know when she'll be back?'

'Sorry.'

'Thanks anyway.'

Doris could see she was upset. 'You all right, love?'

'Yeah. I'm fine. I've got to go. If you see Nan, tell her I'll be back, will you?'

'Course. But you're sure you don't want to come in and wait? Have a nice cuppa tea?'

'No. Thanks all the same.'

Doris pulled the window closed and went over to the stove to boil the kettle. Something was going on, and she'd lay good money that that little creep Jameson was at the root of it. She just hoped that a soft touch like Sarah could handle it. Whatever it was.

By the time Angie sat down in her mum's kitchen, she was exhausted; the mixture of fear, weeping, and simple, undiluted terror at what she had witnessed had drained her.

Vi, who was in her usual position in the kitchen – in front of the mirror over the sink, touching up her make-up – didn't take much notice, putting her daughter's pale complexion and red eyes down to too much burning the candle at both ends. She rather liked the fact that someone so young could look so wiped out. She didn't even notice that Angie was trembling as if she were suffering from a tropical fever.

'Nice outfit,' Vi said, checking out her daughter's reflection in passing as she outlined her lips. 'I fancy a trouser suit.' She turned round to have a look at Angie's feet. 'And matching red patent shoes. Blimey.' She smiled nastily, knowingly, as she returned to studying her own face. 'That new job must be paying well.'

Angie clasped the side of the table, trying to stop the shaking.

'And able to afford a flat as well. Who'd have thought it. My little Ange.'

Angie stared down at the greasy kitchen floor. How it got that way, she couldn't imagine, her mum certainly never did any cooking. It must be all the scraps of fish and chips and saveloys that had been dropped on it since Angie had stopped skivvying for her. How long had that been? Two months? Three? When had she got her hair cut?

She felt dizzy.

'Aren't you going to ask me how I am?' Vi admired her completed face, lost in thoughts of Craig moving down south, of being in bed with him and of him treating her like the queen she knew herself to be.

'How are you?' Angie managed to ask. Her tongue felt too big for her mouth.

'Managing, just, to get along without my little girl. But I've got some lovely news. Craig's—'

'I'm in trouble, Mum.' Angie broke in. 'Terrible trouble.'

Vi spun round and stuck her fists into her waist. 'I might have known. That explains why that grandmother of your'n turned up earlier. It was obvious she wasn't coming to see me.'

Angie looked up, trying to focus. 'Nan was here?'

'Yeah. Bloody woke me up she did. And in a cab if you don't mind. When I said I didn't have a clue where you were, she cleared off.'

Angie buried her face in her hands.

'Don't worry, Ange. I know someone who can get rid of it.'

This was all too hard for Angie, too difficult for her to understand.

'And you will have to get rid of it, you know. I can't be any help, not with—'

With considerable effort, Angie lifted her head. 'Get rid of what?'

Vi nodded at Angie's middle. 'The baby, of course.'

'But I'm not pregnant.'

'There's no need to pretend to me, Angie.' She sighed self-pityingly. 'You don't know how hard it is to raise a child alone. I fought so hard to keep you. Maybe I should have let them take you, then you'd have had a better life and wouldn't have wound up in this state.'

'Mum—'

'You're a daft little cow.' Vi pinched Angie's pale cheek. 'Fancy getting yourself in the same boat as me.'

Angie stared at her mother, with her lipstick just a shade too bright and her hair tinted just a shade too red and with the cigarette burns in her mauve nylon housecoat. 'Same boat as you?'

'Pregnant before you're eighteen.'

'I'm not pregnant. I'm in trouble.' The tears brimmed in her eyes. 'Mum, I'm so worried.'

'Worried? You? You don't know what worry is.' Vi lit another cigarette. 'You'll learn though, before long. When your looks start going.'

Angie's panic had earlier dissolved into confusion, but it was now sharpening into anger. Why wouldn't this woman – her own mother – help her?

'You've had it too easy, Angela, that's been your trouble all along. You should have had my terrible life, then you'd really have something to complain about.'

'Your terrible life?'

Vi glared at her daughter. 'How dare you use that tone with me? I hardly know you any more.' She picked a fleck of tobacco from her lip. 'I've never known what it's like to be free. Not like you. Always at the beck and call of a child, when I was barely more than a child myself. And now look at me.'

'What, at a selfish, spiteful woman, who didn't even know she had a child most of the time? I was practically brought up round Nan's until you fell out with her. Then, when we got this place, I was always at Jackie's. You've never cared about me. Never.'

Vi looked at Angie as if she had just stabbed her through the heart. 'Angela!'

'Leave off, Mum. We both know what you're like. Anything you ever do is only for yourself!'

Vi couldn't be bothered keeping up the charade of

345

being hurt, it took too much effort. She shrugged. 'I'm just not the motherly type.'

Angie looked at her as she flicked her ash into the sink full of dirty plates and cups. 'Do you know, Mum, I'm beginning to feel sorry for you. Your own daughter comes to you for help and what do you do? You moan about how life's treated you.'

Vi snorted unpleasantly.

'You reckon you've never been free. If you ask me, you've been a bit too free. You never took any responsibility for me. None. All you cared about was yourself, and going out, and your latest, useless boyfriend.'

'You watch your tongue. I'm still your bloody mother.'

'Mother? Mrs Murray's been more like a mother to me than you ever have. And you know it. And she's never gone on about being free. Her and Mr Murray have had kids and they've looked after them.'

'Stifled them, you mean.'

'No. They've just done their best.'

'So have I.'

'Have you, Mum? Who for?'

'This is getting boring.' Vi sighed wearily, but, in the moment it took her to register that someone was knocking on the door, a sickly smile had spread over her heavily made-up face. She pulled her housecoat demurely to her throat. 'Get that for me will you, love?' she wheedled. 'I can't go to the door looking like this, can I?'

'I'm leaving. I'll get it on my way out.'

Vi listened as her daughter opened the street door.

'It's for you,' she heard Angie call.

'Is that you, Craig?' Vi's voice was light and girlie.

'It certainly is,' a loud Scottish voice replied.

Vi dashed out of the kitchen and into the bathroom. 'Put the kettle on and make Craig a nice cup of tea, will you, Ange?' she yelled from the other side of the door. 'Just while I finish putting my face on?'

Doing her best to hold back her tears, Angie pushed her way past Craig, and stood for a moment on the grimy, unpolished step. 'I said, I'm leaving,' she called over her shoulder, then hurried down the path, shoved open the gate and ran off down the street, in too much of a hurry and too preoccupied to hear Craig's long low whistle of appreciation.

Martin opened the Murrays' front door. 'This is not a very good time, Squirt. There's been a bit of a row.'

'Let me come in, Martin. Please. I need to see Jackie.'

He hesitated. 'She's upstairs with Mum.'

'Please.'

Despite not wanting an audience for the ructions that were going on in the house, Martin could hardly refuse her, not with the distress she was in. 'Go through to the kitchen. But no noise, eh?'

She sniffed miserably. 'What's going on?'

Martin could kill his bloody sister. He handed her his handkerchief and she blew her nose loudly.

'There's no need to pretend, Squirt. Jackie's been along and told you my news, hasn't she?'

Angie tried to summon up interest in Martin's ordinary – appealingly ordinary – little life. 'No, Mart. She hasn't.'

Martin knew she had, the interfering cow, and he knew how much Angie had always fancied him. Anyone could see it was breaking her heart. Jackie could be a spiteful bitch at times. Just because Angie had grown up into such a looker.

'Ange, I know she's your mate, but you don't have to protect her.'

Angie wracked her brains for a clue as to what this was all about. 'Have you messed up your exams?' She was speaking automatically, platitudes that she didn't have to organize or think about. 'And you worked so hard.'

Martin sat down next to her at the kitchen table. She really didn't know. Jackie hadn't blabbed for once. 'It's nothing to do with exams. The results aren't out for ages yet. It's . . .' He bent forward and clasped his hands over his head, as though he could hide himself away from all this. 'It's something more personal. And it's bloody terrifying. I'm getting married.'

Angie lifted her chin and looked at him, hunched over like a beaten dog. He looked as if he'd been condemned to the scaffold.

'That's nice. When?' What else could she say? There she was, the witness to what might well be a murder, frightened out of her life, desperate for someone to tell her what to do next, and here was Martin, about to get married, acting as if he was carrying the weight of the world on his shoulders.

If her situation wasn't so genuinely terrifying, she might have found Martin's melodramatics quite funny.

He straightened up, throwing back his head and staring at the ceiling. 'In about a month. Mum went mad when I told her. She's been in her bedroom bawling her eyes out ever since.'

'Doesn't she like the girl?'

'She loves her. She's posh and rich and comes from a

good family, whatever that might mean. In fact, she's all her dreams come true.'

Angie noticed that he hadn't said she was all *his* dreams come true. 'So what's the problem?'

'She's pregnant. And Mum reckons it's the most disgusting show up of all time and I've brought shame on us all, and she's never going to speak to me again. Her and Dad scrimped and scraped to give me a chance in life, and this is how I repay them – act like I'm straight out of the gutter. Oh, and I mustn't forget this bit, it'll kill Dad stone dead when he gets home from work and finds out.'

What should she say? She didn't even care that much. Just like no one seemed to care about her.

'It's Jill. You remember. You met her at that party.'

'I remember.' Why hadn't the toffee-nosed idiot gone on the Pill?

Martin looked at Angie's tired, tear-stained face, reached out and stroked her cheek. She looked great, even with red eyes and smudged make-up. Why had he got out of his depth with Jill when Angie was just along the road all the time? 'You all right, Squirt?'

'Fine.'

He stood up and pulled her to him. 'I've always been fond of you. You know you can tell me anything.'

'It's nothing,' she said, backing away. 'I've just got all worked up.'

'I want to help.' He stepped towards her, closing the gap between them again.

Angie managed a thin smile. This was all she needed. On top of everything else, Martin making a pass at her. 'I've had a bit of boyfriend trouble, that's all. And I just got everything out of perspective.'

He had her backed against the sink. 'If only things had been different.'

'Angie.' It was Jackie. She didn't sound, or look, very pleased. 'Martin, why didn't you tell me she was here?'

He moved away from Angie and sat down sulkily at the kitchen table.

'You're obviously not going to answer me,' she sniped at her brother, then turned to Angie. 'Has he upset you as well?'

'No. Look, I've got to go, Jack. Nan's expecting me.' Angie hurried out to the hall. 'Give my love to your mum,' they heard her call before she shut the street door behind her.

'What's wrong with you?' Jackie poked him in the arm. 'Upsetting Mum. And now you've had Angie in tears. You are such a pig.'

'Me? I never did anything? She was upset when she got here.'

'Yeah, course she was.'

'Why don't you keep your mouth shut, Jackie?'

'And why didn't you keep your trousers on?' Jackie flounced out of the kitchen into the hall. 'Just you wait till Dad gets home.'

Angie wasn't sure how she dragged herself back to the tube station and then made the journey to Mile End before getting the bus over to Poplar to her nan's. But somehow she'd made it.

She turned the corner, and saw the familiar walls around the estate, but something was different today. Blocking the entrance to the courtyard, where vehicles turned in for the car park, there was a crowd of chanting, jeering women, many of them with toddlers, prams and pushchairs. Standing to one side were half a dozen police constables, looking distinctly uncomfortable at the prospect of having to attend a demonstration made up of women and their kids.

Stop the killing now! read one of the many placards. *Murderers!* read another.

For a moment, Angie froze. Was it anything to do with David? Did they know she was his girlfriend? Girlfriend? That was a joke. Didn't she mean his *bit on the side*? God, she'd been so stupid.

Finding one last surge of energy, she fought her way through the demonstrators and made her way up the stairs to her nan's flat.

'Thank goodness you're here, darling.' Sarah folded her arm round her granddaughter's shoulders, shut the door tight and hurried her through to the sitting-room. 'I've been so worried.'

Angie felt ill. 'Nan, what's going on down there?'

'It's awful. They've started selling this LSD stuff in the buildings. And round the school. A young boy, thirteen he was, died up on the corner by the Eastern last night. Jumped off the top of a building.'

Angie was ashamed of the relief she felt at it having nothing to do with what had happened in Greek Street, that it was nothing to do with her or David.

'That's sad,' she managed to say.

'Angie, is there something you want to tell me?' Sarah thought about that little turd Jameson and how he had been shouting the odds about Angie's boyfriend being in trouble – pity he didn't use his time tracking down the drug-pushers.

Angie shook her head. She couldn't involve her nan.

'I popped round your mum's earlier. To see if I could find you.' Sarah spoke as if her turning up on Vi's doorstep was the most natural thing in the world. 'I've been a bit worried about you. You know what I'm like. You've been such a stranger lately.'

Angie said nothing.

'I'll make us a cuppa tea.'

Angie followed her through to the kitchen, wanting the comfort of her presence.

'Nan,' she said quietly. 'Why is Mum like she is?'

Sarah put the teapot on the scrubbed wooden draining board. She had her back to Angie as she spoke. 'I blame myself, if you really want to know.'

Angie moved closer to her nan. 'Why?'

'Let's take our tea through and sit down, shall we love?'

'Your mother was a strong-willed, difficult girl, Angie. And I never checked her.' Sarah slowly stirred sugar into her cup. 'I spoiled her, because I was trying to make up for things.'

'What things?'

'Her not having a dad for a start.'

'But that wasn't your fault. Grandad Pearson was killed down the docks.'

'There's an old saying, love: the tragedy of a happy marriage is that it can never have a happy ending.'

'I don't understand.'

'One of you has to go first, and leave the other one. Grieving. Broken-hearted.'

'That's so sad.'

'But not for me.'

Angie frowned. 'I thought you idolized Granddad.'

'Sweetheart, that's what most people thought. It's what I let them think. But I was just a good actress, exactly like your mother. There was no Granddad Pearson. I was a stupid young kid who let her head be turned by a good-looking Swedish sailor. He could hardly speak any English. And he was dark, funnily enough. Not what you'd expect of a Swede at all. Lovely rich chestnut hair, he had. Just like yours.'

'Don't upset yourself, Nan.'

'I felt so bad, I wasn't as strict with her as I should have been.'

'How did you get by?'

'It wasn't easy in those days, bringing up a kiddie by yourself. There wasn't much help. But I managed. I found ways.' She paused, remembering. 'And Doris was ever so good to me. She guessed almost right away I'd never been married. But she never looked down on me.'

'I don't know what to say.'

Sarah fiddled with her teaspoon, straightening it in her saucer. 'It wasn't too bad. Not really.'

They drank their tea in silence for a while, then Sarah shook her head and said, 'But then when your mum went and did the same thing . . .'

Angie almost dropped her cup. 'Are you saying Mum was never married either?'

'I shouldn't have blurted it out like that, darling, but no, she wasn't. There was no Billy Knight who got run over on the Mile End Road, but there was this bloke she met in some night-club up West. A Canadian, she said he was.'

'And his name was Knight?'

'No. She'd seen this film about knights in shining

armour.' She smiled fondly. 'You know what a dreamer she is.'

'So Knight's not my real name?'

'Don't worry, babe, it's all legal, all on your birth certificate and everything.'

'And I'm half-Canadian.'

'I suppose you are.'

'Do you know who he was? Is?'

'Sorry, Ange, I don't. But I do know he never realized she was carrying. By the time she found out, he'd already gone back home. He never did a runner on her. Nothing like that. Not like my Swedish bloke. He was thinking about settling in the East End when he met me, he liked it here. Then, when I told him I was in the family way, he was off on the trot like a carriage horse.'

'Did your mum help you?' Angie had never thought of her nan as having a mother before now.

'No, she chucked me out. But you get over it. You have to. You cope. And you try and make a decent life for yourself and your baby.' Sarah paused again, thinking about how she had gone on the game just to buy food, and how Doris had taken them in to her little terraced house, where they had lived until it had been bombed out during the war.

How differently her own daughter had 'coped' . . .

Violet had tried to get rid of the baby she was carrying, and when that plan had failed, she had insisted she would give it up for adoption on the day it was born. It was only because Sarah had promised to help her out, had promised to do everything for her – give her money, care for the child, whatever she wanted – that Violet had relented and had agreed to keep the baby.

Sarah had always vowed that her granddaughter would

never know she was unwanted by her own mother.

'I spoiled your mother rotten, when she had you. Mollycoddled her. She never lifted a finger from the day you were born. That's why it's all my fault. She thought she could get away with everything. Treat everyone like a servant. Including you when you were old enough. We had a terrible falling out over that. I didn't mind how she treated me, but you were my little princess. I wasn't having it.'

'Is that why you never see her?'

'Partly, but it was when she started talking about . . .'

'About what, Nan?'

Sarah closed her eyes and shook her head at the memories that came flooding, unbidden, into her mind; memories of Violet flying into a temper because she reckoned having a child around the place was putting off her men friends, and swearing she would send Angie away to a home. Sarah had pleaded with her, but Violet, as usual, knew she held the trump card, and only stopped talking about children's homes when Sarah had promised to keep her nose out of her daughter's business and to send her regular weekly payments. Sarah could only thank God that Doris had been around to help her. But Angie would never hear any of this, not from Sarah's lips. Nobody deserved that.

'Nothing, babe. We just disagreed, that's all. I shouldn't say anything against my own daughter, but she's plain selfish, and that's the simple truth of it. She had me to help her, and could have done whatever she wanted. Gone to night school. Got herself a decent job. Anything. But she was a lazy mare, always was and, I suppose, always will be. I should have been stronger, should have insisted. But guilt's a terrible thing. You think you can go out and have a laugh when you're young and that there's no consequences for what you do. That you can just mess around and it'll all be all right. Then you look back on your life and you realize.'

'Me not having a dad never had her spoiling me. She never let me do what I wanted. She even made me leave school.'

'She only wanted to make sure you could look after yourself. That she never had to worry about you depending on some bloke.'

Angie knew that was rubbish, just as well as Sarah did, but she had other, more pressing, things on her mind.

'Nan,' she began slowly. 'You know you asked me if I had something to tell you?'

'Yes, love.'

'I've been involved with someone. I thought he loved me. Then I started to find out things about him. And now I've found out he's . . .'

'Married.'

She nodded miserably. 'How do you know?'

'Darling, I had a visit from someone who knows him.'

Angie's heart started pounding, but before she could run through all the horrible possibilities of who might have traced her to her nan's flat, the doorbell rang.

'I'll get it, pet. You pour us another drop of tea.'

'Evening, Mrs Pearson.' It was Detective Constable Jameson.

'You again. What do you want? See if I'm selling drugs to schoolchildren?'

'No, Mrs Pearson, I've come to question Miss Angela Knight.'

Sarah paused just long enough for it to register with Jameson. 'She's not here.'

'That's funny. Her mother said she was,' he lied. 'It's serious, Mrs Pearson. Very serious.'

'It's all right, Nan.' Angie was standing in the hall behind her grandmother.

'No, Ange, it's not. Policemen don't come to talk to young girls by themselves.'

'They do if they want to be discreet, Mrs Pearson. It's to do with David Fuller.' He looked at Angie. 'And a murder investigation.'

Sarah was in shock. Murder? David Fuller? Hadn't Jameson said that was Angie's bloke's name?

'You'd better let him in, Nan.'

'Bobby, will you tell me what this is all about?' Maureen shoved aside the suitcases that Bobby had just lifted down from the top of the wardrobe and sat beside them on the bed. 'I'm not packing a thing until you do.'

'Sorry, Maur, but Mr Burman—'

'Who?'

'Bloke who works with Dave. He's sorted out a job for me. In property maintenance.'

'Bobby, what are you talking about? You can't knock a flaming nail in.'

'It's not exactly that sort of maintenance, Maur. And there's something else.'

'Surprise me.'

'We've got to go right away.'

'How do you mean?'

'Tonight.' He rubbed his hand over his bald head. 'And it's in Cyprus.'

357

'Why would we want to go to flipping Cyprus? I don't even know where it is.'

'Maur, we've got no choice.'

Sarah Pearson could hardly take it in. When Jameson had come round before, he hadn't even hinted at a fraction of what he was saying now. This David Fuller was a proper gangster. Involved in terrible things. Not some twenty-year-old who'd made a few mistakes. And she'd been sitting here chatting away to Angie about her and her mum, and all the time the bloke was out there on the run. Say he'd come looking for her?

'Angela,' Jameson said, leaning forward and trapping his long, pale fingers between his knees. 'I want to get David Fuller. I want to get him for the murder of two people. That's the two people I know about, never mind all the others, and all the victims of his drug-pushing.'

Sarah tasted the bile rising in her throat, and Angie was finding it hard to control her breathing, it was as though she was swimming under water and couldn't catch her breath.

'The others won't be as nice as me, Angela. And if the big boys get involved at this stage, maybe they won't turn a blind eye to all your nan's little enterprises either. I could protect you. And her.'

'Leave Nan out of this.'

Sarah gripped her granddaughter's hand. 'Mr Jameson, do you swear that if Angela tells you everything she knows that she won't get into trouble?'

Jameson smiled like a lizard. He had them. 'Mrs Pearson, your granddaughter is a little girl who got involved with a grown man. An evil man. I'm not treating her as any sort of a suspect.'

'But if she acts as a witness . . .'

'I have plenty of witnesses to all sorts of things, Mrs Pearson. I just need Angela as a source of information, confirmation if you like, to tie up one or two ends that I can't quite match.'

'How do we know you're telling the truth?'

'Mrs Pearson, I'm by myself here. If it comes to it, you can just deny everything I say. That I was even here. After all, who'd think a nice little girl like your granddaughter would have got herself involved with the likes of David Fuller?' Jameson was telling the truth. Well, partly. He wasn't going to bother with charging Angie with anything, because he wasn't sure if he had anything to charge her with. Involving her in any serious way would need time and effort, and if he failed, it would distract his superiors from what would be his great success: nailing Fuller.

And he rather liked the idea of having Sarah Pearson and Doris Barker – two women with some interesting contacts – in his debt.

For now, anyway.

'Angie, what do you think, babe?'

She couldn't look at her nan. 'All right, Mr Jameson. What do you want to know?'

David was sitting on a tea chest, the only seat, in a prefabricated office building in a scrap yard on the Beckton Marshes. He was speaking on the phone, which, apart from a pad of scrap paper and a stub of pencil, was the only nod to office equipment in the place.

'This is important, Bob. I want you to make sure that when Jeff clears out all the other gaffs, the snooker clubs and that, that he clears out the desks and bureaux in all the flats as well. Got it? Even the legit-looking stuff.'

'Sure, Dave.' Bobby, who was listening to David with one ear, and to Maureen's wails and complaints as she continued to pack with the other, couldn't bring himself to say that he had already spoken to Jeff and that Bill and George had apparently done the job for him. He didn't want to mention it because Jeff had been a bit concerned – just as Bobby was a bit confused as to who had told them to do it – and he'd thought it best not to worry Dave with all that now. Not with all this Mikey and Sonia business on his mind.

He would have liked to have asked Dave about him and Maureen going to Cyprus, but Mr Burman had said not to, that he was keeping Dave up to speed on all of that. It was all making Bobby's head go round, keeping straight what he had to say and not say to people.

'Right, thanks, Bob. Now I'm gonna be amongst the missing for a few weeks, but I'll be in touch. OK?'

He put down the phone before Bobby had the chance to reply, and immediately rang Peter Burman.

'Peter. Hello. It's me, David. David Fuller.' He had a light laugh in his voice, but a lead weight in his gut. 'I've been thinking about that business you were interested in. In Marbella. If you still fancy going ahead with it, I thought I could go over there. Check things out.'

There wasn't an immediate response from the other end, just some mumbling as though Burman had put his hand over the receiver while he was talking to someone else.

'Are you still there, Peter?'

'Excuse me, David, I had someone talking to me here in the office. So, you're interested in going to Spain, you say? Are you in trouble?'

'No. No. Nothing like that. Just need to get away for a bit, that's all. Bit of woman trouble. You know.' He tapped his passport nervously on his knee, the passport with his photograph in it, but in the name of Stephen Joseph Townsend. 'What do you think?'

'I'll make some phone calls. Then I'll get back to you. Are you at Greek Street?'

'No. I'm on a private number. Hold on.' He rubbed the centre of the grease-covered dial with his finger, trying, and failing, to make out the faded numbers. 'Look, how about if I ring you back? Say in an hour?'

'Make it two.'

Two hours to kill.

David stood out in the scrap yard in the warm evening air. It was half past eight and getting dark. The nights were beginning to draw in. He hated the thought of autumn coming, knowing that winter was not far behind. That time of year had never suited him. Not since he'd been a kid and he'd dreaded going home from school, knowing the house would be cold, empty and in darkness.

Still, why worry about that now? He'd be in Spain in a few days. Sunning himself on the Costa. But before he cleared off abroad, he had a job to do.

He opened the back of the Jaguar and took out a petrol can. It was a shame, but he had no choice, the motor had enough forensic in the boot to put him away for life.

He shook the petrol can, spraying the fuel over the gleaming dark green paintwork, saving a drop to pour over an old piece of rag. Then he stood back and struck a match ready to ignite it before he threw it on to the bonnet of his precious car.

'Fuller!'

Startled, David looked up to see three uniformed coppers clambering over the high wire fence. 'If you don't want a good kicking, drop that match.'

'Don't say that, you'll scare me!' David touched the flame to the rag and then flicked the petrol-soaked cloth at the car as if he were shaking out a duster after a bit of light housework.

As David was being led away from the yard in handcuffs, his ribs aching from the rather half-hearted beating the young coppers had given him, Burman was sitting in his office, contemplating the depressing sight of the worn-out prostitute standing in front of his desk. She was almost dribbling with anticipation as she awaited her reward for the second-rate shop-soiled information she had been so eager to pass on to him.

Why were people so stupid?

Burman jerked his head towards the door, and began trimming a cigar ready to smoke. 'Get rid of her,' he said.

Without a word, the two men hauled the now terrified Christina kicking and screaming from the room.

Burman stuck the fat Romeo y Julietta between his lips and thought about David Fuller.

It had been a foolish mistake, no, more of a weakness, to let a parvenu such as Fuller anywhere near his business. The *naïveté* of the man was breathtaking. He had never even suspected that Bill and George, two of his supposedly most loyal workers, had gladly gone on to his, Burman's, payroll as soon as he had approached them.

It was something Burman always made sure of, that he had insiders in other people's business. For security reasons.

Good security pleased him. Just as much as amateurs annoyed him. But not nearly as much as dumb, loud-mouthed prostitutes, who thought he would pay for their pathetic gossip, infuriated him.

Chapter 16

'I don't feel right being here, Doris. Look at that lot.'

Sarah Pearson, feeling uncomfortable, but looking elegant in her broad-brimmed straw hat and beautifully cut, lavender two-piece – especially acquired from Selfridges by one of Doris's more talented girls – nodded to the other side of the ancient, flower-filled Sussex church. There sat Jill Walker's family and friends, in colourful clusters on the ornately carved pews, decked out like an illustration in an etiquette book, demonstrating how the middle classes should dress for a late-summer country wedding.

'If it hadn't been for missing out on seeing my Angie all done up, I would never have dreamed of us coming here.' Sarah tugged at her skirt. 'Never.'

'Just enjoy it, Sal.' Doris was craning her neck to get a good look at everyone and everything, taking it all in. 'This is the only time the likes of you and me are gonna get to a do like this.' She took her lace-trimmed hankie from the sleeve of her lemon duster coat, and held it to her mouth as a shield for what she was about to say, despite the organ music echoing around the hammer-beam roof providing more than enough privacy for even the most intimate of conversations.

'Here,' she hissed under her breath. 'Look behind.'

Sarah twisted round and saw her daughter, Violet, done up to the nines, walking up the aisle on the arm of a handsome, smiling man.

'Blimey, Sarah, look at her, will you? Bold as brass.

How the hell did she get an invite?'

Sarah sighed resignedly. 'Soon as she heard Angie was going to be a bridesmaid, she launched her campaign. Chance to come to a classy do like this, she wouldn't have missed it for the world. And you know what she's like when she wants something, Doris. The Murrays never stood a chance of refusing. Angie was so embarrassed when Violet told Tilly Murray that Angie wouldn't come if her mum wasn't there.'

'Tilly wouldn't have fallen for that old flannel.'

'No, but you know how much she hates any awkwardness. Especially in front of her new in-laws. And when Martin – and his young lady, of course – insisted on having Angie as bridesmaid, to match Jackie, I suppose, they had no choice. You know Violet, she'd have caused murders if she hadn't got her own way. She'd have mucked it up somehow or other.'

Doris shook her head in wonder at Sarah, such a good woman, having a daughter like Violet. 'Yeah, but all that said, and much as I begrudge the words even coming out of my mouth, Sal, you've got to hand it to her. She really looks the part. Like that Jean Shrimpton.'

'Being so good-looking was part of that girl's downfall.'

Doris and Sarah watched as Violet glided effortlessly into a pew near the back, smiling graciously at the man, who stood politely until she was comfortably seated.

'You'd never have her down as an Eastender though, would you? It's like she was born to it.'

'Always was a good actress.' Sarah turned and faced the altar again.

Doris did the same. Still hiding her words behind the

cover of her hankie, she said, 'Did Angie ever find out that she tried to get rid of her?'

'No, and she never will if I've got anything to do with it. When that dirty old sod along the landing got done for doing abortions for the local toms, Angie was so shocked when she found out. I could hardly tell her that her own mother had gone to the very same bloke when she was carrying her sixteen years earlier, now could I?'

'Just thank gawd he got it wrong that one time, eh?'

'He didn't get it wrong, Doris. She just never had enough money to pay him. So he turned her away. If I hadn't been down Leysdown with you in your chalet, she'd have tapped it off me and . . .' She sighed. 'Well, things would all have turned out very different.'

'I never knew that, Sal.'

'No. Well, it's all in the past now.'

Doris shoved her hankie back up her sleeve and looked at her watch. 'Here, look at the time. Nearly a quarter past two. What do you think's causing the hold-up?'

The cause of the delay was simple: the bridegroom, Martin Murray, was round the back of the church vomiting spectacularly into the yew hedge.

'I can't handle this,' he moaned, wiping his mouth with the back of his hand.

Tilly, his mum, was being no help at all, having collapsed into hysterical weeping against a monument of a broken pillar that marked the passing of an eighteenth-century vicar; and Stan, his dad, would only comment that he knew too much education would only lead to some things. So Jackie and Angie had been brought round by Jill's brother, Guy, to try and talk some sense into the reluctant groom.

They were now standing on either side of him, a matching pair of increasingly cross, cream and lilac, fairy-tale bridesmaids.

'*What* can't you handle?' demanded Jackie, shaking him by the arms and making the flowers in her hair bob furiously. 'A lovely church? A fantastic sunny day? Stone-rich in-laws? A brilliant job waiting for you after you've finished college? A bloody rent-free home? A gorgeous sodding bride? Who, I think you should know, is being driven around the buggering village for the fifth bleeding time, and is probably getting fit to come in here and deck you. And I wouldn't blame her. In fact, I might bloody well do it for her, if you don't pull yourself together.'

'Listen to that child's language,' wailed Tilly. 'And in front of all these strangers. The shame of it. I'm going to pass out. I just know I am.'

'Go and see to your mum, Jack.' Angie picked up Martin's top hat from the grass and led him over to a moss-covered, stone bench.

'Sit down, Martin,' she instructed him wearily. 'You are really getting on my nerves.'

He slumped down, his head falling to his chest. 'Don't you start on me as well, Squirt.'

'Stop feeling so sorry for yourself, will you? This is real life. Not some game you can stop playing just because you don't think it's fair, or you don't like the rules, or because you've got bored with it all. Get a flaming grip on yourself.'

'Why should you care what I do?'

'Because Jill's having a baby, that's why. Your baby. Your flesh and blood.'

'She'll be all right. What does she need me for?' He

glared at Jill's brother, who was standing smoking and chatting, surprisingly amiably, with a very solemn-looking Stan Murray.

'Her precious family can give her everything she needs.'

'And what about the baby?'

'That won't want for anything either. Believe me.'

'How about a father?'

He didn't answer.

'Look, Martin, I'd have given anything to have had a dad like the other kids in the street. I used to lay in bed thinking what he'd be like. Inventing little stories about where we would go out for the day during the summer holidays. Down to Walton-on-the-Naze and Jaywick and that. Like you and Jackie did with your dad. Like every kid should be entitled to. You don't want your baby winding up like me, do you, making up lies at school about what we did and where we went?'

'Why can't you all just leave me alone? None of you have got a single clue about what I feel, or what I want. I'm not much more than a kid myself. Why should I have to go through all this? Whatever you say, it's not fair.'

Angie threw his hat down next to him. 'I'm getting fed up with people being selfish. I've got more worrying me, Martin, than you could ever imagine in your stupid, narrow little world. You can't begin to imagine the problems I've got, and yet I'm standing here trying to coax you and be nice to you. Well, I'm fed up with it. And as if that lot's not bad enough, I've even got my mum flipping well sitting over there in that church. And I know she's going to show me up and start queening it over everyone.' She hauled him up by the lapels. 'So just get on your sodding, stupid feet, and start acting like a bloody grown-up for once, and decide what you're going to do.'

'I don't know what I want to do.' He stood there, a picture of self-indulgent misery. 'Help me, Squirt. Please.'

'Oh no, you're not doing that to me. The choice is yours. No one can make it for you. *You*, Martin. You make up your mind. Are you gonna be a grown-up or a stupid whiny kid for the rest of your life?'

Before Martin could even think which choice he would make – adult or child – Jackie had stomped over to them, ploughing her way through the waving churchyard grasses, her dress clutched up around her knees.

'Satisfied are you, Martin?' She looked and sounded as if she were about to detonate. 'Jill's mum's out here as well now. Crying her sodding eyes out. You've had your fun and now you've got to pay the price.'

'Look,' Angie said, her face almost touching his. 'Just get in that bloody church, will you?'

Then she turned on her heel and started dragging Jackie back towards the cluster of little bridesmaids, who were waiting for them, increasingly noisily, by the lychgate. But suddenly she stopped, almost tripping Jackie over, then turned her head and called over her shoulder. 'And stop calling me Squirt, will you, Martin?'

Despite the drama, the tears and the delay, Jill Walker eventually became Mrs Martin Murray at a ceremony that everyone agreed was as moving as it was beautiful, and, as the wedding party made its way across the fields, back to the marquee that had been set up in the Walkers' garden, even Martin was smiling.

'I know you were scared,' Jill said to him, as they led the guests through the five-bar gate that separated the

369

sun-dappled wood at the back of the churchyard from the Walkers' manicured lawns, 'but you won't regret it, Martin. I promise.'

She kissed him tenderly on the lips, and a cheer went up from the crowd behind them.

'And I promise I'll make all this up to you, Jill.'

'I should hope so. You can show willing by asking my mother to dance immediately after we've had the first waltz.'

'Why don't you go over and speak to her, Sal?' Doris, still full from the wedding breakfast, but managing to work her way through a plateful of goodies from the evening finger buffet, inclined her head towards Violet, who was dancing animatedly with a puce-faced, guffawing, elderly relative of Jill's.

Sarah watched her daughter flirting outrageously with the no-doubt rich old man. 'It's been a long time since we've had anything decent to say to one another.'

Doris sorted through her plate for another of the miniature boiled eggs that she had developed such a taste for in the past few hours. 'Didn't you pop round there about a month ago?' She lowered her voice. 'When that copper came sniffing round.'

'Yeah, I did. I was going to talk to her about Angie. But it was so awkward I just left in the end.'

'Remember what they say, Sal. This ain't a dress rehearsal, girl. Don't you go leaving it too late.'

'You're cheerful.'

'Just honest, Sal. Just honest.'

'You all right, Nan?' Angie, with Jackie and her boy-friend, Andrew, in tow, bent down and kissed her grandmother.

Sarah stood up and held her granddaughter at arm's length. 'Don't these girls look lovely?'

'I should say they do,' Doris mumbled through a mouthful of mayonnaise-covered quail's egg. 'And to think I used to have a figure like theirs.'

'Aren't you going to introduce us to your young man, Jackie? Angie's told me ever so much about him.'

'Andrew, this is Mrs Pearson, Angie's nan. And this is Mrs Barker, Mrs Pearson's friend.'

Flashing the dimpled smile that had made Jackie want to leap on him the first time she had set eyes on him, Andrew sat down and set about charming them as only a handsome young man could charm two ladies who had reached a certain age.

Jackie rolled her eyes. 'Watch this, Ange, he's a right flipping professional.'

Angie didn't reply.

'What's up with you?'

'I was just thinking that at least one of us got a decent bloke.'

Jackie stepped back to allow a tipsy-looking middle-aged couple, who were experimenting with a strange variation of the Twist, gyrate unsteadily by. 'Still haven't heard anything from you-know-who?'

'No.'

Jackie didn't know anything other than what Angie had told her: that she had broken up with her boyfriend.

'Not even a note, or a bunch of flowers begging you to come back?'

'Nothing.'

'Do you miss him?'

'Can we drop it, Jack? Please.'

'All right, touchy.' Jackie tapped her foot idly to the

band's rather good stab at 'She Loves You'. 'Don't look now,' she whispered excitedly, 'but Jill's gorgeous brother Guy's staring at you again. He's hardly taken his eyes off you all day. Shall I take you over so he can ask you to have a dance?'

'No thanks, Jack, I'm going outside to get some air.'

'Hi there. Jackie said I'd find you out here. I'm Guy. Jill's big brother? I came to thank you for working your magic on Martin earlier. And to ask you for a dance.'

Angie slowly opened her eyes and looked up at him. She had been sitting alone on the grass, in the cool evening air, in the ridiculously pretty garden, leaning against a fairy-light-bedecked tree. In her mind she had been going over and over the past four months, wondering how so much could have happened. Some really exciting things, but also some terrible things, frightening things, and she was wondering how she would ever get her life back to some sort of normality. And, all the while, just a few yards from where she was sitting, people were dancing and laughing, acting as if they didn't have a single thought in their heads other than enjoying themselves.

'I'm sorry, Guy, you've caught me at a bad time. I'm off blokes at the moment.'

'Not even a dance?'

'No. Not even a dance.'

He kneeled down on the grass, stretched out and rested his hand against the tree, trapping her against the trunk. 'Someone must have hurt you really badly.'

'Yes. He did. And a lot of other people too.' She lifted his hand away. 'If you don't mind.'

'Can't I just sit with you for a while?'

'I'd rather you didn't, but it's your garden.'

He settled down next to her. 'What are you thinking?'

'Nothing really,' she lied. 'I'm just passing the time until we can go to the hotel for the night.' She flushed scarlet, the moment she registered the embarrassing double meaning in her words.

Then she smiled, as Guy, to his credit, hadn't even hinted at a suggestive remark.

'I'm sorry if you don't care for the way I'm preparing your case, Mr Fuller.'

'*You're sorry if I don't care* . . .' David erupted from his chair, and grabbed the table that stood between him and his lawyer, Thomas Frazier. He was that close to raising it above his head and smashing it into the little prick's face, but he knew he had two warders sitting behind him, willing him to lose his temper. That knowledge quickly brought him back to his senses. He held up his hands in surrender and sat down again.

'I apologize. It's this place. It's getting to me.'

Me too, thought Frazier, as he ran his finger round his neck, loosening his collar, wondering, yet again, what on earth had possessed him to opt for criminal law when he could have been working in the overpaid and coddled corporate world alongside his father in the City.

'But, let's face it, Frazier, you're not exactly getting results, are you, moosh? I've been stuck in here for nearly a month now on these ridiculous drugs charges, and, if you don't pull your finger out, they're going to try and stuff me with something far worse.'

'Mr Fuller—'

'Don't waste your time Mr Fullering me. You just get up off your arse and get something, anything, on Burman.

Then maybe he'll shift *his* arse and start helping me the way he should have been all along.'

'Mr Fuller. I am doing my very best.' He took out his handkerchief and wiped his sweating palms. 'But I should warn you, if this continues: these outbursts, and these ridiculous demands to see me at weekends – do you know how far it is from Hertfordshire to Brixton, and how heavy the Saturday evening traffic can be? And as for treating me as if I were an amateur detective. It's quite ridiculous. I'm afraid if this continues, I'll no longer be able to represent you.'

David gritted his teeth. 'I said, I'm sorry.'

'I think that's all we need to discuss for now. I'll be in touch.'

It took all David's will not to smack him across his pathetic, pasty face.

Disappointed as the two warders were that they hadn't been given an excuse to give that cocky bastard Fuller a good hiding, they were content in the knowledge, as they led him back to the remand wing, that he would soon be getting a visit to his cell that they would have paid good money to have witnessed – had they not already been paid good money to stay well away from it.

David stretched out on his bed, with his hands clasped under his head, staring up at the ceiling. He'd always known that just because a bloke had a snotty accent, it didn't make him clever, but that lawyer, he was as thick as shit. First thing Monday morning he'd get something done about him. It was only a shame it was a Saturday or he'd have got on to it right away.

As David thought about how much he'd like to kick the stupid berk right up the jacksy, he heard the sound of approaching footsteps outside his cell, a key turning in the lock, then someone asking from the doorway, 'David Fuller?'

David ignored him. He hated the screws as much as he detested that stinking lawyer, almost as much as he hated being locked up in this rancid pisshole for twenty-three hours a day.

But at the sound of the door closing with a slam, David sat up.

It wasn't a warder. Standing in the cell were two heavily built men, men who had only recently come on to the wing, but who were already swaggering about the landing as if they owned the place.

'What do you want?' he asked, now completely alert.

'We've been requested to remind you that gossiping isn't very nice, Mr Fuller. And to make sure you remember who your friends are.'

David stood up. 'I ain't got any friends.'

The man who had not spoken walked slowly across the tiny room towards David, but didn't stop until he was behind him.

'Not even Mr Burman?' asked the other man.

'Never heard of him.' David knew he was trapped. He looked over his shoulder. The bloke was just standing there.

'That's funny, cos he's sent you a message. And, if you don't understand it, your life's gonna be hell, chum. Absolute fucking hell.'

With that, the man standing behind him grabbed David's arms and twisted them hard up his back, and the other man began smashing his fists into David's handsome face.

*

'Ronald, may I introduce Chantalle Turner.' Peter Burman with his mannered middle-European accent and his flash of gold teeth, gave a stiff little bow, as he gestured to the girl who was standing by his side. 'She will be sitting with you this evening.'

Delighted by his lovely, and very young, dining companion, Detective Chief Inspector Ronald Leigh helped her into her seat.

There were eight seats all together, spaced around the big mahogany table that took up most of the private dining-room in the exclusive, and very discreet, club in St James's, that Burman had invited him to for 'an evening of pleasure and maybe a little business'.

'Charmed, my dear,' said Leigh, thinking how exactly Burman had matched his taste for buxom redheads.

'Will you excuse me for one moment?' Burman backed away from the table with another little bow, and left the room to speak to the uniformed man at the reception desk.

'Messages,' said Burman, holding out his hand.

'One just arrived, sir.' The man handed over a letter, wishing he had spat on it first.

Burman ripped it open and tossed the envelope, without a glance, on the counter, then turned his back on the man, went over to the fireplace, which despite the unseasonably warm weather was, as usual, burning logs, and read the note.

Satisfied that his orders to pass on a message to David Fuller had been carried out that evening, Peter Burman tore the note in half and threw it into the fire.

Chapter 17

'Bobby, I'm telling you, I can't stand it here no more.'

Maureen was sitting with her husband on the balcony of their villa, with their two Alsatians, Duke and Duchess, and Denise, her parrot, thinking about pouring her first gin and tonic of the day, and it was barely half past twelve. Half past ten back home. If she was there, she would just be going down Rathbone market to sort through the bargains, to have a laugh with the stall holders and to have a big, steaming plateful of pie, mash, stewed eels and liquor for her dinner. Christ, she could go a plate of pie and mash. If she saw another bit of battered squid in a harbourside flaming restaurant . . .

'But, Maur, what's not to stand?' Bobby gestured to the picture-postcard view in front of them. 'Blue skies. Lovely warm sea. A beautiful home. Plenty of dough to spend on whatever takes your fancy.'

'I fancy pie and mash.'

'Maureen . . .'

'Bobby . . .'

'What's really up, babe?'

'I told you. It's this place. It's driving me out of my brain. *I want to go home.* I want to go down Rathbone Street. I want to see me friends. Speak to people who know what I'm going on about and who know how to have a joke. I don't even know where Cyprus is on the flipping map.'

'I'll buy you one.'

'I don't want a map.' Maureen clapped her hand to her forehead. 'I want to go home.'

'How about the animals?' Bobby ruffled Duke's silky black ears. 'They'd have to go into quarantine. And you wouldn't like that, would you?'

Maureen pursed her lips and glared at him. 'Don't make up ridiculous excuses, Bob. If you managed to get that bloke to fetch them over here for us, then you know, as well as I know, that you'd find a way to get them back again.'

She went over to her husband, sat on his knee and put her arms round his neck. 'Please, Bob,' she said in a girlie little voice.

'Sorry, babe, we can't. But I have got a surprise for you. I was saving it till later.'

She loosened her hold. 'What's that?' she asked flatly. 'You gonna plant another palm tree?'

'No.' Bobby sounded hurt. He'd taken a lot of trouble making the garden nice for her. And he thought the palm trees looked great. 'Jeff and Jean are moving over here. Mr Burman's letting them have that little place just along the track.'

'Terrific.' Maureen threw up her hands. 'I never liked them two at home. Especially her, the mouthy cow. Why should I like them over here?'

Bobby didn't know what to say.

'So, this is it, eh, Bob?'

'What?'

'Trapped in sodding paradise.'

Bobby flinched at the sound of Maureen swearing. She was doing a lot of that lately. It wasn't like her. 'You should get a hobby, babe. Knitting or something.'

She jumped off his lap and stomped through to the kitchen to make herself a very large drink.

'I should get a job,' he heard her call from the fridge.

'This is nice. Us sitting down together like this.' Sarah looked warily at the tea-stained cup and saucer her daughter had just handed her. A good soak in boiling water with a handful of soda wouldn't have gone amiss. But she wasn't here to criticize, she was here to try and build a few bridges, and to try and sort out a few things about Angie. And now her granddaughter was staying with her – safely out of the way, up in Lancaster Buildings – Sarah thought she could afford to be generous to Violet.

'It was your idea to come here and have a *little chat* about her future.' Vi lit a cigarette with little enthusiasm. Half past ten on a Saturday morning. She would rather be asleep, rather be having her toenails pulled out with pliers, than sitting here in her kitchen having a *little chat* with her interfering old bag of a mother.

'It's an important time for her.'

'It's up to her what she does.' Vi spoke with a weary wave of her hand. 'I've washed my hands of that girl. I've told her everything she wanted to know, and now she can take up nude tap dancing for all I care.'

Sarah felt a glow of triumph surge through her entire body: Violet wasn't going to try and stop her, wasn't going to try and spoil things.

'Still seeing that Craig?' she asked pleasantly.

'What if I am?'

'Don't jump down my throat, Vi. I was only asking. He's a nice-looking feller, that's all I was going to say.' She thought about the oily little git and how he had tried to smooth up to Angie at the wedding. 'I didn't really get the chance to say very much to him at Martin and Jill's do.' She took a tiny, trial sip of the tea. Stewed, of course. 'So I don't really know what he's like.'

'You should try going to bed with him. He's cracking in that department.'

Sarah blanched at such smutty talk, but refused to be baited. 'I heard you'd been seeing some Nick feller as well. He wasn't the same one you used to go out with when Angie was a kiddie, was he?'

'Lovely. Tilly Murray been blabbing to you about my private life, has she?'

'Violet—'

'Don't worry, I couldn't care less. What that old bag thinks doesn't matter a shit to me. But, yes, if you must know, I was seeing Nick again for a while. Satisfied?'

Sarah noticed the grease-heavy cobwebs above the back door. The kitchen could do with a good disinfecting, and a lick of white paint round the skirting board wouldn't go amiss, and as for the mucky fingerprints round the light switch . . . 'I liked him. Nick. He was a nice man. He was good for you, Vi. Not like that married bloke from the shop. What was his name, now? Sam. That's who I mean. What's he up to nowadays?'

'I'll compile a list, shall I? Fill in the bits Tilly's not sure on? OK, let's see: I am not seeing Nick any more and I am not seeing Sam. They were both boring bastards. All right?'

'There's no need for that sort of talk, Violet. It's very unladylike.'

'Well, they were.'

'Nick was well off, if I remember.'

'So's Sam.'

'But Nick was ever so good to you. And single. He treated you with such respect. Like a proper lady.'

'And he bored the arse off me.'

Sarah could only take so much. 'A bit of boredom

wouldn't do any harm at your time of life, if you ask me.'

'I'm not asking you. If you don't mind.' Vi took a deep lungful of smoke and blew it childishly towards her mother. '*My time of life*. Cheek.'

'I just don't want a daughter of mine winding up like some old brass.'

'And I don't want to die of boredom. Now. Really. If you don't mind.' Vi ground out her cigarette butt in the slops in her saucer and stood up. 'I'm going to have a lie down. I think I've got one of my headaches coming on.'

As Sarah walked along the street, back towards Becontree tube station, she looked at Tilly Murray's neat little end-of-terrace house, with its sparkling windows, snow-white nets and tidy, colourful front garden, and then back at her daughter's run-down mirror image of it.

She sighed, exasperated.

She had tried to get through to Violet this one last time, tried as hard as she could be bothered to try – which, to be honest, wasn't really that hard at all – but, she had to admit it, her daughter just wasn't much good, and that was all there was to it. It was very sad, sad as a woman like Sarah could imagine, but it was true: Violet was nothing more, nothing less, than a trollop.

Still, maybe this Craig would at least make her happy.

'Won't be long, Nan.'

'All right, girls.' Sarah kicked off her shoes and settled down into her armchair. The journey back from Dagenham had taken ages and all she wanted to do now was to have five minutes to herself before she had to think about popping down Chris Street before they started closing away the stalls. 'There's no rush.'

'Just the bottle of sterilized and a crusty loaf?'

'That's it.'

'I'll call into Doris's on the way out, see if she needs anything.'

'Good girl, Ange. Sure you've got enough money?'

'Plenty.'

'Use the change to get yourselves a nice lump of that seedy cake in the café, and a nice glass of milk each.'

Jackie and Angie smiled at one another. They both knew, as well as Sarah, that they would creep into the Britannia for a lager and lime and a packet of fags rather than into Pelligi's for a bit of cake and a drink of milk.

Angie put down the two half-pint glasses on the table, and handed Jackie a bag of crisps.

'You won't be able to afford this, going to pubs, when you go to college,' said Jackie, tearing open the crisp packet.

Angie, who, for the past two weeks, had been putting up with Jackie's increasingly pessimistic list of reasons why she should go back to work with her in the City rather than to college, swallowed a gulp of lager and lime and smiled mockingly. 'I'll get a Saturday job.'

'That won't pay you enough to buy new clothes though, will it?'

'Lucky you taught me how to make them at home then, eh, Jack?'

'Angie,' she whined. 'I'll really miss you.'

'But you've got your loverboy, Andrew.'

Jackie poked out her tongue.

'Anyway, the college is only in East Ham.' She grinned, as she tore the Cellophane off her packet of

Number Six. 'I'll be able to go round and see Marilyn in my lunch hour.'

'Might only be East Ham, but it feels like you're going to the other end of the world.' Jackie munched forlornly on a crisp. 'And how about Guy?' she added slyly.

'I've told you a million times, Jackie Murray. He keeps phoning, but I'm not going out with him. I'm not going out with anyone. Ever again. Not after what happened.'

Jackie leaned forward and poked her friend in the arm. 'Here, we could have a double wedding. Me and Andrew and you and Guy.'

'Will you stop it?'

'All right, humpy. And I suppose I'd better keep on the right side of you. I mean, I don't know when you might turn into a tycoon and earn your first million, do I? That'd be handy, though, if I needed to borrow a few bob.' She shook her head. 'Fancy you going back to study.'

Angie rolled her eyes wearily. 'Jackie. I am doing a few O levels. At a further education college. While I decide what I want to do with my life. I might even be able to do them at evening classes.'

Jackie smacked the table enthusiastically. 'That's a fantastic idea, Ange. You could still work up the City with me. It'd be really fab. Just like it used to be.'

'It's nothing definite, Jack. I'm not sure yet what I'm going to do.'

Jackie sat back in her chair, folded her arms and regarded her friend. 'I always knew you'd make some-thing of yourself.'

'You liar.'

'Well . . .'

They sat in silence for a while, with Angie smoking and Jackie picking at the crisps.

Then Angie said: 'Give my love to Martin when you see him next.'

'Come round ours later and you can do it yourself if you like. He's back home for the weekend.'

'What, him and Jill?'

Jackie shook her head. 'Jill's family are going to some horsey do and he couldn't stand the thought of it. So he's pretending he's got work to get done before the new term starts. And that he needs to stay at ours because he's using the library at Mile End. I'm a bit worried about them two, to be truthful. They don't act much like newly-weds.'

'They'll be all right, Jack. They'll have to be. Just like the rest of us.'

'They've already almost come to blows over what they're doing for Christmas. The baby's due around then, but Martin's still insisting he wants to be with Mum and Dad. I can't see Jill taking it lying down. She's got a right temper on her. You'll have to be there, Ange, or I'll go mad if they're at one another's throats all the time.'

'You make it sound so tempting,' she said sarcastically, 'but I might not be able to. I've had a word with Mum—'

'Angie, you are *not* still letting your mum tell you what to do, even now you're at your nan's, are you? Not after everything that's happened?'

'No. This is nothing to do with Mum.'

'But you said—'

Angie shrugged. 'Not exactly, it's not. It's just that I've been trying to trace—' She paused and gulped down the last of her drink. '—my dad. There, I've said it.'

'Your dad?' Jackie sat bolt upright, as though she was still at Campbell Mixed Infants and a teacher had just come into the classroom. 'But he's dead.'

'It's a long story, Jack, and I didn't want to say anything till I was really sure, but I don't think he is.' She held up her empty glass. 'Another drink?'

Jackie pushed her friend's hand away. 'Never mind no drinks. First that David bloke you were seeing turns out to be a big-time drugs-dealer and gets his gob splashed all over the papers—'

'He's not been found guilty yet, Jack.'

'Yeah. Yeah. All right. I'm not thick. And now you reckon you've found your dad. Any other little secrets you've got to tell me while you're at it?'

Angie shrugged. 'Not that I can think of.'

'You weren't swapped by the fairies at birth or anything.'

'Who knows?'

'You're making all this up, right? About your dad?'

'No. This is as real as these empty glasses.'

'Blimey.'

'Yeah, blimey. You're right. I think we could both do with another lager and lime, don't you, Jack?'

Angie set the fresh round down on the table. 'I'm thinking about trying to see him during the Christmas holidays.'

'Where's he from? Round here somewhere?'

'No. He's from Vancouver.'

'Vancouver? Where's that?'

'Canada.'

'Canada? Are you sure?'

'You sound just like a parrot.'

'Very funny. Now, are you going to tell me the whole story?'

'I'm not sure of it myself. Not really. Not yet anyway. It was something Nan started off. She told me a few things about my dad. My real dad.'

'The one who's still alive?'

'Yeah. Then, when Mum knew I wasn't going to leave it, she eventually gave me all the information she had. It wasn't much, to be honest, but I got lucky. I got a really good lead. And, if I get the letter back I'm hoping for, I'm going over there. Imagine that. Me going all the way to Canada to meet my dad. Nan said she'll treat me to the fare if I do go.' She grinned at Jackie across the rim of her glass. 'I'll have to go on a jet.'

'What do you think will happen?'

'Well, I'll pack my bags, and then I'll go to the airport—'

Jackie spluttered with exasperation. 'Angie!'

'Sorry. I don't know, Jack. It might all be a terrible mistake or it might be the best thing I've ever done. All I know is, I feel strong enough to do it. And it's not anyone else telling me to, or making me, or even trying to kid me. It's just me. I'm doing it because I want to. Because I choose to.' Angie flashed her eyebrows. 'Fancy that, eh, Jack, a timid little thing like me, being brave enough to go all the way to Canada to find my dad.'

She took a sip from her glass and then licked the sweet foam off of her expertly outlined top lip. 'I get really scared when I start thinking about it. Think how rotten it'll be if I go all the way over there and he doesn't like me.'

Jackie studied her friend closely, watching the girl she had once known so well, and tried, honestly tried, to

386

understand what she was feeling. She was saddened to realize that it wasn't possible. Not any more.

'Yeah, that's likely, Ange,' she snapped, her abruptness a cover for her sense of loss. 'Someone not thinking you're fantastic. The bloke behind the bar's been practically dribbling over you since you came in, and all your nan's neighbours think you're the sweetest girl they've ever met.'

She licked the end of her finger and dipped it in the last of the crisp crumbs. 'In fact, Angela Knight, you make me sick.'

Angie grinned at her. 'Good. That's always been my sole purpose in life.'

Jackie sighed. 'Things have changed so much, Ange. And I get scared as well sometimes. Knowing I've got to grow up and that.'

'Know what scares me?'

'Apart from meeting your dad and that?'

Angie nodded. 'How I acted like a cheap little tart, and what I nearly got myself involved in.'

Jackie leaned forward. 'You haven't heard any more from the police, then?'

Angie shook her head. 'No. And I don't want to either. I hope I can put all that behind me.'

'No more Angel then?'

She grinned wickedly. 'Come on, I never said that, now did I? How could I get rid of Angel without going back to being that pathetic little thing who wouldn't say boo to a goose? And, I'm telling you, there is not a single, solitary chance of me doing that, thank you very much.'

'I can't say I'm surprised.'

Angie put down her glass on the table and watched her finger as she rubbed it, slowly, round the rim. 'You know, things always work out in the end. One way or another.' Then she raised her eyes, looked at her friend and, in an unconscious imitation of David Fuller, she winked reassuringly. 'Even if we don't always realize it at the time, eh, Jack?'

Postscript

Detective Constable Jameson flicked through the buff, cardboard file as he drank his tea, alone, at his desk. He no longer bothered going into the canteen.

After his success in getting David Fuller put away for a good long stretch, on drugs and forged-passport charges, he had been ready to spread his net wider and to make a real name for himself. But he knew now that it wasn't going to be quite as easy as he had hoped, that it was going to be damned hard work, in fact. His hoped-for progress with his boss, Detective Chief Inspector Leigh, had been disappointing to say the least, and his contribution to getting Fuller banged up was hardly acknowledged in the final reports. But Jameson had determination, youth and efficiency on his side, and every moment of his spare time was now concerned with beating a foolproof path to the well-hidden, but very crooked, door of Peter Burman.

No one would be able to ignore Jameson if he nailed a genuine Mr Big, a real player like him.

Jameson had dismissed a couple of leads as being a complete waste of his time, but had now found a very interesting new direction to follow that had caused him to seriously consider spending his annual leave in Cyprus.

The focus of his interest was Bobby Sykes, who, during the past eighteen months, and despite his apparent stupidity, seemed to have risen rapidly in the ranks of Burman's organization over there. Rumour also had it that Sykes's wife, Maureen, had been taking an active interest in the business, and that she was a bit of a powerhouse.

Jameson was very curious to see what he could dig up over there.

Then there was Sonia Fuller. Although she was still in a coma after all this time, he knew she was the key to what had happened to Mikey Tilson – which motorway fly-over he'd been cemented into, or which Essex smallholder had minced him up and fed him to the Dobermanns.

He jotted down a note to remind himself to give the London Hospital a ring. She would have to wake up one day and Jameson wanted to make sure the consultants knew who to contact.

He flicked over another sheet of paper. Sarah Pearson. Was she worth a follow up? He read through his neatly typed notes. Worth keeping because of her association with that old fence, Doris Barker, but anything more? He put her details to one side, on the pile he had yet to decide on.

Now, who was this?

Angela Knight.

She'd not shown any sign of involvement in Burman's world for over two years now. Never really had any serious involvement in the first place.

He studied the photographs of the smiling, glossy-haired girl. One of them showed her arm in arm with Fuller, as they made their way along the King's Road, in the summer, that would be, of 1965, mingling with all the other Saturday afternoon shoppers.

She was a pretty girl. Very pretty. But totally insignificant. And no one got anywhere by playing around with the tiddlers. No one got anywhere playing around, full stop.

Jameson screwed up the sheets of paper headed *Angela Knight* and the photographs of the smiling, glossy-haired girl and tossed them into his bin.

He had far bigger fish to fry.